Farewell to South Shore

Charlene Wexler

Books by Charlene Wexler

Laughter And Tears Series
Book 1: Lori
Book 2: Murder Across the Ocean

Farewell To South Shore Series
Book 1: Farewell to South Shore

COMING SOON!

Laughter And Tears Series
Book 3: Milk and Oranges
Book 4: Elephants in the Room

Farewell To South Shore Series
Book 2: We Will Not Go Back

NOVELS
Murder on Skid Row

For more information
visit: www.SpeakingVolumes.us

Farewell to South Shore

Charlene Wexler

SPEAKING VOLUMES, LLC
NAPLES, FLORIDA
2024

Farewell to South Shore

ISBN 979-8-89022-072-1

This book is dedicated to my sister, Cookie/Bobbi, and to family and friends who grew up in South Shore during the fifties, and sixties.

Acknowledgments

A special thank you to my agent Nancy Rosenfeld/AAA Books Unlimited; my publisher, Kurt Mueller, Speaking Volumes; and my editor William S. Bike. I also want to thank family and friends who have encouraged me to keep writing.

Part One:

The Family Building in the Traditional Years 1959 to 1968

Chapter One

"Jake, close the store and get home quick," Tillie shouted into the phone. "We have a major problem."

"What is it this time?" Jake asked, as he stared up out the store window at the children walking home from school with their heavy books jangling in their arms.

"It's Pa," Tillie said. "He's on the roof."

"What is he doing on the roof?" Jake inquired calmly.

"Stop the questions and get home!" Tillie shouted.

"What about Izzy?" Jake asked. "He must be home. He hasn't got a regular job, and he isn't working in the store for me today."

"Jake, you know Pa won't listen to him. He's the youngest! Izzy went up the ladder, and Pa made him come right down. You know Pa never forgave Izzy for spilling the bucket of green paint all over the front porch."

Jake hesitated a minute while he remembered endlessly scrubbing the porch. He smiled to himself as he pictured sparkles of green paint still on the white stones next to the red brick entrance. *"Would be a great look if we weren't Jewish . . .," he thought.*

"Jake, are you still there?" Tillie yelled.

"Tillie, I'm thinking," Jake replied. "There is no one here who can run the grocery store if I leave. I can't just close it in the middle of the day. Get another family member. My customers need food for their families' evening dinner, and my helper Ira is making deliveries."

"Just put a sign up that Pa is on the roof," Tillie shot back. "Everyone in the neighborhood knows Pa."

Jake smiled at her comment, and thought, "Yes, everyone in the neighborhood knows Pa, and will understand."

A new voice took the place of Tillie's. "Jake, it's Sarah. You better come home quick! Pa will only listen to you. We are all here. If our father falls, it will be on your conscience."

"Okay, okay, I'm coming," Jake sighed. When his sisters got together with their guilt stories Jake knew he was licked. He could just picture all ten of his adult family members standing around the building shouting at Pa who was going about his project, ignoring them.

"You never let me know why he is on the roof," Jake said as he took a deep breath. "He never told me he was going there, and he usually talks over most things with me."

"The pigeons," Sarah replied. "You know they are driving him crazy. He is putting nails on the roof to keep them away. If he told you, you would have argued with him about it."

"Okay, okay, I'm coming," Jake repeated as he prepared to close the grocery store. Just as Tillie had said, as soon as he told customers that Pa was on the roof, they shook their heads knowingly. Mrs. Abrams, as she checked out her groceries, commented, "Your poor mother, may she rest in peace."

* * *

I was born in 1944, but this story begins in 1959 when I was fifteen years old.

My name is Sherrie Paul, and I am a member of the crazy family whose members found themselves gathered outside the three-flat red brick building in which we all lived. The building was in Chicago's South Shore neighborhood. The patriarch of the family, my stubborn, but lovable, 82-year-old grandfather who owned and cared for it, was the one on the roof.

My Aunt Tillie, her husband, Hymie, their son, Yale, who was a fun-loving kid, daughter Lizzie, who was an in-charge homemaker like her mother, little Rachel, who was quiet and sensitive, and their old bulldog, Prince, all lived on the third floor. Uncle Hymie was a short, bald man with a perpetual cigar in his mouth, and Aunt Tillie ran the clan, though Pa still had the last word. My uncle Izzy and his family lived on the first floor. I lived with my dad, Jake, and my mom, Bess, on the second floor. Aunt Sarah and her son, David, lived with Grandpa across the street in another one of his buildings. Aunt Sarah's husband died in World War II fourteen years ago, and she never remarried, even though she was still attractive.

We had the sandwich apartment, the one on the second floor between family on the first and third floors. My third-floor aunt and uncle, Tillie and Hymie, communicated by fighting and shouting, the dog barked and snored, and the girls whined. Once they forgot to turn the bathtub faucet off, and we got flooded. I don't understand how that happened as the bathroom is the most used room in the apartment, especially when there were five of them sharing one toilet.

We thought we were quiet, but Aunt Dora on the first floor complained that we stayed up too late and she could hear us walking around. Maybe it was because Mom always wore high heels while the rest of the women wore sensible, low-heeled black shoes. Mom promised to walk in stocking feet instead of heels, though that could be expensive if the stockings tore. I would have preferred lush carpeting like my friend Gail had in her apartment, but that would have been too expensive. Instead, we had area rugs over hard wood floors.

It was 3 p.m., and I was on my way home from high school. Down the street, about three and a half blocks from the bus stop on Jeffery Boulevard, was home. Getting off the bus with all the books I carried was a struggle. Tests in school tomorrow, so I had more books than usual to balance. I missed the convenience of O'Keefe Grammar School, only a half a block away, and easy to come home for lunch, as opposed to Hyde Park, my high school, at 63rd Street and Stoney Island Avenue, which was several miles away. Dad sometimes dropped me off, but coming home was usually a city bus ride, unless a group of us teenagers decided to take the long walk home through Jackson Park's Public Golf Course. The boys loved to chase after the lost golf balls, while we girls quietly chased after the boys.

A jumble of voices increased in volume as I walked across the tree-lined street featuring red-and-yellow brick, three-flat apartment buildings. I stopped a minute to watch the boys playing ball in the middle of the street, and the girls jumping rope on the sidewalks, double-Dutch, something I could never accomplish. I moved over to a cute little girl in a blue pinafore.

"Hey Lucy, what is the commotion about?" I asked. I was certain they could hear it from where they were playing.

"I don't know," she answered. "It's your family again." The crack of a bat made me look up. Dodging a ball headed towards the gutter, I continued home.

This was not the first time I'd come home from school to find all the family members shouting at each other about some perceived crisis. I wasn't surprised to find Grandpa on the roof. Grandpa had shown me the wooden boards with nails he was going to use.

The pigeons weren't surprised, either. A whole group of them sat on the telephone wires contemplating how to outsmart him.

I placed my hands on my ears to block out the continuous chatter and shouting, pushed my way past everyone, opened the heavy oak front door, and inhaled the lingering Jewish cooking smells of fat, onions, garlic, and sweets coming from Aunt Tillie's apartment. Her kitchen was her universe. I climbed up the wide wooden stairs to our apartment.

Grandpa would be fine. He was a construction worker before he started to buy real estate, and the roof was flat.

I opened the unlocked door to our second floor apartment and dropped my schoolbooks on the light-colored wooden hall table. Smoke from the cigarette lounging in the green glass ash tray stung my eyes. I backed away from it.

"Hi, Mom," I said, loud enough to block out the sounds of Frank Sinatra crooning *Anything Goes.* Mom did love her small, white-and-gold RCA radio. I preferred the new, small, black-and-white television with shows such as *The Lone Ranger, I Love Lucy,* and *The Ed Sullivan Show,* or my 45 r.p.m. record player with the latest rock and roll entertainers such as Chuck Berry and Elvis Presley.

She moved from the window, letting the lace curtains drop back in place. "What is the commotion about outside now?" Mom asked.

I opened the icebox looking for something to munch on. Nothing good there, all diet stuff. I shook my head in despair. A cookie, one little cookie or just one candy bar would be great to find some day, especially since Dad owned a grocery store.

Mom stood there with hands on her hips.

"Grandpa is on the roof trying to stop the pigeons, and the rest of the clan is trying to coax him down," I answered while still searching through the icebox.

"I guess they will bother your poor dad," Mom said, as she handed me an apple. "No one in his family can do anything without him. It is bad enough that he feeds everyone from the store. Your father is just too nice."

"Isn't that why we love him?" I asked, smiling.

She smiled back at me. "You are so much like your dad. Watch that you are not taken advantage of, my sweet," she said with a hint of playfulness in her voice.

More conservative than Dad due to her experiences in Europe during the war, Mom watched her money carefully. She had a terrible time understanding Dad's family, where crisis or party was group-funded and participation was demanded. Life with the family consisted of laughter and tears, mishigas and tumult, many times in the same situation.

Mom wasn't from Chicago, not even from the USA. Dad and Mom met when he was stationed in London during the end of the war. He brought her home to Chicago. The only photograph of them in London sat on the entrance table. Taken in 1943, it pictured my dad in full U.S. Army captain uniform next to a stunning looking girl who was perched on three-inch black heels and fitted into a tight black strapless dress. They were standing on the famous Westminster Bridge. There must be a better story there than the one they tell—that they met at an officer's club in London and immediately fell in love.

Oh, she was Jewish like the rest of the clan, but a different kind of Jewish. She was tall, five feet seven, blonde, very thin, quiet, reserved, private, and she never kept kosher or played cards. She never even owned a rolling pin! Her hands were soft and smooth. No matter how hard my aunts tried, they couldn't get my mother to join the traditional weekly *kalooki* card game or the weekend family penny poker game, which was played by all the adults on Aunt Tillie's large mahogany dining room table.

Actually, I couldn't blame Mom; we kids played our games quietly compared to the adults who argued constantly.

"This is poker money, pay up now!"

"You're bluffing! I don't trust you."

"You don't need another card."

"You ate the whole bag of candy, you 'chaser!'"

"It's your turn, my God you are so slow, you can't quit now."

"Tillie, more tea!"

"To hell with the tea, Hymie, bring out the schnapps!"

It took me years before I realized shouting and interrupting each other wasn't normal for all families.

Most of the conversations were mixed with Yiddish phrases we kids couldn't fully understand, though we kept trying. When we heard, "*zug gornisht (*say nothing)," we knew they were talking about something they didn't want us to hear, usually swear words or juicy gossip.

Rather than playing poker with the family on Sunday nights, Mom went out with her friend Sofia. Sinai, a very reform synagogue in the Hyde Park neighborhood, had a lecture series about life that Mom and Sofia liked to attend. Sofia was different than other family friends. She was not a neighbor or from the synagogue or South Shore or the West Side, and she wasn't even Jewish. We were told that we should be pleasant to non-Jews whom we encountered in stores, at work, in school, or in other common places, but to have a non-Jew as a best friend was incomprehensible to my dad's clan. Once Sophia wore a red skirt and a tight pink sweater to a Passover Seder, where she drank too much of the blackberry Mogen David wine and laughed during the hour of seder prayer. My aunts were not fond of her.

The only time I really heard my mom and dad have a major argument was over Sophia.

"Jake, I just don't understand why we can't spend Thanksgiving with Sophia's family," Mom had said. "It's not a Jewish holiday."

"The family wouldn't understand," Dad argued. "We spend every holiday together. It's traditional."

"I'm sick of *the family, the family*," my mother uttered as she walked into her bedroom and slammed the door. I stayed quiet in my room, where I imagined the tightening of Mom's jaw, and the head-shaking of Dad as he settled in his recliner.

Besides Sophie, Mom had another friend who tested the family. It was Etta, the black girl who cleaned house one day a week for each family, which meant she was in the building three days a week. We all loved Etta, with her high-pitched voice and friendly, open attitude, but my mom stepped over the line between help and friend. Many days when I came home from school, I found Mom at one end of the yellow Formica kitchen table and Etta, with her large-boned body, perched on a red vinyl chair between the other end of the table and the icebox.

Mom, dressed in a red print dress, stockings, and low heels like she was going someplace fancy, sat with a cigarette in hand. Etta, in an old but colorful house dress, laughed in between drinking wine and puffing away on her cigarettes.

"Hi, baby girl," Etta had called out. "I made you an apple pie. Go check out the icebox." She knew how to win my heart, especially in a household without a baker.

"Don't you go telling nobody . . ." was her introduction to some family gossip, like when Yale stole money from Aunt Tillie's purse or when Aunt Dora started yelling that Uncle Izzy couldn't do anything right anymore.

Now, Etta had a cat. Nobody had a cat as a pet then; dogs and birds, people had.

This cat, named Geronimo, was a scrawny yellow attack cat who hated Pa. Etta spent so much time in the building that some days, she brought Geronimo with her.

One day, I heard a commotion upstairs. I ran up to Tillie's apartment where I found the cat attacking Pa, and Pa hitting him with a broom, yelling in Yiddish, *"Ga aveck, you momser (Go away, you monster)!"* and Etta screaming "Geronimo, Geronimo" while she pulled on the cat. That was the end of the cat coming with her. I figured if Pa took the cat on the roof, the pigeons would go away.

* * *

Mom did light candles on the Sabbath, using very straight-lined modern candlesticks instead of the traditional copper ones everyone else used. She hated the conservative synagogue we went to because everything was in Hebrew, and she couldn't read or understand it. Actually, after all my years of Hebrew school, I could only read it, couldn't understand it either, but the synagogue was a good place to socialize. My grandpa and my uncles spent most of their free time at the conservative synagogue called South Side Hebrew on 74th Street. I do wish we had lived closer to it as we were not allowed to drive on the Sabbath or the Jewish High Holidays, and it was a schlep from our house, especially when we were dressed in our finest clothes and walking in heels.

Mom tried to get along with my aunts, but she really danced to a different drummer, which made my aunts crazy.

The day my mom walked out the front door in tan linen pants right past family members sitting outside enjoying the warm fall evening, I thought Aunt Tillie would pass out.

"Bess, what are you wearing, and where are you going?" Tillie asked, wide-eyed, and with an outstretched hand pointed to my mom's pants; Tillie had virtually jumped out of her lawn chair.

Mom answered, "Pants! If Katherine Hepburn can wear them, so can I."

Aunt Sarah looked up, defiant. "Not a Jewish woman,"

Mom walked right by them and entered Sophia's waiting car. Tillie and Sarah ganged up on my dad. After that encounter, Mom still wore pants, but never near the family.

I had wished that I could wear slacks to school, especially during Chicago's freezing winter days. But Mom had made sure I was dressed in the current fashions. Back then, I had at least six cashmere sweaters with matching skirts, plus my trusted penny loafers. My friend Fern teased me because most of my sweaters were in shades of blue.

Our apartment was different from the other family apartments. The layout was the same on all three floors: a large living-dining room, small kitchen, two bedrooms, one bath, and a sun parlor. The difference was in the furnishings. Light-colored, straight-lined, modern pine furniture, free from tchotchkes and plastic covers, adorned our rooms instead of heavy, dark, wooden furniture. Just one mirror hung in the front room, and only two or three pictures hung on white walls, and for sure no artificial flowers would be seen anywhere. Even the linoleum on our kitchen floor was one color, not patterned, and we never used tablecloths, just something called placemats. Our apartment looked bigger than the others, but it felt sterile.

Hidden in a corner of the living room, between sparks dancing against the tan and white stone fireplace, was one exception to the modern furniture. It was my dad's old, saddle-leather, tan and brown cushioned recliner with the torn arm that was covered by Aunt Tillie's multicolored crocheted quilt. Being settled into that chair next to the tall brass lamp with the paper opened wide was my father's way of relaxing after work. Some days he added his brown Kaywoodie pipe from Kaufmann Bros. & Bondy Company. If he fell asleep, Mom and I made sure we removed the pipe from his mouth.

Everything possessed a place in our apartment, and the floors sparkled from Etta's polishing.

Mom, who constantly smelled of lemon, was so attractive, with her straight, shoulder length, champagne-blonde hair that accentuated her honey-brown eyes.

I wished I looked like her, but alas, my genetic pool was bent more towards Dad's family. Five feet, four inches tall, with unruly, curly black hair and a too-big nose. I would get the traditional nose job when I was older when and if Mom would let me. I did try hard to keep from getting too fat, which wasn't easy, being part of a Jewish clan. My large, sparkling, dark brown eyes and heavy black eyebrows made up for some of my other physical faults.

Dad's family came from Poland, and then the West Side of Chicago. They were noisy, loving, clannish, outgoing people. The women were small in stature and on the plump side, especially their bosoms. They had black curly hair, or dyed red hair, except for Aunt Tillie, who had a shiny head of silver hair tinged with a touch of pepper. She was the only one who didn't have a standing appointment at Andre Pierre's beauty shop on 71st Street.

When Tillie went to the beauty shop for special occasions, Pierre started on her, saying "Tillie, you are a beautiful young woman. How can you go around with gray hair? Let me fix you up. The first dye will be free."

Tillie wouldn't give in. "If God wanted me to have red hair, he would have given it to me. First, he gave me black, and then silver. I will keep it. *Amen.*" She tapped hard on the table to emphasize her position.

Sarah, who was taller and more into appearances and clothes, would never contradict her older sister. She quietly mumbled, "Tillie is the only woman under sixty in the synagogue with gray hair."

There were no secrets between them, and to my mom's horror, they become involved in each other's business to a fault, such as the trivial fight over how much time my dad needed to walk to the temple one Friday that he closed the store late. Tillie said an hour, and Sarah said only a half hour because he walked fast. While they were arguing, my dad went to sleep and skipped Sabbath dinner and temple.

The family functioned sort of like an old-fashioned village in the tightly knit, predominantly Jewish section of the South Shore neighborhood which ran from Lake Michigan on the east to Stony Island on the west, from Jackson Park on the north to around 79th Street on the south. The area was originally farmland. Then the 1893 World's Fair opened in Jackson Park. The Illinois Central Railroad and the annexation of South Shore to Chicago turned the farmland into a large community of shops, parks, churches, and synagogues populated first by Christian and then by a mixture of ethnic groups. Each group stayed within its own territory, while still being tolerant of others.

There were some non-tolerant groups in the neighborhood, such as the restricted South Shore Country Club, built on 71st Street in 1905 where very wealthy white people played golf, rode horses, ate expensive catered food, and kept everyone who was not like them out of their fancy place. As kids, we snuck in through the lake beach and pulled down the signs that said: "No dogs, blacks, or Jews allowed."

Chapter Two

The hum of a motor slowing down alerted us to my dad's arrival. Through our opened window, we heard Aunt Sarah say, "Oh Jake, thank God you're here!"

Jake, my father, the oldest of the five siblings, was the family fix-it man. He could fix a car, a roof, or a fight between family members, especially when it involved Grandpa.

I walked over to the opened glass pane near Mom, who was peeking out through a crunched curtain. We watched Dad quietly move up the ladder. He picked up some nails and joined Grandpa in his hammering. They talked together in Yiddish, the language they brought with them from the old country. Of course, it kept us kids out of the conversation.

Though Dad was dressed in shirt and tie and was about four inches taller than Grandpa, except for the thin black mustache covering his upper lip, he still looked like a young boy helping his small, thin, bald dad. In only a few minutes, Grandpa and Dad were down from the roof and marching with the clan up to Aunt Tillie's apartment. Another family crisis resolved!

"Come *Essen* (to eat), supper, strudel for all," Aunt Tillie announced as she led the march through the front door and up the stairs.

Mom went into the bedroom. It's not that my mom disliked my dad's family; it's more that, being English, she was uncomfortable with the continuous tumult. She would rather listen to music or read her books. She had a whole bookshelf full of classics such as Kafka's *Metamorphosis,* and popular books such as *Peyton Place,* and she let me read them all, even the juicy parts, so long as I was willing to analyze them with her. From the time the teachers put "Dick and Jane" books into my hands, Mom taught me to fall in love with books.

I hesitated, not sure where to go. "It's okay," she said, "though I have a hard time believing that you enjoy all your aunt's greasy food." I knew she was referring to schmaltz, the Jewish staple in almost every recipe. I wasn't going to answer her. Mom already knew I wasn't a follower of her bland healthy diet. I followed the clan upstairs. At least Mom didn't use guilt as a weapon as my aunts did. My cousin David told me, if his mother yelled at him, he felt guilty for straining her voice.

* * *

Twenty-some family members crowded into the red-and-yellow tiled kitchen. Though small, it was warm and inviting. We were met with the sweet smell of honeyed strudel mixed with whiffs of garlic-laden brisket and fresh challah. Aunt Tillie always had a house full of Jewish food, even on non-Sabbath and non-holiday days. She spent her days in a loose fitting floral house dress, cooking and baking. Sometimes she even appeared with a pink apron over the house dress. People were always coming and going in her house, dogs barked, and kids screamed and laughed, and nobody ever left her home hungry.

Mom had said that it would be nice if she did some cleaning, but Aunt Tillie's house was always a comfortable place to be for me, and her food was delicious. As a young girl, I loved to help Aunt Tillie cook. Stirring and tasting was how we could find her most days. She was the only one in the family who made light, fluffy matzo balls. Aunt Sarah's could be used as weapons.

When I asked for Aunt Tillie's recipes, she looked at me like I was crazy and said, "Recipes! Get over here and help." She grabbed my arm and pulled me over by the burners of her white porcelain stove.

"I learned by helping, watching, and tasting like my mother did with *her* mother," Aunt Tillie explained. "Get a spoon - taste the soup." I opened the *fleshig* (meat) drawer, took out a soup spoon and dipped it into the simmering pot. "Blow on it so it doesn't burn you," she ordered, and I did what I was told.

"So does it need more salt, pepper?" she asked.

I glanced at my cousin Lizzie who stood in the kitchen doorway laughing. I answered, "Maybe a little salt."

Aunt Tillie put her lips together and shook her head, saying, "Okay, put in a *bissel* salt."

I looked at her, and asked, "Aunt Tillie, what is a *bissel*?"

"Where have you been? A bissel is a little."

She glanced towards Lizzie, and ordered, "Stop the laughing. You're not that much better. You are both in school during the week, so we will have the 'Cooking Jewish' class on Sunday."

Those Sunday and holiday lessons were how I became a good Jewish cook. There were some drawbacks to our lessons. Some foods I quit eating after I learned how they were made. I learned that *Kiska*, which I loved, was made from stuffing a cow's gut, and pickled tongue was *really* tongue.

At our house, dinner was a guessing game, except for Sabbath when the whole family gathered at Aunt Tillie's house and Sunday when we went to a restaurant. My mom hated to cook, and I think she never mastered what was and what wasn't kosher.

My cousin David said, "Grandpa insists that my mom follows her mother by keeping a weekly food schedule. Monday, lamb chops. Tuesday, veal chops or chicken. Wednesday, dairy. Thursday, meatballs or stuffed cabbage. Friday and Saturday, a Sabbath dinner of soup, chicken, brisket, *kishkey, challah*, etcetera. And Sunday is bagel, lox, herring, and smoked fish."

Because Pa lived with them, they had to be Orthodox, doing things like praying all Sabbath and not driving, writing, or turning lights off on the Sabbath while the rest of the family were Conservative Orthodox, which gave us a little leeway. We kept kosher, but we could do some things on the Sabbath, like talking on the phone, writing, and visiting with friends after temple. Also we could eat *milichg*, (dairy), at non-kosher restaurants.

Aunt Tillie was loud, sometimes argumentative, but she really had a heart of gold. Everyone always got a big hug from her while the kids received a cheek pinch from Uncle Hymie with the inevitable question, "Who's your favorite uncle?" Your answer had better be "Uncle Hymie" or you got an extra pinch. Occasionally when you gave him the right answer, he slipped you a nickel. He had some kind of a political job, so he was home a lot.

He usually had either pieces of food, a big fat cigar, or a wide smile on his face in spite of the fact that his high blood pressure required him to slow down on eating and smoking. His excuse to the young doctor was, "I'm Jewish. This is the way we eat." Then he went back to his friend, the old, retired doctor, the one he prayed with at synagogue, the one he played poker with, the one who wouldn't lecture him. In Yiddish, Uncle Hymie was called a *kibitzer*, a joker.

My family believed their strong Polish blood would protect them. Their genetic pool was made up of ancestors who made it through pogroms, freezing temperatures, and starvation. Over and over I heard how Pa had fled Warsaw with the Polish army on his heels. Polish Jews never got out of the army alive, we were told. I don't know about that one. Grandpa, though short and thin, was stubborn and tough.

* * *

"Hymie, get that damn dog out of here," Aunt Tillie yelled as Prince grabbed a bagel off the table. Everyone called Prince a big dumb dog, but I think he was pretty clever when it came to food. Once he stole a whole brisket off the kitchen table. We thought either Prince or Uncle Hymie were going to be dead meat that day. All the windows were opened, up and down the block, when Aunt Tillie started to scream and howl.

"Tillie, Tillie, what happened? Who died?"

"What's with the screaming and howling?"

"Did you hear someone crying?"

"Oy vey!"

So went the neighborhood "phone"—the one with heads sticking out of the window or women sitting on the steps outside, which was so much more efficient than the real phone hanging on the wall. We never saw Prince or Uncle Hymie move so fast as they did that day.

As I filled my plate with some of Aunt Tillie's brisket and chopped liver, David came up behind me. He was my favorite cousin, the only one older than I was. He was a high school senior, while I was just a sophomore. He also was an only child like I was, so we were connected without worrying about sibling rivalry. We were the only ones with bedrooms all to ourselves. The other cousins had to bunk up with one or two other sisters or brothers. Aunt Tillie's girls were always fighting over missing clothes, toys, or games, while Yale, the prince, had his own room.

Chapter Three

"Sherrie, let's take a walk," David said. "I have something important to discuss with you."

"Not until I'm done eating," I replied. "I don't get this kind of food at home. The best my mom could do is bagels and lox on Sunday." Even though Dad had modernized our kitchen with an electric refrigerator that had a real ice maker, and a new electric stove that burned your fingers if you were not careful, Mom's food was lacking.

"The food must be terrible in England if my mom is any example of their cooking," I said as I took a sip of the sweet Mogen David ceremonial wine instead of the grape juice provided for the kids.

A *barcha* over the wine was chanted by Grandpa before every clan meal.

"Baruch ata Adonai, Elohim Melekh ha olam bore p'ree hagafen . . ." ("Praise to You, Adonai our G-d, Sovereign of the universe, Creator of the fruit of the vine.")

Actually, the real family drink was tea. The tinkle of a spoon against the glass as family members sipped hot tea could always be heard at these gatherings. That is, except for Uncle Izzy, who always yelled across the table, "I'm sick of this tea. Bring me some pop." A 6-oz bottle of Coca-Cola would be produced just for him.

Aunt Sarah stirred her tea while she held a sugar cube in her hand. With plate in hand, I sat down next to her at the triple-leafed, mahogany table with the carved lion paw legs. Contrary to the plastic covers on the red silk sofa, the dining room chairs were covered with leather, and more comfortable. As I lifted my fork, she touched my hand and looked straight into my eyes, "Sherrie, take care of my David. He is so unhappy lately, and he won't talk to me about it."

I scrutinized her face, looking for some reason for this statement before getting up and moving towards my cousin. He seemed fine to me. Most of the time David's problems revolved around Pa, with Aunt Sarah pressuring David to conform.

"David, I'll be right there," I said. "I need a bathroom break, and it is finally empty."

David waited for me. The younger kids gathered around him. He ruffled the thick black curly head of hair on Yale. "How is your bar mitzvah practice going?" David asked. "I bet you can't wait until it's here."

Yale reached up and whispered something in David's ear. David burst out in laughter.

Gail, a small, brown-haired, ponytailed six-year-old cousin in a fluffy blue lace dress jumped him. She held out her wrists, "David, smell my perfume."

Lilac permeated the air. "Wow, you make me think of beautiful flowers," David said with a broad smile across his face. He was so charismatic.

With a flirtatious giggle, she answered, "David, take me with you."

He picked her up, hugged her, and then put her down. "Gail, the streetlights will go on soon, and you can't be out anymore today."

While she narrowed her big bright eyes and thought about that rule, we slipped out. I grabbed a piece of rugelach on the way, the only dessert on the table besides those awful stewed prunes the adults enjoyed.

Handsome, tall, and slender, with two adorable dimples, plus a full head of thick black hair, David fascinated me. He wasn't the classic competitive first-born. Sensitive and quiet, he loved to read, work on artistic projects, and go to museums. Two years older than I was, he took me places I couldn't go as a girl alone, like the real live theatre. I spent time with my friends at the Jeffery Theatre to watch movies every

Saturday afternoon, but it was different than the live theatre. About three times a year, David took me to downtown Chicago to see real actors perform. We spent time together because we had so much in common. Too bad he was my cousin. Girls who thought they could get to him through me tried to be my best friend. He never kept a girlfriend for long.

Slowly we walked down the street towards Lake Michigan. The old city neighborhood had full majestic natural oaks and maples. The sweet, perfumed fragrance of the magnolias only added to the delight of a spring day. Flowers were just starting to peek through the lush green ground. Only a few red tulips were visible. Blue jays, sparrows, and several other colorful birds chirped loudly, and bushy-tailed gray squirrels scurried up the trees, while the "Pop Goes The Weasel" tune from the Good Humor cart was heard coming down the street. Spring was definitely in the air.

"Do you want an ice cream? We could chase the cart," David suggested.

I rubbed my stomach and replied, "Are you kidding? After eating at Aunt Tillie's, I am stuffed."

He smiled as we continued towards the lake.

We sat down on the massive grayish-white concrete rocks and watched the icy blue water beating against them. Not much wind made for a calm lake today. I longed for the summer and the 76th Street Rainbow Beach. It was a real beach, where there were no rocks, and the water lapped gently over the white sand. When we would spend the day there, we would park ourselves down on the sand with our sun umbrellas, blankets, towels, and Coppertone lotion. We swam, or, if adventurous, we rode on a big, large inner tube out into the lake, or we just stood waist-deep in the warm water. The food stands provided a cold drink, an ice cream, or a hot dog while us young, freckled-faced, skinny-legged teenagers in our one-piece bathing suits flirted with the boys from South Shore and Bowen high schools, as well as Hyde Park, who tried to be macho to impress us.

There was no sunbaked beach here, but I could still reach the water from my rock. I took off my penny-loafer shoes and socks and dangled my feet in the tepid waves. I scooped up a handful of water and splashed it against my face. A welcomed light northern breeze swept by us.

In the winter we stayed away from the rocky shore, as the fierce cold winds blowing over the rocks made them treacherous. Several years ago a young boy had been swept off the rocks and drowned.

David wasn't in a hurry to talk. I assumed it was another conflict with Pa. I loved Pa dearly, but I wouldn't want to live with him, especially without a dad in the house. He was too old school, and his word was the law.

It felt good to be by the lake, because the crowded apartment had been stuffy with so many people and no air. We had two of those new miracle window air-conditioners, but Aunt Tillie didn't. She depended on old fans situated near the windows. In our apartment the air conditioners sat in the bedroom and front room windows right over the grinding radiators. Windows closed, air conditioner on, no more worry about cross-ventilation, sticky wet skin, and total frizzy hair in the summers.

A young boy peddled by on a ten-speed Schwinn bicycle with wheels that made a weird whirling noise. Sounded a little like cicadas.

David reached into his pocket and pulled out a cigarette from a Chesterfield pack. He covered the match with his hand in order to block the wind as he lit it. He took a deep puff, letting the smoke spread out through his nose and sail over the water. I had tried a cigarette once and ended up coughing and coughing while my friends laughed and laughed.

"David, what did Yale whisper to you?" I asked.

David smiled as he turned in my direction. "The kid said, I can't wait for my bar mitzvah because it is my get-out-of-Hebrew-school card.'"

Realizing how true that was and how that statement reflected Yale's so very maneuvering personality, we both grinned and shook our heads. Aunt Tillie always said, "That kid of mine tells it as it is."

Then I asked, "What do you want to talk to me about? Did you write another poem for me to check?" His poems contained fascinating thoughts and language, but weak grammar and spelling, so he always asked for my help. I so admired his artistic talent and his ability to focus on only one thing at a time. I found myself analyzing everything. Mom said I should be a lawyer. A woman lawyer, that would be something.

"No," he mumbled, as he tensely stared out across the water.

I could tell that there was something serious on the tip of David's tongue, but somehow, he couldn't let it out. An uneasy feeling took over me, one I never felt with David. Normally, I felt relaxed with him and knew what to expect from our meetings.

Finally, I said, "David, you are acting like a nincompoop. Tell me what's wrong. You and I have been honest with each other, always sharing our secrets, since I was five years old. I even told you when I stuffed socks in my bra to look like I had bigger boobs." I thought that would make him laugh. It didn't.

I tried to be more serious, "Remember when we mixed our blood and pledged to be soul mates forever, just like our uncles and aunts have been with each other?"

David pressed his lips together and turned his head away from me. "Sherrie, I don't like who I am," David said. "Thoughts floating through my head torment me at night, and I don't understand what my body is telling me. I am so baffled and afraid. I'm especially worried about what I'm going to do after graduation next year."

Not understanding, I answered, "That's nuts. You are smart, charming, and handsome, and every girl in the high school is crazy about you. Life for you has always seemed swell."

At fifteen in the 1950s, love and sex constituted a romantic concept between a boy and girl, not a physical one, so I never had a clue to what David was trying to tell me about his body talking to him.

Another thought entered my head. Though many dads never came back from the war, David's was the only one in our extended family who was killed. Oh, Uncle Izzy did come back a little messed up, but that doesn't count as the same. Dad says Izzy was in the battle of Okinawa and he will never get over the war. So what? He is sweet and nice to everyone and always seems happy, even though he has a slight limp.

"Do you think, not having a father had made a big difference in your thinking?" I asked. "Our uncles and aunts always said you have a remarkable resemblance to your dad, and they talk about how much they miss him. Possibly you are trying too hard to take his place." My mind pictured the photograph on Aunt Sarah's mantle of a handsome young man in a tan army uniform who was just a few years older than David.

He hesitated before he answered. "Yes, it does have something to do with my dad. I don't want to be a doctor. I hate blood," he said as he grimaced and lit another cigarette.

I shrugged my shoulders, "So, don't be a doctor."

"It's not that easy," David said. "I am the oldest boy, and I will be the first one in the family to go to college. My father wanted to be a doctor. I've been told the whole clan had put away money for me to go to medical school."

A selfish thought occurred to me. "David, is there money put away for me and the other cousins to go to college?"

"For Yale maybe, but the rest of you are girls. You get married and have babies."

Angry, I got up and started to walk away. Then I turned towards him. "My mother had two years of college before the war. She wanted to be a teacher. Not every woman is satisfied with just cooking and cleaning. Some of us want to use our minds."

He reached out and grabbed my hand. "I'm sorry, that was insensitive of me. Will you help me, Sherrie? You can have the money they saved for me."

I sat back down on the rock just in time to be splashed by the waves. I threw my black cashmere cardigan over my wet blouse. The tension diminished with the water and we both started to laugh.

"I hate blood, too," I said. "I want to be a writer. What do you want to be?"

"I would love to become a decorator," David said.

"Wow," I exclaimed. "You did fix up your room nice. Too bad Grandpa made you take down the fountain. I thought it was neat—so clever to paint those drainage pipes white."

"How can I tell them?"

"Let's think about it, You do have another year of high school. Can I talk to Mom about it? She's not like everyone else. She can keep a secret, and she is more worldly than the rest of us."

I had a hard time understanding why he would be willing to give up a chance to go to college. College was my dream. The thought that he could be drafted into the army also occurred to me. The war in Korea had ended, but there was a new conflict starting in a place called Vietnam.

"I could get a job in a furniture store, and get some experience in decorating, but I am expected to work in your dad's store this summer," David explained.

"Me too," I replied. "I would love to have the summer off, but . . ."

The shine of city lights, the bright crimson sky, and the sparkle of fireflies circling around us meant night was now approaching.

"We better go," David sighed, as he ground out his cigarette on the rock. "They will be looking for us." By the time we reached home, the streets were clearing, the crickets were starting their evening concerts, the birds were swooping over the treetops in search of their nesting grounds, and the lights in the houses were glowing. We parted in the middle of the street.

David had set into motion a plea for help, so I went to Mom and told her David's story. She had lost family in the war like David had.

She smiled slyly, "I'm not surprised. Tell him to wait until the summer and the holidays are over, and I will help him talk to everyone."

I gave her a big hug.

"Thank you, Mom. I knew you would help."

She stopped me. "Sherrie, you need to continue to be there for him. David is different."

"What do you mean, Mom?"

"When he is ready to tell you, he will."

I wasn't sure why being a decorator instead of a doctor was such a big deal, but I let it go for now. I was a busy teenager.

Chapter Four

The summer flew by with just two family crises.

Little Gail fell off the playground swing and broke her arm. To the horror of the doctors, we all took her to the emergency room, all twenty of us, because that is what close families did.

"Everyone, *please*, wait outside. You can sign Gail's cast when we are done," young Doctor Cohen said, with a desperate edge in his voice.

Gail cried when the cast came off. "Nobody can sign my cast now. I won't be special anymore."

David carefully lifted her up on his lap, and said, "Gail, honey, the cast didn't make you special. You were special because you didn't let the cast depress you. You learned how to do things with it, like writing and cutting your food. You will always be special to me."

That cousin of mine was so compassionate and clever.

The other one happened right after Aunt Tillie's and Uncle Hymie's dog, Prince, died. Izzy came home from fishing at Navy Pier, carrying a brown-and-white mixed-breed dog and a big yellow doghouse. The kids who were outside playing ran towards him. With a wide mischievous smile, he shouted up to Tillie's open window, "Tillie, I brought you a new dog."

Before Tillie responded, Sarah leaned out her window and yelled, "That dog is pregnant. Make him take it back."

I felt sorry for Uncle Izzy. When he came home with fish that he caught, Aunt Dora would yell, "Throw those fish back in the lake. I'm not cleaning them." Now he had to take the dog back, too.

* * *

David took a job at the furniture store down the street from my dad's grocery, so he was busy after school, and we didn't see as much of each other. In fact, he dropped away from most of his old high school friends, too, spending more and more time in the furniture store, or talking to my mother.

"What happened to your cousin? He never participates in our activities. He dropped out of the writing club and the AZA club, plus we never see him at the usual hangouts—the bowling alley, Mitchell's Ice Cream, the baseball field." This was a familiar line of inquiry from several of the girls in my school, plus a few of the boys. I wasn't sure how to answer. The last time I saw David, he was coming out of my apartment after talking to my mother.

I tried to make conversation, asking, "David, how was the game? Did you see Little Louie?" My dad and the uncles had taken the boys in the family to Comiskey Park to see the White Sox play. The Sox were on a winning streak, and everyone on the South Side was hopeful for a 1959 pennant and a World Series win.

"Sherrie, we were so high up and it was cold and dark," David said. "The dough pretzels were delicious, though." He knew I was jealous, so he tried to minimize the experience just like old times. I was grateful.

I missed him, but my third year of high school was more challenging and busier, and I had a boyfriend. He went to South Shore High School on 76th Street while I went to Hyde Park High School on 63rd and Stony Island. Both schools were tied together socially with sororities, fraternities, dances, football, etc. so it was no big deal.

With disheveled brown curly hair, tall and lanky with an angular handsome face was my Jeff. Jewish, of course, otherwise I would be thrown out of the family like my Aunt Barbra was. I was told Grandpa sat shiva for her and no one was allowed to see Aunt Barbra ever again. Marrying out of the faith was worse than eating a sausage pizza!

From the first time that Jeff and I started to date, he made life exciting. My petticoats swished back and forth as he twirled me on the dance floor at school parties. No jalopy for my boyfriend; Jeff had this gorgeous, white Chevy convertible with a red leather interior, which meant we could travel to downtown Chicago instead of spending our Saturday nights on 71st Street at the Jeffery Theater and The Peter Pan restaurant, or parking at La Rabida Children's Hospital by Lake Michigan to watch the submarine races.

"Why do you always order a grilled cheese sandwich and a Coke when we eat downtown?" Jeff asked. "Aren't you hungry, or are you afraid that I don't have the money?"

I twisted the curls on my forehead as I thought about how to answer. "Well, once you did shuffle me out of a restaurant pronto because we couldn't come up with enough money for a tip, but really it is because I don't know what is kosher."

He smiled. "Never thought of that. We don't keep kosher anymore, except for the restriction on pig and shellfish. Sorry Sherrie," Jeff answered as we left. "I guess we will stick with the delis. The prices are right, and they are kosher."

I felt a little funny. More and more kids in my generation were pulling away from the kosher life and experimenting with all kinds of foods. I really longed to try a hot dog at Carl's, the hot dog stand hangout on 83rd Street, or a barbecue beef sandwich at The Tropical Hut in Hyde Park, or one of those 15-cent hamburgers at the new drive-in called McDonald's, but I was still bound by tradition.

The lake was different downtown. We parked by Oak Street Beach and gazed out at the reflection of glass and steel high-rise buildings or rested our eyes on luxurious white yachts and dreamed of a different life. Engaged in innocent flirtations, we kissed, hugged, and petted a little while listening to the new rock and roll singers like Chuck Berry. If it was late enough, we romanced with Franklin McCormick as he recited love poems over the radio. The radio was our license to the world and to all the new hit tunes.

I did have a midnight curfew, which was hard to meet sometimes, like the day I quietly opened the door to our apartment and found my dad with crossed arms waiting on the other end.

"Sherrie, it is 12:44," Dad said with his eyebrows raised and lips pursed. "Why are you late?"

Never Mom, always Dad was the one I had to answer to as Jeff mumbled goodnight and hurried down the stairs.

"I'm sorry, Dad, but we went to see the colorful lights and music display at the Buckingham Fountain," I stammered. "It was so fantastic that I couldn't pull myself away."

"Sherrie, the display is over at 11 o'clock. I know because it was always one of my favorites."

"Dad, we had to walk to the car."

His eyes pierced through me, his lips compressed into a small line. The stare and the absence of sound coming from him terrified me. The family used guilt as punishment. It worked much better than violence, especially when it came from my dad. I felt a shiver up my spine.

"Dad, Dad, I promise, I won't be late again," I begged.

"Adjust your blouse and go to bed," he finally said.

My world was a simple place back then. School was good. I was keeping all A's and I had a fulfilling social life. The worst thing I could do was disappoint my dad or a family member. I was never late again, nor were my clothes ever in disarray again.

Jeff promised to teach me how to drive when I turned sixteen. None of the women in the neighborhood drove. They didn't need to. A shopping stroll down 71st Street was almost a daily chore. What their metal carts couldn't carry was delivered by the stores.

I was the one who broke the tradition and learned to drive. It wasn't a quick easy learn. I put a significant dent into my boyfriend's beautiful white Chevy when I slid it into a utility pole. It put a significant dent into our relationship too. Thank God for insurance, and a smart boy who quickly changed seats with me and took the rap for the accident. I then had to wait another six months before dad took over the driving instructions and let me near our automobile.

Never could parallel park well. Always turned the wheel too much or hit the brake too hard. Having the neighborhood kids cheer and tease me as I practiced for the driving test didn't help. I was thrilled when I passed the test. So was my cousin Lizzie. She now inherited my blue Schwinn cruiser bike and my pink pedal pushers, because I now had access to real wheels. Mom and Dad now had an unpaid employee to do the errands. Freedom was when I got the car for myself, which wasn't often because like, most families in the late fifties, we were a one-car-only family.

Finding a parking space near the apartment building was hard enough for a one-car family. There were no garages in the area. I can remember Aunt Tillie yelling, especially in the winter, "Yale, there's a parking spot in front. Quick go save it for your father and Uncle Jake!"

Yale would answer to no avail, "Ma, it's cold out. Dad could be late."

"Then, young man, you can shovel and scrape off the ice and snow in the walkway while you wait," Aunt Tillie would answer.

In order to save parking spaces, some neighbors put chairs in the spaces in front of their apartment building, while they watched from a window.

Besides my dad's grocery, there was Rosenblum's Drugstore, a good place for a soda while waiting for prescriptions, especially when the soda jerks were cute young guys. Fialkoff's Kosher Butcher was the perfect place to use one's haggling skills. (Oh, how I hated the raw acid smell in that store. As a kid I dropped my ice cream cone on the sawdust floor and ran out.)

Then there were the beauty shops where the neighborhood gossip flowed constantly, and a little ways east on 71st Street was South Shore Deli, and next door was South Shore Bakery. The bakery had an unusual marble cake with alternating white and chocolate squares covered by chocolate frosting. Between delicious bites, we kids puzzled over how it was made.

The many dress and millinery shops for those special occasions popped up across the shopping street. Trying on hats until Mrs. Munishkin threw us out was a favorite of us young girls. "Go, Go," she would wave us out of the metal and leather chairs while we sat in front of the large ornate mirrors, admiring the many hats with bird feathers.

"I spend all my time putting hats together, and you delinquents, you mess them up. *Gay awek* (Go away)!" she would shout as she picked up fallen ostrich feathers. That was probably the most mischief we girls got into in the 1950s. Mrs. Munishkin got even with me by selling my mother a very expensive orange hat that Dad and I both hated.

Seders Dress Shop was where we had our own saleswoman. It was the place to go for special occasions, like my bat mitzvah, and the high school prom. The sales ladies brought dresses to us in a separate dressing room like the rich people of the world experienced, not like most stores that sold clothes from racks.

David and I spent many Saturday afternoons munching on buttered popcorn while watching a double feature at the Jeffery Theater. Once, when we were little, we fell asleep and stayed there until our folks and neighbors sent out searchers. The teenager who managed the theatre was busy with a girlfriend and paid no attention to us. He got into more trouble than we did.

I can't forget the jewelry store, the one the women of the family took the train to around once a year, or for special occasions, when a ring was needed for a wedding, a watch for a bar mitzvah, or a bracelet for a special anniversary or birthday. The women picked the items out, but the men made the actual purchase. Aunt Tillie said Jews liked jewelry because the stones were easy to smuggle out of the country when the pogroms came. I think we modern Jews like it for its value and beauty. The store, owned by a relative, was in the Art Deco Pittsfield Jewelry Building on Washington Street in downtown Chicago.

"Nice to see you again, Mrs. Paul," Bill, the blue-and-red uniformed elevator operator said as he opened the brass gate. We entered the ornate gold and marble trimmed elevator on our way to the twelfth floor, where shining diamond engagement rings sparked dreams of the future for us young girls, and memories of past days for our mothers. This day we shopped for Yale's bar mitzvah gift. A watch, the symbol of adulthood, was the traditional family gift for a boy. I lingered by the mirror as I fingered the beautiful sterling silver Star of David hanging around my neck. It was the bat mitzvah gift I had received three years ago. A gold and pearl sweet 16 charm sitting in one of the cases caught my eye.

Lizzie came up behind me and whispered, "Heh, Sherrie, that charm would make a good addition to your traditional bracelet, wouldn't it?"

Soon, I was surrounded by the whole clan. "Marty, let's see the charm," Tillie ordered. Marty took it out, and Tillie looked it over and over. "So, how much?"

Marty gave her the price as I tried to find a place to hide.

He said, "Sherrie will be sixteen in two months. The gold charm with the one pearl and the words *sweet sixteen* would be perfect. You know she already has the bracelet with her bat mitzvah charm. You'll talk to Jake about it. Maybe you could work something out. For the holidays, I bet you could use a case of whiskey."

As she walked away from the case and the charm, she looked Marty in the eye.

"Marty, I know your jewelry is only top quality, but that charm has a tiny nick."

Marty came around from behind the case and he hugged Tillie. Then with a slight grin, he said, "Tillie, you are still so good at maneuvering. Show me where the nick is!" They both started to laugh.

We left the jewelry store and walked on down Michigan Avenue. We shopped for clothes and accessories until we were ready to drop. Marshall Field's, Chicago's famous department store, had a special salad made with almost a half a head of lettuce, hard-boiled egg, Swiss cheese, turkey, and a slice of rye bread. All was covered by a thousand island dressing and ordered without the turkey because we were kosher. Eating in the Walnut Room with its Tiffany glass ceilings, white marble counters, and thick carpeting completed the day for us.

With sore stocking feet resting beside high heels, we quietly endured the thirty-minute train ride from the Randolph Street station back to 71st Street and Jeffery Boulevard. Back at home, we took off the girdles and fancy dresses that were required for a trip to downtown Chicago.

On the train in the summer we needed to find seats next to open windows as there was no air conditioning. I was always willing to ride backwards when we turned back the cane seat so we could face each other. It was hard to talk over the clicking noise of the wheels meeting the rails and the screeching sound of the brakes at each stop, but we were a family used to shouting so we managed to carry on a conversation over the noise.

My family did love jewelry, especially Aunt Tillie. She always wore small, pierced diamond earrings, plus a gold heart on a chain, and we were always hunting for jewelry she took off while baking.

"Sherrie, Sherrie, help me find the ruby and diamond ring," Aunt Tillie would say. "It was Ma's and since you're the oldest daughter, it will be yours one day, so you better find it."

If the rings weren't on the sink ledge they were in her pocket. But it was a fun game to play when I was young, and I did get the ring and a gold bracelet from the grandmother I never met. She was larger than I was, so they flopped around on my hand and arm, and I was afraid to change their size or wear them. I didn't want to lose the family heirlooms. I resolved to pass the jewelry on to my children or nieces so they would stay in the family.

Aunt Tillie also was the keeper of the family silver. Every Rosh Hashanah—the Jewish New Year—the mahogany box would be taken down from the top shelf in her closet, and her daughter Lizzie would knock on my door.

"Sherrie, it's polish the silver day," Lizzie would say. With a frown on her face she would complain, "What is wrong with the stainless? It takes us all day to get the tarnish off the sterling. I don't think God cares."

I differed with her as I kind of got a high from making something ugly turn into something sparkling and beautiful. I couldn't understand why we didn't use the sterling more often, especially since most family dinners used meat silverware, and the sterling was for *fleishig* (meat) meals.

As we were busy polishing and chatting, I asked Aunt Tillie, "Where is Aunt Dora? She usually joins us."

"She's lying down," Aunt Tillie said. "She's been feeling nauseated this morning."

Lizzie and I both raised our eyebrows. "What is wrong?" I asked.

Avoiding the question, Aunt Tillie went over to the kitchen window and opened it. "It's warm in here," she said as she removed her sweater, and went back to cleaning the silver.

"Mom," Lizzie said. "I saw her knitting a yellow blanket. Is she pregnant?"

"Isn't she too old?" I asked, eyes wide open.

Tillie put down the fork she was cleaning, stared at us, and said, "She is only thirty-eight. You young people think we're ancient. "*Ptew, ptew, ptew*, stop talking about pregnancies, you will bring on the evil eye."

Chapter Five

My mother and David still spent time talking to each other. In fact, he spent more time with Mom than with me. They finally decided to confront the family at the Yom Kippur breakfast. It was a time of forgiveness. A twenty-four-hour fast was tough to handle, so Mom decided to start the discussion while everyone was anxious to get to the food, thus cutting down on any arguments.

Right in the middle of the family settling around the large dark wooden table filled with food, Mom, dressed in a long tan skirt and a lime-green cashmere sweater, banged on a pot, and in her rich, sharp, British accent, she told the family to be quiet. Mom never did this, so all conversation ceased as everyone froze into a shocked state.

I heard Aunt Tillie say, "Could she be pregnant?"

Mom ignored her.

"David has something to tell you," Mom said. "It is a hard decision, and he needs you to listen." With that, Mom sat at the table, and we all waited for David to speak.

Looking as handsome as ever in a white, button-down shirt and brown khaki pants, David stood up and took a deep breath before talking. I knew he had been practicing for days.

He said, "My family is so wonderful. I want to thank all of you for being there when my father died. It kept Mom and me going. I know the family wants me to follow my Dad's dream of becoming a doctor, but I must follow my own dream. My dream is to become a decorator. I know you have saved money for my college years, and I am forever grateful. I hope you will use whatever money I don't use for Sherrie and the other kids."

For the first time ever, the family actually became quiet. *Tick-tock* went the wall clock, a sound I never remembered hearing before. They sat there, staring at David, while David turned to me with lips pursed, face pale, and head down. I reached over and squeezed his cold hand. He squeezed back hard. I knew he was struggling to keep it together. He was afraid of what Pa would do.

Mom stood up and clapped, and so did I. I was proud of David, and of Mom, too. It was the first time she actually became part of the family. Soon, most of the family came forward and hugged David. Dad put his arm around Mom and whispered something in her ear. A big smile covered her face.

Grandpa didn't go near David. I heard Grandpa say to David's mother, "I told you, Sarah. The boy needed to do man's work. You babied him too much."

The color drained from Aunt Sarah's face while her hand stretched over her heart. Her reprieve from grief for her husband centered around protecting her son. David's recent changes in behavior she attributed to adolescence, and she paid no attention to Pa's warnings, not that it would have made a difference in David's nature.

Uncle Hymie clenched the top of his chair while he stared at David.

A teacup chattered as Aunt Tillie's shaking hands put it down. With tightened jaw, she rose from her chair and walked over to David and to my mother. Then she took them to where Grandpa was sitting, and she said, "Pa, it's settled. The boy must follow his dream. When you were young, you and Ma followed your dream and came to America. Your parents weren't happy when you left them."

Grandpa ignored everyone, got up, cleared his throat, and pronounced the Jewish cure for everything: "Let's eat."

It was the early 1960s, and I didn't have a clue about what David was really telling us, or why kids would whisper, "Your cousin is a *homo.*" I tried to look it up in the encyclopedia without much luck. It said *homo* meant *man*!

After graduation, David continued to work for the furniture store full time, distancing himself from the family mainly because Pa asked him to move out. He still came to Friday Night dinners and saw his mother regularly. We stayed in contact, but our relationship was not the same.

About four years later, David introduced the family to a tall, muscular, blond, narrow-faced young man named Jeffery, who, like David, resembled a handsome movie star.

"Jeffery is my design business partner," David said, "and life partner." As I watched David, who was now dressed to the hilt in Polo shirts and pants, give Jeffery a passionate smile, I remembered a time when I taught David how to *cha-cha* before he went to a dance with a girl named Doris. I then realized sometimes people aren't who they seem to be.

With lingering nostalgia, I thought about all the girls who were so crazy about David. It was hard for me to process that David preferred boys to girls. I swallowed hard and brushed away the few tears that ran down my cheeks before congratulating them. The David I knew growing up was no longer the same person, but it felt good to see him happy.

My mother sat by me. As she put her hand on mine, she said, "Be happy for David. A few years ago I was afraid he would do something terrible to himself. With Jeffery, he has confidence and a renewed passion for life."

I turned away towards the rainbow colors reflecting off the windowpane before I answered, "Yes, Mom, I will try to understand." Though, truthfully, I still didn't quite get why the word *decorator* triggered so much emotion.

* * *

Every fall around the Jewish holidays and on the anniversary of a loved one's death, the family piled into my dad's sharp, blue Cadillac convertible and Uncle Hymie's old white Hudson sedan and drove out to Waldheim Jewish Cemetery on the West Side. The women wore their special dresses and coats, while the men came in their overcoats and fedoras. It was the custom to honor the memory of a loved one rain, snow, or whatever. We recited the prayer to preserve the soul of each departed member and left pebbles on the large monument markers to show that we were there. Lunch time in a near-by restaurant was where memories and stories of the departed flowed.

"Do you remember when Izzy threw the tomato at the wall?"

"It wasn't at the wall. He was trying to hit me and missed," my dad said.

"He ran out the door in his underwear."

"What could he do? Pa was chasing him. Pa had just finished papering the wall with that terrible red and gold Chinese flock wallpaper."

"The tomato was red, so it matched," said my dad.

My uncles playfully punched each other and laughed. Surprisingly, Pa kept eating without saying anything.

Tillie looked at Sarah. "Did you realize how young Ma was, only fifty-six?"

"She always seemed so old," Sarah added in an uncharacteristic quiet voice.

Tillie reached across the table and put her hands on Lizzie and me. "Our mother would have loved you two girls."

Izzy broke the mood. "Sherrie, Lizzie, if you're not finishing your food, pass it down to us, especially that half of a corned beef sandwich.

We can't waste anything." We were an extended loving family that lived together and functioned like a small village.

I was the first girl in my dad's family to go to college, thanks to David. His coming out gave me the courage to follow my dream. He taught me to be myself even in the midst of fear and uncertainty. While my friends were getting married, or becoming secretaries or teachers, I was taking the Illinois Central train and then a bus to the University of Illinois branch located on Chicago's Navy Pier with the hope of going on to law school.

It helped that we were in the 1960s by that time, which was a much different decade than the quiet, innocent 1950s, when homosexuals had to stay underground, and girls could only look for a "MRS" degree. I could be more than a housewife, secretary, or a teacher. I thought of law with a sideline as a writer. I wanted to be the first woman in the family to be able to support herself. Even though college classes were so much harder than high school, they gave me my first feel of freedom. Just traveling beyond South Shore to downtown Chicago daily made a difference. I suddenly saw a world outside of the family building.

Little did we realize that the fall of 1963 would alter our safe lives. It would alter the lives of all Americans. On November 22 right before Thanksgiving, an era of peace and innocence ended.

It was on a balmy sixty-degree fall day. On the way to my classes, I walked along Navy Pier watching the waves breaking against the actual pier when I witnessed boys and girls glued to handheld radios.

I stopped one of them asking, "What is wrong?"

"The president has been shot! Classes are canceled, everything is canceled," he shouted.

"What president?" someone asked.

"Kennedy, the president of the United States!"

I joined the shocked group. We made our way to the school union where there was a television. A gray-haired lady in a flowered dress told us, "I was watching a television soap opera when Walter Cronkite broke in to tell the nation that President Kennedy was dead. Cronkite took off his glasses and paused briefly to maintain his composure." A girl I barely knew melted into my arms as tears rolled down our faces. I hardly remember how I made it home that day. Everyone walked around downtown like zombies. For days, at home, we hardly did anything but gather around the small black and white television until we watched John Kennedy being buried. The image of his three-year-old son saluting would stay in everyone's memory forever. We were a stunned nation. Camelot fell, and with it the calm, innocent, easygoing world we lived in.

Chapter Six

Life went on, but the nation changed. Suddenly, we were paying more attention to what was going on in the world, not just our neighborhoods.

One day, David called me, all excited, and said, "Sherrie, the 1964 Civil Rights Act has been signed! No longer will there be discrimination based on religion race, color, or sex. Jeffery and I have been going to rallies and meetings to help get it passed, as it will also help gays!"

"That is great news, but the escalation of the Vietnam war isn't good news," I replied. "Jimmy Schmitt, my good friend from high school, was just drafted, along with other boys we know."

In another time, David and I would only have been talking about The Beatles and the movies we'd seen. Now that the '60s were here we, like other young people, were becoming more involved with the world beyond our neighborhoods—reading newspapers, and watching television programs that talked about ideas.

* * *

The shattering of glass from Chaim's heel was greeted by clapping and shouts of "Mazel Tov, Mazel Tov" by the one-hundred and twenty guests at the wedding of Cousin Lizzie and her high school sweetheart. I gave Lizzie a quick kiss before she and her husband left the chuppah (the canopy representing the future home of the couple) and charged down the aisle to be congratulated by family and friends.

Being Lizzie's maid of honor I was at the signing of the ketuba (Jewish marriage contract between the bride and groom), and I held Lizzie's long veil while she circled her future husband the traditional seven times. Her ivory-colored pearl inlaid dress was a gorgeous secondhand find. She and I had answered an ad, but nobody needs to know. A wedding dress is only used once anyway. The two gold rings they exchanged were engraved with the traditional saying, *Ani L'Dodi V'Dodi Li* (I am my beloved's and my beloved is mine).

This was my third bridesmaid performance for 1964. My closet had pink, yellow, and lilac dresses I'll never wear again. All my young friends and young family members were getting married, while I was struggling my way through classes at the University of Illinois Chicago campus, and praying that I would get into law school next year.

The room in the temple's gathering hall was transformed into a beautiful wedding festival. White padded chairs and pink tablecloths with red and white roses in glass vases replaced the old cardboard tables. Nameplates and pink matchboxes were next to every serving. On the stage was a six-piece orchestra, and there was a bar. This was the fanciest wedding we'd attended.

Uncle Izzy, looking out of place without his cigar, cut the three-foot-long challah and made the prayer over it as Chaim's dad did the prayer over the wine. Pa stood with them, but a stroke had slowed him down. It was sad to see him not in charge.

The buffet table was attacked after the traditional cry, "Let's eat."

Aunt Tillie, wearing a long pink gown, matching shoes, and purse stood next to the buffet, which was loaded with silver platters filled with three different salads, brisket, turkey, small lamb chops, potato pancakes, rolls, and fruit. She was standing next to a sign that read, "Catered by South Shore Deli." She was crying.

I walked over to where she was standing and hugged her. "Congratulations on your daughter's wedding," I said. "You look gorgeous, especially with your shining gray hair. Why the tears?"

She wiped her eyes with an embroidered handkerchief and answered in a stiff voice. "Sherrie, they hate my cooking," Aunt Tillie replied. "I can make better food than the deli, but Lizzie wouldn't let me. Did you taste the brisket? It's dry with no flavor. A caterer they needed?"

"Aunt Tillie you are the best cook in the whole world, but you have to stay back and enjoy your daughter's wedding," I explained. "You would be exhausted if you tried to cook for over one hundred people. Lizzie said you made the strudel and rugelach for the dessert table."

"Chaim's mother wanted the caterer for her fancy-schmancy North Side family," Aunt Tillie said. "They are paying for half the wedding so they get to make noise. Did you see how many fur coats are hanging in the temple closet?"

"Be happy for Lizzie," I advised. "Come with me. The band is playing a hora." I pulled my aunt over to the dance floor where we joined everyone holding hands as they circled the room, kicking and singing.

I went back to my table exhausted. I sat down and quickly drank a glass of Coca-Cola. I turned to my Dad and said, "Why haven't you and Mom joined the dancing?"

My mother took a drag on her cigarette and said, "I've been very tired lately. Probably menopause."

I had noticed that Mom was doing less, and was much thinner. Before I asked whether she had seen a doctor, David whirled me onto the dance floor.

"Sherrie, it's a cha-cha. You spent hours teaching it to me."

We did make good dance partners. I noticed that David didn't bring his partner Jeffery to the wedding. Just as well. He couldn't dance with Jeffery among this crowd. Anyway, he needed to take care of his mother, Aunt Sarah.

It was Sunday night and I had school the next morning so I left the wedding early. It felt strange to have Lizzie married. She was going to Roosevelt University to become a teacher. I hoped she didn't become pregnant before finishing. Unfortunately, once girls got married they usually gave up working.

Chapter Seven

The year 1965 was a sad one for the family. It was a year that made me realize how fragile we were, and how little control we actually had over our lives. Man plans, and God laughs.

Since Grandpa had suffered his stroke, he couldn't walk or talk like he used to. He even stopped putting on his prayer shawl to *daven*. Aunt Dora had a second miscarriage and stayed in bed in a state of depression. I helped take care of both Grandpa and my cousins when I wasn't in college classes.

After spending two hours with my grandfather, where I tried to get his feet to move one foot in front of the other while his trembling hands waved me away, Aunt Sarah brought me into the kitchen.

"Sit down," Aunt Sarah said as she padded the red vinyl kitchen chair next to her Formica kitchen table. "I appreciate your help with Pa, but you have a full college schedule, and we are all helping to watch him. You have to realize he won't get better."

"Aunt Sarah, you don't understand, I love him so. He is my only grandparent. Yale, Lizzie, and Rachel have two other grandparents."

"Yes, but Dora's parents live far away on Devon Avenue, so Pa is special to them too, and Hymie's parents live in Florida, so those cousins only have Pa nearby too," Aunt Sarah explained.

She got up and went by the stove to pour herself a cup of tea. While Aunt Sarah was dipping the tea bag in the water, she turned towards me, "Honey, you are young and haven't lost anyone like I have. My mother died twenty-years ago, my young husband . . ." she trailed off before continuing, "Pa is eighty-six, and it is natural for him to die at that age."

I didn't understand Aunt Sarah, and believed that she had become a cold, uncaring person. I thought the family had gone through the worst of times. That is, until my mother was diagnosed with lung cancer.

My mother died right before my college graduation, six months after her lung cancer diagnosis. She went so fast from a beautiful young woman to a chemotherapy shadow of what she had been. Her life had become in and out of the hospital with surgeries, hair loss, needles, and nausea. I was at the hospital with her at the end. Twelve long-stem roses sat on the nightstand. A basket of apples, oranges, and grapes rested untouched, while she was taking her last breaths. Her nurse told me that the hearing was the last sense to go. I leaned in close to her and told her I had been accepted to John Marshall Law School, and that I would be going for her. Her head turned towards me, and her eyes smiled. Only about five percent of the law school's classes had women students. She had encouraged me to apply. She had always pushed me to go where women hadn't tread, while my aunts were happy with the status quo.

Up until my mother's death, the family at Waldheim had consisted of relatives I had heard stories about, but never knew. From now on, I would visit with a different purpose, I thought, quietly fingering the black ribbon attached to my clothing. The ribbon that was the Jewish symbol of mourning for the immediate family. Now the stones and flowers I left on my mother's grave would come from a broken heart.

At the funeral, David was almost more upset than I was. He leaned on me while we walked past her body lying in the casket at Weinstein's Funeral Parlor. I think I was still in shock.

"Sherrie, your mother was the only one who ever understood me. "If it wasn't for her, the family would have ostracized me. I loved her so."

It took a while before he controlled his crying. I gave him some of my Kleenex. The ride in the mourning limousine to Waldheim cemetery from Piser's South Shore Funeral home was a very long and unusually quiet ride, maybe because Aunt Tillie rode with her family in their car, while David and I rode only with my dad and David's mother Aunt Sarah.

As we sat on chairs under the canopy by her grave site while the rabbi spoke, instead of joining the prayers, I gazed on a red-breasted robin, ear towards the ground, busily searching for the early morning worm, which might have been for the bobbing heads peeking out of the nest resting between the branches on the ancient oak tree located near my mother's grave. I thought Mom would be happy that she was buried next to life being renewed. To this day, when I see a robin, I think of her.

I couldn't eat a thing at Aunt Tillie's, where the shiva took place. I know my eyes were red and swollen, but all the mirrors were covered as the tradition demands. The seven days went by slowly. Pa was too sick to even come to the shiva. A haze was cast over the week, as everyone was waiting for him to be next. I hardly remember it, though it was rewarding to hear how well my mother was liked.

After my mother died from lung cancer at the very young age of forty-eight, Dad asked me to go through her things and take whatever I wanted. For sure I knew I wanted Mom's collection of books. Her typewriter, open and set up on her desk, made me believe I might locate that novel she always planned to write. If it was there, she hid it well. All I found were scribbled notes with sayings from famous people. There was a file folder labeled *David* which I planned to read at another time. She had recognized his situation early on.

It would be hard to find someone thin and tall enough to wear her clothes or even her gloves. Those delicate small hands were unique to my mom. Maybe her hats. I smiled as I tried on the orange Mr. John hat with the one green feather. Dad and I teased her about it, and she never wore it. I tried to stand in her shoes, but they were too high, too tight, and, most of all, they represented a steadfast resolve and maturity I hadn't reached yet.

Chanel No.5, Mom's favorite perfume, was in the air. Breathing in the sensual flower fragrance made me feel closer to her. I remembered her turning the bottle over and lightly pouring a few drops of the perfume on her fingers before adding it to her wrists and her neck. I looked through her dresses before I came to one of her favorites, a green flowered dress. I took it off its hanger and held it close to my skin. It, too, still had her scent.

I tried to think of her life instead of her death. Just six months after her diagnosis, she'd been lying in a hospital bed among tubes and oxygen tanks, taking her last breath. So fast, it was still hard to believe, even though it was a time when the word *cancer* was usually associated with a death sentence, but not usually with someone so young.

Even though I was surrounded by Dad's large, loving family, it was still hard to imagine life without my mother. Her soothing quiet voice had always been a comfort in a sea of family tumult and loud conversation. I did a lot of crying and thinking. I was glad to have the summer off. On the surface, Dad was doing better than I was, but men kept everything inside. I needed to talk about my feelings, and fortunately David was there for me. My aunts tried, but they were too dependent on religious answers. Truthfully, I was angry with my God, and refused to talk to the Rabbi.

My mother was never bitter or scared. A week before she died, she said, "Remember me the way I looked before that terrible chemo made me look like Kafka's insect, hairless and mutilated." I will always remember her as the beautiful young woman she was. I really thought my mother would live forever, at least into old age. Besides grief, I also felt anger. Anger that she was so young, anger that I would be mother-less at such a young age, and anger at myself for the times I fought with her over trivial things, and anger at her for being different and making me choose between her and the other family members so many times.

* * *

I spent a lot of nostalgic time in her closet and drawers gathering pictures and personal items before finding a box filled with costume jewelry, plus one very disturbing item I had never seen before. It was hidden in a brown envelope.

Dad, seated at the round wooden breakfast table, was drinking cof-fee and reading the morning paper when I entered the kitchen with the box. I could hear my heartbeat in my ears and feel my hands shake. I waited until he took a drink of his coffee and a bite of his Danish, before I removed something from the box. I held it out towards him, pressed my lips together, stared at him, and demanded, "Please explain."

He put his Danish down and wiped his face with a napkin before taking the large gold cross out of my hands. I was hoping he would tell me that it belonged to a friend of Mom's. Instead, he said, "I didn't know your mother still had her cross."

"Her cross! Dad, was Mom . . ." My voice cracked before I finished the sentence. I took a deep breath and started again. "Dad, was Mom Jewish, or did we just live a big lie?"

"Sherrie, please try to understand," Dad said softly, as he nervously fiddled with his coffee cup. "It was a different time. Mom's grand-mother was Jewish, Mom's parents were Protestant, and she was raised Christian. I loved her so, and I knew Pa wouldn't let me marry her if he knew the truth. If I did it against his will, he would have torn his clothes and sat shiva for me like he did with Barbra.

"It was a different time," he repeated. "My mother and father came from an arranged marriage. At birth, my mother was promised to my seven-year-old dad. Love wasn't considered. Religion, family, economics, and obedience came first. There was a war going on . . ."

Those big, bright, dark eyes that I had inherited pleaded with me as my father gently caressed my hand. I pulled away from those strong loving hands that had always made me feel safe. "Dad, who else knew?" I asked, wondering if the whole family had betrayed me.

"No one, but I know Tillie and Sarah suspected, but they never asked me."

I sank down into a chair, tears flowing down my cheeks. "This explains the blond hair, small nose, the different food, and the fact we never went to London to meet her family. We lived a lie. You told me she was raised very Reform. You and Mom *lied* to me. That is what hurts the most. You both lived a lie!"

"Honey, when I met your mom, her mother had died from cancer and her brother had been killed at Dunkirk, and she wasn't sure where her father was," Dad explained. "She had no immediate family. I'm sorry. We should have told you."

"What does this make me? Am I Jewish?" My gaze was fixed upon the cross. I unconsciously rubbed the gold star hanging from my neck. If only Mom were here to tell her side. I wondered, was she miserable all these years being someone else? No wonder she understood David.

"Of course you are. Your father is Jewish, and your great-grandmother was Jewish, and your mother was part Jewish."

"Is this a lie or can I believe you?" My dad had always been the voice of reason, the calming of the waters. How could I ever trust him again?

I wanted to find the truth on my own. "Do you have any information on Mom's family?" I begged. "Somewhere there may be a father, a cousin, a . . . a family member that wondered what happened to their Bess. She never talked about them!"

Tears filled my eyes as I thought about the lies my mother had to live with. I felt like I was on an emotional roller coaster, something like Holden Caulfield when he lost his teenage innocence. *Yes, people die young, and your parents aren't always truthful.*

From that day forward, my goal was to find my mother's family. Dad gave me the little he had, like her maiden name, but my attempts to find my mom's family were unsuccessful. Believing that her friend Sophia might know something, I ravaged through mom's desk, looking for Sophia's number. I went into the kitchen and took down the phone book from the shelf near the wall phone and looked through it. I even walked around the Hyde Park neighborhood, trying to remember the one time I was in Sophie's apartment. Unfortunately, neither Dad nor any family member remembered Sophia's last name, or her address or home phone number, or her friends. The fact that she hadn't shown up at the hospital or for Mom's funeral made me wonder if she was still around. She may have gone back to London. There was a funeral notice in the newspaper for her to see. I shelved this idea for now, but not forever. I knew that someday I would extend my search overseas.

I did find Aunt Barbra, my dad's sister who had been shunned by the family when she married a *goy* (non-Jew). That would have been my dad's fate had Pa known my mother wasn't Jewish. Aunt Barbra was divorced twice and living in California. Her sisters never lost total contact with her. They were obedient to Pa, but family was family, no matter what.

I felt disillusioned with my perfect world. Suddenly, family secrets seemed to be popping up everywhere. Rules that I thought were sacred had been broken and hidden. I decided someone knocked outside of the family circle may be able to help me understand why my parents lied to me.

Chapter Eight

I went out to California to visit Aunt Barbra. She was quite different from the rest of the clan - big blonde dyed hair, movie star makeup emphasizing her dark brown eyes, and a revealing blue patterned jump suit covered her paper thin body. Her bra pushed together enormous breasts that didn't seem to go with her body. A memory flash of brown frizzy hair came to me, but I would have been very young when she left, so I didn't mention it. My dad was the oldest, and Barbra the youngest.

After greeting me at the door with a big hug, Aunt Barbra paid the limousine driver, who had picked me up at the airport, and then she ordered her gardener to take my luggage to the blue room, while she guided me into an enormous open spaced room with high ceilings, and large windows that opened to a view of the Santa Monica Mountains, my first view of real mountains, not the hills of Wisconsin. I stood mesmerized by their massive expanse of green rising to meet powdery snowcapped tips in the middle of summer.

"What can I get you? A drink, gin, vodka, something else?" she asked while I stood, glued to the windows.

I turned towards her and sheepishly answered, "A Coke would be great."

She laughed, "I forgot how young you are." She called to someone named Angie, who magically appeared with a Coke in a crystal glass, plus a delicate China plate of delicious looking pastries.

Aunt Barbra sat down on a beautiful red-and-white flowered silk sofa. Alternating between the slim cigarette in one hand and the glass of vodka in the other, she said, "Sherrie, I was a rebel, always fighting with my mother, hating the old ways, hating being poor.

"One Saturday night while my boyfriend, Dennis, and I were petting in the back seat of his Ford, the door opened and my father's hands pulled me out of the car and dropped me on Garfield Park's grass," Aunt Barbra continued. "My father yelled, 'You are nothing but a *kurveh*'—a loose woman. My sister Tillie put my clothes back on me while the other cars of making-out teens sped away. Tillie held me in her arms and walked me home. My mother was waiting in the kitchen. I sat down on the metal kitchen chair, while Tillie brought me some Kleenex to wipe my tearing eyes.

"Mom stood there with both hands held high. She shook. "Why, Barbra, why? *Little girls are made of sugar and spice and everything nice.* They don't talk back to their papa. They listen to the rules and obey. Go ask your father for forgiveness or he will make you leave the house."

"But I told her, 'I won't ask him anything. I hate him.'

"Pa walked into the house. He turned to Tillie and said, 'Get her out of my house. I won't have the whole neighborhood know my daughter is a *kurveh,* with a goy.' With eyes opened wide, he pointed towards the door and yelled, 'Out, out.' Tillie, who was recently married, put her arms around my shoulders and we walked down to her place.

"At sixteen I ran away with Dennis just to be free," Aunt Barbra recalled. "I knew that Tillie couldn't keep me, even though as my older sister she had always been my protector. Sarah would have thrown me under the train! She was Pa's girl. My romance with Dennis, the goy, only lasted a few months, but it did get me to L.A. I never forgot that my father had kicked me, and my mother never stood up to him to protect her daughter."

Laughing, she shook her head, "Honey, I've had a wild life. Someday, you can write a book about your old Aunt Barbra. Was this your first flight?"

I sat down across from Aunt Barbra on one of her cushy, green, silk chairs. I couldn't relate to the Pa she was talking about.

"Oh, Aunt Barbra, thank you so much for the ticket. I could have come on the train for forty dollars, which would have been one-third the price."

She waved her cigarette-holding hand, "Honey, I wanted you to have the experience."

I bit into one of the small cheesecake pastries, and savored it around my mouth before I answered, "It was a magical experience. I dined in luxury on a chicken, corn, and mashed potato dinner, stretched out on the sleeper seat, marveled at the sights through the window, bored my seat mate with my enthusiasm, and bothered the stewardess with a million questions. I will always treasure my Pan American Airways travel bag with its mouthwash, toothbrush, and eye masks! Thanks for getting me a ticket in the front of the plane, away from the smoking section. My only problem was clogged ears, like I was on an elevator in a high-rise building."

Dangling a shoe from perfectly painted ruby red toes, Aunt Barbra said, "Ah, honey, you needed to chew gum upon takeoff and landing. Didn't anyone tell you that?"

"No, but you are the only one I know who flew on airplanes."

I picked up my Coca-Cola glass and turned and glanced out the window at the swimming pool surrounded by the majestic mountains and blue sky, thinking how different this scene was from Chicago's West Side where she grew up. There wasn't another house in sight. Was she lonely by herself? Did she even know any of her neighbors? I never spent a day in South Shore without running into someone who knew me or one of my family members.

I carefully put my crystal glass down, looked into my aunt's dark brown eyes, and asked, "Did you ever miss Chicago and the family?"

Her demeanor changed. The vodka and cigarette were placed on the marble end table, and she produced a handkerchief from her pocket. Tears welled up in her eyes and smeared her mascara, and she wiped at her eyes before she answered, "Never Chicago. But, in later life, I so missed the family. I wasn't allowed to come to my mother's funeral. The old Orthodox ways were set, and Pa never let me come back into the family."

"Aunt Barbra, you know my mother died just a few months ago," I said. "To not be allowed to go to her funeral would have devastated me. My mother pretended to be Jewish, and my dad and she lied to the whole family. I'm devastated."

She started to laugh, "I love it! Thank you Jake for getting even for me. Does Pa know now? I need another drink for this one." She walked over to the bar and filled her glass.

I spoke carefully when I replied, "Pa had a stroke and doesn't re-spond to anything. We are upset because we don't think he will last long."

"Let's forget the subject of the family now," Aunt Barbra ordered. "I can tell you have had a good upbringing with them and I don't want to ruin it.

"Sorry about your mother. I never knew her. Too young. Enough about old ideas. They make me angry" She stood up and raised her arms in a pushing away maneuver.

Then my aunt came over and hugged me. "We are going to have fun this week," she said with a big smile.

With Aunt Barbra, I had my first taste of pasta that didn't come out of a Franco-American can or was served with kasha. Delicious it was, but most likely not kosher, and I'm still a little guilty. I didn't take to the expensive wine that was served with it. My tastebuds were used to Sabbath's sweet red Mogen David wine.

In California, I had my hair cut into a blunt-cut bob and learned how to put on real makeup.

"How old are you?"

"Twenty-one," I replied, as I thought about how naive and protected I had been for the first twenty.

"Why are you not wearing makeup?" she asked, bringing me back to the present.

"I have lipstick on."

"Awful too," Aunt Barbra asserted. "Orange lipstick on a rose complexion."

She grabbed my hand and pulled me into her warm and cozy pink bedroom, which had mirrored walls, thick pink carpeting, and a huge round bed that was covered with pink, blue, and green fancy silk pillows, plus a fluffy white Pomeranian who gave me a low growl when I tried to pet her.

"Don't worry about my Tiny. She growls at everyone. Pomeranians are one-person dog."

"Sit," she said to me as she motioned to a small pink-and-blue pillowed chair in front of a dressing table. When she opened the table's drawer, I gazed at more makeup than I had ever seen, even in a store.

She pulled out a rose-colored lipstick. "Try this one."

After I applied the lipstick, she said, "Look in the mirror. Can you see the difference?"

"Yes," I said as I started to raise myself from the chair.

Aunt Barbra pushed me back down, saying, "We've only just begun. You are lucky to have those thick black eyebrows. They do need some plucking, though. Does my sister-in-law, Dora, still draw on asymmetrical brows?" I burst into laughter while my mind pictured my Aunt Dora's face. "Yes!"

Aunt Barbra just shook her head.

About forty minutes later, I could hardly recognize the girl in the mirror. Aunt Barbra then packed several containers of makeup in a bag for me to take home. She tried to give me a few of her dresses, but they didn't fit. Aunt Barbra then went to her dresser and pulled out a tan cashmere sweater with a fur collar and tossed it to me.

"Here, honey, your first mink."

"Thank you, but I can't accept an expensive fur," I said as I lovingly ran my hand over the soft plush sweater.

Aunt Barbra held my chin in both of her hands as she stared into my face. "This is a lesson you should never forget. Never, ever, refuse mink or diamonds!"

I was going to laugh, but then I realized she was serious.

The makeup made me think of Mom's friend Sofia, and the pictures of my mom in London. Just like Mom, I wouldn't wear all that makeup when I got back in the family fold.

"My sisters are feeding you too much. I can hear Tillie, 'Eat, eat, you're too thin!'" Aunt Barbra said and smiled a devilish grin.

She then tossed a lightweight jacket at me, grabbed her purse, keys, and cigarettes, and headed out the door. "We're going shopping," she asserted. "You need to look like a law student. That wool sweater and plaid skirt will *never* do."

I held on for dear life as we sped down the mountain road and into a busy highway in her small white sports car, with live cigarette butts flying out the windows and my thick black hair flying across my face.

On Hollywood Boulevard, in front of a fashionable store, she abruptly stopped, whirled out, threw her keys to a doorman, and pulled me inside of the store.

"Good to see you, Barbra," said a sales lady. "What can we help you with today?" Coffee cups, ash trays, and lighters appeared instantly.

She pushed me forward. "My niece is going to law school. She is going to be one of the few women lawyers, and I'm so proud of her. She needs an appropriate outfit." With a knowing smile, the sales lady shuffled me into a fitting room. The sales lady picked out outfits and paraded me in front of Aunt Barbra, who kept waving her cigarette held hand in a negative gesture until I walked out in the suit. The brown tweed two-piece with the gold buttons covered my young body perfectly.

Barbra stood up and waved her arms triumphantly. "It's perfect. Whose is it?"

"It's a Givenchy," the sales lady smugly answered. It came out as *"Gauv-awn-SHEE."*

"Get matching shoes, purse, and hat," Aunt Barbra ordered.

"Aunt Barbra, please, it is too expensive," I protested.

"Nonsense," she replied.

As she paid, I listened carefully to the celebrity gossip between Aunt Barbra and the sales ladies. It seemed like everyone in Hollywood knew each other. Debbie Reynolds had been in the store earlier. Wow, that would have been a real treat for me. Though I probably would have passed out.

I was afraid to ask how my aunt had made her money. She had mentioned that, though she hadn't married that well, she had divorced very well.

It was hard to believe Aunt Barbra belonged to our family. She had married a goy, obtained a divorce, eaten pork and shellfish, and didn't observe any of the Jewish traditions. I was ready to modernize, but never to that degree. My visit with her was like entering another world.

I needed to borrow one of her suitcases to get everything back home.

Right before I left, Barbra brought out a small jewelry box. Inside were two half-carat diamond studs. She handed them to me. "As the youngest daughter, Pa gave these to me when Ma was sick."

"They are yours as the oldest," I protested.

"Pa sat shiva for me," Aunt Barbra recalled. "He wouldn't want me to have them. By the way, you do have pierced ears . . . of course," she answered herself, "the rite of passage was to get your ears pierced at sixteen by Dr. Shores and his shaking hands!"

This gave us a good laugh. We parted with a hug and kiss before the limo took me to the airport. If I stayed much longer, I would have become too spoiled.

As I looked out the window on my return plane trip, my breath increased and my heart beat faster when Lake Michigan - with tiny boats and the outer drive with miniature cars - came into view. Chicago was still home, and Jeffery - spelled with an "ery" - still meant you were a Chicago South Sider, one who traveled almost every day on Jeffery Boulevard, spent your Saturday afternoons at the Jeffery Theater, and spelled your son's name with that *ery*.

Dad kept staring at me while he picked up my suitcase and led me out of Midway Airport to the car. Finally, I asked him, "What's wrong?"

"When you get home, wash your face and re-do your hair. She fixed you up to look like the *kurveh* she is."

I put my lips together and kept quiet while I waited until we got home. My aunts and cousins didn't even comment on my clothes and makeup. They did bombard me with questions, however:

"Tell us about the plane ride!"

"What was California like?"

"Did you see any actors?"

"Where does Aunt Barbra live, what is she like?"

"Did you take pictures?"

They were interested in their lost aunt and sister, the one who had ventured outside of their world. Truthfully, I couldn't remember how to keep my California look, but I always remembered how it felt to be a princess for a weekend.

* * *

A few months after my mother passed away, Grandpa died and joined her in Heaven. He may have come back as a pigeon because more of them were resting on the roof than ever before! I missed him. I still miss him. There were not many family patriarchs anymore, nor apartment buildings completely filled with family and love. It was the end of an era, and the beginning of another one. One where I would go from a naive little Jewish girl to a modern woman determined to make a difference in the world.

Part Two:

A Former 1950s Girl Comes of Age

Chapter Nine

It was one of those beautiful late Chicago summer days. Lake Michigan's turquoise blue reflection shone brightly against the dimming light of dusk, and the evening calm. The boaters and swimmers had turned in for the night, and the fish no longer jumped. Even the waves hardly splashed against the rocks I occupied.

He snuck up behind me, throwing his arms around my shoulders. I held on to his strong hands for a few seconds before I turned around and hugged my favorite cousin. "David, it is so good to see you. It's been a few weeks," I said with a genuine smile. He sat down on the smooth-edged large concrete rock next to the smaller one I sat on. We had been meeting since we were kids on these rocks, which were located one block away from our family building. They were there as barriers between the deep lake water and the land. Most people congregated on the beaches where the soft sand merged with the warm lake water, especially since the beaches were conveniently located just a mile north at 55th Street and a little over a mile south at 76th Street. We loved the quiet scene, the convenience, and the privacy our special rocks afforded us.

"Sorry, I'm late," David said. "Before meeting you, I checked in with Aunt Tillie to let her know I was here for Sabbath dinner. Otherwise, she would worry."

His eyebrows knit as he scrutinized my look and said, "You look like the little girl I used to play with, hair in a ponytail, no makeup, and gym shoes. I thought you had to be dressed for law school, or did you take the day off?

I turned towards him. "Day off, are you kidding? I changed. When I am home from law school, I can't wait to get rid of my business clothes and dress comfortably. You are looking very chic."

Since David paired with Jeffery and was working as a decorator in the city he dressed in a business outfit: suit, long sleeve shirt, and tie. Today, he brought along a towel to sit on and left his tie and jacket in the car so they would stay dry and clean. He did look handsome, but he was so good-looking with that tall physique, broad shoulders, narrow waist, and dimples, that he looked good in anything. Lucky Jeffery.

"Sherrie, we need to get you on your own and out of the family building. There is another world out there," David said, as he took out a Salem cigarette and lit it. I accepted his offer of one.

After two tries to light it, David took the cigarette, cupped his hands around it, and fired it up for me. I inhaled and slowly exhaled while he smiled and shook his head at my attempt to smoke. He was the one who taught me.

"I know I have to move closer to the school but I am afraid of the city," I said. "I'm afraid of this new world we are living in. I thought nothing could be as bad as the loss of Camelot when Kennedy was shot in 1963. In the last five years, my mother and our grandfather died, and the world has gone crazy."

David took a deep drag on his cigarette and looked out across the lake. I swatted a group of flies. We both jumped as a black cat slithered around the rocks. Feral cats were new to the neighborhood.

He answered, "It does seem like the world has changed with Robert Kennedy and Martin Luther King's assassination just this last year."

I shifted onto a bigger rock closer to him and reminded him, "You weren't living here for the riots after King was killed, in fact, you and Jeffery were in Florida decorating a client's house. We were scared. We found ourselves in the middle of violence after Dr. King's assassination in April. The riots that started on the West Side moved to the South Side. There was destruction and chaos. Buildings were burned down, stores were looted, people were shot. We were lucky. Most of the damage happened in the Austin and Lawndale communities west of us, but we still had destruction. I still have trouble believing things like that happened in our neighborhoods."

David turned towards me and explained, "Do you know why South Shore was saved? South Shore had damage, but not as much due to a deal the Blackstone Rangers made with the other South Side gang called the East Side Disciples. A deal motivated by Mayor Daley."

I shook my head, pressed my lips together, and replied, "These gangs are scary. We had groups called fraternities and sororities in high school. The worst they did was ostracize you. Shooting, killing, destroying property never happened here. I do remember a knife fight between two girls during my last semester at Hyde Park High School."

"Mayor Richard Daley's edict to the police—'Shoot to kill any arsonist, shoot to maim anyone looting stores in our city!' at the Democratic Convention last August saved the rest of the city," I said. "We were glued to the television all that week, worried that violence would come back to the West and South Side. Aunt Tillie paced up and back, saying a prayer for the mayor, whom she had met several times, and lamented the fact that two leaders of the Democratic Convention protest, Jerry Rubin, and Abbie Hoffman, were Jewish."

"Heh, Jeffery and I lived in Lincoln Park where most of the action took place," David said. "The Yippie protesters were tenting in the park, where more of them were busier smoking and strung out on drugs then rioting, while the police and National Guard were bent on removing them."

"I was upset with both sides. Violence is no solution." I said.

"I agree, but unfortunately sometimes people feel that there is no other way to get attention," David answered. "Sherrie, more reason for the whole family to move north where there are no riots. I'm going to bring it up at dinner. Will you support me?"

The streetlights went on. We looked at each other and laughed. While growing up in the fifties, that was our signal to go home. We put out our cigarettes and started back to our family building and Sabbath dinner. On our way, I asked him, "Why don't you ever bring your partner, Jeffery?"

"Sherrie, why would you ask?" David replied. "He goes to his family alone and I go to mine alone. His Catholic family is worse than mine in accepting our love for each other."

"Sorry, I thought things were better and they were more accepting now. Jeffery is always welcome with me. I really like him, and I think he has been good for you."

David's face lit up and he said, "Your mother and Jeffery helped me come out and acknowledge who I am."

We entered our three-flat family building and walked up the steps in silence, letting the familiar loud conversations from Aunt Tillie's apartment take over, while we inhaled the garlic and onion smells of chicken and brisket stewing next to sputtering wax from the Sabbath candles.

During dinner, David brought up the fact that it was time to give up the family building. To his surprise, they were already talking about it. They had stayed through the real estate falling prices scare, and the gang takeover of the streets, but they caved after the riots and looting of 1968. That scared them, especially for the younger cousins who were still going to grammar and high schools in South Shore.

Chapter Ten

When the family building was sold in November of 1968, the eldest cousins had been out of the neighborhood. I was in law school in Chicago's downtown area, my cousin Lizzie was married and living in a northern suburb, and my cousin David was living in the up-and-coming Lincoln Park area.

The day the rest of the family moved out of the building was filled with emotional goodbyes, even though we all would only be, at most, twenty-five miles apart from each other. The hard part was saying farewell to the memories that went with the family building. Grandpa had purchased the red brick three-flat thirty years earlier when most Jews left the West Side of Chicago and scattered either farther north or south.

For weeks Lizzie and I assisted with the packing—actually, Lizzie more so, because I was busy with law school. Lizzie's brother, Yale, who seemed to grow taller every day, moved the heavy boxes for us. Items that were family-owned became items for debate—things everyone wanted, and things no one wanted. Thank God for the Temple resale shop.

Aunt Tillie was the worst. She couldn't part with anything. She constantly made comments such as, "Don't put that plate in the resale box. Ma used it to make gefilte fish."

"Tillie, it has a crack in it," Aunt Sarah had said as she took it out of Tillie's hand and tossed it into the give-away box. Aunt Tillie was the more emotional sister and Aunt Sarah the practical one.

I understood Aunt Tillie. The items involving my late mother were incredibly hard to let go of. I could see her in high heels with her sun-bleached blonde hair bouncing back and forth, dancing around the almost empty front room, singing along with a Frank Sinatra record, or busy sitting at the modern Danish kitchen chairs, pencil behind her ear, reading a book in which she might write comments or notes. That is why she hated the library—she needed to own the book to scribble her thoughts in it. Some would say she ruined the books; I felt she personified them with her interpretation. Now those notes in her handwriting are treasures to me. I'm a reader and a note-taker, with scraps of paper in every book and in every one of my pockets. Someday, I'll put them together into a novel—the novel my mother wanted to write, but never got to it.

On the last day, as the moving vans took off, and before the new owners took over, I stood outside with shoulders slumped and watering eyes as I stared up into empty windows that held the ghosts of my first twenty-one years. Except for my mother's death, they had been very happy, loving, though naive years. Now I would be entering the real world without the comfort of going back to my family building. I was scared.

My cousin Lizzie motioned me to follow her through the archway, separating our building and the neighbor's building ending in our backyard. This city arrangement of the building's archways made privacy difficult. If you wanted to open a window or pull back the shades, you would end up staring into your neighbor's bedroom. In the backyard, I noticed that the lawn was sparse, and the fence needed painting. With Pa gone, and my dad depressed by my mother's death from lung cancer, repairs had been neglected.

"Why did you want to come back here?" I asked her. Lizzie pointed to the flower bed against the red brick building. Snapdragons and tulips came up every year. They had been our grand adventure in gardening, something city people didn't typically do. The school had given us free seeds and bulbs, so we tried it, and, to our surprise, flowers came up every year, even though we were negligent in our watering and weeding, being city girls. Memories I forgot about. We continued down the alley and across to our old grammar school playground. No one was around. It was a weekday, and the kids were in school.

"Let's say hello to Queenie," Lizzie said. We walked over to O'Keefe's field house, where we had spent so many days hanging out with Queenie, the woman who helped us with after-school activities. No Queenie. The wooden rectangular white field house at the end of the school playground was boarded up, and the large playground adjacent to the brick three-floor kindergarten to eighth-grade school had busted swings, cracks in the asphalt, and shards of glass. How sad for the boys and girls going to school there now.

I found myself glaring at the graffiti-marked boards with anger. Why would they close the field house? It was the one place where kids could comfortably socialize and engage in sports or art projects without getting into trouble.

We left the school and continued walking down Merrill Avenue to the Corner Drugstore on 71st Street, which was the neighborhood's shopping mecca. It, too, was closed and boarded up. There was a group of blue-jeaned and black gang-jacketed teenagers smoking and hanging out on the corner. Empty beer containers and wine bottles lay strewn in the alley behind the closed store.

I felt so out of place in my colorful knee-length skirt and black flats, but my main concern was the closed-up drugstore. I grew up in that store, especially at its soda fountain. I turned to Lizzie with a sad pouting face and mused, "Now that the drugstore was gone, we will never again get to sit by their small metal table and wrought iron chairs, drinking milkshakes and crunching on Salerno cookies."

I guessed it would be useless to look for Mitchell's Ice Cream Parlor. Probably closed too. My mouth watered at the thought of their hot fudge sundaes. The dress shops, butchers, and beauty parlors were long gone, replaced mainly with empty stores. The wind blasted us as a train flew by. Good to see that the Illinois Central trains were still going, I thought.

As we walked back, I asked Lizzie, "Did your mom talk to you about how different the neighborhood had become?"

"You were here for Friday night dinner two weeks ago. Did you notice the difference"? Lizzie replied.

I shook my head. "Lizzie, I just came with my dad, parked in front, and went upstairs," I answered. "I never looked around or paid that much attention to the difference in the neighborhood, especially since it was dark already. Though I did get upset when I heard the Jeffery Show closed. We spent every Saturday afternoon there."

With a smirk on her face, she answered, "The movies were so stupid that it didn't matter when we joined the film. Cowboys always won, and nobody ever got hurt in the cartoons."

We walked back to find an angry Aunt Tillie, who was worried about us. It never occurred to Lizzie and me to be afraid in South Shore.

Aunt Tillie and her immediate family moved into a bungalow in Skokie, a predominantly Jewish suburb north of Chicago. She was the one who took Ma's good gold Austrian dishes and Ma's sterling silverware and copper Sabbath candlesticks because Tillie's house would still be the gathering place, especially now that grandchildren and new pets were joining the family.

Aunt Sarah, who was now alone, moved into a two-bedroom apartment near Tillie. My two aunts never could be apart. They depended on each other. They took most of the furniture, antiques, and tchotchkes, but Aunt Tillie's new home still wasn't the family building.

The North Side and the northern suburbs were different from the South Side—quieter, and not as friendly. Maybe it was air conditioning that kept most people inside, or just a more secretive atmosphere. No kids played ball in the streets. No alleys, just manicured landscaped backyards, with barbecue grills, and an occasional swing set. Yes, Devon Avenue had numerous Jewish delis and Jewish-owned restaurants, groceries, and clothing stores, but it still wasn't South Shore where everyone knew each other. Growing up, we were always told, North Side Jews were different. They were more into style, furnishing, the right clothes, clubs, etc. and now my family was moving north.

Gail, the only cousin who would be going to high school on the North Side, stood around outside of the family building impatiently, twirling her long, straight, black hair through her fingers.

I asked her, "Gail, are you afraid to go to Senn High School with all the stuck-up and spoiled North Siders?"

Gail's eyes opened wide, her face lit up, and her shoulders straightened as she replied, "I can't wait, Sherrie. You have no idea how bad Hyde Park has become. I have no friends anymore. Dad drives me every day because I'm afraid to take the bus. My wallet was stolen last month and there are fights between colored and white boys all the time. Not just fistfights, but knife fights too!"

"I'm surprised," I said. "The only problems my friends and I had while going to Hyde Park was an occasional slur about being Jewish, and it usually came from the Mount Carmel High School kids who joined us on the bus. There were a few colored kids in my classes, but they usually stuck together and never caused any problems. One girl, Rosemarie Gulley, is a television news reporter now."

"That was five years ago. It's different now with all the kids. There is less discipline everywhere except with our family," Gail answered. "Were the kids smoking weed in the bathrooms then?"

"Just cigarettes," I answered. "We didn't know what weed was."

"Did you see the musical, *Hair*?" she asked.

"What?"

She looked at me like I was weird. "The musical. Some of my friends saw it. I didn't even ask to go. No way would my parents have let me see it. They still won't let me wear blue jeans to school."

"The one with nudity and burned draft cards? No way," I said. I wanted to add that I was still in love with *The Sound of Music.*

Boy, did I suddenly feel old. I realized I had been so entwined into my new world of law school that I hadn't noticed what was going on in South Shore, or the world of the late 1960s. My undergraduate world during the early 1960s was a quiet, prim, and proper place. For me, it was made up of going to school in Chicago and living at home. I knew by 1965 there were dramatic social and political changes such as marches, drugs, anti-war protests, war protests, the sexual revolution, musicals like *Hair,* rock 'n' roll replaced by protest music, and groups like the Beatles, but I ignored all of it. I had one goal, which was to be one of the few girls who could get into law school, which meant my world consisted of study, study, study. One B grade could stop me from attaining my goal. This gave me no time to do or think of anything else.

Chicago's downtown world, where I now hung out, was made up of people from different countries and religions, contrary to Chicago's neighborhoods, which were segregated by country of origin and religion. Growing up, we knew which street lines would put us into the Italian, Polish, Greek, Jewish, Black, etc. areas, and we avoided these areas in order to stay away from territory fights. We accepted the ghettos or villages our immigrant grandparents formed. America's melting pot was just a group of simmering pots that were now exploding.

Speaking of things that were different in the late 1960s, David and his friend Jeffery were living and working together in a North Side region of the city that was a gathering place for homosexuals, who were becoming more open about their relationships. The young Vietnam protesters were opening up avenues that my friends and I never dreamed of doing, not only about the war but about other areas of society as well. Liberals were making their demands heard. Blacks were leaving the racist South for jobs and better living conditions in the North. Civil rights groups were marching and demanding more equality. I wondered if we could achieve equality for all races and sexes without tearing the country apart.

As the moving van drove on, Lizzie and I, the older cousins, hugged in a silent promise to carry on the scattered family. David, also one of the older cousins, should have been with us, but he found an excuse to stay away. He found it too emotional to be here. Liz and I went our separate ways, driving down streets that were echoing with the sounds from screeching police sirens, and ambulances.

When I turned onto the Dan Ryan, an expressway I've driven for years, I shifted my concentration to the road and the speeding, crazy lane-changing drivers. I glanced at my gas gauge and realized that it was close to empty. Not wanting to get stuck on the Dan Ryan Expressway, I pulled into a Texaco. While the attendant filled my tank with gas, checked my oil, and washed my windows, I thought about how my attitude was changing. I was now afraid to drive to the South Shore!

"You needed gas," he said. "Your twenty-gallon tank was down to one gallon. Your oil and tires are good. That will be $6.00."

I opened my purse and pulled out a five and a one, thanked him, and continued home.

My dad was reluctant to leave South Shore. He tried desperately to hold on to the grocery store, even though the customers were no longer predominately Jewish or white. Unnecessary panic caused by real estate agents, who continually preached, "the value of your property is falling every day!" helped make the merchants flee with the residents. Dad wouldn't budge. He just made adjustments to his merchandise, less Jewish food, more of a variety of things. Slowly a new group of customers shopped in his store, and he treated them the same as all of his old customers. Instead of calling him, Joncle, his Jewish name, the new customers called him, Mr. Jake.

The North Side was too far from the store, so my dad moved into a modern high-rise rental apartment in Hyde Park. I hated it. Out of every window, all you could see were cars and traffic—no alleys, no trees, no people. Apparently, he had hated my mom's modern furniture, as it all went to the Hadassah resale while he took the French Provincial antique bedroom set from the 1920s that had belonged to Pa, my grandfather. Mom's furniture would have fit into the modern concrete and steel plain-looking boxy apartment, with its white walls, white kitchen cabinets, and white stove and refrigerator. Dad's second bedroom was cluttered with his father's tools, which were mostly obsolete by now. I guess they represented the main thing father and son had in common.

I sat down on Aunt Tillie's old red vinyl chair, which was now my dad's, and peered out the window. "Dad, how can you live in this cold, enormous hi-rise where nobody knows each other after living in a real neighborhood?" I asked while I sipped the hot lemon tea he had put before me.

"Sherrie, it's an apartment in a convenient place. My wife is gone, my home with my family is gone," Dad replied as he puffed on his pipe and glanced out the window. He was having a hard time with the move and the loss of his wife and father. Maybe this place would make it easier for him to cope. At least he didn't have to drive that far to get to the store, I thought.

Tillie and Sara tried to get my dad to close the store, but their shouts were now coming from too far away to have the same influence. The close family living together was no more, and Pa wasn't around to make the final decree, "Because I said so!"

Chapter Eleven

I was attending a law school located in the downtown part of the city in an old high-rise building. It was a law school separate from any other university; thus, most students were from Chicago, many already working, or even married. The middle 1960s were still a male chauvinistic world, even though the feminist movement was sprouting its wings. Being one of the few girls in law school, I had to work twice as hard to stay and convince my fellow male students that I had a brain that went with my boobs and legs.

I filed into the large wooden walled and marble two-storied lecture hall, seated myself as far high up and back from the front as possible, in order to avoid being called upon. It didn't work. "Miss Paul, will you please explain why you believe that the plaintiff should be awarded such a large sum of money?" the professor had asked.

As I stood up to answer him, someone in the back of the room whistled. I felt my face grow hot, and I consequently bobbled my response.

"If you were dressed properly with a longer skirt, we won't have this type of interruption," the professor said.

I wanted to remind him the school dress code in the middle 1960s was a shirt and tie for the men, and dresses and heels for the few women and dress styles were short now, but I slid back into my seat, holding back my tears as muffled laughter echoed through the room.

Suddenly, three years of living through ridicule for being a woman seemed impossible. To avoid talking to anyone, I hurried to the bathroom before the class ended, where I washed my teary face and re-applied makeup. My next class was a small group seminar on taxes that went better, though my only goal that day was to make it home.

Times like that humiliating scene made me think I should have given into the 1950s rule: get married, have kids, and play it dumb, like the main female characters in the Doris Day and Debbie Reynolds movies we loved, instead of trying to compete in the big boys' world. It was a tough and lonely world.

When I arrived home, the first thing I did was to call my cousin Lizzie to complain.

"Sherrie, stay in school. Taking care of a household and dealing with a crying baby is not the Cinderella story we dreamed about," she advised.

Then I called a friend from undergraduate college. She never let me complain. She answered with, "Sherrie, I was thinking about you, can you babysit Saturday evening?" Reluctantly I answered, "Yes."

"Thanks, you are the only one I know who is not married."

At twenty-three I was considered an old maid. I hung up and plopped down on my sofa, depressed.

Things were changing in the outside world, but not inside the institutions. The older crowd who ran the schools and government institutions just thought that the younger crowd was being rebellious.

A view that would soon pass. It started with a group of young people called hippies, who were protesting the Vietnam War. They wandered the countryside dressed in sandals, long skirts, beads, and jeans while either burning American flags or strumming on guitars and singing new tunes about the freedom to choose their own destiny. Their music was different, too. Large, unstructured outdoor concerts like one planned for next year, Woodstock, with stoned groups singing protest songs, were popular. Some were serious protesters hoping for change, while others used this time to embrace drugs, free sex, free merchandise, and the new commune living idea. Others were joining the protests in hopes of better conditions for women, gays, blacks, and other minorities.

Inside my law school, there was no freedom. Everything still was structured around ancient rules. I started law school feeling excited about paving the way for women; I hadn't realized how hard it would be.

Chapter Twelve

My freedom came in the form of a rented apartment in the Lincoln Park neighborhood, which was just a few miles north of Chicago's downtown, near the lake and the zoo. Young people, both gay and straight, had invaded Chicago's Near North Side; a neighborhood where poor ethnics lived for years was becoming a neighborhood of expensive apartments, condos, and restaurants. A few years ago, a girl living alone in an apartment in the city was taboo, but now, in 1968, it was becoming accepted. What also changed things for me was that my grandfather, Pa, the head of the family, had died. He would have believed it was scandalous for me to live alone, and his opinion was law for the family, though in the later years Aunt Tillie and Aunt Sarah had learned how to maneuver him. David had assured the rest of the family that he would watch over me.

David wanted me to move into an old mansion that had been cut up into apartments. It had original marble fireplaces, colorful stained glass windows, and high ornate ceilings with hanging gas fixtures, all restored by David and Jeffery. They were rehabbing old buildings they had bought at good prices before the area took off as the place for young adults to live on their own. They rented out some, and sold others. David was still the same warm, loving cousin I grew up with, but there was a difference. He had confidence in himself now, and his creative juices were flowing.

David stopped the car in front of the old, three-story, white stone mansion located two blocks north of the Lincoln Park Zoo.

He took my hand as we scaled wrought iron stairs and entered through a heavy stained glass wooden door. The old mansion had been broken into six two-bedroom apartments.

I stood in the middle of the large room on the first floor, turning round and round.

"Oh, David, it is charming!" I said as I clapped my hands.

He smiled at me with that old charismatic personality I loved. Grabbing me by the arm and leading me around the two-bedroom apartment, he said, "Sherrie, let me show you how we've put this place back to its glory, yet still keeping it efficient and affordable. Someday, we hope to restore these mansions to their grandeur of the turn of the century."

The fireplace in the common room had brass wrought iron besides white and maroon marble tiles. David pulled me down so we were looking into the fireplace opening, and pointed to a knob. "We've converted the fireplace to gas, so you can use it easily, though there is nothing better than the sweet smell of burning wood," he enthused. "Here is how to turn it on. I can picture you wrapped in a soft blanket curled up on the old comfortable green sofa being warmed by the red flames dancing in the fireplace."

I smiled and replied, "In your fantasy, you forgot to put a book in my hands!"

"Of course," David said as we stood up and he swung me around.

David had placed a heavy oak roll-up desk against the living room wall facing three tall windows that spilled late afternoon sun into the room, causing the desk and the rejuvenated, newly sanded oak floors to glow a rich golden brown. All were animated by the light that changed through the stained glass windows. They reminded me of the many churches I had read about. In the bedroom sat a lace canopied bed I could die for. A warm red-and-gold patterned antique Oriental rug with a slight hole at one end covered the floor. I was afraid I would end up killing the potted plants David had added, as gardening wasn't one of my strong suits. The only drawbacks were the bathroom and kitchen, which were still creatures of the 1940s—small with white porcelain sinks, a tub, a toilet, linoleum floors, sparse cabinets, and bad lighting.

"You are so talented, but I can't move in as a single girl even though you are giving it to me at a reasonable rent," I had said to David when he first showed the apartment to me. I wouldn't admit that the thought of suddenly being on my own was terrifying. However, there was no family building to fall back on, and I was still hurt and angry with my dad over secrets concerning my mother's religion and wouldn't accept his invitation to take over his second bedroom.

"Sherrie," my dad had tried to explain, "stop dwelling on your mother's cross. She kept it as a reminder of her youth. She became Jewish."

He had expected me to take this poor excuse as a legitimate reason to keep the truth from his own daughter. This made me crazy. "No, she didn't," I asserted. "She never converted. She just acted Jewish." I had grabbed my coat and left his apartment, yelling, "You *both* lied to me! That's the problem!"

After that scene with Dad, I realized I couldn't live with him. I was ashamed for being disrespectful to my father and called to apologize, but I was still hurt.

* * *

David helped me move into his remodeled mansion. I left most of my things in Aunt Tillie's basement since this was just a temporary place, and because my pink flowery bedroom spreads, curtains, accessories, and stuffed animals had been perfect for my growing up years, but not for a law school student. My mom's record player, records, and books did come with me.

On the first night, I woke at 4:30 a.m., in shock, screaming, "Where am I?" I turned the light on, looked around, and started to cry. No stuffed animals or fluffy pink blanket. The stained glass windows I had thought gorgeous now reminded me of demons. Never before had I lived alone. We lived on top of each other in the family building. Even as early as 4:30 in the morning, I could always find somebody noshing in one of the apartment kitchens. Not here; no one I knew and loved was around this building and, worst of all, there was no phone to call family.

The hardest part of my move-in was getting a telephone installed. I spent days running to the drugstore to make calls in the telephone stall back in the corner.

I visited Aunt Tillie, missing face-to-face talks with family. Aunt Tillie wasted no time making me feel at home. "Sherrie, your father and I are upset," she said. "You won't give us your phone number, and you don't call."

"Aunt Tillie, I can't get the phone company out to install a phone."

Aunt Tillie's hands went up in the air. "Aha! It is done." To make sure I understood, she asked, "Sherrie, why didn't you tell me? I'll take care of it."

After I had spent a month without a phone, Aunt Tillie, with her West Side political clout, had a pretty blue princess phone installed the next day. The Jews and the Irish still ruled Chicago. "*Long live Mayor Daley*," I said to myself, and my first call was to Aunt Tillie. Some things never changed, at least in Chicago.

It turned out that after the first two months, David had found me a suitable roommate. I was now living with Judy Rosen, a nice Jewish girl from the suburb of Lincolnwood. My aunt played mah jongg, a strategy game featuring dice and tiles, with Judy's her mother and they had become friends. The fact that her boyfriend stayed over on the weekends, and that the smell of marijuana leaked through her door, were our secrets.

Marijuana and other drugs had now become like the illegal alcohol of the 1920s—a symbol for the young people who were against the establishment.

I had hoped for a friend in Judy, as most of my girlfriends from high school and college were already married with children, but the girl was wrapped up in the new world and her boyfriend. After pleading to be allowed on my own, I would never let my family know how lonely I was. I missed living in my loud, loving, busy family building filled with the wafting scent of garlic brisket and sugary cinnamon desserts.

Instead, I was struck with the odd smells of cumin and oil from Middle-Eastern food, and the high-pitched Eastern European sounds echoing through the hallways. Wailing sirens from ambulances and police cars echoed through the windows all day and all night. The neighborhood had one foot firmly in the hardscrabble past and one tentative foot in the upscale future.

Instead of girly talk about boys and clothes, Judy said things such as, "Sherrie, I can't believe you, a law student, aren't participating in the rally against the Vietnam War, or taking any interest in the women's movement!" She could be very sharp-tongued with her criticism. I had entered her room in an effort to have a friendly conversation when she attacked me with her beliefs.

"Judy, I don't have time," I replied. "I need to study every minute."

"You can't bury yourself in books," Judy asserted, with wide-open eyes and rising voice. "The world is changing. Boys you knew in high school are coming back from a useless war without limbs, or in body bags. Join the rally this Sunday."

Before answering, I looked around her room with the various rebellious posters, especially the one with the burned remains of an

American flag. My family was always very patriotic. Pa considered America wonderful after fleeing from Poland.

I looked directly at her to emphasize how important my response was, and said, "Judy, getting caught at a rally could get me kicked out of law school."

That didn't go well. Judy shot abstract theories back at me that I think she read in those pamphlets her boyfriend, Jesse, passed out; socialistic ideas that he embraced with his no-work ethic. He seemed to believe that the rich should support everyone else no matter if they worked or not. I hated to think my taxes were going to his marijuana habit. I didn't buy his no-addiction theory.

My Aunt Tillie used to say, "Sherrie adheres to peace at any price." I never let Judy know that I disagreed with the protests and the burning of the American flag. My father and my uncles had served in the military, and we were proud of it. I used the school as an excuse. Not wearing a bra every day sounded good, but I didn't have the nerve to participate in that protest. Though the male students would have enjoyed it, as I was very busty.

I had finally conquered the art of smoking. I had been inhaling everyone else's smoke for years. Salem cigarettes helped keep my weight down and eliminated my nail-biting. The drug scene wasn't something I wanted to be involved with, so I stayed clear of it, especially after seeing how it had taken over Judy's life. Most of the time, she was out of it, either sleeping, hardly functioning, or over-functioning.

Judy, wearing torn jeans and a loose peasant blouse, entered the kitchen while I waited for my cheese pizza to bake. She picked up my Salem cigarette out of mom's green glass ashtray.

"You need to smoke something good," Judy asserted. "I can't believe how straight you are, like someone stuck in the fifties." She tried to give me the joint she was smoking.

"No thanks, I need to be alert and conscious in my studies," I said as I backed away from her.

The buzzer sounded and I took my pizza out of the oven. I turned to Judy, who was just staring at me. "Would you like a piece of pizza? I only eat cheese."

She sat down on the red vinyl kitchen chair next to the white Formica table while pizza, weed, and smoke filled the air. "I'll have a piece of pizza if you will join Jesse and me tonight at a gathering in a house close by, no rally, or public place," Judy negotiated. "I need to show you today's world."

She took a beer out of the fridge while I drank my Coke. We shared the pizza in our small white kitchen, avoiding conversation about everything but her mother and my aunt, who both came from the West Side of Chicago, and liked to cook and play mah jongg.

I finally agreed to join Judy and Jesse at a meeting in a private home, where I believed I wouldn't be seen by someone from my law school or be arrested for rioting.

I thought I looked good. Judy stood in the doorway, shaking her head, and said "Sherrie, you are dressed for a fifties party. This is the sixties! It is a hippie meeting, a gathering of young people for a cause. We are fed up with the rich, and powerful establishment, who are busy with material things."

She threw a pair of blue jeans and a strand of colorful beads at me. "Take off that ridiculous cashmere skirt before Jesse gets here," Judy ordered.

Jesse arrived before I changed. With his long pony-tailed reddish-brown hair and beads, he nonetheless had the nerve to laugh at me in my attire. "Sherrie, what the fuck are you wearing, a skirt, red nail polish, and fancy heeled shoes?" Jessie asked. "Where do you think you are going? You are a fucking mess."

"Leave her alone, Jessie, anything goes now," Judy said in my defense.

I was about ready to forget the whole thing. For sure I wasn't used to his casual use of swear words. Once I answered my dad with the word *shit,* and he exploded.

Judy picked up her jeans and handed them to me. "Please, come with us. You need to get a feel of what is going on in the country."

I ignored Jesse, changed into Judy's jeans, which were tight and a little long, but I didn't own any blue jeans.

We walked about four blocks to a small apartment on Orchard Street in Lincoln Park. In front of the apartment sat an orange, flowered VW flowered van with peace signs painted all over it. I noticed one side of the van had painted words that read, *We won't go!* I was so out of it, it took me a while to realize they meant Vietnam. Law school had put me into its own world. No class talked about, nor did it deal with, the protesters.

Instead of furniture, all sizes of colorful pillows for sitting on, leaning on, and laying on, were scattered around the apartment. A Joan Baez recording blasted through the room. The sweet scent of marijuana mingled with the heavy smell of cigarettes was the first thing that hit me.

Shortly, long-haired, bearded, blue-jeaned, college-aged, (mainly) white boys and girls with beads or flowers in their long, shoulder-length hair plopped down on the pillowed interior or hung out on the packed back balcony. Fringed and wild-colored clothing was everywhere. One girl without makeup in a long loose dress reminded me of a pioneer from the west. Guitars and tambourines ready to be played, hung over shoulders. One good-looking, long-haired blond with a diamond in a pierced ear had me fooled—was this person a he or she?

Wine was the drink of choice, and joint smoking the norm. Plates of odd food such as tofu, brown rice with cumin, and turmeric-spiced vegetables were being passed around. I ended up chain-smoking my cigarettes to keep from being offered a joint. I think some drug was being passed through needles in a bedroom, but I wasn't sure. Groups of people were in heated conversations, wiped out, or even engaged in sex.

"Girl, let that hair down," a guy with a dyed red ponytail said as he grabbed at my pinned-up beehive. I slapped his hand, yelling, "Don't touch me." He backed away.

I started to leave, but Judy stopped me, saying, "The poet is here."

All activity and noise stopped as the group gathered around a small bearded man. He was treated like a guru as he sat down on a pillow in the middle of the room where he proceeded to read a poem called *Howl* that was a little too sexual for me. He ended his recitation with an ear-blasting shout, "I declare the end of the war!" All in the room, with the exception of myself, loudly echoed his declaration.

He turned towards me. "Don't you believe the end of the war in Vietnam is here?" he demanded.

I sank into the sofa and quietly answered, "No."

"How would you end the war?" the poet asked.

"By negotiation," I answered more boldly.

He turned towards the group and smugly said, "Did you hear her? 'Negotiation.' She still believes we can negotiate. She doesn't realize the old order will not give up their control. We must demonstrate, and challenge."

Suddenly he was on the floor, crossed-legged, chanting the mantra, "*Om, om, om.*"

I felt sick and only wanted to escape from this group when Judy rescued me. I did agree with some of their complaints, but not their self-righteousness and illegal methods.

Judy stood up, poked the poet, and said, "Allen, leave her alone. She is a law student, and I dragged her here."

A sly grin covered Allen's face. "We can always use a law student in the group," he said. Allen then stood up, handed out some flyers, and departed. I left a few minutes later. One evening with a hippie group was enough for me. I understood their wants, but not their methods. In my mind's eye, peaceful demonstrators were dressed in business clothes, approaching their elected representatives, not half-dressed, shouting demands.

I left. As soon as I exited the apartment, I took off Judy's beaded headband and colorful scarf. It was quite late to be walking alone in the Lincoln Park area. Staying alert to my surroundings was something my dad taught me. My eyes surveyed the streets, alleys, and stores, while I fingered the whistle he had given me. The bums and druggies didn't scare me half as much as the rats in the alleys, scurrying around and through the garbage cans. Like chalk across the blackboard, the screech of their claws against the metal of the cans made me cringe. Never had I felt scared walking to our family building in South Shore. Never had I been vigilant about locking my doors or keeping check of my personal property while growing up in the fifties.

Home from school, planning to crash into my books in preparation for the next day's tests, I undressed and wrapped myself into my cozy pink chenille bathrobe, a gift from Aunt Sarah. The cup of tea and bag of popcorn by my desk would do until I became hungry. Then I would order something from one of the many restaurants in the area or raid the limited supplies in the kitchen. Law school was hard and challenging, yet at the same time, I was excited by it. It wasn't all fact; there were many shades of gray of interpretation, which I enjoyed.

My concentration was soon interrupted.

"Please don't go," I heard Judy say, crying. Next, the outside door slammed, and her sobbing increased. I wasn't sure what to do. She always seemed so strong and in charge; she was the one who did all the screaming and ordering in their relationship. After about fifteen minutes, I slowly entered Judy's room. There was a strong smell of smoke from overflowing ashtrays. Clothes scattered across the bed and floors, lying next to printed circulars and almost covering Judy's coiled-up body.

"Did you and Jesse have another fight?"

With lips clenched and eyes narrowed, she looked up, "He may not be coming back."

"He always does," I said as I thought about the many fights they had. She was his meal ticket, but I never understood what she saw in the ponytailed, bearded, nonworking druggie.

She wiped her eyes with one long sleeve of her, embroidered blouse, before saying, "He's not happy about the baby."

"A baby! You're having a baby without a husband?" I almost shouted.

I was trying not to judge her, but it was hard for me to realize that a Jewish girl could let herself get into this situation. I know she was living a double life, acting like she was still taking classes at Roosevelt, and dressing normal the few times she went home to visit. I guessed her parents knew nothing of Jesse. What about this new miracle birth control pill? Why wasn't she on it, if she was so progressive? I was still a virgin, saving myself for my future husband.

She looked up at me with red, swollen eyes. "A baby or an illegal abortion! My mother will kill me either way," Judy moaned.

My aunt had just told me Judy's mother, Ida, was all upset that she hadn't won at mah jongg in three weeks. She had bought herself a new dress to make her feel better. *This will take her mind off of mah jongg, that's for sure*, I thought. *If I were Judy, I'd be more concerned about my father.*

In any case, I was back in the fifties, not understanding the sixties, and I didn't know what to say.

Jesse saved me from having to speak. He came back, and the shouting and arguing continued. I retreated to my room and my books and the comforting sounds of Frank Sinatra on my mother's record player, though I wanted to venture into the kitchen for a piece of my leftover cheese pizza. By the time I fell into bed, they were hunky-dory next door.

Chapter Thirteen

April's nice weather brought people out from every nook and cranny. It was a welcome relief from winter's snow and freezing temperatures. The competition at my law school was so intense, and the work so difficult, and the lunchroom full of locker-room talk, that on many sunny days I walked over to Buckingham Fountain with my lunch in one hand and my books in the other.

Since my high school days, I had been fascinated by Buckingham Fountain, which was designed after a fountain at the Palace of Versailles. It was at its best on summer evenings when special lights turned the waters into colors of the rainbow—red, blue, green, and yellow.

The lake, shimmering bright blue, would soon be dotted with all sizes and styles of boats, but for now, it was still peacefully shaking off the long, cold winter. As I approached the group sitting on recently painted white wooden benches near the fountain, I heard one of the men, named Nick, call out, "Sherrie, I think I just fed your grandfather!"

Laughing, I sat down next to Nick and two other gentlemen dressed in baseball caps, t-shirts, and gym shoes. I had become friends with a group of retirees who spent their day feeding the pigeons. Chicago had enough of them. Nick had remembered my story about Pa and his love of pigeons.

"They don't flock away when I approach now," I said as I bent down to offer a piece of my cheese sandwich to Gertie, the all-white lady pigeon who was always around the fountain.

Nick grinned. "They recognize you as a friend. You know they are really intelligent birds."

I threw my hands up to the sky. "Forgive me, Pa."

Harry, a retired lawyer, said to me, "Let's see what you are studying today. I need to test my memory." He rested his cigar on the end of his portable lawn chair.

"Torts test,"

"Oh yes. We, lawyers, get our bad name from torts—she thought the dog was friendly, so she petted the dog, who bit her hand. She ran away, falling on the neighbor's stump, breaking her arm. Now the dog chasing her was joined by another dog who scratched her leg as she ran into the neighbor's thorny rose bushes, cutting her face, etc., etc. Who sues whom?"

"Oh, yes," I said as I laughed at his accurate evaluation of torts, or what is commonly known as personal injury.

"I love it! A girl in law school." He slapped his leg and smiled. "What do the boys think of it?"

I hesitated before answering, "Some are nice and helpful, but most resent me. Just this morning, one fellow student said, 'Do you realize you've taken away the slot from a man who would become a lawyer for life? Not like you who, in a few years, will have children and stay home where you belong.'"

I stated that encounter like an attorney stating a fact, but those bitter words had made me run out of the school and towards the fountain to calm down. The confrontation had so unnerved me that I was shaking while I described it. Of course, I hadn't mouthed back to the rude class-mate. My family had taught me to be polite. I could have pointed out that I was paying the same tuition as he was paying.

Before Harry could respond I heard a stern, deep, commanding voice say, "Dad, I've been looking all over for you. Mom is worried. What are you doing here?"

Harry didn't move off his chair. "I'm busy feeding the pigeons and visiting with my friends, "Leave me alone."

"I would, but Mom keeps calling me. The two of you better communicate. I have an important job and can't be running around town looking for you."

"Go back to your important judge, Ronnie," Harry said.

I watched the young man cringe and press his lips together at the name *Ronnie*. I guessed he must go by the name Ronald, or maybe even Sir Ronald.

As Ronnie stood there staring at his father with a pompous look, two thoughts came into my head: *He is a rude, inconsiderate son, but boy, is he gorgeous*. Tall, trim, with broad shoulders, big, bright green eyes, a head of full black, slicked-down hair, plus two dimples hidden behind that stern expression. He was dressed impeccably in a double-breasted pin-striped suit with matching blue shirt and tie. The gold watch on his left wrist looked expensive; perhaps it was a Rolex. Quite different than our pigeon-feeding group, or the young hippies rioting against the establishment. He was the personification of the establishment. *His judge must be a chum of Mayor Richard J. Daley*, I thought to myself.

I wanted to either tell him off or grab and kiss him. Never have I had a reaction like that before. An electric current went through me just at the sound of his deep voice.

He must have felt my stare. He took a hard look at me before silently turning around and leaving. I noticed that when he stopped to light a cigarette before crossing Michigan Avenue, he also turned back in our direction.

"That woman of mine drives me crazy," Harry said. "Married forty-two years, and she needs to know where I am every minute, and that kid of mine is so self-righteous. Thinks he can change the world. It sure won't work in this city. He called me an ambulance chaser. The father that made it possible for him to go to law school and hobnob with the mighty! Hey, let me see your case."

I checked my watch. "Thanks, Harry, but it is time for me to get back," I handed Nick the rest of my sandwich, suggesting, "Feed it to Gertie when she comes back."

Whenever I was able to get away, I joined my pigeon-feeding retired friends, half to enjoy the beautiful spring, and half in the hope of seeing Harry's son again. I never asked about him, afraid to be too inquisitive. That was a mistake. I should have remembered that a moment lost is a moment that cannot be retrieved. A month later, Harry had disappeared, and no one knew his last name or where he was. After a few months of inquiring, it began to feel like Harry had disappeared from the face of the earth. I tried to forget him, but I couldn't get that son of his out of my mind, even though I suspected Ronnie would definitely be trouble.

I shuffled into my apartment, loaded down with law books and thinking I may have taken on more than I could handle. I started out of my room towards the kitchen when I heard doors open and close, first the front, then the bedroom door, then the front door again.

In a very weak, pleading voice, Judy yelled, "Jesse, Jesse, please don't go." He went anyway.

Not wanting to interfere, I went back to my room until her sobbing and moaning got to me.

Entering her room, I gasped at the weak, pale figure curled in a fetal position upon the bed. "Judy, what happened to you, you look awful." I was really worried about her.

She looked up at me with swollen red eyes and a slightly bizarre smirk on her face. "What do you think?" she said. "I had an abortion."

My eyes opened wide, and I said, "An abortion! They are illegal!"

"Sherrie, you are so naïve," Judy sighed. "For the money, you can always find a backroom abortion doctor. Do you really think I was going to have the baby?"

She pulled up the covers and turned away from me. "Please go, leave me alone," she said, as she waved me out with her hand.

Not knowing what to do, I left as she had directed.

I stayed in my room, reluctant to leave Judy alone in the apartment. Picking up my law book and lighting a cigarette, I tried to concentrate on my studies, but my mind kept wondering and questioning. How could a nice Jewish girl like Judy end up with an illegal abortion? Okay, she wasn't so nice anymore, twenty, into drugs, alcohol, and the hippie crowd, but an abortion?!

Should I call her mother? Her mother still believed Judy was studying at Roosevelt University to become a teacher. They paid her tuition even though she never went to school. As a law student, I questioned morality vs. the law I was learning to interpret and uphold. To me, illegal was illegal, even though having an unwanted baby was not a great alternative. Truthfully, I never even thought about abortion or the pro-life issue before this.

At home, in my family building, this wouldn't have happened. The neighborhood pipeline would have known Judy's problems, and everyone would have rallied around her. I stubbed out one cigarette and lit another. She was different, she grew up in a house, a different neighborhood, a more secret environment, more like this apartment building we were in. Face it; I didn't even know the other five tenants beyond a nod, and I guess I never really knew my roommate. Even though Judy was the one who made the most noise, Jesse made the decisions. So different from South Shore.

I tiptoed near the door to Judy's room. All was quiet, so I retreated to my territory. I worried about her but wasn't sure how to help, or if she wanted help.

About an hour later, I was standing near the counter in the kitchen, making myself a cup of tea when I heard Judy scream, "Help, help!" As I flew into her room, the teacup dropped, burning my hand from the scalding water. Laying on the floor in her hippie white linen embroidered dress—covered by bright red blood— was my friend. I felt panic. Where was my family to take over?

"Keep it together," I kept telling myself. Trembling, I dialed the fire department at FI5-1313 and sat by her side until help arrived. She was pale and sweaty, and the towels weren't stopping the bleeding. I offered Judy some water, but she refused. It felt like forever for the paramedics to come, but it was only fifteen minutes.

When the paramedics loaded Judy on the gurney, she said, "Don't tell my mother." Of course, I ignored her. Calling her mother wasn't easy, nor was it any better meeting her mother and married sister at the hospital, though they acted differently than my family would have. No loud, emotional demonstrations, just quiet anger, pain, and questions. I was the one with tears in my eyes.

She lived, but the botched abortion left Judy with a uterus that could never bear children. Her mother was angry that I hadn't called her sooner, to let her know what was going on, but thankful that I was there to save Judy's life.

Judy either didn't know how to find Jesse or decided not to tell on him. I was mixed up about my actions. I sure hadn't been prepared for the sixties and my sought-after independence.

My cousin David had told me that I needed to get my head out of the safe family building and gain some street smarts to survive in the city. I left the hospital angry at Judy and angry at a medical and legislative system that would make someone risk her life for the right to choose whether or not she wanted to have a child. It was my first significant experience with a law that affected me. It brought me closer to the brewing women's rights movement.

My aunts had trained me well. Even though I was angry, I cleaned Judy's room. I didn't want her mother to witness all that blood. David also would be upset. He took such pride in his remodeled buildings. It took a lot of scrubbing and washing. I was beginning to feel like Lady Macbeth. Blood everywhere, the bed, the floor, the sink, and my hands. When the room was clean, I went into the bathroom, turned on the hot water faucet, took out a fresh bar of soap, and scrubbed my hands repeatedly. Then I sat down on her one chair and took out a cigarette. After about three puffs, I put it out, went back to my room, and cried.

I felt guilty. I'm not sure why. It wasn't my job to protect Judy. If you are Jewish, you are guilty; there doesn't have to be a logical reason. I decided I might stay a virgin forever, which wouldn't be easy.

I had a hard time sleeping that night, waking several times to wash my hands. I felt like returning to my safe family building, but it was gone.

I called Aunt Tillie to tell her. She was shocked and kept repeating, "Oy vey, her poor mother."

"Aunt Tillie," I asked carefully, "what is the Jewish law on abortion?" The Christian view on abortion was much easier to find, as it was in the news often.

I could hear her gasp, and go *ptew, ptew, ptew* to ward off the evil spirit. I realized I had made her uncomfortable. Finally, she answered, "We don't talk about those things. Ask the rabbi."

I was afraid to call our Orthodox/Conservative rabbi and ask about abortion, so I called two reform temples. The rabbi wasn't available at either, but a librarian from one of the temples called me back with this quote from the Torah: *"A woman's life, pain, and concern take prece-dence over those of the fetus. A fetus is considered part of the pregnant mother."* I did know scholars spent their lives interpreting every word of the Torah. I wanted to pursue this with a rabbi on another day. Living every day in the real world, I realized how sheltered I had been in my family building. I wanted to talk to Judy about it, but she wasn't an-swering my calls.

While in class, Judy and abortion were on my mind all day. The bottom line for me was that the woman wanting an abortion should be able to get one in a safe place. I knew many people had different views, especially Catholics. Since I was in law school, I needed to check out the laws related to this topic because we were a nation of separation of church and state.

I waited for my last class to clear before approaching one of my younger professors.

"Professor Wilber," I said as I approached him at his podium, "a friend had an illegal abortion, and it has made me realize we have never dealt with a case about abortion, and we have had just one case about women's rights."

He picked up his briefcase and started to leave the classroom. Part-way out the door, he turned to me and said, "Miss Paul, I hope it *was* a friend we are talking about. If you want information on the topic, check out the law library. It is very well stocked."

My face flushed at his accusation. I had purposely picked this pro-fessor because I thought he was only around forty and a cool dresser in plaid jackets, so he would understand. Instead, I felt his mistrust and resentment, but I wasn't going to let it stop me.

I swallowed hard before I made my way down the marble stairs to the library. Luckily, the law librarian was a woman. Approaching the desk, I asked, "Mrs. Fillmore, where can I find information on abortion and other women's rights?"

"Depends how far you want to go back. Most information starts in the late eighteen hundreds."

"I want to look at today's laws."

I was impressed by the rows and rows of colorful, hard-covered books occupying walls that reached up several floors. The librarian directed me to the proper section, which had an attached ladder that reminded me of the ladders linking the medicine shelves in South Shore's now-closed Rosenblum's drugstore. As I climbed the ladder to find the right books and journals, the light off the antique brass show globe, ceiling fixtures shot light across the wood-paneled floor.

I approached one of the expansive oak tables and sat upon a green leather upholstered wooden chair, surrounded by tons of books and journals, and realized even more than usual how my years with my family had sheltered me from the outside world. Oh, I had heard about women's turn-of-the-century efforts to gain the right to vote, and today's fights for other rights, but until Judy, I never related any of it to myself. My quick scanning made me realize that, besides the abortion issue, women were denied equal pay, couldn't keep their jobs if pregnant, couldn't get credit, and needed a reason to get divorced, plus a slew of other injustices.

I had dismissed the hippies. I wasn't one to march or break the law, but now I wanted to find other women, possibly other lawyers who were involved with the women's rights movement.

Almost as if in answer to a prayer, Mrs. Fillmore came to my table and slipped a piece of paper to me. "These girls may help you," she whispered.

The paper read, *Shirley Greenwald and Paula Platt. Specialists in women's law.* There was an address in Lincoln Park, but no phone number. I tucked it into my pocket. Just mentioning abortion produced awkward and hostile reactions. On the way home, I bought a copy of *Cosmopolitan*.

I wasn't emotionally stable enough to stay in the apartment after Judy's abortion. I was having a hard time sleeping, and every time I went near her room, I thought I saw blood by the door. When she refused my phone calls, guilt was added to my pain.

My cousin David was the only one I talked to about it. We sat at the kitchen table in my apartment, drinking coffee and smoking cigarettes.

"David, you know how much I've loved this place, even though Judy and I lived in different worlds. Since the abortion, I'm freaked here, and I need to get out." I ground my cigarette out in Mom's green glass ashtray and pressed my lips together to keep the tears from forming.

David stood up, moved the chair aside, and hugged me. Pulling away, but still holding my hands, he said, "Sherrie, it's no problem. We'll get you out of here and into your own place. I have another idea that may also help. I've been seeing a great therapist. She has kept me sane. It still isn't easy being gay in this world. There is still a lot of discrimination against us. The family doesn't need to know. I will pay for you to go to her."

I wasn't ready to take on therapy, though it seemed to be in fashion now. I squeezed his hands and replied, "Thank you for the offer, but I don't have time for therapy and law school. I think I need to be in a building with younger people."

I went from old to modern when David put me in one of his one-bedroom rental condos in the 2020 N. Lincoln Park building with the famous Original Pancake House. I was now really on my own and I loved it, especially the view of Lake Michigan through the window of my twelfth-floor apartment. The old mansion had been fantastic, but I felt much safer in this building populated with young adults. Along with the restaurant it had a doorman, garage, a cleaners, and a grocery. David, dressed like a professional in Polo jeans and a button-down shirt, helped me furnish the condo in modern decor. We used high brown leather bar stools around the kitchen counter, a flowered sofa with matching green fabric chairs, and Aunt Tillie's cedar chest for the coffee table. He talked me into one of the new queen-size mattresses, which took some getting used to after sleeping on a twin bed my whole life.

When the mattress was delivered, David was there directing. After the delivery men left, for old time's sake I threw one of the oversized pillows at him. He responded by tossing it back at me. Soon we found ourselves reminiscing about life in our beloved family building.

"David, do you remember when, in the middle of one of our pillow fights, Etta's cat jumped at the pillow?"

"Of course I do. Feathers flew all over your bedroom, and we were cleaning up forever. What about the walkie-talkie I tried to stream across the street from your apartment to mine?"

"Oh, yes, a car got caught in the wires," I recalled. David and I burst out laughing as we bounced on the new mattress like kids from the past. How I loved that cousin of mine. He could make anything fun. I bestowed a special hug around his neck before he left.

I abandoned my beloved blue color for the earth tones in fashion. I even let David paint the walls green. They went with the copper-colored fridge, stove, and dishwasher. It felt more like home, so much so that I put my family pictures up on the walls and unboxed some of the antiques from my dad and Aunt Tillie. Bright colored majolica vases and dainty English china cups and saucers were placed on my dark wood china cabinet, making me feel as if I were back in my family building. I picked up a yellow ceramic jar with an Indian design. As I opened it, I immediately thought of Lizzie's dad, Uncle Hymie, and his El Producto cigars. The lasting aroma of tobacco was throughout the jar, and my eyes watered.

I called Lizzie, "Did your dad hide cigars in that Indian jar?" I opened it and there are broken cigars everywhere."

Laughter came over the phone. "Lucky you, just tobacco," Lizzie said. "My mom sent out that old hickory-hickory dock clock for repair. The clock man called all upset. There was cocaine hidden in it."

"Yale?" I asked, shaking my head.

"Who else?"

We both laughed before continuing our conversation about the rest of the family.

David popped in every couple of days. One day upon entering my apartment, he put down a box of donuts on the Formica kitchen counter, looked around, shrugged his shoulders, and waved his hand like his mother did. "Sherrie, you've made this place look like Aunt Tillie's house! Too, too many things," he said as he rearranged the shelves in the rich mahogany and glass china cabinet he had brought me from his mother's house. While he was busy, I poked my head into the donut box, removed a chocolate nut-covered donut, and took a big bite, catching a broken-off piece of donut in my hand. I didn't want to miss any of the sweet, syrupy taste.

After rearranging things, he stood back to admire his work. Then he smiled and handed me half of the tchotchkes. "Put these away for when you get a bigger place," he directed. "All my Jewish clients add extra stuff to the rooms after I set them up. Why?"

I smiled and replied, "You are Jewish too. I guess we are collectors, or maybe we can't let someone else be in charge."

He knit his eyebrows and gave me a quizzical look.

"Moving to this condo worked better than therapy," I explained. "Your visits cheer me up. My nightmares have disappeared, and I've met some very nice people in my age group. Unfortunately, I don't have a lot of time for social life because of the pressure to get top grades in law school," I told him.

"So glad to hear that," he answered sarcastically, as he grabbed his coat and took off.

Chapter Fourteen

"Schoolwork is no excuse for missing Shabbat dinner," Aunt Tillie asserted. "The family misses you."

"Aunt Tillie, I am in law school now," I replied. "It's different. My life is studying. You know I come when I can."

"Different, you've always worked hard and gotten good grades," Aunt Tillie said, dismissively. "You were in all the honor societies, while I couldn't get Yale to open a book. You will be here this Friday at sundown and bring that new young man of yours. I hear he's a law clerk for a judge. Yale got a ticket. Maybe he can help us out. In the old days, you gave the ticket to your alderman, and it was taken care of. Boy, do I miss the boys in the 24th Ward."

Aunt Tillie was referring to the West Side of Chicago, where the Jewish aldermen ran their part of the city. The South Side Irish ran the rest. I had asked her to use her connections to find out about Ronnie, but I hadn't seen him since that day at Buckingham Fountain.

"Aunt Tillie, Ronnie doesn't work in traffic court," I replied. "He works for a federal judge, and he isn't my young man yet. I asked if you knew anyone whose son was a law clerk for a judge because you know everyone in Chicago who is Jewish."

"This one I don't know, but I do know a lot of good Jewish boys to fix you up with," Aunt Tillie replied. "Mrs. Goldberg, the matchmaker, has a list of boys your age. Benny Cohen would be a good match. He runs the family clothing store on Devon. You would always have beautiful dresses. Don't be putting that other boy on a pedestal because he works for a judge.

"Ninety percent of the Jews in Chicago have roots on Maxwell Street, and the other ten percent better not brag about being German," she added. "The war took care of their arrogance."

Thinking about Benny Cohen, a young, freckled-faced redhead came to mind, and I asked, "Did he live in South Shore?"

"Yes," Aunt Tillie replied. "But now he is a young man with money, and he doesn't stutter that much anymore."

I loved her dearly, but there was so much she didn't understand about the sixties and the changes being made in society. The Daley machine still ruled in Chicago, but not in the same open way, and the matchmaker game was dead. How dumb of me to start with my aunt. If Ronnie felt anything about me, he would be able to find me, so I better get this young man out of my mind. It was going on a month since he captured my attention.

It wasn't as if I lacked dates. There was Ted, the veterinary student with the pet snake, the balding head, and the tongue always working its way between my teeth; there was Henry, who was good looking and knew it, and there was blue-eyed blond William who was not Jewish and whom I couldn't bring home to the family even though he was a super-intelligent nice law student, who took me to some of Chicago's top restaurants.

Of course, I was prepared to go to another Friday night dinner for the family tradition and for the food. I did miss the smell of garlic roasting in the hallway of my building. My aunts were specialists in the Jewish guilt department, and I definitely could use a real home-cooked meal instead of the cold tuna, chicken sandwiches, and cheese pizzas on which I was living. I so missed the loud chatter and the friendly arguing about everything.

A bright orange sun peeked through the Chicago skyline as I left my school and walked towards the Chicago Transit Authority el (elevated train, instead of a subway) station. The day was warm, and I tied my jacket around my waist as I boarded the train. The el train rocked and clattered much more than my South Side Illinois Central train, and it sped by unfamiliar buildings, except for Wrigley Field, which was forbidden territory to a South Side White Sox fan. I took the el to the end of the line on Howard Street where my cousin Yale, now wearing those new contact lenses, and at least a foot taller than last month, picked me up in his new white Chevy Impala.

I asked, "Where did you get the gelt for the car?"

"My looks and charisma landed me a top job in a high-class men's clothing store," was his cocky answer.

I laughed, "I'm guessing you're dating Widman's daughter, Rachel."

He gave me one of his crooked grins. "Yeah, I am, but her dad's a tough boss."

Yale was the family maneuverer. He would either become the president of some big company or, God forbid, end up in jail.

I stretched out in the comfortable seats. The el car had been so crowded that I had to stand most of the way, barely hanging on to support while the train lurched back and forth. *Thank God Dad will be driving me home,* I thought.

Yale and I hardly made it through Aunt Tillie's door before the family surrounded me.

"Don't take off your coat. We have to go. Your father is in the hospital."

Aunt Tillie was moving up and back, chanting, "Those lousy bums, those drug addicts. I told him to get out, but no, he wouldn't listen."

"Like Pa," Aunt Sarah added as she picked up her black pocketbook and tan knit sweater.

Everyone was talking until I yelled, "Stop! Is he alive? What happened? One person tell me." A cold sweat covered my face at the dreaded thought that my father may be dead.

Uncle Izzy came forward and said, "Jake is alive. Your dad is tough. He will be all right. The bum kids on drugs robbed him again. Only this time, one of them shot him in the hip. He is at Michael Reese Hospital. Let's go."

Michael Reese Hospital, where all the cousins were born, where most of the Jewish doctors ended up, was located south of downtown at 2929 S. Ellis Ave. next to Lake Shore Drive, which runs along Lake Michigan. The hospital, founded in 1881, was a major research and teaching hospital.

The drive seemed to take forever. Skokie was a lot farther away from Michael Reese than South Shore was. The daylight was disappearing, and the rush hour traffic and the increasing raindrops against the windshield made the driving more difficult for Yale. No one talked, which was unusual for my family. Each of us sat still, absorbed in prayer or, worse, in fear of what we would find. I told God that I was sorry for being angry with Him and Dad over my mother. I needed to make peace with my dad. I bargained for my father like the family taught me. I even asked Pa for help.

The man lying in the hospital bed didn't resemble the father I knew. Besides being attached to all kinds of tubes, I noticed a receding hairline and wrinkled skin resembling a man much older than someone in his late fifties. Since Dad was in recovery after surgery, I only had a few minutes with him.

Waiting for Dad to wake up and for the doctor to talk to us seemed like forever. I felt too young to have to acknowledge that my parents weren't immortal. I was only twenty-three, my mother was gone, and now my father was teetering between life and death. I still felt anger on my part regarding secrets my father kept from me concerning my mother's religion and history. Dad and I had to deal with these issues in order to patch up our relationship.

I flipped through the pages of my law books while I waited, but concentrating on them was almost impossible. I craved a cup of coffee and a cigarette. On my way to the cafeteria, I nearly bumped into a young man hurrying down the hall. I could hear the beating of my heart as I immediately recognized the man as Harry's son Ronnie. To my dismay, I soon realized the squinting eyes and silent stare belonged to someone who was trying to place me. Feeling awkward, I didn't know what to say to him.

"Do I know you?" he finally asked as we stood face to face.

Trying to keep from trembling, I answered, "Not really. We met once at Buckingham Fountain when your father was feeding the pigeons."

He laughed, "Of course, you were the young girl among the old guys. What were you doing feeding the birds?"

"Taking a break from law school," I answered as I played with a tendril of hair.

"A law student. I would have never guessed," he said, grinning and laughing out loud. "Where are you going to school?"

His tone was much friendlier than at our first meeting, and his attire less formal—in fact, he looked a little rumpled. I even detected a five o'clock shadow.

As my trembling voice answered, "John Marshall," Yale grabbed me and said, "Sherrie, your dad's doctor wants to talk to you."

Reluctantly I hurried off, again losing this young man who made my heart flutter and my breathing shallow. What could I do? My dad's life was in danger. Later when I reviewed the meeting my rage increased as I realized that, while I kept thinking about him, he didn't even remember who I was. I knew I wasn't a beauty, though I had lost weight since high school, and now had an attractive hourglass figure.

To hell with Ronnie, I said to myself. Though I did wonder who he was visiting in the hospital. I hoped it wasn't his dad.

"Mr. Paul is no longer in a life or death situation," Dr. Michaels explained. "We were able to remove the bullet, give him a blood transfusion, and stabilize him. He may have some difficulty walking. Bone was shattered in his hip."

The family silence was broken, and the poor doctor was bombarded with questions, moans, and tears. We were an emotional Jewish family, after all.

"How long before he will be released?" "What do you mean he can't walk? He climbs roofs." "*Oy, Oy*, how could this happen? "Why, my poor brothers? Why, God, should they both have limps?"

Then Tillie asked the main question. "What about the store?" The doctor said it could take months before Dad could go to work.

Chapter Fifteen

The old neighborhood had not remained the same. After President Kennedy was shot, the nation pulled together in a shared grief. Five years later, when Martin Luther King Jr. and Robert Kennedy were assassinated, our country was pulled apart. Rioting and looting on Chicago's South and West Sides replaced King's peaceful demonstrations. The realtors were the only ones happy about it. They made money by blockbusting. They put fear into white homeowners' minds—fear that riots would come to their neighborhood, fear that the value of their homes would go down as soon as minorities moved in. Owners sold and moved out of South Shore. Gentiles moved south and west to suburbs like Oak Lawn, and the Jews ran to the northern suburbs like Skokie.

In just a few short years, the streets of my beloved South Shore were scattered with rubbish, and stores were vacant or exhibiting boarded-up windows. The 71st Street business strip had been a thriving shopping street with high-class clothing, grocery, beauty shops, restaurants, etc. Now it looked like slum property. Even the overgrown grass seemed to be calling for help. High school in my day had social clubs that competed in sports or musical exhibitions. Now, gangs of teenagers competing for drug dealing turfs were sprouting up. No wonder there was a massive exit of the more affluent white and black residents. The riots and looting on the South and West Sides in April of 1968, after Dr. Martin Luther King was assassinated, didn't help. People became scared and left.

The hardest thing for me was seeing the family building. Paint peeling off, weeds instead of flowers, a broken doorbell, and, worst of all, no pigeons! I was told our large apartments were broken into two per floor. Thus, more than one family lived on each floor in most of the apartment buildings. The newer individual houses and the neighborhoods further south than 80th Street seemed to be kept in better shape, possibly because those families were property owners instead of renters.

My grammar school, only a half of a block down the street, had in its former playground several outside structures to relieve student overcrowding. The changes saddened me. I pictured dear teachers and fellow classmates walking the corridors and settling in the classrooms. It was years before I again went back to the building. It represented the happiest days of my life, where I felt love and security. Innocence too, but I wouldn't talk about that now.

My dad's store, a place where I always felt safe, suddenly felt threatening. The gated windows and gated front door covered the ads my dad spent hours making. It made me feel sad. An enormous black metal and glass walk-in telephone booth stood in the front of the store. A hanging telephone book and a black dial phone with heavy metal cords were located within. In the past, it was a convenience that was hardly used. Now it was continually used by customers who couldn't afford a phone, or by policy wheel operators or drug dealers.

Nobody knew me there, neither the help nor the customers, except for Uncle Izzy who was nervously puffing on a cigar while going over my dad's book of credit that he gave to customers and Aunt Sarah who was trying to familiarize herself with the inventory, which was no longer Jewish-oriented. I tried something new, a bag of barbecue chips with a hot sauce that almost sent me to the emergency room.

We were trying to keep the store open for my dad. We were family, and in crisis, family members came together and covered for each other.

I had the summer off from school. Instead of working as a law clerk, I was helping in the store.

A customer, a big, tough-looking black woman with one of those new hairdos called an Afro, said to me, "You Mr. Jake's daughter? Come here, girl."

"Yes," I answered.

She grabbed my arm and pulled me over to an isolated part of the store. Initially, she scared me, but then she softened, saying, "You tell Mr. Jake we are sorry, and we will make sure those boys will never hurt him again."

"If you know who shot Dad, let's go to the police," I replied, as I peered into her eyes.

"Listen, girl, we don't trust the police. We take care of it ourselves."

Then she was gone before I could respond.

Some other woman tried to sell me a policy wheel ticket. Policy was a lottery type of game people in the black neighborhoods bet on. You had to pick the right six numbers. The woman assured me if I played the right numbers, I would win a lot of money. When I asked if it was legal, she disappeared.

In just a few short years, my South Shore neighborhood had undergone a radical change. I felt sorry for all who stayed. Taverns were in place of restaurants and delis.

I was shocked by the number of people who asked about my father. He had developed a new following with the black and Latino population of the new South Shore. Of course, it helped that he was the only grocery store that stayed in the changing neighborhood.

Real estate agents scared people into selling, and then they turned the large apartments into multiple dwellings, thus attracting the poor, leading to gang wars over drugs, similar to the Mafia wars over alcohol in the 1920s.

I was especially touched by a little black girl, no more than three or four, who approached me.

"Miss Jake, will you tell the Mr. that I'm sorry I took his stuff without paying for it," she said, handing me some soap and hair clips. "I can't give back the candy 'cause I ate it."

The family wanted to sell the store, while my dad kept talking about how he missed *kibitzing* with the customers and couldn't wait to get back to work. A family dilemma.

I blamed South Shore because I so wanted the home where I grew up to stay the same, but it was not only South Shore that had changed since the fall of Camelot—it was all of the country that had erupted into violent protests, aggressive behavior, and disregard for the law. As a law student learning to interpret and uphold the law of the land, it was hard for me to understand what was happening. My cousin David saw things differently, however.

Complaining to him over a cup of coffee while we sat in my kitchen, he told me off.

"Sherrie, you were kept so naive and sheltered in South Shore, and the family ghetto," David asserted, as he put his cigarette out in Mom's green glass ashtray.

"How dare you call it a ghetto?" I sat up straight in protest. "We were protected and loved."

"In a way, but we were not allowed to be ourselves, to follow our dreams," he said as he stubbed out his cigarette, "or to go against the family rules."

I shook my head, looked up into his face, and said, "I don't understand. You didn't marry and go to medical school like the family wanted you to do. You became a decorator and are living with a male partner, and I am a single girl in law school, instead of a married woman with a kid in each arm. Isn't that following our dreams? Remember how the family sat shiva for their daughter and sister Barbra when she ran off with a *goy*?"

"Okay, Sherrie," David replied. "You have some good points. Some of our luck came from your mother's help and, truthfully, Pa was getting old and senile. He wasn't really the in-charge patriarch he had been all those years. Remember, I lived with him."

David got up and moved towards the refrigerator. He reached in and pulled out the carton of milk. He poured some into his coffee and returned to sit by my red Formica table.

"In his last years, Pa looked so small and frail that it was hard for me to believe that I had been so afraid of him," David recalled. "What also helped was that the outside world changed, others protested, and we took advantage of it. But the battle has just begun. You will agree with me that it isn't easy to be a woman in a man's world, or for me to be a homosexual in today's world. Yet, because some people chose to fight for their rights, you are a woman in law school, and I was able to come out. I plan to join the fight."

I stared at him in his business attire, slicked-back hair, and button-down shirt. Nothing *free-spirited, hippie of the 1960s* about him. He was determined to make it as a gay decorator. This flair for design was in David's blood. I still had one foot in each world. I wanted to be a lawyer and I wanted to be a wife and mother. I leaned my chin against the palm of my hand as I thought about this.

I thought about how Aunt Tillie had humored Pa as she attempted to take over the family's leadership. Yes, so much of David's opinion of the family and the world today was true, but he missed how women had to learn how to work around men.

"Yes, David, you've given me more to add to my agenda. Now, let's get to the hospital to see my father."

I put out my cigarette, finished the last cheese pastry, and laid the cups in the sink. While David helped me put on my coat, I realized I still had trouble with the word "homosexual," and coming to terms with what it really meant. *Gay*, the new term being used by homosexuals, was more comfortable for me to use. David would always be the cousin I grew up with, no matter what he called himself.

Outside, David had to give me a little push to get into his large blue Chevy business truck. We drove along the Outer Drive past Grant Park, past the fountain and the Field Museum by a calm blue lakefront dotted with early spring walkers and bicyclists. We got off on 22nd Street and drove onto 29th Street to the main building of the enormous Michael Reese Hospital complex.

Michael Reese Hospital had kosher food for its many Jewish doctors and patients. The tray on my dad's table extending over his bed smelled like the family building with fewer spices. As the days went by, I was pleased to see my father eat more and more, gain strength, and respond positively to his post-surgical care. By the end of the second week, he had moved from wheelchair to walker, while I was traveling from hospital to store to my apartment, a schedule physically and emotionally tiring. More tiring than the law school schedule I had complained about.

When Dad was finally released from the hospital, he reluctantly stayed in Skokie with Aunt Tillie while Uncle Izzy stayed in my dad's Hyde Park apartment so he would be closer to the store. By the time my dad returned two and a half months later the family had had it, especially after the grocery store was broken into through the roof, and Uncle Izzy had to respond to the alarm at one o'clock in the morning.

The showdown happened during a Friday night dinner at Aunt Tillie's house. After the last piece of rugelach was eaten, and the Sabbath candles were almost burned out, Aunt Tillie, the spokeswoman, stood up from her chair and faced my dad.

"Jake, the family has had a meeting, and we want you to close the store," she asserted. "It is not a safe place for any of us to be."

My dad's face turned bright red. Pointing his finger in her direction, he answered, "Who are you to tell me what to do? I am the oldest in the family. How *dare* you tell me what to do?"

In a huff, he tried to get up but fell back. This triggered everyone to surround him and start arguing.

"You can't even stand without your cane! We are all working the store while you are recovering. Are you going to wait until one of us gets killed? You have to get out of that neighborhood. Jake, they burned down the West Side and half of the South Side after Dr. King was murdered. There are no more peaceful demonstrations."

"Stop, stop," Dad said. *"Los mer alain*—leave me alone!" My dad put his hands on his head. I rushed to him and put my arms around him. Aunt Tillie kept moaning and complaining.

Dad looked up and said, "I'm only fifty-eight. My wife is gone. What can I do? The store has been my life. The customers are my friends."

A smile broke out on my Aunt Tillie's face. "It's taken care of," she said. "I've talked to Arty from the old ward. He can give you a political job in the Park District, by the city golf courses."

"Golf?" my dad said, incredulously. "I know nothing about golf!"

Dad had no choice. He wasn't capable of running the store by himself, and the family was done. The store was sold for very little and a few months later he went to work for the city.

According to Aunt Tillie, Dad would be a figurehead, while the daily business and events in the three- to four-hundred city parks were carried out by employees who had been there for years. My dad, a hard worker, and faithful employee was determined to learn the ins and outs of working for the city. His slackened pace due to his limp didn't stop him. He wouldn't take up golf, but he did integrate things like club-houses and senior recreation centers on the city parklands, plus some food pantries for the poor. Also, flowers soon sprouted up all over the city due to my father's orders. Flower catalogs were scattered over his desk as he became interested in gardening.

Not being a politician, he made a few mistakes, like the time he was interviewed by a newspaper reporter.

"Mr. Paul, your city park gardens and golf clubs are beautiful, but considering you are paid all year round, we would like to know what you do in the winter," the reporter said.

My dad—again, not a politician—gave an answer that almost ruined him: "I do all my planning in the winter, and then I work twice as hard in the summer!"

The newspapers had a field day with that quote, and my dad swore off any other interviews.

The family was worried about my dad losing his job after his catastrophic interview, so I spent spare time visiting him at City Hall as it was close to my school. I was impressed with the eleven-story stone building, with its marble staircases and bronze tablets. I was told that the roof had a garden, but I never saw it.

Dad sat behind a big comfortable-looking wooden desk and chair. The sun shone through the large windows, which opened to the busy downtown streets. Black and white family pictures and a large calendar sat on his desk. The walls had colorful maps and pictures of the different Chicago parks. Dad was dressed in a suit and tie even though it was a warm spring day. He seemed impressed with his status but bored, though he wouldn't admit it. He had never been a white-collar sitter.

I met Howard on one of my visits. Howard, a hardworking employee without clout, was my dad's assistant and teacher. First, we became friends. Then he asked me out on a date.

At Valois, a famous cafeteria in Hyde Park, Howard was piling my plate with homemade roast beef, chicken, hash browns, and cake, as we walked down the cafeteria line. I was mesmerized by the vivid picture menus on the wall above the matching cafeteria food.

"Whoa, I can't eat that much," I said as I tried putting the food back.

"Sherrie, this place is a famous institution," Howard countered. "You won't get food like this anywhere else. You don't have to eat everything."

He didn't come from my family. Howard took my plate and I followed him through the crowded aisles of people from all walks of life to a metal, four-seater table which sat adjacent to a wall adorned with pictures of Mayor Daley and other dignitaries and celebrities.

Howard was much taller, heavier, and older than anyone I had dated. His dark, receding hairline was showing tinges of gray. I noticed that, though his hands were large, his fingers were long and trim, and he had these sad brown eyes. He was kind, and considerate, pulling out my chair and taking care of my tray.

These thoughts and observations distracted me from my original reason for joining him for lunch.

I sat down on the red vinyl seat of the chair, draping my sweater over the back before approaching him with my problem.

"Howard, my family is upset. After my dad was shot in his grocery store, we went to great trouble to get him this job and out of the South Side of Chicago. Now, we find him in the worst neighborhoods like Jackson Park and Garfield Park. What can we do? We are afraid he could be attacked again."

Howard opened his hands and shook his shoulders. "Sherrie, it isn't the job, it's your dad. He could just sit at a desk in his city office and send others out, but he insists on checking everything on his own. I go with him to protect him, but, believe me, when your father is in a Chicago car, no one will bother a Daley man."

I sat back in the chair, smiled, and said, "That's my dad, the perfect employee." I could just see Aunt Tillie and Aunt Sarah ganging up on my father after I gave my report.

Howard and I started on a routine type of dating—movies at the Chicago Theater and a German dinner at The Berghoff until I finally dared to ask for a restaurant change.

"I'm sorry, Sherrie," Howard said. "I should have asked you. I thought you liked the Berghoff. How about trying the Italian Village?"

He was quiet and always apologizing. Howard was just too nice. Why he didn't even kiss me until the third date. I was confused about his behavior until I talked to Aunt Tillie.

"Sherrie, Howard is afraid of your father," Aunt Tillie explained. "He doesn't want to lose his job. Howard's dad died, and he helps support his mother. He is a real mensch. The type of son Yale should be."

Howard was a good man, maybe too good and too old for me. We had fun together, but there was an emotional spark missing. He thought Woody Allen and Peter Sellers were absolutely crazy, and he read only technical journals. He had no idea who F. Scott Fitzgerald was, and the law in Chicago was what Mayor Daley told him to do, while I was still a romantic who wanted to see stars with every kiss, laugh at stupid things, and be surprised once in a while.

It was almost two years since I had seen or thought about Ronnie. We met again while I was in my senior year at law school at a class tour of Superior Court Judge Marcus' courtroom, located on the fourteenth floor of the Dirksen Federal Building.

Judge Marcus was a federal judge appointed by President Kennedy in 1963, right before Kennedy was assassinated. Judge Marcus was known and loved by everyone. This man came from poor immigrants living on Chicago's Maxwell Street and made it to the top, a true-life Horatio Alger story. The judge was a small, thin, bald man with an enormous capacity to be there for everyone. He was friends to politicians, actors, and the shoeshine man.

In his long black robe, he delivered an encouraging speech, emphasizing the need to do what is right, and how important it was for us to keep an honorable name. After the speech, we were invited to look around the courtroom, which was adorned with signed pictures of famous actors and political figures plus collections of Abraham Lincoln paraphernalia, bookshelves and bookshelves, and even a small jail cell, with iron bars.

I was staring at a signed photograph of Frank Sinatra, thinking of my mother, when Ronnie approached me. I immediately knew who he was, by the smell of his shaving cream and the fact that my heart pounded a little more quickly than usual, as I turned around and stared into his large green eyes. *He's got nicer eyelashes than I do . . .*

"Haven't seen you in a long time," Ronnie said. "Nice to see that you've made it to your last year of law school."

I immediately became defensive, standing up straighter, pressing my lips together, jaw clenching. "Because I'm a girl, you expected me to drop out or to fail," I exclaimed.

Ronnie smiled, exposing his two dimples. "I'm sorry. It's Sherrie, isn't it? I shouldn't have said that. I'm just not used to women lawyers. Come, let me introduce you to my boss, Judge Marcus. He does better with women lawyers than I do."

I followed, keeping my gaze away from him. Suddenly the judge approached us with open arms. Before Ronnie could say a word, Judge

Marcus pulled me towards him and surrounded me in one of his bear hugs. "How is that aunt of yours?" the judge asked. "I'm still angry with her for picking that cigar-puffing blowhard over me."

He then looked at Ronnie, "So, you've met. Take good care of her or you will answer to me and her Aunt Tillie."

I left Ronnie staring wide-eyed while I went to the ladies' room to have a good laugh. My Aunt Tillie knew everyone in Chicago. My grades were tops, but a letter from the judge in 1967 did help get this girl into law school. I wondered about Ronnie's father, as he has never been back with my pigeon-feeding friends where I originally met Ronnie. But I refused to ask him and spoil that great scene so I left the courthouse, knowing he could always find me, and I had to keep playing hard to get.

About a month later, on a cold snowy winter day, I saw Ronnie standing outside the door to my law school. I almost didn't recognize him, in his brown tweed winter coat and pulldown wool hat, and at 5 p.m. the street was busy with people rushing on their way home. If I hadn't stopped to button up my heavy sheep-skinned coat, we may have missed each other.

"Hi, Ronnie, what are you doing here?" I casually asked.

"Looking for you. You never answer your phone, are you never home?"

He rubbed his gloveless hands together, "It's cold. Let's go across the street to the pub and get some coffee."

He took my books out of my hands and marched a ways ahead of me across the street. The wind was blowing, and the streets were icy, so I followed carefully, stuffing my hands into my pockets to keep them warm. He opened the heavy pub doors for me and we slid into a long leather booth near the back of the place. With a sly smirk on my face,

I settled in the seat across from him. I was determined to not let him know how much I became rattled at his deep voice and strong touch.

The waiter came over, and, without asking me, Ronnie ordered two black coffees. Matter-of-factly, he stared at me and stated, "It's been around a year since you've been playing a cat-and-mouse game with me. I expect to get an answer when I leave a message. I think it is time you stop it, and we get to know each other." It was actually two years since I laid eyes on him, and knew I wanted him, but I wasn't going to tell him.

I don't know where he left a message, but I never got it. Anyway, I wasn't going to give in to demands. I moved out of the booth. Turning towards him, I said, "What a romantic invitation. Send me the contract to check over, and then I will consider signing it and legally spending time with you." I left. I wanted to look back to see his face, but I resisted the urge. Shivering in the twenty-five-degree weather, I slipped into the adjacent garage to retrieve my car.

This was a new independent me, one who started to take shape after my mother died. I realized to capture this guy would be a challenge, and I wanted him. I longed for him so much that he was on my mind constantly. I imagined his lips on mine and his long slender fingers over my body. He occupied my dreams, now that he was back in my life— dreams of dancing with him around a beautiful flowered Jewish wedding chuppah. The Jewish Pipeline had informed me Ronald was not the marrying kind, and once he thought you were his, he lost interest. There was a long list of girls he had hurt. So far, my game was working.

Just when I thought that I had overplayed my hand with Ronnie, an envelope arrived from the office of Superior Judge Marcus. I signed for it and quickly tore it open. Inside was an official-looking ten-page dating contract from Ronald Greenspan, Esq.

After a good laugh, I grabbed my cup of coffee, my new keep-awake liquid; a cigarette and an ashtray, and prepared to cuddle up on my plastic-less red floral sofa for a fun read.

I wasn't disappointed. Skimming through the pages, I could tell Ronnie had spent time on it. In my three-and-a-half years of law school, I never ran into a contract for dating. For pre-marriage, there were many, and he was using some of the legal language, such as the number one statement.

1. *We agree that whoever decides to disobey the terms of the contract will give the injured party the sum of to be decided.*

Number two angered me the most until I found it in a pre-nuptial marriage contract.

2. *We agree not to engage in any sexual activity with anyone other than each other.*

I would have to set this man straight. I was still a fifties girl set on being a virgin until marriage. To hell with the sixties' free sex. I had seen what it did for Judy.

3. *We agree to allow the male partner to make financial and business decisions, while the female partner manages the house.*

Wow, male chauvinist. Did he forget that it was the sixties, not the 1900s, and that I was a female law student?

4. *We agree to discuss our differences and not fly off the handle and walk out.*

I guess I had upset him when I walked out of the pub. Oh, well. Fiddlesticks! That one brought a big smile to my face.

There were four or five other points that were a real stretch, like respecting each other, and dressing in a dignified manner. They were all written in lawyers' jargon. Instead of studying, I spent the evening preparing my response, which I intended to send officially. I needed a lawyer girlfriend to call, but there was none around.

His contract was typed neatly on official-looking paper while mine was clicked away on my mother's ancient typewriter with the C that stuck. I was efficient but not a perfectionist, a problem in school, but not here. I did re-do the page I spilled my cup of coffee on.

I waited patiently for Ronnie's response. Every time the phone rang, I ran into the kitchen, pushing open the swinging door and dodging the swing back. I needed a longer cord on the phone. Classes helped me from worrying that it may not come. About five days later, my official negotiated contract came back. Again, I dropped everything and settled on my comfortable sofa. The timing was good. It was now winter break, and Mother Nature had covered her world with a blanket of white, so I was stuck in the apartment anyway. I heated some of Aunt Tillie's chicken soup and removed a small challah from the freezer.

There were several interesting responses. One bothered me. It referred to contract point number three. His response was: "I agree that I sounded a little male chauvinistic, but I was only referring to the fact that it was still difficult for a woman to get a job with a major law firm."

I hated to admit he was right. This made me think about the names of the two women lawyers who concentrated on women's rights. When the weather cleared, I would look them up.

Our contract was becoming more and more like a letter than an official paper. I was relieved to find out that even though his dad had had a heart attack two years ago when we met in the hospital, he was doing well now. I wrote to him about my family building, and we were both surprised to find out that our mothers were not Jewish, even though they raised us in the Jewish faith. In his case, he was aware of his mother's faith and had spent time with her family for holidays such as Christmas. His mother was raised on the North Side of Chicago and his father in New York. That explained why Aunt Tillie's expert Chicago pipeline didn't know Ronnie's family.

Outside of mandatory family dinners and necessary shopping, I hardly left my apartment during the two-week Christmas vacation. I had several New Year invites that I turned down. I had hoped Ronnie would ask me out as 1969 turned into 1970. He talked about how fast the seventies had come, and that he wasn't sure what he was going to do, but he never officially suggested that we get together.

Late afternoon on Dec. 31, expecting David, still in my PJs, coffee cup in one hand, chocolate donut in the other, I responded to a knock on my door. When I opened it, big arms encircled me, pulling me into a warm embrace. Then a gentle hand raised my head upwards, and a very special kiss pressed against my lips. That strange electric feeling ran through my body.

"Ronnie!"

He put a finger on my lips, "Get dressed in something pretty. We are going to celebrate the signing of our contract."

He reached into his pocket and produced a pen and a ten-page dating contract. New Year's Eve as 1969 became 1970 was the beginning of a special courtship. Of course, with us being two lawyers, not everything went smoothly.

Chapter Sixteen

I thanked God that I wouldn't have the store to help out with this summer. I would need every single moment to study for the bar. That unbelievable two-day twelve-hour exam that hardly anyone passed on the first try had to be my focus now that graduation from law school was over.

The whole family was at my graduation, all dressed up, cheering, and clapping as I received my diploma. My body ached for my mother while I also beamed with the love coming from my support system.

I had warned Ronnie about my family, especially Aunt Tillie, so when she first surrounded him with a big bear hug and then the interrogation, he was ready.

"I hear you come from Lake Forest," she began. "How did that happen when Lake Forest is restricted, where Jews and other minorities were unwelcome?"

"I told Sherrie Lake Forest on purpose so you couldn't tap the Jewish Pipeline and find out about me! We lived just north of Lake Forest in Lake Bluff," he answered with those great dimples showing. I knew he was teasing her. He did tell me Lake Bluff, which also probably had very few Jews. When we were growing up, many neighborhoods wouldn't allow Jews or blacks to move in.

Tillie, dressed in her temple outfit—long black skirt and white buttoned high blouse—wasn't happy. She stood with hands on her hips, face wrinkled, lips together, and eyes wide open—her determined look, the one that always scared the cousins.

"Nobody gets to our Sherrie without family approval, and my informers actually can reach past the West Side and South Side, young man," Tillie asserted. "I want a straight answer, none of that lawyer *mishigas*. Are you Jewish?"

My Dad stepped in, saying, *"Ga nuck*. Let the young man alone. Sherrie is happy. No more shiva business. If someone married out of the faith, they were considered dead."

"Wow, everyone, stop interrogating Ronnie. He is Jewish like I am Jewish. His mother is a WASP, and his father is a Jew, the same as my family."

That shut everyone up, though I did see Tillie give me a stunning look. I'm sure she knew I was talking for my mother, who I truly missed today, and not just being disrespectful to my family, something I'd never done.

I still hadn't met Ronnie's mother and sister, which bothered me. We did have a corned beef and chopped liver sandwich lunch with his dad at Ashkenaz's Delicatessen. He was thrilled that we were dating and really happy that me, a girl, had graduated from law school. I thought that after meeting my family today, Ronnie might never want to see me again.

We celebrated with an old-fashioned Jewish dinner in Skokie at Aunt Tillie's house, which was an old bungalow with large rooms and picture windows highlighted with stained glass. The familiar black and white wooden clock, twelve-rack spice rack, Shabbat candlesticks, and the traditional Bubbie and Zadie (Grandma and Grandpa) statues were in the flowery wallpapered kitchen, plus a bouquet of assorted colorful flowers brought to my aunt from Ronnie.

Pine picnic tables painted a bright red with matching umbrellas, and a new swing set could all be found on the green grass in the cozy back-yard. Lizzie's golden retriever ran around the yard looking for food. Uncle Izzy and Aunt Tillie never replaced Barney, who lived to be sixteen. Still, out of habit, most of us gathered in the kitchen. To supplement the strudel and rugelach, David brought a decorated *congratulations* cake from Levinson's, a Jewish bakery on Devon Avenue.

The whole family was there, even Aunt Dora, with her crooked drawn eyebrows and her orange lipstick on her teeth. My girl cousins, who were younger than I was, were already married with babies. Aunt Tillie's house was alive again with tea kettles whistling, family members shouting, dogs barking, and little children running after each other while televisions blasted.

As a graduation gift, Ronnie gave me a beautiful brown leather Gucci briefcase with my name on it.

Aunt Tillie hit the glasses to quiet down the room as she stood up next to my dad.

"Sherrie, come here," she said, pulling me to her. "We are so proud of you. The first girl in the family to go to college. You were always the best learner, even when it came to making challah."

Izzy yelled at her, "Enough with the challah, give her the card."

"Okay, okay, keep quiet." She turned towards me and handed me a card. "There is a check in here for a down payment on a car. Just a down payment, you will have to take out a loan for the rest of the vehicle, but you are a big girl now with a profession. Soon you will be making your own money."

"Jake, take her to Simon," Hymie said. "He'll take good care of you."

My dad waved his hands in the air, saying, "I know, I know."

"Be careful with him," Aunt Tillie warned. "Yale's car had trouble in a few months. The brakes, right, Yale?"

"No, Tillie," Hymie said. "It was Yale's fault. He never put oil in the car."

"It's always my fault," Yale said as he took a drink of wine and lit a cigarette.

I started to cry. "I don't know what to say. You all have been so wonderful in your support of me. I never expected this. I believed I would get the traditional watch."

Aunt Sarah waved her hand in the air and said, "See, I told you she wanted a watch."

"No, Aunt Sarah," I replied. "I need a new car so much more than a watch."

Aunt Dora said, "You don't need to tell the time? What if you need to go to court?"

"Aunt Dora, I have my mother's watch," I replied.

"*Sha*, I'm not done," Aunt Sarah said. "Sherrie, you are now the family lawyer. Here is your first case. Another ticket for Yale. Fix it. I think the family should take back their payment on his car."

Every eye turned towards Yale, who gave us his shoulder shrug and winning smile that always said, "Who, me?"

My dad stood up. "In the immortal words of Pa, let's eat." With a smile on all faces, we proceed to consume the family feast.

* * *

For Labor Day, I decided to make dinner instead of going out.

Ronnie and I were sitting in my apartment, finishing my attempt at making an Italian dinner that didn't mix meat and cheese. Ronnie had enjoyed my chicken soup and brisket meals. Funny, I was a female lawyer who still needed to be admired for her cooking and cleaning skills. Women's lib?

My family didn't need a cookbook for their Jewish meals. We learned by watching and helping our mothers or, in my case, Aunt Tillie. I decided to branch out for Ronnie's sake and had purchased a recommended cookbook called the *Antoinette Pope School Cookbook*.

My apartment kitchen was small, but I still managed to set a beautiful table with a white linen tablecloth, gold china plates, and crystal glasses. I had spent the afternoon shopping carefully, moving through the boxes of fresh vegetables, looking for the best tomatoes, peppers, onions, and the meatiest chicken breasts.

Following a cookbook was new to me, especially since I had to improvise to make the chicken dish kosher. I worked all day chopping, frying, baking, and stirring. The pungent aroma of the sizzling vegetables before they went over the chicken and into the oven made me believe I had made a winning dinner.

Instead of wearing my universal black pants, I traded my apron for a pretty green knit skirt and top.

Ronnie, still dressed in his work suit, was on time. My heart did a flutter when he kissed me and handed me a bouquet of red roses.

We started with a chopped salad and a bottle of red wine. *So far, so good*, I thought. Then I served the chicken, which I thought was very good.

"How was the Italian chicken?" I asked as I glanced at Ronnie's almost full plate.

His voice had a cold edge to it. "Sherrie, it's missing the Italian cheese, and I think you used schmaltz instead of butter. Can you only cook Jewish? Take a course in cooking," he said as he pushed his plate away.

I took his plate and threw out the chicken. He took a drink of his red wine, got up, and walked over to the window. I knew I better change the subject before I said something I would be sorry about.

"If I take a course in anything, it will be a review course for the bar," I shot back.

Ronnie turned around to face me. "Nonsense, I'll help you. Everyone fusses about the bar. I passed the first time."

Angry and hurt, I started to clean up, forgetting to serve the apple strudel I had labored on all afternoon. Oh, well, it was Jewish cooking anyway.

Ronnie grabbed his suit jacket and briefcase, gave me a peck on the cheek, and left, using work as an excuse to get out.

When Ronnie went home, I looked at my two drawers of silverware and two cabinets of dishes. *If we get married, he won't keep kosher. The family would be upset*, I told myself while I finished cleaning up.

I signed up for a review class for the bar anyway.

Besides worrying about the bar exam, I needed a job. In the early seventies, not many law firms hired women, and when they did, the woman's job was more like that of a secretary: paper-pushing. Ronnie had lined me up with one of those jobs, but I wanted more, yet I was afraid of all of it. None of the women in my family had ventured away from the job of housewife, mother, and family organizer. It was 1970, and the world still wasn't ready for professional working women. Most Jewish women went to college for MRS degrees and teaching degrees, not law.

Clark, the main street in the Lincoln Park neighborhood, was busy with cars zooming by from both directions while both fashionably dressed and shabbily dressed individuals skirted around them. Scanning for a building with an Egyptian décor, I drove slowly down the street. I parked my new blue Chevy Impala in front of the building which actually had painted figures of pharaohs and pyramids on its facade. I approached the store next door, which was the antithesis of the Egyptian one, but the one with the correct address. The cool breeze over my skin helped calm my rising temperature in anticipation of my meeting with the two female lawyers. I remembered to put change in the parking meter so I wouldn't receive another ticket.

I tried the peeled, green-painted wooden door before I noticed a bell. I rang it, and a voice answered with, "Sherrie, is that you?"

"Yes," I said.

"Be right down," the voice replied.

While waiting, I looked around. It seemed like the twenty-hundred north blocks of Lincoln Park hadn't turned around as extensively as farther south by Wells Street. The twenty to thirty-year-olds had taken over this area, called Old Town. It was a beautiful area just north of downtown next to Lake Michigan and Lincoln Park Zoo.

It had deteriorated for several years. Now it was in a revival, something my beloved South Shore needed. Several old brick three-flat buildings and non-hippie stores still were in the area. A 1900 glass antique show-globe in the fifties style corner drugstore's window reminded me of my now closed Rosenblum Drugstore in South Shore. Young people's restaurants like the Claim Company, famous for hamburgers on black bread, were taking over old stores. Bicycle riders, like the one who just cut me off, were taking over the streets, and apartments. I knew there was a famous children's hospital not far away. I was still a South Sider discovering the North Side.

Shortly the clopping of shoes grew closer, then stopped, and the door opened. A pretty, auburn-haired little thing in blue jeans and an oversized button-down shirt offered me her hand.

Painted nails and beauty-shop fixed hair were requirements for the big law firm interview, but not for these lady lawyers. I felt totally out of place. Yes, David, I needed some street smarts.

"Hi, I'm Paula. Jesus, you're all dressed up. You'll never make it up these narrow wooden stairs in those heels. This is a no-elevator building, and we are on the third floor. If you take them off, the splinters will kill your stockings."

"I'll take it slowly," I said as I started up. It took a while as those old steps *were* narrow, and some were missing pieces of wood. My mind began to think pushing paper at a big law firm may not be bad.

The office was really sparse, as the lawyers had just moved in, but it held two wooden desks, a couple of chairs, lamps, a typewriter, two file cabinets, and bookshelves upon bookshelves. Large radiators were stationed near the windows. I hoped they weren't still being used. David had converted the ones in the mansion to central heat. On one of the cluttered desks sat a framed letter from Gloria Steinem, the guru of the women's movement.

Shirley, who was the complete opposite of Paula—tall, big-boned, with very short straight black hair—got right to the point.

"We make very little money because we represent many poor or welfare clients," Shirley said. "We are very dedicated to the cause. We want to make abortions legal, sexual harassment of women obsolete, equal job opportunities, equal pay to both sexes for the same job, a chance for working pregnant women to keep their jobs, and a place for working mothers. Have you heard of the Equal Rights Amendment?"

I had grown up among chaos, with an underlining of stability and a kind of normalcy for our Jewish South Side neighborhood. I liked these two girls, one Jewish, one Protestant, both very knowledgeable and dedicated, but I needed to feel there was some order and hope to their mission. For sure I would be taking a cut in any salary I could make elsewhere. I told them that I would let them know in two days.

I left Paula and Shirley's office confused. I loved what they were doing, but I needed to start making some money. I called David. He was still my sibling substitute, and he lived not far away.

We met at the Original Pancake House in my 2020 building. Whenever I saw him, I couldn't help thinking, *What a loss to the women of Chicago.* Drop-dead gorgeous. Loved him from the time I was a little one. I realized Ronnie looked very much like David, with the same tall muscular build, head of black wavy hair, and those adorable dimples. That must be part of my attraction to Ronnie. For sure, their personalities, goals, and interests were not alike.

Flicking the ashes from my cigarette, I watched the girls in the restaurant ogling his gorgeous body as he approached my table and bent down to give me a cousin's kiss.

"You sounded agitated on the phone. What's up?"

I explained my problem, and the first thing he said was, "Do they own the building? Property in this area is going sky high. The gays started moving into the area a decade ago. Now the straight community is buying up the property, too. All those stores and restaurants in Old Town are demanding sky-high rents."

"I doubt it. I would love to work with these two women but they are broke, and most of their cases are on welfare. I think Shirley's family subsidizes them."

I stubbed out my cigarette as David leaned in close to me.

"Sherrie, it is time for you to make money and pay back the family. They have paid your tuition amounting to over one thousand dollars. They are getting older. Jeffery and I are doing very well. I am supporting my mother and helping Uncle Izzy, and I will always be there for you if you need it. Nice car, that blue Chevy Impala of yours."

"Yes, you are right. I owe the family. I have good taste and, consequently, large car payments, but no tuition payments."

"Does it have air conditioning?"

When I said yes, he gave my hand a tender squeeze, "Way to go, cuz. By the way, I really like your Ronnie, super intelligent with an optimistic personality to counter your pessimism."

"I'm not pessimistic."

"Sherrie, you carry an umbrella on sunny days, just in case," David noted.

I took my fork out of my blueberry pancakes and quickly tried to punch down the umbrella sticking out of my bag. David glanced over my shoulder and gave me his famous raised eyebrows and dimpled grin. We both burst into laughter. I knew he was right. I owed a lot to my family.

Ronnie, who was more conservative and old-fashioned when it came to women's rights, gave me a good suggestion: "Take a good-paying job, and help the girls on weekends and evenings."

As it turned out, I was more helpful to Paula and Shirley by working at a law firm that had access to all cases, judges, and records. I had a passive role in my working law firm and an active role with Shirley and Paula, which was very satisfying. Writing and handing out pamphlets, counseling one-on-one, and doing research were my high points, while Shirley was the dynamo who preached, shouted, and made it to all the meetings and rallies, and Paula found the money and the people who could help.

With Ronnie's help and the review course, plus my devotion to studying, I passed the bar the first time I took it, and I was able to officially work for Mitchel and Greenspan, Ronnie's father's old personal injury firm, thanks to him, not Ronnie. His father, now in a delicate state due to severe heart problems, still managed to meet me for lunch and tell me how happy he was that I was with Ronnie. He did give me this piece of advice, "Don't let him boss you around. Be tough with him."

While my priorities were to help get laws through for equality for women, my upbringing made me very obedient to my male bosses and silent about my other job. From the time my alarm started buzzing at six in the morning until I left the office at five in the evening, I played the role of an early seventies woman lawyer who kept her opinions to herself while she pushed papers and made the coffee in the morning.

Though the seventies were calmer than the era of the riots of the sixties, many women's issues were now on the table with an increased likelihood for success. We had a hero, a lawyer named Ruth Bader Ginsburg, who was leading us through her work for the American Civil Liberties Union, where she fought for equality and participated in over 300 gender discrimination cases. She became a model for female lawyers.

I stared at the enormous sign Shirley was pushing into her new red Chevy station wagon. On it were all our hopes:

EQUALITY OF RIGHTS UNDER THE LAW SHALL NOT BE DENIED OR ABRIDGED BY THE UNITED STATES OR ANY STATE ON ACCOUNT OF SEX.

Twenty-two states had ratified the ERA in the first year after the House and Senate had passed it. Only sixteen more were needed. We were all on a high.

"Shirley, I wish I could go with you,"

"We could use you in Springfield considering that Governor Ogilvie is a Republican, and he would recognize your boyfriend's name. Can you believe Illinois is one of the few big states that hasn't passed the amendment! We are going to change that."

I watched this powerful, wired, blue-jeaned, recently divorced blonde jump into her loaded wagon and take off. Paula and I waved to her. "If anyone can do it, Shirley will," I said.

Paula gave me an approving nod.

Chapter Seventeen

All was well in my life—everywhere but with Ronnie. We had been dating over a year. I had an apartment, he had an apartment, and it was the birth control seventies—but not for me.

"You are unreal," Ronnie said, exasperated. "Sherrie Paul, who is working so hard for women's rights and independence, is still old-fashioned, living in another era. We both want the same thing. Get. On. The. *Pill*." He shouted as he got up from my sofa tossing his clothes on the floor.

Oh, he was angry. I was putting my bra and blouse back on. Again, I had gone to the brink and abruptly jumped up and stopped. I was raised where it was important to be a virgin when you married. It may be the early seventies, but I was still a product of the fifties.

"Do you love me?" I asked.

"Of course I do," he answered.

"Then let's get married," I said.

"I told you, not yet" Ronnie replied. "I just started a new job with a high-pressure law firm, and my dad is sick."

"I told *you*, I plan to be a virgin when I get married," I shot back.

He got up, put his shirt and pants on over his extraordinarily handsome muscular body, grabbed his shoes and jacket, and stormed out of my apartment.

I yelled after him, "You can take a cold shower here!" Actually, I was the one who needed the cold shower. Had he pushed me, I would have given in, even though I was using sex as my *get-into-marriage* card. My nights were full of dreams of romantic lovemaking with Ronnie, especially after hearing stories about his free days.

As days turned into a week with no call, letter, or appearance of Ronnie, I began to worry. Maybe I was stuck in old behavior patterns, perhaps Judy's abortion did a number on me, but what was love without respect? I missed a mother with whom to talk things out. Crying didn't help ease the pain, nor did trying not to think about him, especially since when I sunk into my sofa, the pillows still carried his scent.

I thought of calling David, but he had his own problems. He was getting used to a new lover, and he was still pining for Jeffery, who, after ten years, had said goodbye.

On the tenth day of no contact with Ronnie, when I believed all must be over, an official envelope appeared at my door.

Inside was a marriage contract. I laughed and cried. I even poured myself a glass of white wine. My hands were shaking so much that I almost burned down the house while I lit a cigarette before reading the document.

There was only one page with five silly points. The last one said:

Sherrie Paul, Esq., I realized, I can't live my life without you. I love you and hope that you will agree to marry me.
Ronnie Greenspan, Esq.

I wanted to jump into my car and run into Ronnie's arms, but I decided to play the game. I started to write my response to the contract . . .

Ronnie Greenspan, I received your marriage contract, and I agree with four out of five of your points. Point number three states that once married, I am obligated to have sexual relations with you. I request we be married in the Jewish faith according to the laws of the United States and the laws of the Jewish Ketubah.

In the Ketubah, you are obligated to please me based on your job.
If you are not working, sex every day, but if you are working, sex once
a week - unless you are working as a camel driver. Then it can be once
a year! Over the course of marriage, the husband traditionally has
three primary obligations to his wife: He must provide her with food,
clothing, and sexual satisfaction.

I, Sherrie Paul, love you, Ronnie Greenspan, very much, and would
be so happy to become your wife as soon as we negotiate point number
three.

On Saturday, I sent this contract by special delivery. It was worth
the extra money.

The day drifted by while I patiently waited for a reply. Oh, I could
be out and about shopping with Shirley or my cousin Lizzie, or I could
be working on research for the women's movement, but then I might
miss the contract reply, so I stayed home, pretending to read a book. At
the same time, I smoked a package of cigarettes, gulped down cups of
black coffee, munched on oatmeal-raisin cookies, and stared at the
green wall telephone or out the window at the cars rushing by. I even
took a shower with the bathroom door open, so I could hear the phone
if he called.

Relief fell over me when the contract came back by special mes-
senger: Ronnie himself. As I opened the door, the first thing he said
was, "Where in the hell did you find that Ketubah quote - a camel
driver?" Then he handed me a bottle of Dom Perignon champagne.

"I'm a good lawyer, and five years of Hebrew school helped," I
said. "Would you like to come in? I baked a cake."

"Were you expecting company? You baked a cake!" he said as he
entered my apartment and kicked the door closed.

"You cut your hair," he added, frowning, as he ran his hand through my hair. I had been wearing my black wavy hair shoulder length with one side pinned back. Now it was in a short pageboy style, straighter with my curls turned under.

"I thought it would make me look more professional."

"I loved your long, flowing, black waves."

"Put it in the contract and I will grow them back."

Ronnie brought his briefcase over to the table and pulled out an official-looking document.

"We both need to sign it," he said.

He reached across the table and ran his finger through the frosting on my cake. As it touched his lips, he said, "*Mmm*, chocolate, my favorite."

While he was busy helping himself to a piece of chocolate cake, I pretended to scrutinize the contract, before picking up my pen and signing under his name.

Immediately upon the signing, he grabbed me.

Up into his arms I went, and down on the floor fell Ronnie, the chocolate cake, and I. We burst out into bubbling laughter. Oh, how I wished we could have held onto that funny, happy moment forever.

Licking the cake from around his mouth, Ronnie said, "Honey, I love you because you, and only you, can bring out the little boy in me."

Utilizing a napkin to wipe chocolate frosting from his face and his disheveled black hair, I answered, "No, I bring out the part of you that comes from your dad."

I'm not sure he was happy with that, but he did take my jaw in his hand, turned my face towards his mouth, and landed a big, sweet chocolate kiss on my lips.

Not many people got to see this side of Ronnie, or even call him "Ronnie" instead of "Ronald." One day I watched a different Ronald

Greenspan in court, one who was in total control, unemotional, leaving his opponent in fear of his next move. I admired and feared that Ronald.

Two days later, we visited the Jewelry Building on Wabash and became officially engaged. My two-carat, pear-shaped diamond ring dazzled on my left hand, and I spent most of my days showing it off, or just staring at it.

We celebrated at Armando's, a new Italian restaurant on the Near North Side where I had a taste of a pasta dish that wasn't Jewish kasha or kugel.

"What am I eating?" I asked. "It is delicious but different."

"Sherrie, where have you been?" Ronnie replied. "It's called lasagna."

I put my fork down and asked, "Ronnie, does it have meat and cheese together?"

"Sherrie, if we are getting married, we better get one thing straight," he said. "I cannot live in a kosher house. I never did. My mother fed us ham and seafood, while my dad cooked his own Jewish food."

I pressed my lips together, dropped my head down, and stared at my sparkling ring. I realized that since I was on my own, I had kept a very loose modern kosher home, though I did keep separate dishes and silverware for meat and milk foods. Actually, more of my meals for one were eaten on paper plates.

I looked up into Ronnie's lawyer face.

"We need to compromise," I said. "I will give up on separate *milkic* and *fleshic* dishes and silverware, but I can't allow any pig or shell-food in my kitchen. Out of the house, you can eat whatever you want. Also, while we are talking, I've assumed that our children will be raised Jewish."

He answered, "I agree, so long as our children are allowed to celebrate with my mother on her holidays."

I laughed, "Counsellor, you need to revise the marriage contract."

Ronnie called the waiter over and ordered me some spaghetti with a meatless sauce. I looked up past the colorful murals of Italy, and whispered, "I'm sorry, Pa, next year in Jerusalem," and to myself, I said, *Aunt Tillie and my father will have to understand. Times are changing.*

We raised our wine glasses and clicked *congratulations* on our engagement and compromise. He paid the bill, helped me into my coat and scarf, and we retrieved his black Lincoln.

Ronnie helped me out of the car in front of my apartment. "Are you coming in?" I asked.

"Too tempting, and among my workload, I now have a marriage contract to make some changes on," Ronnie replied.

With that said, he gave me a big kiss and took off. Before entering my building, a light wind touched me. Looking up, I noticed the clouds had opened a space in the sky, exposing a beautiful setting sun. Smiling, I said, "Hi, Mom."

I hardly slept, waking up many times to look at my ring and think about our compromise. I also decided to let my black hair grow loose, wavy, and long even though short hair gave me a more serious lawyer image.

Ronnie wanted to set the wedding date for May, three months away, because his dad had suffered another heart attack, and he wanted him to be there. I liked his dad and hoped he would keep going for a long time. I bargained for June, just to give me a little more time to plan. My family had always married in the temple, but our temple in South Shore was no more, so I went along with Ronnie's suggestion of the Ambassador West, and his Ultra Reform Rabbi.

We were an older couple for the times, Ronnie thirty-four and me twenty-six, so we were more dependent on each other than our families for the wedding arrangements and payments. However, I did solicit my cousin Lizzie and Aunt Tillie to join me at Marshall Field's to register for china, cut glass, and silverware and pick out wedding and bridesmaid dresses—one of the ceremonies most brides in our circle engaged in, though more dresses were bought at Margie's on the Southwest Side than at Marshall Field's. Anyway, the fun began a week after I received my ring.

Aunt Tillie, Lizzie, and I sat with the Marshall Field's woman in charge of the bridal registry.

"First, what are your colors?" the saleslady asked.

"The wedding colors are pink and blue," I replied.

"Here, we are doing the register for your gifts, so I need to know what colors you will need for your towels, sheets, furniture, and accessories," she said.

I hesitated in my answer. Ronnie was thirty-four, established, and living on his own for seven years. I was moving into his two-bedroom condo, and I wasn't sure how much I could change in his furnishings.

"Let's skip those things and go to the china department," I said.

"You love pink, since you were a little girl, what is the problem?" Aunt Tillie asked.

When I explained, she answered, "Sherrie, the woman gets to take care of the house and kids."

I just smiled and walked over to the china department. *Thank God Shirley isn't here*, I thought to myself. I was a walking contradiction.

Chapter Eighteen

Ronnie and I met with Aunt Tillie and my dad so Ronnie could explain that he was older and in a position to pay for the whole wedding. He explained that we wanted the family to be involved and be a part of the wedding ceremony, but he had hired a wedding consultant to help with the band, dinner, flowers, etc. He had told me that most of Chicago's dignitaries would be invited, and he needed things to be right. I asked him not to mention that to my family.

My dad said, "Whatever makes you and Sherrie happy is good with us, as long as it is a Jewish ceremony."

Aunt Tillie started to talk, but Dad hushed her. You could tell from her pinched lips that she wasn't happy about it.

The only thing my family had to do in the planning was to give me a bridal shower, which they did. I made sure they were invited to the other showers and parties.

Working with the wedding consultant and planning the parties became a full-time job, literally.

At Ronnie's apartment during one of our planning sessions, Ronnie told me, "Sherrie, you won't need to work for the law firm anymore since I've made associate partner with Cohen and Field."

"Wow, that is great!" I said. "Congratulations, Ronnie. I know you have been working overtime in anticipation of the promotion. I will be happy to quit the firm since I've never felt like I was more than a law secretary there. My work and my pay have never reflected my schooling. Any time I tried to do something that men had always done, I was quickly corrected. Anyway, I will now have more time to help Shirley. She needs it now that Paula has married and retired."

I did realize that I was very much in love with an ambitious in-charge guy who wouldn't tolerate competition from his wife. Yet, I wanted to practice my profession. I would need to find my way.

Ronnie never paid attention to what was going on in the women's rights movement, but I vowed to become much deeper into it after the wedding. With Shirley, I had gone to a lecture by ACLU lawyer Ruth Bader Ginsburg, and was impressed by her use of the law versus just rallies, magazines, and noise to further the movement.

But first, the wedding. Until the planning of the wedding, I hadn't realized that Ronnie's mother came from a wealthy, politically connected Republican family. Actually, from where and how I grew up, I didn't think Illinois had any Republicans. To everyone's surprise, a Democratic, Jewish judge sat together with a non-Jewish Republican senator at my wedding. At the same time, the ten-piece band alternated between a hora and a proper waltz.

The wedding was truly perfect—the fairytale I'd been told since I was a little girl. I walked around, afraid the clock would strike midnight, the pumpkin would appear, and I would become Cinderella. My ivory silk wedding dress with its tiny pearls made me look like a princess. I wore my thick dark hair up in a beehive and had my makeup done professionally. I carried a basket of pink roses. My mother's pearl and diamond earrings were a gift to me from my father. They matched the long, large pearl necklace from my husband. I had missed my mother every day of my life, but never as much as on my wedding day. Even though I really didn't believe in an afterlife, I talked to her all day, making my mascara drip down my face as the tears fell. I knew she would have been proud of my graduation from law school and of my choice for a husband.

My dad, handsome in his black tux, and Aunt Tillie, in a floor length pink beaded dress—minus an apron—walked me down the aisle while a vocalist sang *Sunrise, Sunset* from *Fiddler On The Roof.* Peonies, lilies, and roses arranged in chandelier form adorned the chuppah we stood under. My heart beat double time until Ronnie cracked the wine glass to mark the end of the ceremony. I repeated to myself, *Mr. and Mrs. Ronald Greenspan*, with a heave of accomplishment. After all, it was a tough three years, between my two goals—to become a lawyer, and to become Mrs. Ronald Greenspan.

The receiving line, where stranger after stranger congratulated us, gave me a glimpse into my future, but I was too happy to think about it then.

After hors d'oeuvres and champagne, we served tenderloin steak for the majority of the guests, and white fish or a fruit plate for my kosher family. Flaming baked Alaska was the grand finale for the dinner. My dad made the *brocha* over the wine and the challah. My favorite part of the meal was the sweet table with everything from toffee apples, Eli's cheesecakes, to ice cream sundaes. I danced throughout the evening mostly with David, which I guess didn't sit well with Ronnie, but David and I had spent our high school days practicing the chacha and the other popular dances.

Lizzie, much pregnant with her second child, couldn't be my maid-of-honor, so I asked Ronnie's sister, Inez. She was a tall, thin girl with her mother's delicate features and confident attitude. I missed Ronnie's dad, my greatest fan. A stroke took him two months before the wedding. He was so proud that he had brought us together. My family loved him. Ronnie's mother was distant and hard to warm up to, no matter how hard I tried. I wondered how they had connected.

I hoped Ronnie would have asked David to stand up for him, but he didn't. I knew he really would have liked David to come without a partner, but I put my foot down on that one.

"Ronnie, you should get to know the real David instead of looking at him and only seeing *gay*," I said. "Why, most of the time, I forget that he is gay."

"That is because you grew up thinking he was your straight Jewish cousin," Ronnie countered. "*Family* and *Jewish* do not go with *homosexual,* so you blocked it out. I only met him as a homosexual, and I won't have him stand up at my wedding."

I pursed my lips together and refrained from starting a fight over the issue. Even though there was some truth to his statement, it irritated me because David was special to me and because it, again, illustrated how far apart Ronnie and I were on so many issues.

Strong, self-sufficient political women weren't on his list either, but Shirley, Paula, and their families were definitely at the wedding. On this I also took a stand.

Through the preparation of the wedding, we learned new things about each other.

On a day before the wedding took place, I was in a bathroom stall at the ladies' room of Fritzel's Restaurant when I heard two girls talking.

"Have you heard that Ron Greenspan is finally getting married?"

"Is it one of the models he usually dates, or someone well-politically connected to advance his career?"

"She is just a fat, mousey little Jewish girl. We can't figure out how she caught him," the first girl answered in a high-pitched voice.

"Maybe she is a wizard in bed! You would have to be to keep up with him."

At first, I felt panic. After all, I wasn't as attractive or polished as those women, then a "ha-ha" feeling came over me, something like identifying with the small, unimportant cat who caught the big fat mouse. I almost blew my cover with a sarcastic laugh. I was dying to see what they looked like, but I chose to stay back for a while so that I could keep that conversation to myself. I heard the clicking of spiked heels, the kind the young fashion crowd wore, along with their designer clothes and perfect hair and nails. I couldn't handle heels that high. *Mousey*, I thought to myself. *That hurt.* They never even mentioned I was a lawyer.

Before I exited the bathroom, I pushed the loose hair from my forehead, hid my one chipped nail, and stood up very straight. I glanced around but most of the women in Fritzl's looked like they just came out of *Vogue* magazine. As I walked back to my table, I listened carefully to the conversations because I knew I could recognize one of the high-pitched voices. No luck.

"Are you okay? You were in there a long time," Ronnie said as he lifted his Jack and Coke in a crystal glass.

"Just fine, honey," I answered, slipping back next to Ronnie into one of the cushy booths. I savored my waiting coffee, sipping it slowly, but I just tasted the slice of cake I had ordered. I was now determined to go on a serious diet. Perhaps I would try that new grapefruit diet that was popular. I would never be tall, but thin I could become now that I was away from Aunt Tillie! With practice, I may be able to wear those three-inch heels, too. My wedding night was now taking on new anticipation.

I had to wait for that wedding night twelve hours after we left the hotel. It took place in a suite of the Ritz Hotel in London. Me, Sherrie Paul, who had never been out of Chicago any farther than South Haven, Michigan, or my one flight to California, was now sipping champagne in one of the most expensive hotels in the world in London, England. Wow! And I lost fifteen pounds before the wedding. Never again would I eat another grapefruit! Ronnie was a "tit" man, so though he liked my thinner figure, he worried that too much dieting would take away from my bust. Thus, I started eating normal food again.

The suite was bigger than my apartment. It was lushly decorated with crystal chandeliers and wall sconces, patterned silk ivory couches, fresh-cut flowers in antique porcelain vases, thick beige carpets, and a canopied bed with feather comforters. Luxury fit for a queen. Aunt Tillie would have been in heaven.

My wedding night and the week that followed was fabulous. I was naive and Ronnie was experienced, and he loved teaching me. His lips embraced mine, his tongue explored every part of my mouth. At first, I jumped as his hands and tongue explored my whole body.

"Relax, honey, I won't hurt you. My job is to please you," he whispered in my ear.

I soon relaxed and enjoyed the new sensations. I anticipated pain, but when Ronnie entered my virgin body, there was some blood, but very little pain.

Afterward, while we sat up in bed smoking, Ronnie laughed, "You really were a virgin."

"Why would you doubt me?"

"You are twenty-six, and you've played one hell of a game with me," he replied. "I think it is great, my love."

It bothered me that he hadn't believed me. Ronnie then took on the role of teacher, directing and calculating our every move, losing some of the romance I had dreamed about, but he did know how to please me, bringing me to orgasm several times an evening. I liked to flirt, which worked while dating, but not now. Ronnie was in control, and I was a happy follower.

After three days of lovemaking in an oversized queen bed with silk sheets and a feather comforter, plus delicious room service food, Ronnie left me for business. His firm was international, and I found out that he would often be traveling. He set me up with a private tour of London's highlights and a shopping spree at Harrods Department Store. Touring with him would have been more exciting, but I understood he had been to London many times and his career was very important to him.

My first instinct was to stay in bed or to go on my own without his guide, but I knew Ronnie would be angry. Luckily, I stayed with the tour guide who, with his VIP passes, slipped us in and out of the exhibits with no lines. London was mobbed with tourists, and I was like a schoolgirl on a magical trip. We did all the highlights: Museum after museum, the changing of the guard at Buckingham Palace, and my favorite—The Tower, where the crown jewels had been kept since 1303.

The priceless diamonds, emeralds, and pearls sparkled in their vaults. I wondered if my mother had visited here as a schoolgirl and had also dreamed about being a princess. She never talked about growing up in London, just about hiding from the bombings during the war. My guide mentioned the only time the jewels were ever moved was during World War II when they were hidden in Canada.

I was fascinated by the fact that Queen Victoria and the present Queen Elizabeth II had worn the solid gold St. Edward crown as leaders of the British Empire. In the USA, very few women had leading government positions, and the thought of a woman president would never occur to most people. A late lunch of fish and chips and a short trip around Harrods completed my day. A whole day would be needed to explore and shop at Harrods. By the time I reached the hotel, I was exhausted and needed a bath and a nap before dinner.

The suite was equipped for a princess, and I actually became one by treating myself to a Jacuzzi bath, something I had never had before. When I pressed the on button in the large pink tub, the hot water bubbled and gurgled, tickling my feet and back as I sank down in the tub.

When Ronnie came through the door, I convinced him to join me. We had a late casual dinner that night.

The next day, when my guide, Godfrey, picked me up, I asked to be taken to Portobello Road antiques market.

"Well, Miss, your mister gave me a guide, and that wasn't on there," Godfrey said. "He wants me to take you shopping to some specialty shops, and we missed Parliament yesterday."

"Godfrey, I have some say so on my tour," I said. "First, I want to go to the outdoor market. I've heard so much about it." My mother had compared it to Maxwell Street the first and last time my mother had gone to Maxwell Street with Dad and me.

"Yes, ma'am," Godfrey said. When we pulled up to Portobello Road in Chelsea, he advised, "If you are walking please do take along the bumbershoot—I mean umbrella. You never know when the rains will appear in London."

I thought of David as I took hold of the large black umbrella, and quickly exited the car on Portobello Road. "Pick me up here in three hours," I directed, and I watched him drive off.

Yes, Portobello Road did remind me of Chicago's bustling Maxwell Street. The stalls were selling everything one could think of, from posters, door knockers, jewelry, clocks, to yams. The noises, people shouting, dogs barking, and especially the mix of ethnic smells delighted me. Missing were the Vienna hot dog carts and the pushers, but in exchange in front of most stalls and storefronts sat brightly colored lilies, roses, daffodils, and pansies that mixed with and sweetened the aroma coming from the food carts. Londoners kept gardens everywhere. The red, pink, green, and blue painted ancient buildings were squeezed next to each other, and several of the adjoining streets were still cobbled.

I couldn't wait to develop and send my dad the pictures I was taking. Recollections of Sundays with him on Maxwell Street floated back to me. I still had the leather jacket we bought at Grace's when I was twelve.

I had been leisurely walking down the street, taking in everything when a small, lace curtained window of a shop caught my eye. I walked into it and had started to scavenge among the linens, glasses, and jumbled garments when I stopped cold. I began to shake as I ran after the woman who had just walked out the door of the shop. I clutched at her jacket about halfway down the street. With the little breath I had left, I said, "Sophie, is it you?"

"Do I know you?" she asked as she disentangled her jacket from my arm and stared down at me.

"I'm Sherrie Paul, Bess's daughter. Bess from Chicago." I answered in-between huffing and puffing.

She glared at me in disbelief. Finally she knitted her eyebrows and asked, "How did you recognize me?"

I smiled, "From photographs! You still have that gorgeous long blonde hair, and your gait, you always moved with such assurance. I just . . . had a feeling, it *must* be you. Or someone doing a pretty good impression of you!"

She gave out with the strong hearty laugh I remembered from years ago. "Are you on holiday, or did you move here," she asked while moving her eyes over all of me. "My, you're no longer Bess's little girl. You are a grown woman."

"Holiday, sort of," I replied. "Please, can we go somewhere and talk? I have so many questions about my mother."

Sophie took my arm and led me into a store called the Grain Shop. We sat down at a worn wooden table, and she ordered us something called cheesy pasta, and a pot of tea. She kept staring at me in disbelief.

Somewhere in the back of my mind when I heard Ronnie and I would be honeymooning in London, I thought I might find a connection to my mother, even though she had never wanted to go back. The telephone books in the hotel were of no help, but the market—the one my mother talked about—came through.

"You must try this pasta," Sophie said. "It is one of my favorites. If you want something stronger than tea, they make a great hot toddy. I still can't believe it . . . Bess's girl!"

Then with her loud, hardy laugh, she asked me a barrage of questions. Halfway between answering, I realized she had told me nothing about my mother.

"Sophia, when my mother died, I found a cross among her things," I said. "When I questioned my father, it seems he knew very little about her life before they married. You are the only one who knew her then, and you disappeared."

I took another forkful of cheesy pasta. "This is different and delicious."

She took a deep breath and leaned back in her chair before answering, "Your mother and I were cousins. She died so young, only in her forties. You know, I quit smoking after she died of lung cancer. It was so hard to watch her gasping for breath and being so sick from those terrible chemotherapy drugs."

I took out a tissue to wipe my tearing eyes at the memory of those days. I was just twenty then, not realizing my mother could die.

"Sophie, please tell me about her family. I would love to meet them. Was my mother at least part Jewish?"

She waved her hand away from her body. "Hell, no. She told your dad that to keep him happy. We came from impoverished farm people, miles from London. We did some things we were ashamed of to get a better life. She was a smart, wonderful person, but her father was abusive, and she had to disappear where he couldn't find her, especially after her mother died, and her brother went off to war. America looked like Heaven to us. It was better to Bessie than to me. The soldier I married wasn't like your father, and I divorced him and returned to London, right after Bess died. Without her, I couldn't stay there."

"She adored you, but your aunts really drove her crazy. Is Tillie still around?" Sophie smiled. "God, I can just picture her in her house dress and rolling pin."

Sophie loaded her teacup with cream and sugar before drinking it. I hardly understood her very British diction.

I pushed my chair in closer to her. "Sophie, in the States, you were almost American in speech, and here . . ." I said, my voice trailing off, as her hand waved in front of me and she said, "God, Bess and I practiced for hours to pass like Americans."

"Did she love my dad?"

"Oh, my love, Bess loved your dad's gentleness and the way he took care of her. She was terrified of her drunken, abusive father. Her most enormous pride and love was in you, the daughter who wanted to make a dent in the way men viewed women. She knew you would achieve your goal of going to law school."

She was talking so fast that I needed to stop a moment and think about what she was saying. "Sophia, did you really say my mother's father abused her?" I asked. "What type of abuse, did he give her orders or possibly hit her?"

Sophia looked down at her teacup, her brows knit. She continued, hesitating, and finally said, "He was an alcoholic who did things to Bess after her mother died that were . . . that were *very wrong* between father and daughter."

I looked at her, horrified at the thought that my mother was sexually assaulted by her father.

155

Sophie then shook her head and spoke quickly. "Let the past be the past, with your mother and with your young man," she said. "Good seeing you."

She was up and out before I was able to get an address or phone number. I ran after her, but she was faster than I was. I had to stop to adjust my fancy shoes and take a breath.

"Mom," I whispered, "Why didn't you trust me enough to tell me your story?" I asked aloud. I wanted to know about my mother's early years, and I didn't.

Tears rolled down my cheeks as I stared down the crowded street. Anger at my dad overwhelmed me. On the surface, things were fine with Dad and me, but beneath the surface, the hurt from the lies about my mother still simmered, especially since he just wouldn't talk about them. Now maybe we could discuss things. Now that I had confirmation that he had lied to me about my mother's religion.

I walked to the end of Portobello Road. Down one street was a kosher deli, and a bit down from there was a small church. I walked into the church and stared at the stained glass windows and the large gold cross, thinking, *half of me belongs here*.

When Geoffrey picked me up, he asked, "No shopping bags? I told you Portobello wasn't for elegant ladies like you."

"It was perfect," I answered with a smile.

Chapter Nineteen

When I got back to the hotel, I called Lizzie, even though it cost some extra money. "Lizzie, everything is great. I just needed to tell you I saw Sophie."

"Your mother's friend from London who lived in Hyde Park?" she asked sleepily. "She was a fun lady. My mom didn't like her, but we did. Are you keeping in touch with her?"

"I wanted to, but she disappeared on me."

"Too bad you didn't get her number or address," Lizzie said. "I know you would love to find your mom's family."

"Yes and no." Then I told her what Sophie told me about my mom's dad.

Lizzie was in shock, too. "I can't believe that could happen to your mom. Do you think your dad knows?"

I thought, maybe Ronnie could supply Sophia's number, as she seemed to recognize his name. Though at dinner, Ronnie had no idea what I was talking about. My honeymoon was like a dream, but meeting Sophia, and getting a small glimpse of my mother's world before she met my father, was the highlight of my trip to London. Sophie's story about my mother being abused by her father was not what I expected to hear. I then realized that my father rescued her, and that was why she put up with the family. Thinking back, when Mom didn't understand a ritual like the lighting of a *Yahrzeit* candle, Dad always excused her by saying her family was very English Reform. Her past gave me another reason to go back to work on laws to protect women from abuse.

When we got back home, I made a trip to Waldheim Cemetery to see my mother. The family still made their frequent trips to the cemetery, but lately I'd been pulling further away from my family and their traditions.

On my own, I had a hard time finding the family plot. I cursed myself for wearing new sneakers as I squished through the mud and passed over broken monuments. Waldheim was an old Jewish cemetery just west of Chicago's city limits that had fallen into ruin due to lack of upkeep, while newer ones were being built closer to where we lived.

When I finally found the right location, I just stood and stared at the five occupied graves. Buried here were three people I never knew—a grandmother, an uncle and a baby. The other two were occupied by my grandfather and my mother. I had put all my anger on my father. Now I was angry with my mother. She had died and left me with all these unanswered questions about who she was before marrying my dad. I looked at her picture on the headstone, and said, "Mom, you were such a good actress that they buried you in a Jewish cemetery. We should have buried you with your cross to ward off the rabbis!"

My mother's headstone was in English, while the others were in Hebrew, something I don't remember seeing before in a Jewish cemetery. Suddenly, it occurred to me that all Jewish markers only listed the dead person's father's name, not the mother's name. An example would be Pa's stone, which said in Hebrew, Benjamin, son of Jacob. My mother's only had her birth and death date, no parent's name. The women were ignored. *I will have to ask my non-Jewish friends how their stones were. Something else to ask the rabbi and my feminist friends.*

Raindrops pounded my car's windows, and teardrops poured down my face as I drove home.

Back home, in Ronnie's Lake Shore Drive condo, I settled into a quiet life. No longer working for the law firm and living in Ronnie's large, uncluttered, designer-furnished place with domestic help, I found myself waiting for Ronnie to come home and entertain me, which wasn't healthy for either of us.

The refrigerator running, the hum of the overhead lights, the building elevator creaking, sirens wailing through the windows, and the invitations to attend luncheons, play bridge, or go shopping all were driving me crazy. I missed my loud, middle-class family building, where these sounds would never be detected. Though this luxury apartment was a real blessing with its twenty-five hundred square feet of glass, marble, and leather, plus three bathrooms compared to growing up in a small, one-bathroom apartment, some days I found myself sitting and staring out the window, looking at the lake with a cigarette in one hand and a book by Betty Friedan or one of the other feminist movers on my lap. Funny, just a few months prior, I had dreamed about having time to do nothing. By now, I couldn't stand listening to another television show about Watergate, especially after Nixon was inaugurated for his second term. Camelot, where were you?

Outside it was snowing lightly, but I needed to get out. I showered, brushed my teeth, and threw on a pair of jeans, a sweater, coat, boots, gloves, and made a thermos of coffee before heading for a walk along Lake Michigan. Halfway out the door, I heard the phone ringing. I sped back into the kitchen, catching the phone before the last ring.

It was a very excited Shirley. "Sherrie, we desperately need you to be here with us!" she said. "Linda called to tell us a decision should be made soon. 1973 could be our year!"

I retrieved the car from the garage and started out down Lake Shore Drive to the Planned Parenthood office.

The light snow was now getting heavier, masking the windows and clouding out the sun. The temperature was in the thirties, not bad for winter in Chicago, but perfect for snow accumulation. I should have taken a cab. At least I had boots. At red lights, I wrapped hands around my coffee thermos, my icicle fingers welcoming the warmth.

My heart beat faster as I recalled Ronnie's cold voice and his direct stare as he warned me, "Do *not* involve my name in any of your friends' women's nonsense—no abortion rally, no ERA."

Until then, I had stayed in the background, writing most of the pamphlets without my name attached, and attending the rallies as a participant, not an organizer. But I had to be with my friends when the verdict on the Roe vs. Wade case was announced.

Three years ago, Shirley had met Linda Coffee, one of the lawyers on the case, at a convention of Women's Equity Action League, and our group of lawyers and volunteers had helped to get this abortion case before the Supreme Court. It was going a lot better than the Equal Rights Amendment.

In the late sixties and early seventies, Cook County Hospital in Chicago was the place for Planned Parenthood, and the dispensing of birth control pills, and where many of the See Jane workers were available. (Jane was the Chicago based women's underground abortion service established in 1969.) I had a hard time working there, as it brought back memories of Judy's destructive abortion.

Paula and Shirley, who were members of the group, moved their women's freedom law office down the street from County Hospital into an old, two-flat bungalow, although more deals were still made at The Greek's, a tavern across the street from County Hospital.

I parked the car and walked two blocks. The January cold caught my breath. Laughter and joyful sounds came through the door of Shirley and Paula's office. It was so crowded with people that the old wooden desks, extensive collections of file cabinets, and vintage typewriters were hardly noticed. The haze of smoke from the many cigarettes made breathing difficult. We, mostly women, from all religions, races, all walks of life, and all styles of clothing from girdle tight sheath dresses, leather boots, and mini-skirts, to long muumuus, were waiting for the phone to ring to confirm that the Supreme Court had voted affirmative on Roe vs. Wade.

I walked around, greeting women and a few men I knew and had worked with. I'm such a chocolate lover that I couldn't resist the tray of pastries next to the large coffee pot. I took a slow bite of the chocolate cake, letting it dissolve on my tongue before swallowing. I savored the moment because there were no sweets in our house. After all, Ronnie and I were eating healthy and dieting. I had discovered that not all vegetables came out of a can!

Paula came out of the private office and asked for quiet. She stood on one of the makeshift podiums and yelled, "I am proud to announce that today, January 22, 1973, the Supreme Court issued a 7- 2 decision in favor of Roe that held that women in the U.S. have a fundamental right to choose whether or not to have abortions and have therefore struck down the Texas abortion ban as unconstitutional."

The room erupted in loud cheers.

It took a while for Shirley to calm everyone down, so she could continue talking, saying, "This was a fantastic achievement. Our daughters will no longer have to endure back-alley abortions, unwanted pregnancies due to rape, youth, the lost father, disease, or the inability to care for a child! But . . . ." she was interrupted by the cheers and applause of the crowd, but continued, "keep in mind, we have a long way to go!"

She held up one of our pamphlets.

"Some things to think about in our pamphlet," she continued, and noted the following:

"One: We need to work hard to get the Equal Rights Amendment passed.

"Two: We will have to work hard to defend and make Roe vs. Wade work. Opposition to Planned Parenthood and abortion clinics will be rapid. Not everyone agrees with us.

"Three: Women still can't get a credit card in their name.

"Four: Women get fired when pregnant.

"Five: In some states women can't serve on juries.

"Six: Women can't go to several ivy league schools.

"Seven: Women cannot play in several sports.

"Eight. Women cannot receive the birth control pill and Planned Parenthood counseling in many cities and states.

"Nine. Women can't take legal action against sexual harassment.

"Ten. Women do not get equal pay as men."

The crowd started clapping after each demand, but shortly Shirley had to give up. Though this was a crowd that agreed with her, at this moment, they just wanted to celebrate today's victory. Paula brought out the champagne, and everyone headed for their celebration drinks.

I snuck out the back door—or so I thought, "Sherrie, where are you going?" Shirley asked. "The celebration is just beginning."

"Ronnie will be looking for me, and it's getting late," I replied.

Shirley's face dropped into a deep stare. "You preach the Gospel, but you don't practice it. Think about it."

There was a happy, noisy crowd inside and a cold, angry reception waiting for me at home, but I had to leave. I buttoned up my coat, pulled my hat down, and trudged through the snow to my car. I brushed the snow off the windows and carefully drove home on the icy streets, that hadn't yet been plowed.

I left the car with my building attendant and walked towards the door, while the cold bit at my face and stunned my hands. I nearly knocked over a woman exiting, as I was contemplating an argument with my husband. She was not happy when her mink stole slipped off her shoulders and fell into the snow. *Oh, well. When the mink was alive, I'm sure it trudged through the snow many times.*

I tip-toed into the apartment, hoping Ronnie would be asleep. Only one lamp lit the front room. Smoke rising from the green silk sofa told me he wasn't in bed.

The shadows cast across the floor as Ronnie rose made him look so much taller and powerful. He put out his cigarette in the green glass ashtray and walked around the sofa to face me.

"You went to the rally," he said.

"It was a celebration," I replied.

"Not for long," he shot back. "The conservatives will fight back. Remember, you are my *wife*. It is your job to support *my* career."

I said nothing, though there were a million things I wanted to say. I just stood in the entranceway, still bundled in a coat, scarf, and boots. He turned around and went into the bedroom, slamming the door shut. I went into the den, tears rolling down my face. I understood that Ronnie had different beliefs from mine, but until tonight I hadn't acknowledged that the man I loved *scared me.*

I slept on the sofa, still in my dress, waking several times to see if the bedroom door ever opened.

Around six in the morning, I awoke to clanking and banging mingling with the aroma of strong coffee coming from the kitchen. My first instinct was to throw the blanket over my head and go back to sleep, but I knew we had better talk before he left for work.

I went into the bedroom, threw on my slippers and bathrobe, and slowly made my way down the hall to the kitchen.

We stared at each other. Then, as my husband, the lawyer, made his case against me, I concentrated on his full head of salt and pepper hair and his wide-open, green-and-speckled-brown eyes. My hands tightly gripped the table's edge for balance. I was used to the volume increasing when a family member was angry; not Ronnie, whose volume and tone stayed calm and even, which was scarier.

I stood still as he paced. "Sherrie, I've been working very hard to become a partner in one of the most prestigious law firms in the country," Ronnie said. "I can't have a wife who is fighting against me."

I looked down at the paper on the kitchen table. My picture was on the front page along with the rest of my friends. I thought I had dodged the news, but they caught me by the food table.

Looking up, I said, "Doesn't it matter that I have beliefs too?"

He answered, "If you keep them between us, fine. If you must be a part of troublesome groups that rally against the conservatives I work with, then we are wrong for each other!"

Ronnie then picked up his coat and briefcase and left.

I sat down in his chair next to the untouched coffee and scrambled eggs and cried. Married just a few months past three years, and it was over. I reached for his still-lit cigarette and finished smoking it, one long puff after another. I picked up his Zippo lighter with the words, *Love, Sherrie* on it and pocketed it.

The phone kept ringing with messages from excited colleagues over Roe vs. Wade, but I couldn't answer them. I was a Liberal Democrat and my husband was a Conservative Republican.

I had no mother to talk to, but I did have my family matriarch, Aunt Tillie.

I drove north on Lake Shore Drive that cold but clear winter morning. The sun sparkled on the frozen lake like stars dancing. I smiled as I turned into the suburb of Skokie. It wasn't South Shore, but it was spiritual, with its delis and synagogues.

Aunt Tillie's house was all lit up and toasty warm. Of course, the front door was open, just like it had been at the old South Shore building. The decor was similar, only there was more space for all the tchotchkes, pictures, and furnishings. Smiling, gap-toothed, and pony-tailed little girls popped out from wall collages, most likely made by Lizzie. A step into the kitchen with the wonderfully sweet and sour aromas made my mouth water. Standing by the stove, hands busy, rolling matzo balls into the simmering chicken soup while drops of sweat rolled down her brow stood my Aunt Tillie.

"Something smells delicious in there. I'm coming in."

Aunt Sarah pushed her large, old-fashioned glasses up her nose. She turned towards me, twisting her mouth into her famous guilt stare, and said, "Sherrie, what are *you* doing here? We thought you and your husband were too fancy for us." Aunt Sarah remained seated at the kitchen table, her mouth still sneering.

Before I could answer, Aunt Tillie, sensing what I needed, hugged me and said, "*Sha, sha*, what's wrong, my baby?"

Words poured out in between tears. I had really missed my family building with women I trusted, not the fake ones I now spent time with to please my husband, women I went to country clubs and museum events with, where we impressed each other with our knowledge of clothes and designers, and we pretended our lives were wonderful.

Tillie asked, still embracing me, "Do you love Ronnie?" She then let me go and retrieved a box of tissue and a piece of freshly baked challah.

I wiped my eyes with the tissue. Clearing my throat, I answered, "Yes."

Sarah asked, "A girlfriend? It will pass. They all stray."

"Of course not," I replied. "I told you, he wants me to stay home and give up being a lawyer and an active worker for women's rights. All the things I worked so hard for."

With outstretched hands, Sarah said, "For this, you are crying? Why, every girl . . ."

I saw Aunt Tillie give her sister the famous family look that said, *Keep quiet.*

Sarah stopped in mid-sentence.

Aunt Tillie sat me down at the familiar red kitchen table where she added strawberry jam to my bread and said, "Then you need to realize you married a strong-willed man who honors the old traditions of the husband being the head of all of the family and the wife being the submissive one in charge of the household."

I added more jam to my challah and took a bite before responding. "Aunt Tillie, it is 1973," I said. "Times are changing. Women are asking for and getting their rights. Why, Roe vs. Wade was just passed, and the Equal Rights Amendment is not far behind."

"Like Moses had to wander the desert for forty years to get rid of a generation of slaves, it will take at least another generation or two of men before they will admit that women deserve equality," Aunt Tillie said.

"What can I do?" I asked as I reached for another piece of bread.

Aunt Sarah, who hadn't said a word after Tillie warned her, spoke up: "Have a baby."

Aunt Tillie rose and began setting plates of brisket, potatoes, and kugel in front of me.

"My sister is right," Aunt Tillie said. "I would tell you also, learn to maneuver him. You did it before you were married."

I smiled as I acknowledged to myself, I'm just too much of a pleaser to be a skillful manipulator, though I did a good job while we were dating, but that was exhausting, not something I thought I would have to continue. Another reason why I couldn't be a trial lawyer, but I was a great writer and researcher.

Chapter Twenty

I didn't get it. Just one month off the pill and I could be pregnant. I thought my period was probably just late. Irregularities were common after being on the tablet. It was still relatively new. *I won't think about it yet,* I told myself.

Four weeks later, overwhelming dizziness, stomach pains, and nausea confirmed that I was pregnant, though the rabbit still had to make the ultimate decision. I decided I wouldn't tell Ronnie until I made a trip to the doctor.

That didn't work. Dressed for dinner, Ronnie pulled me close. "Hey, babe, you look great. You are filling out that dress," he said as he squeezed my bloated breasts.

"Ouch," I whimpered.

He stepped back, eyes wide open he stated, "You're pregnant. Why didn't you tell me?"

"How do you know? I have an appointment with the doctor Monday to confirm it," I replied. "It is only a little over two months since I had a period."

This scenario confirmed for me why women needed the right to an abortion. I had a husband, my baby was conceived out of love, we could afford it; still, I was worried that my husband might not be happy about it. Of course, having the right and being able to get it were two different things. Shirley had made me aware that it was extremely difficult to keep abortion clinics going because of protestors and new rules made to make getting an abortion difficult, such as building restrictions or doctor restrictions. Ronnie startled me with . . .

"You were on the pill! Why did you go off without discussing it with me?"

I stiffened.

A smile replaced his narrowed lips. "Never mind, I think it is fantastic. I need a son now before I get too old."

Then Ronnie gave me a big hug and a sweet kiss. A sigh of relief swept over me. Ronnie walked over to the bar, took out two crystal glasses, filled them with red wine, and handed me one. We leaned forward to hit our glasses together in a toast to our new baby.

After the first three months of morning sickness, my pregnancy went well. I felt like a princess. Everyone, including Ronnie, watched over me. I got to eat and eat and gain weight, though, as I filled out, there were many places I couldn't go. Once pregnant women got too big, society demanded they stay home.

My cousin Lizzie and I had become much closer now that we were adults. Our three years difference in age meant much less. She had grown a few inches taller than I was, and she still wore her sandy-colored hair shoulder length and wavy. I spent my days at the beauty shop to keep my hair in the fashionable straight hairdos. Though she was younger, Lizzie was experienced in the ins and outs of pregnancies and child-rearing as she married right out of high school and already had two little ones. Her looks and mannerisms reminded me of her mother, my beloved Aunt Tillie, especially when Lizzie did the *ptew, ptew, ptew* fake spitting to ward off the evil spirit after talking about my pregnancy.

Lizzie picked me up for lunch at one of Chicago's famous downtown restaurants, Marshall Field's Walnut Room on the 7th floor of the department store. I stuffed my big body into the passenger seat of her car, just short of sitting on knitting needles.

"Lizzie, are you trying to kill me?"

"Sorry. She picked up the yellow and white yarn attached to knitting needles and tossed the bunch onto the back seat.

"What are you making?"

When she answered, "A blanket for your baby," I felt ashamed.

"Thanks! I could never master knitting or sewing, something you and your mom are so skilled with."

"You have little patience for manual skills, but you can write," she said as she pulled into the garage across from the store.

We parked the car and entered Marshal Field's through the State Street entrance under the famous ionic green clock. I loved taking the escalators instead of the elevators because the great wall reaching up to the Tiffany crystal circular dome was elegant.

When we reached the seventh floor and the Walnut Room, we admitted to each other that it was a goy's place, but what an elegant one with its crystal lights, enormous open decorated ceiling, a fountain with palm plants, dark wood paneling, and the waitresses in their black dresses and white aprons. Christmas, when there was an enormous tree in the middle of the room, was the special time to visit if you weren't Jewish. Christmas at the Walnut Room was a Chicago institution dating back to the turn of the century.

Lizzie whispered, "I would love to take my kids here to see the Christmas tree, but the family wouldn't understand."

Even though my maternity clothes were getting tight, I finished the restaurant's special salad, turkey without cheese, while Lizzie just nibbled on hers. I felt self-conscious as some older women gave me disdainful looks.

Lizzie turned around and frowned back at them. "Forget it, these old biddies think you should stay home for nine months. I got fired from my teaching job because, at five months, I was showing too much to teach third grade. I doubt that eight-year-olds still believe the stork delivers babies. Speaking of that, Sherrie, have you given up on your work to get the Equal Rights Amendment passed?"

"Of course not," I replied. "The house ratified it Oct. 23, 1971, and the Senate, March 22, 1972. Presently, we have to get thirty-eight states to ratify it for it to become an amendment. Because of my pregnancy, and Ronnie, I'm not as much involved. Still, when they need me, I help write the pamphlets and briefs. Anonymously, of course. Also, being home so much has given me the time to make calls requesting women to let their representatives know about the amendment. Illinois still hasn't ratified it."

"How is that going?"

"I am totally amazed at how many women have never heard of the ERA."

"Sherrie, most of us are so busy with the house and kids, that we leave business, finance, and laws up to our husbands," Lizzie replied. "Wait until your baby is born."

I finished another roll while Liz puffed on her Salem cigarette. "Lizzie, I know you think I'm crazy for working on all these causes, but things like no more draft for your son to worry about and better pay and facilities for your teaching job have come about because we are working to establish new laws."

Per usual, she avoided my box office statements. I let it go.

"Do you want to go shopping for more maternity clothes?"

I looked at Lizzie who wore a pink and blue tie-dyed top over slim pants on a thin body. After two kids, she looked great. This was needed encouragement for my ugly fat pregnant self.

"Thanks, Liz, but everything looks alike, tent dresses to hide the fact that you are pregnant, or black pants with an open panel. I think I will add to our women's rights demands the right to look pregnant and to go everywhere until you deliver."

"While we are talking about it, how about the right to nurse your baby in public," Lizzie added.

"You want to really shock those old biddies, like they did in the sixties."

"Can you imagine Aunt Sarah if I pulled out a tit at a Friday night dinner table, instead of hiding in the bedroom with the baby?"

We both had a good laugh.

I stopped in the bathroom to pee—the pregnant woman's hourly ritual. While washing my hands in the old-fashioned marble sink, I looked into the big steel-framed mirror and asked, "Will you be barefoot and pregnant, or both a mother and a modern, working lawyer?" I sighed as a hard look revealed a puffed up face and a swollen body. At that point, I only wanted to get my body back.

Times were changing, I thought. So I went home and wrote a new paper for our women's rights group, emphasizing some of the things Lizzie and I talked about to make life easier for pregnant women.

Chapter Twenty-One

"David, I need your help," I sweetly voiced over the phone.

"Anything for you, Sherrie."

"I have this craving for a Rainbow Cone ice cream cone, and Ronnie won't go near the South Side," I explained.

David laughed into the phone and said, "Sherrie, you are over six months pregnant. It's an hour drive. Are you up to it? There are great ice cream places closer."

"David, you are a South Sider," I replied. "How can you say that? Nothing better than Mitchell's or Rainbow. It is a perfect day to go. Clear blue sky, warm, not hot, summer sun, low humidity."

Sure, it was a long ride to Rainbow Cone on 92nd and Western, but it was fun seeing some of our old neighborhoods. I got excited when the giant ice cream cone on the roof came into view. David waited in line while I sat on one of the metal seats outside the store. They were uncomfortable for my massive body, but those five flavors (chocolate, strawberry, pistachio, Palmer House vanilla, and orange sherbet) in the ice cream cone were to die for. To David's astonishment, I finished the whole thing.

"David, it is so good to have you back. I guess New York wasn't that great?"

My cousin looked thinner and harder. His checkered shirt was way too big, and his dimples were hiding behind a serious expression. I worried about him. Since he and Jeffery had broken up, he'd been all over the place. David belonged back in design where his talents could be put to good use.

"Truthfully, I followed a lover to New York, and I ended up in a persecution incident which included a night in jail because I am gay,"

David recounted. "I always stayed in the urban subculture, hiding from the public. I'm now ready to fight for gay rights, and I've joined the Gay Liberation Front. We could use your law firm to help us. You know there are gay women too-lesbians."

"Oh, David, I am proud of you. I will help you wherever I can. Just right now, I'm not really involved with the law firm with the baby coming. A new day is dawning for all minorities. By the way, did you know that Illinois was the first state to do away with sodomy laws in 1961?"

The store looked the same with its yellow stucco outside and rainbow cone painted on the front wall. The area around it that had been surrounded by a large grassy field was now in the middle of a busy shopping street, making it a little less special. In fact, the whizzing by of cars and trucks made it harder to hear each other. On the plus side, the ice cream was still yummy and the memories of going here with the family from the time David and I were little was heartwarming.

David brought me back to the present. "Sherrie," David said, concerned. "After toiling through a law school that tried its best to get rid of women, I can't believe you are giving in to past rules - barefoot and pregnant. Are you still Sherrie Paul, or do you only respond to Mrs. Ronald Greenspan?"

"I guess you are right, David. I'm even reading *Good Housekeeping* and Dr. Spock, instead of Betty Friedan and my law books. I do want offspring, many children, but I also want to continue my career."

"You can do both," David assured me.

"Ronnie won't allow it," I replied, taking a Kleenex out of my pants pocket to wipe my eyes.

"Think about what you just said, Sherrie," David shot back. "Ronnie sounds like Pa - the patriarch and the ruler who nobody dared oppose. Remember, my mother and I lived with him. But that was another time. Why, you and your mother are the ones who encouraged me to come out about being gay and to fight for my rights against the establishment!" He leaned back in his chair, took out another cigarette, and lit it.

I felt the baby kick, and I began to tremble and sob. The pregnancy did havoc with my emotions. The mention of my mother, plus all the goals I was abandoning didn't help. The tears wouldn't stop. David went to get a few napkins as I was out of tissues.

"Oh, David, I'm so guilty," I said between sobs. "I agree with the need for women's liberation, but, at the same time, I *want* to be a mother, I want to be home, raising her children like my mother and aunts did!"

I thought about Shirley, divorced, working while raising two kids. How did she do it?

David walked around the table and gave me a big hug. "You'll figure it out after the baby is born," he said, soothingly. "I bet Ronnie wants a boy and you a girl so it can be named after your mother."

Smiling, I answered, "You're right. I want a Barbra—Babs, for short. Bess is too old a name to stick her with."

I squeezed his hand as he helped me get up and maneuver myself into the van. David and I had a special bond from growing up together in the family building in South Shore. We could say anything to each other without worrying about judgment.

* * *

In my eighth month, and nothing to do but wait. Like waiting for Godot, the time went by slowly. I cut back on cigarettes, which only made me eat more. I glanced at my swollen fingers, the ones that would no longer hold my rings, and put down the Danish on which I had been nibbling. I peed constantly, which made it tough to leave the house.

The book in my lap still stayed on the same page as it had been on an hour ago. I couldn't concentrate, and I was feeling like a puffed-up elephant.

I pulled the heavy, brown, velvety drapes back and looked out the window at an empty beach where the waves beat against the wet, gritty sand. Closer to my building there were people; a young girl walked a large blond golden retriever, and another woman pushed a toddler in a stroller. I assumed there was a strong wind as the stroller top was down, the woman had her head covered by a scarf, and the dog's fur was stirring every which way. I tried to imagine myself pushing a baby in a carriage along the lakefront.

Ronnie snuck up behind me and kissed my neck.

I turned around and said, "Ronnie, I would love to raise our child in a house with a yard."

"I've been thinking along the same lines," Ronnie replied, "I'll talk to Renee, the real estate agent the firm uses."

I would have preferred Skokie or even Highland Park, but we ended up buying a house by the lake in Glencoe, a northern suburb that was recently invaded by the elite Jewish community. In fact, it had one of the nicest Reform congregations on the North Shore. So Reform that at least seventy percent of the service was in English. My mother would have loved it.

The house was as big as our three-flat building in South Shore, and the lawn, with its constant smell of newly cut grass, was as large as the park I had played in as a youngster. The garden, with its neatly ordered plants and flowers, would probably cost a fortune to maintain. From this purchase, I was guessing we were in the money, or we were part of Ronnie's mother's estate from her father, who had just died. I wasn't allowed to ask questions about our finances, even though I had handled my own through school and beyond.

The nicest part was being by Lake Michigan again. Only this part of the lake was very quiet—no bathers, just a few boats, and very few police and ambulance sirens screaming. We now lived in very private territory. I would probably miss the noise, I figured.

Now that we were influential North Shore Jews, we hired an architectural firm to redo the fifty-five-year-old North Shore Lake mansion. David was in California finding himself, so I didn't feel guilty, though nobody Ronnie hired could do as well as David, who had been born with a unique flare for design.

I made sure the baby's room and my office had my input in the design and decor, while I gave in for most of the other rooms. On hold, until the baby was born, were the choice of pink or blue bedding clothes, and decorations to go with the mahogany crib and nursery set. Jews were superstitious about having showers and buying things for the baby before he or she arrived. Beautifully wrapped gifts from those who didn't observe or know of my tradition sat unopened on the floor.

Ronnie and his decorator were into mirrors, marble, modern lines, and the projection of money, power, and the right things. Uncluttered and orderly like a luxury hotel was the finished project. The knick-knacks and tchotchkes I grew up with would never fit. I put them in a box to be stored in the attic where I found some Christmas decorations the last owner probably forgot to take.

Sometimes I wondered if I fit in. Ronnie's mother and sister loved the way the house was taking shape. To them, everything had to be socially acceptable and perfect. I've never seen them with a hair out of place. Now, I knew my family would be afraid to sit down in my house. They wouldn't understand a Jewish house with a white sofa minus plastic and a furnished basement with a wine cellar, with pinot noir instead of Mogen David wine.

My labor pains started while I was still in the apartment. In fact, I was listening to one of my mother's records. I think it was Joan Baez. I had dozed off in the oversized leather lounger, dropping my Dr. Spock book when I felt wet. Luckily, Mandy, our cleaning lady, was with me as I cabbed to Northwestern Hospital just off North Michigan Avenue. The traffic, the road, and the pain seemed longer and longer, even though we traveled only about eight miles. I was sure my baby was going to be born in a Yellow Cab.

I was wrong. Seven hours of labor awaited me before birth.

When I woke up after delivery, I took one look at Ronnie, who was sitting in a chair near the bed, and I knew our baby was a girl.

"Ronnie, it's a girl, right?"

"How did you know," he replied, flatly.

"The look on your face. No big smiles or enthusiastic gestures. This baby is for me, the next one will be a boy. Is she perfect, all parts intact?" I asked as I tried to roll over.

He got up and said, "I'll see if the nurse can bring her to you. She is perfect, with a head of black hair."

When she was put into my arms, I was in awe of her perfect tiny little fingers and toes, especially when she wrapped a hand around my own. All the pains I felt disappeared.

"Are you still good with naming her Barbra Ann after my mother, Bess Ann?" I asked.

He swallowed hard and said, "We made a deal, you name a girl, I name a boy. Can we call her Babs?"

Babs she became.

I was overwhelmed by the well-wishers. Flowers and cards not only came from family and friends but from clients and influential Chicago politicians. My aunts were there most of the week I spent in the hospital, pushing the nurses aside as they tried to instruct me in nursing techniques and caring for a newborn. I was so lucky to have them as substitutes for the mother I so missed.

Lizzie was right; that first baby took up most of my time, even with help at home, and Aunt Tillie's constant advice. I finally realized why my mother, a stranger in our world, had stayed in the family building. She knew my family wouldn't let her take me, and she couldn't leave me.

Funny, whenever I asked my aunts about my mother, they totally avoided the issue of her religion, like the elephant in the room. The stories they passed around were different from my version, which was now attached to Sophia's story. I concentrated too much on the past. When we had a baby naming in the Reform Glencoe Synagogue, near our new house, I wondered how my secret Protestant mother would have felt at my Jewish baby naming. My dad just concentrated on how much he missed her. I was hoping that with my baby, I would be able to concentrate now on how much I missed her and be able to send away the elephant in the room.

Dad brought an old photo book to the baby-naming. Album pages with my baby pictures were filled with photos of family members and just a few images of my mother, but I enjoyed looking at her neat, or-ganized handwriting labeling all. Most of the writing was fading along with the small black and white photographs, but we enjoyed bunching together over the kitchen table, reminiscing.

"You were a beautiful baby, Sherrie." "Look at that old wooden highchair." "Pa was still alive. He would never hold the babies." "Where was that picture taken? I think it was by the Midway in Hyde Park, near the University of Chicago at one of our picnics." "I think the men were playing pinochle." "Did your mother really wear high heels on at a picnic?"

Babysitting for cousins while growing up helped me care for Babs, but there is nothing that compares to the bond with one's own child. Babs was my world, especially since Ronnie traveled so much. Most of the families we socialized with had nannies. I refused to let anyone else raise my child, which became an issue between my husband and me. We had grown up in different economic groups and thus held different priorities. I was used to the family being involved in the care of everyone, especially the children, and religion had played a big part in my life.

A nanny mainly raised Ronnie and his sister. He especially had a hard time relating to babies, and he expected to still be my number one priority. I laughed when Ronnie held Babs with stiff arms and a fearful expression on his face. Diaper changing? No way for him. When Babs was potty trained and running around the house, he finally related to her, especially when she perched herself on his lap and called him *Da Da*. She was slender, fair, and sweet, and I always dressed her in beautiful chiffon outfits.

Ronnie and I argued and kissed and made up a lot in those early years. Usually, I was the one who gave in, so long as it was an issue that didn't take me away from Babs. He still could make my heart flutter with desire with just his touch, and I only wanted to please him.

Jim, named after Ronnie's dad's Jewish name of Jacob, joined our family two years later. This time, my pregnancy went well. His bris was an expensive catered business affair where most of the guests had to ask each other what was happening, and what were we eating. Where Babs had been an easy baby, Jim was a handful, keeping me up nights and continuously on the go during the day. He was curious and needed to be doing something constantly. If I turned my back, he ran off somewhere.

Babs was my buddy. We hid together when Jim and Ronnie had their disagreements. Yes, by five, Jim was challenging his dad for attention and control, and Ronnie was spending more time with us, I believe because of their interaction.

"Dad, Dad, did you see the baby gorilla?" Jim had asked as he grabbed his dad's arm during one of our visits to Lincoln Park Zoo. Babs and I laughed and laughed as we watched Ronnie running with Jim to the gorilla area, while unaware that a hole in the bag of popcorn he held left a long trail.

One time, Jim was successful in getting his dad to hang up on a business call and rejoin him in constructing a Lego ship, by saying, "Dad, it is your day off, and we are playing together. Aren't I important to you?"

When the kids were young, we even managed a few trips to Florida and California, though Ronnie spent most of his days there in the hotel room on the phone, while I entertained Babs and Jim. He had such a hard time relaxing and letting go of his work, even on vacation.

Chapter Twenty-Two

We had several fun family days until, suddenly, Ronnie became cold and unavailable. I knew that he was under pressure to become a senior partner in his law firm, but it shouldn't have made him mean and abusive to his family. His career was flourishing, and he had a family who adored him. It was hard for us to deal with loving words and hugs that could turn into sudden anger, where even the tone of his voice changed. We tiptoed around him when he was home, as it seemed that none of us could do anything right.

Our palace on the lake turned into a house of horrors when Ronnie's car would pull into the garage. One night, eight-year-old Babs and I were getting dinner together when, hearing Ronnie arrive, we both stood at attention, afraid to move, while six-year old Jim continued to play with his Legos; nothing changed in his life.

"Turn that damn television off! You can hear it throughout the neighborhood," Ronnie bellowed as he stormed into the house.

Unconsciously biting her fingernails, Babs turned off the TV while I went to greet my husband. Trying to defuse the situation, I reached up to kiss him. He moved away from me. "Get me a drink," he growled.

I nervously walked to the bar and poured Ronnie a Jack and Coke. On the way back to him, I tripped and spilled the drink on the white living room sofa.

All hell broke loose.

"You clumsy fool! This sofa cost a fortune! You don't deserve *anything* good," he yelled as he pushed me out of the way.

"You leave my mother alone," Jim yelled as he ran towards us. He then hit his father with his small, clenched fists.

That was it for me. I grabbed my purse, both kids, and hurried out of the house and into the car. I drove aimlessly, while my kids sat quietly. Finally, Jim asked, "Where are we going?"

"Out to dinner. Where do you want to go?" I answered as I changed into sunglasses to hide the tears.

"Lum's," Jim suggested.

A dinner at Lum's and shopping at Toys R Us kept us out long enough to let Ronnie cool down. Driving home down my perfect black-topped driveway, with its adjacent manicured lawn and spectacular view of Lake Michigan's steel-blue waters, I wondered how long I could keep convincing myself that I lived in paradise and was so very happy. I had been fooling myself for quite a while. Ronnie was right, after all; maybe I really was a fool.

He was nowhere around, but the white sofa had been scrubbed clean of the spilled alcohol. *Too bad*, I thought; this house was too white and sterile. It needed some dirt, some spots!

Babs, Jim, and I retired to bed. There was no sign of Ronnie until four o'clock the next afternoon when he came through the door like nothing ever happened.

"I hope you didn't start to cook. I brought home Chinese from a new restaurant by my office. I got beef and broccoli, cashew chicken, egg rolls, shrimp, and those fortune telling cookies." He dropped the white cartons on the table and turned towards Babs. "Help Mom while I go up and change out of my suit." Jim continued to play with his Legos while Babs and I set the table and opened the cartons of Chinese food. I quickly refroze the hamburger meat that was defrosting on the kitchen counter. Ronnie returned, wearing a Polo t-shirt and blue jeans, and sat down at the table with us, and started a family conversation. We had a fun dinner, especially with the fortune cookies.

"Did you know fortune cookies have to be read with the words, 'under the sheets' at the end? Jim, what does your fortune say?" Ronnie asked.

Jim started to laugh as he read, "You will be successful - *under the sheets.*"

I looked at Ronnie thinking, *I'm the one who needs that fortune cookie!*

That night, Ronnie even sat on the sofa with us as we watched *Charlie's Angels* on our modern 21-inch color TV.

"Why didn't you tell me these angels were so beautiful?" Ronnie joked.

I refused to tell my family anything about Ronnie's treatment of the children and of me. In my mind, and to the children, I made excuses: *Dad works very hard. He is under a lot of pressure.* We never knew what to expect from Ronnie in those days. We were the poor little rich family out in the sticks. We hardly saw my family or his.

As I came in from a walk along the Lake with Jim, who couldn't stay out of the water, and Babs, who only wanted to hold my hand, I noticed that the answering machine was blinking. I hit the button and smiled at the message. It was Lizzie. "We heard Ronnie was out of town," Lizzie's message said. "Would you like us to bring Sabbath dinner to your house?" Ronnie had virtually forbidden me to have my family over when he was home, so this was perfect timing. I quickly dialed Lizzie to say we would love to have the family over.

"Babs, Jim," I addressed the kids, "Auntie and family won't be here for another hour, let's surprise them with the family cookie, *Cherries In The Snow* cookies."

Jim clapped his hands while Babs gathered the butter, cherries, and flour. When the doorbell rang, we were still rolling cherries in the dough and messing up the kitchen. In piled ten or more family members and chaos - bags of cooked food, noise, lights, pots and pans banging, kids fighting, and Good Sabbath greetings uttered.

Babs and Lizzie gathered plates, silverware, and glasses, while Jim and I placed the cookies in the oven and turned on the timer. Aunt Tillie opened her packages of garlic brisket, roasted chicken, challah, and kugel, and I warmed them in something new called a microwave.

"What are you doing to my food?" Aunt Tillie asked with raised eyebrows and outstretched arms. "How can you warm it in five minutes? Put it in the stove, we can wait."

After Yale tried to explain the microwave to her, she worried that her food was now full of radiation. Things were changing so fast, it was hard to keep up.

All quieted down when the Sabbath candles were lit and the prayer was chanted. Mogen David's sweet wine was sipped, and the food passed. Friendly arguments started, with everyone waving their hands and talking at once, making the noise level increase and my house seem like an evening in our old family building.

Thank goodness Jim had put on the timer, or the cookies would have burned. I carefully took them out of the oven and put the pan on the stove to cool.

Aunt Sarah held up two cookies, and said, "This perfectly round cookie was made by Jim, and this cookie with the cherry hanging out was created by my Sherrie. Slow down, my kin." She came over to me and pulled me in for a hug.

My dad, sitting at the head of my glass-and-steel kitchen table, shook his head, waved his hands in front of his face, and said, "Nonsense. Who cares what they look like? They taste good, that is important." We ate and shouted back and forth to each other over the state of the world, and other things we could do nothing about.

Babs picked up the powdered sugar container and drizzled the sugar over the cookies. "Now they all look alike, and nobody knows who made them," she said with a smile.

"It is good to hear you laughing. You are too serious lately. Is something wrong?" Lizzie asked me when we were in the kitchen stacking the dishwasher.

I clenched my jaw, looked out the window, and said, "Things are not good in my marriage. Ronnie is under stress and hard to please, but we are trying to work it out." I quickly added, "Please don't say anything to the family. You know how it will spread, and I will have all kinds of advice pouring in."

Lizzie put her hand on my shoulder and said, "You and the children need to be happy too. I'm here if you want to talk, and I will keep my mother out of it."

I hugged her and thanked her. She then put her hand on mine and we stood still for a few seconds until her youngest came over with his complaint about his brother, "Johnathan won't give me the ball." On her way into the living room, she shook her head and laughed. "Four are too many."

My house had become alive with my family, and I loved every minute of that night from the abundance of food, the loud arguments around the table, to the kids sprawled on the floor playing Monopoly while eating candy and popcorn. I didn't even worry about the furniture or the white carpet, but we did stay mainly in the kitchen.

It didn't last long enough. My life wasn't like my growing up in the family building.

Chapter Twenty-Three

When Babs and Jim were in school full time, I agreed to fulfill my role as a society wife to a law partner in a prestigious firm. Charity and museum board meetings, luncheons, and country club dates became my life.

Delilah Benson, one of the partner's wives, became my mentor. I met her at Saks Fifth Avenue. Saks was even a more luxury store than Marshall Field's. It was a four-story stone building located on North Michigan Avenue that specialized in women's clothes, jewelry, and amenities.

Delilah was a tall, slim woman in a black Chanel suit, and three-inch high leather shoes. I followed her as she strode across Saks's second floor, looking down her nose at the clothes on the racks.

She looked back to make sure I was following her and said, "We are going into the designer room where I have a special sales lady. I *never* buy off the racks."

I had one chipped red nail that I tried to hide. Even though I had them done two days ago, they never lasted. I knew her nails would be perfect.

I left the department store loaded with expensive designer clothes— linen pants, silk shirts, Chanel suits, and purses. Ronnie told me to go with Delilah, so I didn't pay attention to price tags.

Delilah helped me get the packages into my car, and said, "I've made appointments at my beauty salon with Albert." She looked me over critically, "We need to do something with that hair of yours."

I just smiled, while seething inside.

My new companions, Delilah, whose husband ran a bank; Marie, whose husband ran a major real estate agency; and Celia, whose husband was a partner in Ronnie's law firm, took over my life. Slim, ultra-white teethed, designer-dressed society ladies became my idols.

I tried to make my marriage work. We hired babysitters and joined our husbands at the *in* affairs and chic restaurants where we ate little and drank too much. Dressed in my new expensive clothes, I'd smile as Ronald walked me around, chatting and shaking hands with the important people in the elaborate private dining rooms, where the tables were always decorated with white linen tablecloths, crystal, and china all set around fabulous flower centerpieces. Gourmet dinners were served by white-coated waiters. I became part of the Ronald Greenspan franchise.

After a while, I had the speeches and greetings memorized, and I could actually recognize what designer each woman was wearing. Delilah was a good teacher; as a woman walked by, I liked to reach over to Delilah and whisper a designer's name. Like the time I whispered "Gucci?" and Delilah smiled and whispered back, "Right on. Marie is always dressed perfectly. You should get to know her. Her husband, Daniel, is one of the firm's most influential clients."

I smiled back and shook my head affirmative, though I really thought Marie was a cold, arrogant person with whom I wouldn't want to associate.

I gave up what was special to me to do what my husband wanted me to do. I closed my eyes to the fact that my husband traveled worldwide and was seldom home, or to the rumors of his affairs with other women, even though it broke my heart, or of his demanding and authoritative treatment of me and our children—until I had enough.

Babs trembled and hid when Ronnie was home, while Jim talked back and ended up being punished, and timid me tried to keep everyone happy.

One day, eight-year-old Jim backed away from the dining room table, tripped on the chair, and knocked over a plate of pasta. Red tomato sauce splattered over the white tablecloth and the thick tan carpet, causing a terrible mess.

Ronnie, eyes wide open, jaw clenched, flung his hand across the table, grabbed Jim by the arm, and attempted to hit him.

Anger overwhelmed me, and my blood began to boil. I jumped up and shouted out, *"Don't you dare lay a hand on my son!"*

Ronnie turned towards me, his eyes opening even wider, as I moved in between both of them.

"How *dare* you tell me what to do?" he shouted back. "While I'm out working my ass off, you are living in luxury, spoiling these children rotten. They need some real discipline!"

I hid my trembling hands and answered, "It would be nice if you worked less and spent more time being a husband and father. We don't need more material things, or a man in the house who is always angry and *abusive!"*

He picked up his coat and briefcase and headed towards the door. The last thing he said was, "You have no idea how lucky you are."

Fighting back changed me, strengthened me, but I wasn't ready to do anything drastic yet. My children were very young, and I still loved Ronnie, or I believed I did. He could be so warm and loving, and then at other times, so very cold and cruel. It was hard to know if I was happiest when he was home or when he was gone. He was fantastic trial lawyer, but an unpredictable husband and father. I wanted to believe in him like I did when we first married.

I tried to act normal, putting hamburgers and steaks on the grill, serving them with a salad and the chocolate chip cookies Babs and I had made.

"Should we wait for Dad to come back?" Jim asked as he put his Matchbox cars away.

"Dad will eat when he gets home,"

We ate and watched *The Brady Bunch* before going to bed. No Ronnie. I had a hard time sleeping. I tried reading my new mystery, but I couldn't concentrate. I went downstairs to turn up the air conditioner and look around. Finally, I fell asleep.

I heard the front door open and close late that night. I glanced at the clock on my bed stand: 1:15 a.m. Additional noise downstairs, but none near our bedroom. I had a hard time falling back to sleep as tension gripped me. I wanted to go to him, but I waited for him to come to our bedroom. When he didn't, I expected him to be gone Saturday morning. Instead, the aroma of fresh coffee and the sweet smell of cinnamon muffins floated through the house.

Clad in a bathrobe, I slowly walked down the long hallway and entered the kitchen. Babs was the first to greet me, saying, "Mom, Dad and I are making a surprise breakfast!"

Jim was sitting at the table, drinking orange juice, while Ronnie, apron-clad, leaned over the stove, scrambling eggs with cheese. I just stood there thinking, *Could we find a pill to keep this side of my husband always?*

I smiled and answered, "I am shocked. Everything smells delicious. May I help?"

Ronnie turned around and smiled, "Just sit down and enjoy."

We had this excellent breakfast together, plus more surprises.

"Sherrie, you're right," Ronnie said. "I haven't spent enough time with you and the kids. What about we spend winter break in Aspen?"

"What about Disney World?" I answered. "We tried Aspen and never saw you. Babs and I don't ski, and Jim ends up in a class away from you."

I could tell he was already becoming annoyed. I dared to challenge his plans. Ronnie turned towards the kids and said, "You decide, Aspen or Disney?"

Jim yelled "Disney," and Babs, hands folded on her lap, quietly answered, "I don't care."

"Ok, it will be Disney," Ronnie decided. "I'll have Myra book it. We'll have a great time!"

He grinned at me. I smiled back, while a little sarcastic voice in the back of my head said, *No way will this work.*

That night, Ronnie reached for me, and I lovingly responded. I became lured into thinking things would get better, and they did—for a short while. No barking orders, and he was actually home for several family dinners and outings.

Then winter break came, and lo and behold, Ronnie had to work. Myra, his secretary, did a great job of booking the kids and me. We flew to Orlando first class, stayed in a suite at Disney's top resort, and toured the park with a guide. No waiting in line for us. I wondered what vacation place she booked Ronnie; probably Aspen. I pretended to not see makeup on his shirt a few days before we left.

* * *

Back at home, Ronnie and his partner, Larry, were working on a case in the dining room when he shouted, "Sherrie! Get in here"

I turned to my children. "Remember whose turn it is," I said. "Mom will be right back."

Nine-year-old Jim clenched his jaw, threw down the dice from the Monopoly game, got up, and yelled, "No, you won't! When Dad calls you, you never come back!" He ran out of the room, and Babs sat there, saying nothing, like an obedient ten-year-old.

Ronnie's voice escalated in tone and demand: "Sherrie! Get in here! NOW!"

I reluctantly went into the dining room.

"What do you want?" I asked. "The kids and I are playing a game."

"Get us some coffee and pastries," he ordered in his most demanding tone.

I looked him square in the face, narrowed my eyes, and in the most authoritative tone I could muster, said, "Get them *yourself*."

As I turned to leave, his partner Larry stood up and clapped. I went back to Monopoly with a big smile on my face, expelling a breath I had been holding the whole time.

As I sat back down to play with Babs and Jim, who had returned to the game. I realized I had taken the first step towards the end of our marriage.

Most people would think it was because of Ronnie's many girl-friends, but Larry made me realize the real reason was that I had had enough of the way he emotionally abused our children and me.

Chapter Twenty-Four

A year and a half of separation had passed, and we were in divorce negotiations. *My* lawyer, Deidra Blum, and I were sitting at one end of a long wooden conference table in one of the modern sterile offices belonging to Ronnie's law firm. He and one of his law friends were sitting across from us when in awe, I heard Ronnie say, "Sherrie is a brilliant lawyer. The children are in school full-time, so she can go back to work and make an excellent salary. Why, in a few years, I will probably come back and sue her for alimony."

He had turned on his charm and innocence, usually reserved for the big shots he wanted to impress.

I sat there in shock. During our married life, Ronnie hardly acknowledged that I was a lawyer. I understood now that he never wanted me to threaten his superiority, or maybe currently, he was just working on reducing his alimony. I kept quiet and let my lawyer speak.

I opened my purse and dug through it until I found a small bottle of aspirin. I swallowed two with water. My head was pounding. I knew I should let Deidra negotiate and come back to me. I thought about those great agreements we made while dating and how I had believed in our romantic courtship. I still loved him, but I couldn't live with him.

Deidra calmly answered, "I'm sure you are right, Ron, but we have to take into account that, for the last twelve years, Sherrie had a non-paying job of wife and mother, and will now have to start from scratch at any law job she obtains. Also, your children are not old enough to stay home alone after school."

As Deidra spoke, I thought back to the fellow law school student who had told me I was taking up space from a male lawyer who would not take off to care for children. I got up and walked over to the coffee pot sitting at the end of the table. With trembling hands, I poured myself a cup of coffee, hoping it would calm me down.

When I go back to work, I thought to myself, *childcare will be one of the issues I will work on.* I had already talked to Shirley about joining her law firm, but these negotiations could take a while, and I couldn't start until they were settled.

* * *

Since my mother's death, Aunt Tillie had been a mother substitute to me, and now that I was in crisis, she was by my side. Besides a divorce, I was reaching my early forties, the age at which my mother had died, and it scared me. Already my hair was turning salt and pepper, my waistline was expanding, and my mind was having trouble concentrating. If she could die young, so could I, leaving two very small children. But I was never one who waited for Godot to solve my problems, so I moved ahead establishing a new life.

I gave up the house to Ronnie for extra money. It had always been his house anyway. For now he was living downtown in a condo, until we moved out. The children stayed with me while he had them on alternating weekends and holidays, and he provided a generous and agreeable childcare settlement. Alimony, based on what Ronnie earned and spent during our marriage, not on what he had before, or what he had inherited, became a sticky point, which I finally gave in to.

Aunt Tillie in her flowered housedress, huffing and puffing from carrying so many boxes, entered my house. A few steps behind was my cousin Lizzie, also loaded with boxes. Lizzie, still thin, wearing a pink and blue tie-dyed shirt, dropped her boxes on the table next to Aunt Tillie's.

"What are you bringing? We are moving, and we have to get rid of things."

Waving her hands, she said, "You have to eat and the *kinder* need to play," Aunt Tillie replied, while Lizzie just looked up and rolled her eyes. It was comforting to know that family was there to help me pick up the pieces.

Lizzie then helped her mother unload plates of brisket, challah, and rugelach, along with boxes of toys. Aunt Tillie was the big emotional Jewish mother I needed, especially since no one ever talked about my mother, who was not Jewish. I understood part of Ronnie's attachment to me was that he also had a non-Jewish mother. My dad's silence on anything about my mother hurt the most. He couldn't acknowledge the fact that my mother was a non-Jewish goy.

Jim and Babs ran right into Aunt Tillie's arms as Lizzie and I left on our mission to find a house for the kids and me. Out the door, Lizzie clapped her hands with excitement as I raised my coat's hood to ward away the light snow.

"I found the perfect house and it is only two blocks from me," Lizzie said. "Get in the car already."

I got into the car, wiped the spots of snow off my face, and lit a cigarette while I let the lawyer in me weigh the location. Lizzie lived in Northbrook in a new Jewish community; but I would be working downtown with a fifty-mile round trip; but then again, Lizzie would watch my kids. I could afford to hire someone, but family was better.

"Sherrie, what's wrong?" Lizzie said, interrupting my thoughts. "I've been telling you about the house and you haven't said a thing."

My Lizzie had criticized her mother for years, and she had turned out the same, not an old Jewish mother, but a modern Jewish mother who also had to be in charge of everything.

Before we got out of the car, she still was selling me the house, saying, "Besides granite countertops, it has a treehouse that Jim will love. The best part is, we can get it before it goes on the market. A divorce, and they just want to get rid of it. Oops, almost forgot about *your* divorce . . ."

My energetic, spirited cousin skirted around the place, pointing everything out better than a real estate agent could have. It wasn't my mansion on the lake, but I had been miserable there. The four-bedroom, three-bathroom, red brick two-story modern eighties house would be good for my family.

"The kitchen has granite countertops, with an island, and more light wooden cabinets than you will ever need," Lizzie enthused. "Take a look at the master bedroom—blue wallpaper, your favorite color, a walk-in closet, an unusually high ceiling that really enlarges the space, and a Jacuzzi tub. What else could you want?" She practically yelled.

Man, I thought, *she is right,* and said. "Okay, Lizzie, I'll take it."

"You'll take it! I'm so happy!" Her voice raised with glee. "It will be like the family building all over again!" Then Lizzie turned towards me. "Wait . . . what do you mean, you'll take it? You don't even know what they are asking! Also, I have three other houses to show you."

I sat down on one of the large spinning kitchen chairs and said, "Lizzie, I looked downtown and ruled it out because of the schools. I looked in Skokie. Do you like this house better than the others?"

"Yes, and they are asking only $69,000," Lizzie said.

"Put in a bid for $67,500," I said, as I checked the kitchen table and chairs. "Also, see if they will sell this blue and pink tiled kitchen set; it was made to match the blue floor tile and the flowered wallpaper."

Right then and there, I put in a call to my father. "Dad, could you and your friend George inspect this house I'm thinking of buying? I trust your judgment. You've always been the fix-it man." When he asked for the address, I felt good.

"Since his retirement, he hasn't been acting right," I told Lizzie.

"My mom feels the same," Lizzie said. "Your dad quit coming out to visit. Mom yelled at him when he refused to go to her doctor, and now he isn't answering the phone when she calls."

I felt guilty for neglecting my dad and pledged to look after him. I was extremely busy putting together a new life. The family building had been easy—everyone in the same space, interacting daily, no chance for secrets!

Chapter Twenty-Five

Ronnie had moved into a condo in downtown Chicago, while the kids and I were trying to pack up for our move into our new home in Northbrook. Boxes were everywhere. I was sitting at my modern glass and rattan desk, busy doing my new job of paying bills and taking care of my finances. "I'm a lawyer, this shouldn't be this hard," I said to myself. Only Ronnie had taken care of everything for so long. I looked up. Through the large plate glass window the lake looked calm and so very blue on this beautiful spring day. Pink, blue, and yellow flowers were popping up around the perfect manicured lawn. Squirrels chased each other among the ancient trees. I knew I would miss this beautiful scene. I glanced at my watch—3:12 p.m. The kids would be home soon.

The housing contract sat to my left, and the divorce papers sat to my right. I had held it together until the divorce papers arrived. Then I burst into hysterical laughter and tears. Finally, with shaking hands I picked up the divorce papers and stared at Ronnie's signature. I was busy preparing a new life, but the divorce didn't feel real to me until I saw Ronnie's handwriting. My mind wouldn't internalize it. I just couldn't sign either one. Instead, I folded my arms at the elbows and laid my head on them. I felt numb, overwhelmed, hurt, and ready to give up. I heard the garage door opening but couldn't respond.

"Mom, are you sick?" Babs asked?

I looked up into my daughter's worried face and realized I had let my heart rule my head. Things would be different now. I had two children to think about, and I have to continue on without Ronnie. I grabbed a tissue out of my pocket and cleared my face.

I faked a smile. "Just tired, honey, Let's get some dinner together, maybe mac and cheese, or pasta."

The three of us had to adjust to a new life, a life without Ronnie living with us.

One day, while the three of us were sitting at the breakfast table Babs brought me the newspaper. On the front page was a picture of Ronnie being congratulated for winning a big case against a utility company.

"That's Daddy, right?" Babs asked.

"Yes," I answered, as I lowered my fork back into my plate of eggs.

"I guess that is why he has no time for us," she said.

"That is one of the reasons why your dad and I got a divorce," I explained.

To myself, I answered, *It's really the mini-skirted young blonde hanging on to him. It looks like they are celebrating at the Pump Room with Melman, the new owner.*

I was never comfortable there, though they did have great cheesecake. I glanced at my jeans, shirt, and sneakers before checking the blonde one more time. He thought he wanted an intelligent wife, but he wanted a showgirl that looked stunning hanging on his shoulder, and who knew how to keep quiet. I wondered if she was the one who contributed to the divorce. Did she also get a soft, thick, white mink coat like the one hanging in my closet? It looks like it in the booth behind them. While I stayed faithful, he never did. Should I tell the children, or keep protecting him?"

Pushing his cereal bowl to the side, Jim got up from the table. "Dad loves me," Jim began, he still buys me presents. It's *your* fault!" Jim pointed a finger in my direction before fleeing the room.

Babs looked at me with head lowered. "I'm sorry, Mom."

"It's not your or your brother's fault," I told her. "Your dad and I still love you both very much, but we can't live with each other. It is our fault. Your father and I tried, but we want different things from life."

I expected the call that came while we were finishing breakfast. I reached for the yellow wall phone. "Yes, Marla, I will tell the children,"

"Dad canceled our weekend," Babs guessed, as she looked up. She never complained. Jim made noise, but Babs was really the tough one.

At first, Ronnie took the kids every other weekend. Now he canceled more and more. Instead of the fights over visitation, and money those other divorcees told me about, it was almost like Ronnie would like the kids and me to disappear out of his life, because he belonged to the elite class, and we didn't. He did regularly pay child support and alimony.

"Yes, I better tell Jim." I said as I went up to his room where he was busy packing his weekend bag.

"Jim, dad's secretary called . . ." He didn't let me finish.

"You're lying, Mom," Jim cried. "He promised to take us to Wisconsin Dells."

"Sorry, his secretary said he has to cancel." Jim threw a football at me.

I left the room thinking, *I better make him go to therapy. I should have never let him quit after two sessions.*

It was the early eighties. Suddenly, the word *divorce* was no longer just a whispered word that meant *shame*. More and more couples in their forties and fifties were splitting. In fact, television sitcoms like *The Brady Bunch* were about second marriages and blended families. More women were college graduates and able to get good jobs, even though they were still paid less than the men in similar positions. At least my children had other divorced kids to talk to, particularly Babs, whose best friend Kaley's parents were already divorced five years. It was harder for Jim. I heard him talking to a friend who asked, "Do you have a dad?" Jim threw his Legos across the room before answering with, "My dad has a job more important than anyone else, a secret job that keeps him away!"

Chapter Twenty-Six

I had joined my lawyer friend Shirley in a new adventure. While her first partner, Paula, and I were stay-at-home mothers, she had become a prominent attorney in the field of women's rights. She always looked the role, wearing designer suits, high heels, perfectly coiffed hair, and no chipped nails, while I was living in comfortable leisure pants suits.

Her new project involved a home for abused women. It was located on the West Side near the University of Illinois at Chicago campus. Having learned that my mother was abused as a young girl, I was anxious to make sure women were protected. Also, I was just angry at the way so many men, like my ex, viewed women as inferior beings to men.

Shirley, in her work over the years, had become angry with the way abused women were not believed and dismissed. She was dead set on taking the abusers to court. Most of the women were scared to death of their abusers, and only wanted a safe place to hide, while the authorities were easy on the offenders, rarely keeping them in jail. This disregard for women's rights was common.

I met Shirley at the building which had been a Skid Row hotel before the area had started to change for the better. Though it was completely renovated with some of my money before the divorce, it still felt cold and sterile. Clean, comfortable, concrete rooms with adequate furnishings and equipment, but no pizzazz to cheer up the occupants. I needed to find David to fix it up.

Shirley was showing me the place when out of an office door we bumped into a pleasant-looking man. He was about five feet, nine or ten inches tall with sandy brown disheveled hair, and a patterned shirt sticking half out of his tan corduroy pants. His large brown eyes emitted compassion. Shirley stopped.

"Gary, I would like you to meet Sherrie," Shirley said. "She is a lawyer who will be working part-time. I am starting her with the depositions for Angela and Marie. I would appreciate if you would help her get started."

She turned to me and said, "Gary Bernstein, our staff psychologist."

He gave me a warm smile and a sturdy handshake.

"Welcome. When would you be starting?"

"In three weeks, after I move into our new home." I really wanted more time after the move, but this job would keep me from applying at law firms which were almost all run by males.

I couldn't handle the rejections: "You haven't worked in twelve years." Or worse, the recognitions: "Aren't you Ronald Greenspan's wife?" And having to answer irritating questions with, "Oh yes, my kids' last name has been shortened to sound less Jewish. I am going with my maiden name, Sherrie Paul, which truthfully was shortened at Ellis Island when Pa came over from Poland in 1900."

On my way home, I felt excited about starting work with Gary. He seemed very pleasant. Also, my mind was swirling with ideas to fix up the shelter. When I reached home, my first call went to Aunt Sarah.

The first few minutes of our conversation consisted of listening to her *kvetch*. As she aged, she complained more and more. I glanced at the kitchen clock; my kids would be bouncing through the door soon.

"So sorry to hear how bad your arthritis has become, but I need to get ahold of David," I told Aunt Sarah. "The number I have is no longer in service. I have two jobs for him, one at my new house, and one at work."

"David," she replied. "David was such a good son before he went to California. Now he forgot his mother. He hasn't called me in over three weeks. I don't know where to find him."

"That doesn't sound like David," I said. "Do you know the name of the young man he was living with?"

"The boy died, and David said he was coming home, and then I don't hear from him," Aunt Sarah said. "Sherrie, find him for me."

I hung up, disturbed. I was so busy with my problems that I hardly kept up with anyone. There was something wrong.

Lizzie was no help, either. "There is nothing wrong," she asserted. "David has disappeared before. Aunt Sarah creates her own *tsuris*."

I let it go, but it bothered me. He normally would have checked in and congratulated me over the divorce. David, like the rest of my family, hated Ronnie because Ronnie tried to isolate me from the family.

The move had been hectic. I felt like a traffic cop directing the movers where to put the boxes. Both Lizzie and Babs were my helpers. Jim spent the time throwing basketballs into the new basket above the garage. Even though I had hired a cleaning service, I still felt the need to do some extra work. We had very little furniture as I left everything with Ronnie. I had hated the masculine luxury hotel look Ronnie and his designer had put together.

Lizzie looked around after the moving truck left. With knitted eyebrows, she asked, "Where is the marble coffee table, the Lalique vases, the Persian rug from your bedroom, and your leather sofa? I loved those things, and they cost a fortune."

"I told you, I didn't take any of that decorator stuff," I answered. "I took the majolica."

Lizzie took a deep breath, shook her head, and said, "The majolica was from our grandmother! You should have fought for more money and half of everything. He treated you like shit and had all those girl-friends!"

I walked away from her, went to my purse and took out a cigarette, lit it, and stared out the windows through the pale green kitchen blinds.

We needed to go shopping for new furniture and accessories to make our house a home. I especially wanted to get rid of the dark green and silver foil paper in the kitchen.

Hopefully, David would show up and help. He could get us into the Merchandise Mart. I wished he would settle down and design instead of chasing boyfriends and causes.

The rooms in our new home were much smaller than those in the house on the lake, but they were engaging with their many built-ins, like the walk-in closet that housed eighteen built-in wooden shelves and the living room's built-in bookshelves surrounding a large twenty-five inch television. The parquet floors were beautiful, but I would have preferred carpet, which needed less upkeep. Already the wood was scuffed from the movers. I needed Etta our family building cleaning lady to do her cleaning magic.

Lizzie and I were busy unpacking the boxes with my kitchen equip-ment when Jim, dressed in his husky blue jeans and Walter Payton No. 34 shirt, appeared in the room's doorway. He was pouting, lips over each other, eyes narrowed. Any minute I thought he would be throwing something. I approached him and asked, "Honey, what's wrong?"

"Why do I have to share a bathroom with Babs? We had our own bathrooms at our other house."

Lizzie burst out laughing. "Boy, are you spoiled! When Sherrie and I lived in the family building, we had to share a bathroom with four or more people!"

Jim gave us a hostile look. "Why did we have to leave our home and Dad? I hate it here!"

Hands on hips, lips in a pout, Lizzie turned towards Jim and shot back, "Your father was a son of a bitch abuser and womanizer, and . . ."

I put my hand on her to shut her up. Jim fled out of the room and out the door.

I ran after him, catching up halfway down the block. I tried to hug him, but he backed off.

"Jim, honey, I'm sorry, but your dad didn't want to stay with me," I explained. "He doesn't love me anymore, but he still loves you and your sister. Things will work out. Give it a chance. It's not easy for Babs or me either."

How could I tell a ten-year-old what it means for your husband to have girlfriends, for him to be intimate with someone else? To know that you were never good enough for him from not knowing what fork to use at a formal dinner party to what moves to make in bed to excite him?

"Why can't I live with Dad?" he asked, fists clenched in rage, tears rolling down his cheeks.

He wouldn't let me near him, but he stopped running away from me. He stood still, glaring at me.

I wanted to scream. Instead, I calmly said, "Children belong with their mother. The courts understand that. Also, your father travels all over the world for business and wouldn't be able to take care of you."

He calmed down and walked back with me, but he wouldn't say another word or let me touch him. He had inherited his father's good looks--long skinny legs, straight perfect nose, cute dimples, and Ronnie's stubborn, unyielding personality. I either coddled him or scolded him. I needed to seek help.

"We are stopping the unpacking and ordering a pizza. What kind do you want?" I asked as we neared the house.

"I don't care," he answered as he slowly went upstairs and made his way to his room and locked the door.

Back in the kitchen, I sat down, lit a cigarette from my pack, and took a deep puff.

Lizzie sat down next to me, reached out and put her hand on mine, and said, "Sherrie, he is only ten. He will come around once he gets used to the new neighborhood and school. And if he doesn't, there is always therapy. Of course, you will never tell the family about therapy. You know my daughter Chava is going? She is having trouble with bullying from the girls in her high school. My mother doesn't know."

I thought about the aunts and outside therapy. They believed problems should be solved within the family only. Lizzie surprised me.

"Funny, Jim was the one always fighting with his dad, while Babs ran and hid," I recalled. "Now Jim is miserable without Ronnie, and Babs is thrilled." I shook my head and took another puff of my cigarette before stubbing it out, saying, "Liz, you know the neighborhood, please order us a cheese pizza, and whatever else you want."

I called Babs. "We are ordering a pizza, do you want anything else?"

"Yes, a beef sandwich too," she yelled back.

Babs got Jim to join us for pizza, though she couldn't get him to loosen up. We let Lizzie go home to her family, and I suggested we three watch a movie on TV. We found a tape of *Sleeper,* an old Woody Allen movie. It gave us a chance to laugh. When Babs and Jim went to bed, I stayed up until after three a.m. organizing the kitchen. I believed the other rooms could wait, but the kitchen had to function.

I undressed, brushed my teeth, and thought about a shower, but put it off until the morning. I was just too beat. I looked at my empty ring finger with its invisible band around it. Then I lay down on my big, lonely bed and softly cried into the pillow. The big box of Kleenex on my bed stand came in handy.

Chapter Twenty-Seven

The first two weeks passed with unpacking, cleaning, painting, shopping in new stores for groceries, registering the kids in a new school, and becoming acquainted with a few neighbors. Lizzie had all kinds of groups and temple committees to line me up with, but I put her off for a while.

Aunt Tillie decided she was our personal cook.

Jim and Babs became accustomed to raiding her bags as they ran through the front door after school.

"Aunt Tillie, where are my cherries in the snow cookies?" Jim asked, searching through her bags.

I smiled at Lizzie, who was her chauffeur, and said, "I feel like I'm back in the family building."

"Yes, you were gone for twelve years," Lizzie said. "I never left, just moved it to another location. You've given my mom new life. She has been lost since my dad died."

I smiled as I thought of her dad with his continuous cigar. "Lizzie, we are losing too many of the older generation, Pa, my mom, your dad, Uncle Izzy, and even Aunt Barbra. We are getting old and moving up the pyramid too fast. Both breast cancer and heart trouble run in the family. We should get checked."

I felt guilty. Ronnie made so many demands on me to become the ideal upper-class woman he wanted that I had neglected my real family. Oh, I had done the right things, funeral, shiva, donations, etc. Now I am back, and my children will reap the benefits of my close, loving family.

* * *

Wild sirens blasted through the kitchen, and I wasn't sure where to go first, the burnt toast, the sputtering eggs, or the alarm. Babs jumped up from the kitchen table and yanked the toast out of the toaster while I turned off the stove. Neither one of us knew what to do to turn off the alarm. I had visions of the fire-department showing up.

Jim came to the rescue. He stood up on the kitchen stool and took the batteries out of the alarm.

I sat down on a chair and held my head in my arms.

My twelve-year-old daughter patted me with a reassuring gesture and said, "Mom, don't worry, you won't get fired on your first day back to work."

Jim wasn't very optimistic. He said, "She will if she burns down the clinic like she tried to do here today." He coughed from the burned scent that lingered in the air even after Babs opened the kitchen windows.

I started to laugh. My kids were taking care of me.

Before their carpool came, I was able to make sure that both kids got an unburnt breakfast of cereal and muffins.

Babs was right. I was a nervous wreck over starting back to work. My sleep was interrupted several times by the steady rain, and my fear. After showering, I stood in front of my closet, picking out an outfit to wear. It was spring, which meant one minute it was cold, the next hot or rainy. One outfit was too fancy, another too casual, and another too sexy. I finally settled on a pale blue, three-piece, knit pantsuit and medium-high heels. My makeup was done in fifteen minutes at a tenth of the cost, instead of the forty-minute procedure I was required to use for those society affairs with Ronnie: False eyelashes, heavy eyeliner, drawn-on eyebrows, heavy cake makeup . . . no more for me, nor would

I go back to the exercise classes and diets I participated in just to be his ideal wife, the one who looked like she just walked out of *Vogue* Magazine; my makeup now was simple, just foundation to smooth out my tan complexion, a small dusting of blush, and my favorite pink lipstick. I could use a makeup mirror as my eyesight was getting worse. Maybe I just needed cheaters.

It took a good hour to get to the West Side. Off and on I turned the radio from news to music and back again. Neither calmed me down. My new, blue, middle-class Oldsmobile replaced the Mercedes I had inherited from the divorce. A good idea, considering where I was working, and a used car would have been even better, I thought as I watched a gathering of teenagers on the corner near the parking lot. It was still a rough neighborhood.

I walked into the shelter, still feeling the back-to-work jitters. It was a little over twelve years since I'd worked as a lawyer. I wasn't sure I remembered anything.

The moment Gary greeted me, my tension eased, and I felt comfortable. He offered me his hand and a wide-open, friendly smile. His Mr. Rogers cardigan sweater and casual, slightly ruffled, sandy brown hair also helped put me at ease.

"Sherrie, we are so happy to have you here," he said, "God, this place needs help. Shirley wants you to do two testimonies today, but I think we can begin tomorrow. You better read the case histories before you start. I know everything is new, and I am here to help."

He walked me into a small, sparse room occupied by one of those old wooden teacher's desks, a swivel chair, and some bookshelves. The one small narrow window offered very little light.

"This is the best I can do for now," Gary said. "Feel free to lighten up the room. It needs a woman's touch."

My eyes gravitated to the center of the desk, where a single rose sat in a small glass vase. I picked it up and turned towards Gary.

"To welcome you," he said as his face turned a shade of red.

"Thank you," I answered as I watched him leave the room. He was shorter and thinner than Ronnie. His brown cardigan sweater gave him an academic look. His sandy-colored hair was sparse, and his black-rimmed glasses made me think of Woody Allen, but there was something about him that was genuine and sweet. I guessed he was in his middle-to-late forties.

The office was dark and gloomy, and the reports were terrifying. Two women had been burned and beaten by their spouses. I looked for an ashtray. None was around, so I had to use a paper cup for my ashes. Luckily, I didn't burn down the place. I had planned to read up on abused women, but with the divorce and the move, the books were sitting unopened on my nightstand. I now knew why Shirley asked me to work with abused victims; she must have silently laughed when I, in my designer clothes and beautiful house, complained about Ronnie abusing the kids and me. Yes, there was emotional abuse, but nothing like this. I definitely needed to explore emotional and physical abuse further.

"How's it going?" Gary asked as he handed me a cup of coffee and a chocolate donut.

I jumped at his voice and he nearly dropped the coffee cup. I was so involved in the file that I was thrown off guard.

"I am horrified at the abuse. Cigarette burns on these women, and one had a broken nose, the other broken ribs, and both were raped by their husbands. Why did they *stay* with them?"

Gary hesitated before answering. He looked somber as he handed me my coffee. "They were afraid to leave, Sherrie, they had nowhere to go," Gary explained. "The first shelter for abused women opened in

St. Paul in 1974, only eight years ago, and laws protecting abused women have only started to appear. I thought you were better informed. I'll give you some up-to-date material to take home tonight. You can meet with Angie in a few days and write up the testimony then. Why don't we walk around the shelter and get you acquainted with it?"

I was surprised when our walk was strictly for a facility tour. "Here are the sleeping rooms, here is the exercise room, the offices, the cafeteria, where the pool used to be," Gary said as we moved from room to room.

"Gary, why didn't you introduce me to anyone?" I asked when we ended back in his office.

"Frankly, you're not ready," he explained, "and the women aren't, either. Just a tip," Gary added, "when you come back tomorrow, wear something more casual. And get rid of those *enormous* diamond studs, and read the info I've given you."

I became very defensive, especially after the pleasant morning we shared.

"I don't like your tone. If we are going to work together, you need to remember that I am a *lawyer*, not someone off the street, happy to get any job."

I wasn't going to be hit by his sense of male empowerment. I wondered, were they all intimidated by working women?

He looked directly at me and said, "I'm sorry, Sherrie. It's just that these women are so vulnerable and fearful. I need them to trust you. I didn't mean to talk against you."

We parted, me on my way home to greet my kids, he back to his office.

Even though I left early enough to miss most traffic, I still made it to the garage door only a few minutes before Babs and Jim burst through the front door.

"Mom! How did your new job go?" Babs yelled as she fell into my arms.

"I'm not sure," I answered. "How was your day?"

Babs began a whole dissertation on her day while Jim dismissed us and went up to his room.

It was another pizza night, so when Lizzie called and asked if Aunt Tillie could come tomorrow, I gave a sigh of relief. We would have homemade food for three days.

That night, I did my homework, reading all the information Gary gave me, even though it kept me up past midnight noshing on choco-late-covered raisins and cups of coffee.

Awake at 6:30 a.m., with the sun peeking through the windows, I hurried with my shower and morning routine to provide breakfast for my children before they had to leave for school and me for my job. I toyed with the idea of wearing a miniskirt to aggravate Gary, but I opted for black pants, a button-down shirt, and flat shoes even though it was as hot as hell.

I left early enough to make it to work before 9:00 a.m. Young boys and girls jumped and splashed around an open fire hydrant, while teen-agers in black jackets stood on the corner, smoking and assessing me and my car. It made me realize where I was working, and I made sure my car was locked. As I walked into the shelter, I thought maybe I was overreacting because of the changes in South Shore, or because I've become a north suburbanite and xenophobic.

Today wasn't as comfortable at the shelter as it was yesterday. Gary was all business from the minute I walked into the office. He never even asked what was in the cardboard box I carried.

"Shirley tells me that you prefer to stay in the background of a case because of your ex," he said as he removed his dark-rimmed glasses and cleaned them with a silk cloth. "She admires your legal writing skills, and that is how we should use you. We are starting with the two cases I gave you to read about. One today and one tomorrow. They both have distinct dynamics. Do you have any questions?"

I smiled, shook my head, "no," even though I had many questions, among them, after twelve years, could I still write, and was I slack in keeping up with the times as far as new laws and rules, and what did Shirley really tell him?

Chapter Twenty-Eight

The shelter was a remodeled one-bedroom efficiency motel that needed a lot of work. Most rooms had a small kitchen area with stove top only and a miniature white refrigerator, and a small kitchen table and one kitchen chair. The small, narrow closets held a folding ironing board on its side with an iron on one of its two shelves. The beds each had a homely but clean, polyester blue and green bedspread. A light wood-colored dresser held a small black and white television, leaving no room for anything else. The shower curtains in the bathrooms had seen better days. It sure wasn't a place to cheer anyone up.

We knocked on Door 27. The door opened, and a buxom black woman in a housedress and sandals appeared.

"Hi, Angie, this is Sherrie," Gary said. "She is working with Shirley."

Before Gary could finish, Angie said, "Forget it. I ain't going through with it. He'll kill me." She turned around and walked away from him towards the bedroom, avoiding the small kitchen area.

I noticed that she said this without much emotion, almost like it was a given, like she expected to get no help.

Gary followed her. "Angie, that is why you are here. We are protecting you. Tyrone can't come here. We even have a policeman on duty all the time."

Through the open bedroom door, we heard her bitter laugh as she said, "Policemen, they don't give a *shit* about women. They don't take us seriously, especially us black women. *Three times* I called the police, and they done *nothing*. Finally, when I ended up almost dying, they did something."

I watched this interchange silently from afar until Gary turned towards me.

I came forward towards the bedroom door and said, "Angie, I'm a lawyer working with Shirley to make sure that society takes abused women seriously. We've been working for women's rights for the last twenty years."

Angie was seated on the edge of the bed upon the green and blue flowered bedspread, the only nice thing in the room. She shook her head and replied, "Talk so I can understand you. I just want you to keep Tyrone from beating me and finally killing me. I'm not into rights and stuff."

I looked around, thinking *everything is clean but drab and depressing.* The only chair in the room was by a small light wood table. I pulled it over by Angie and sat down, facing her.

"We will try our best to put him in jail and protect you," I responded. "If you leave here now, he will find you and hurt you, and we won't be able to protect you."

She eyed me carefully and responded, "I'll talk to you, but I ain't signing nothing right away. You have to put him in jail for more than a few days. He's been away for weeks and let out before."

"Fair enough," I said as I took out a legal pad of paper. "Let's sit here," I added as I pulled my chair into the kitchen near the table. Gary found a folding chair and sat with us.

"Before we start, can we get you something to drink?" I asked.

She smiled wickedly. "Honey, you ain't got what I really need here," she said and turned to Gary. "A Coke will do now," Angie said, settling into the one kitchen chair.

Her story was what we all, at the time, associated abuse with: unemployment and drug-and alcohol-abusing. Less than one percent of ghetto abusers served more than a night in jail. After years of Angie's broken bones and bloodied body parts, Tyrone finally shot her. Amazing that she was still living. Shirley wanted to prosecute him on the disregarded abuse that ended in a gunshot, not just the gun charge. Shirley had said that Angie being discriminated against by the powers that be was at the bottom of this. She was a black woman and, therefore, her abuse wasn't taken seriously.

I wanted to ask Angie why she stayed with him, but I didn't.

Gary brought in a Coke with ice for Angie, a black coffee for me, plus those delicious donuts he had yesterday.

I took a bite of one of the chocolate-glazed donuts. After savoring it throughout my mouth, I turned to him and asked, "Where do you get these out-of-this-world donuts?"

Although Gary had found a chair, he stayed standing with a coffee cup in his hand.

"On the way to work, there is this donut shop in Roseland that has the best homemade donuts you'll ever eat," he replied.

Angie started to laugh and said, "I know where you mean. Old Fashioned Donuts. I used to live in Roseland. They sure are good." Angie helped herself to one of the donuts, savoring the flavor.

I had assumed that Gary was a North Sider.

"Where do you live, Gary?" I asked, putting my coffee cup down on the kitchen table. I made a note on my legal pad to find a larger table and some extra chairs for the kitchen area. How could anyone do a proper interview without a decent table with chairs?

"I grew up in South Shore, Now I live in Homewood."

"What a small world. I grew up in South Shore on 68th and Merrill. Went to Hyde Park High."

"I was across the tracks and went to South Shore High," Gary said. "We will have to explore our common roots one day."

Angie relaxed her posture, smiled, and said, "Here I thought you were some rich lady from Chicago, using me. My cousin lives in South Shore. I'm in Englewood now. You were smart to get out. Tyrone wasn't a bad person until he got hooked up with the gangs that took over the South Side."

I felt sorry for her. She wasn't a bad person either, just stuck in a bad place. What happened to my beloved South Side of Chicago?

Gary excused himself, saying, "I have a therapy appointment. This was good getting to know each of you. I guess we have a lot in common." When he left, Angie and I continued talking, mainly about South Shore. I felt that I had gained Angie's trust. Now I would have to figure out how to help her.

The early morning tension eased. Back in the office, Gary smiled as he watched me empty my cardboard box onto my desk: digital clock, box of tissues, small desk lamp, pen holder, my own coffee mug, pens, books, pads of legal paper, my old college typewriter, window curtains, Windex, paper towels, a picture of Jim and Babs, and my nameplate that read, *Sherrie Paul, Esq.*

"I guess you are staying," Gary said as he left for his sparse office across the way, furnished with only bookshelves, a swivel chair, and a desk. Before entering his office, he looked back and said, "I like those big silver loop earrings, and so does Angie."

"Costume jewelry," I answered with a smile.

I glanced at my watch. The time was 3:10 p.m. I figured I'd better go if I wanted to stop at the John Marshall Law School library. Gathering my coat, umbrella, and files, I stubbed out my cigarette, tidied my desk, and left. Gary was nowhere around, so I just shut the door.

Knowing that Aunt Tillie would be with Jim and Babs, I spent an hour at John Marshall, my alma mater, to look up modern laws and cases on abused women. Not in a hurry to get home, I stopped in the local grocery to pick up some needed supplies. Yawning as I pushed the cart around the store, dropping items, as very little sleep was catching up with me, I realized I wasn't used to working and taking care of kids and a house. Ten years back when we women were struggling to get the right to work in a man's world, did we realize we would still have the job of taking care of the home and kids?

The spring sky was setting into a bright orange ball as I pulled into the garage. A whiff of challah baking produced a lick of my lips and a smile on my face. I could picture Aunt Tillie showing Jim and Babs how to braid the dough. I wondered what kind of grandmother my mother would have been. It was hard to picture her as a grandmother, as she died so young.

Besides challah, my kids and Lizzie's kids had a Jewish cooking lesson from Lizzie's kids' grandmother. "Mom, come try the chicken soup and matzo balls," Babs said. "We made it with Aunt Tillie!" Just as I sat down to eat, Lizzie appeared through the door. She and I sampled the soup and challah. We started to laugh as we reminisced about our youth in the family building. It was great that Aunt Tillie was teaching our children about Jewish traditions.

"Sherrie was good, she listened, like you, Babs," Aunt Tillie said, "My Lizzie, always with the questions." Aunt Tillie waved her hands and shook her head while she piled our plates with roast chicken and potatoes, saying the traditional, *"Es, es (eat, eat)."*

Lizzie stood up. "Mom, kids, we have to go. You have school tomorrow, and we have to drive Grandma home."

Aunt Tillie shook her head, waved her hand, and said, "Lizzie, let them finish eating, and the dishes. We can't leave Sherrie to clean up!"

Babs got up and walked over to Aunt Tillie, and said, "I will help Mom. Go home. Thank you for the lessons and the great food."

Aunt Tillie gave her a pinch and a hug. "She is a *mensch*."

Lizzie rolled her eyes at me while she tried to shuffle everyone out of the house. Her son and daughter helped pack up Aunt Tillie while Babs started to clear the table.

Before I could say goodbye, the phone rang.

Surprise hit me when I heard Ronnie's strong, demanding voice on the phone. He asked for the children this weekend. Since he had already canceled two of his appointments with the children, I almost forgot that he had the right to take them, so I had to agree. Jim was thrilled, and Babs tried hard to stay home, but I made her go. When he picked them up Friday afternoon, I expected Ronnie to at least come in and look at my new house, but he sent his driver to get Babs and Jim. I watched them leave. I was disappointed that he did not come in; I hadn't seen him in months. We ran in different circles.

Lizzie tried to fetch me for an outing, but I opted to stay in and finish my unpacking and my reading for my new job. After opening one of the boxes, my hand slid over the large, leather Gucci briefcase, the one Ronnie had given me when I graduated from law school. Inside were memories of our courtship. I reread the silly contracts we had made for each other and looked at the pictures of happier days. Grief, instead of the usual anger, swept through me. I left everything in disarray, climbed up the stairs, and fell into my empty bed. The only good thing I could think of was that I wouldn't have to endure another night of perpetual snoring. Yeah, the almighty Ronald Greenspan snored!

Sunday night, both kids came back from their weekend with their dad in good spirits with expensive toys: Babs with jewelry and a child's makeup set, and Jim with a Mattel Atari, which was one of the new digital games that worked with the TV. Though I was happy to have him busy every day after school, the video game constantly occupied the family room TV, which was the only one we had in this house.

"Mom, can Kenny and Danny come over after school to play Atari?" Jim asked.

"Yes, of course," I said, and I was thrilled. These were the first friends Jim brought home since we moved, and it seemed to be the first time since the divorce that he was happy. I bought a second television for the bedroom so Babs and I had something to watch. I even forgave Ronnie and Jim when Jim told me, "Dad said you don't have to work because he gives you a lot of money for us."

I didn't answer him. I remembered that Ronnie and I had promised not to talk against each other with our children. I would have to speak to him about it.

I thought about our divorce proceedings. I hated fighting with Ronnie, so per usual, I gave in, instead of letting the negotiations drag on forever. So now, I genuinely needed to work to keep our lifestyle and to accumulate some savings for my children's and my future. But most of all, I was a female lawyer, a feminist who wanted more than cleaning and cooking. I had a mind I wanted to use. The only problem was being there for the children I dearly loved. I wanted to work, and I needed to be there for them. Childcare still wasn't available free or at an affordable price.

I didn't sleep well that night. Ronnie, the divorce, the kids, and my future were on my mind. I was still tired in the morning, but I had to hustle. Gary and Shirley had me scheduled with a new client, one they were treading carefully with. In fact, she was the only one I made an appointment with, and the only one housed in the shelter's one large suite. I decided to pay more attention to my makeup and clothes. I picked out a tan knit instead of the leisure suits I've been wearing and added a little eye makeup to my usual routine. I left the house early enough to be there on time.

Charlene Wexler

I knocked on the door before entering Marie Wilson's suite. I had read that she was in the process of divorcing a wealthy, significant Chicago real estate firm owner who had abused her. It would be a different interview from the one with Angie, whose case I was still working on.

Marie yelled from the bathroom, "Come in. I'll only be a few minutes."

The so-called suite was a disaster too. A separate bedroom with a window treatment was the difference. I needed to talk to Shirley. These women needed to be in a place that gives them some cheer and hope.

When Marie walked out of the bathroom, we stopped cold and stared at each other. Unprofessionally, I said, "Jesus, I hardly thought that you would be the same Marie Wilson I knew."

She nodded her head, put up both hands in a surrender motion, and said, "Yes, I am the same woman who was on the museum board with you. The rich, strong, snobby Daniel Wilson's second wife. It was all a sham. Even my name, which is really Mary. Why are you here? Weren't you married to that high class, good-looking lawyer?"

I smiled and shrugged my shoulders. "I, too, was a fake. I lived a life that was a sham, too. I am now divorced for six months and putting a new life together. I'm here to help you get where I am. Only, I don't understand why you are here in this cold sterile place. I remember being in your fantastic home in Lake Forest. Why, you had original paintings on your walls, Dom Perignon, Moet, Hennessy, champagne, and never mixed nuts, just all pecans."

She started to half cry and half laugh and said, "Sherrie, can you get me something real to drink?" She tossed her Coke into the sink.

I called the restaurant down the street and convinced them to send us some cheese and crackers and some good white wine, which I sipped, and she gulped. We sat down by the table in the small kitchen area of the suite. I took out my tape recorder.

"Marie, do I have permission to record you?" I asked. "It will be used professionally by your lawyers."

"Yes, you have my permission to record me," she said as she began her story. "First, I'm here in hiding under another name because I want to expose Dan for the abuser and cheater he is, and take him to the cleaners, and he understands it and has threatened to have me killed. He is busy checking for me at major hotels and friends' houses." She stopped talking and sipped her wine. I noticed that though her arms and fingers were perfectly manicured they were without any of the diamonds I remembered.

Where was my safe family building? What was I getting into—her husband threatened to kill her! I excused myself, saying, "I need to use the bathroom."

In the bathroom, I wiped my eyes with Kleenex, took a deep breath, and centered myself enough to go back and professionally listen to Marie.

Her story surprised me at every level. I sat and listened in awe. To me she was still the beautifully dressed, tall, thin snob with the chilly voice I had encountered at the Museum of Science and Industry dinners for major donors. Then I thought about my mother. Abuse could happen to anyone. Marie continued with her story, and I continued to listen without judgment.

"Twenty-three years ago, Daniel took me out of a line of Las Vegas showgirls and made me into the wife his family and the world expected," Marie explained. "His mother never really bought the story that I, too, came from an equally prominent European family, but she was widowed, and I believe equally afraid of him. He hired people to train me in the social arts, how to stand properly, what fork to use at a formal dinner, the proper clothes to wear. I was his Eliza Doolittle from

My Fair Lady. I was adorned with jewelry, designer clothes, and trips as my reward.

She stopped talking and poured herself more wine. She looked out the window and pressed her lips together.

"If you want to do this another day, I understand."

Marie looked at me, half smiled, and said, "I need to get this done, and with you, it is easier. She continued. "In exchange, I was physically, verbally, and emotionally abused. He controlled my every move, isolating me from everyone. If he decided I did something he didn't like, I was beaten. Sex became akin to rape. You probably believed that I was a snob who was too good to talk to you."

She stopped talking, rolled up the blouse sleeve on her left arm, and said, "When you are not allowed to go to the hospital, scars heal slower."

I viewed a thick, bulky scar from her shoulder to the inside of her elbow.

She ran her fingers across the scar. "This one bled uncontrollably," Marie said. "He locked me in my room even though I really needed stitches. First, I wrapped it in toilet paper, finally the towel, even when I knew I would be punished for ruining the towel."

"Marie, truly, I'm blown away by this," I said in astonishment. "When we were on the museum committee together, I thought you were a beautiful, arrogant, wealthy young woman, and there was no way I could become part of your group."

I thought I might be sick from her testimony, which wouldn't be very professional. I got up and turned towards the window, took a deep breath, and opened the shade. "We could use some sunshine in here," I said. This faded gray concrete room with its dull lighting was awful, I thought, while I tried to concentrate on something other than her testimony.

Marie laughed and said, "Sunshine won't help. This place needs a lot, but it makes a good hiding place for me. Should I continue? It feels good to finally tell my whole story. I feel like you understand since we knew each other in our fake worlds."

She drank more wine while I nibbled on the crackers.

"I was scared to death to do anything that would anger him," Marie recounted. "Zero was put in my name, so I am broke, but my one ace in the hole is I know about some of his illegal real estate deals and have made copies of the papers with his signature on them. We didn't have children because I wouldn't bring them into my miserable world. Oh, and that luxurious villa was full of paid help who reported on my every move, and all the phones were tapped, and no mail came to my beautiful prison," Marie concluded.

"Amazing how people are never what you think," I responded. "I thought you and Daniel were very arrogant and possibly anti-Semitic. I hated the snobbish attitude of everyone on the board. I came from a happy, noisy, Jewish middle-class family. Shirley and I will protect you and do our best for you," I said with conviction.

Fear permeated the room. I shivered as I now, too, gulped the white wine. The poor emaciated woman was wasting away from her ordeal. Besides therapy with Gary, we needed to liven up this place, maybe even get a hairdresser or makeup lady to give the women something to look forward to, to feel better about themselves. I needed to go back to listening to her story instead of designing the shelter. It just was so hard for me to believe this horror happened to someone I knew.

After another hour of specifics, I left in disbelief; that is, until I was alone in my office and thought about how controlling my husband, Ronnie, had been and how right David had been when he told me I had no street smarts. I believed and trusted everyone and found an excuse for their bad behavior. David tried to tell me that the world was different from my safe family building, but I didn't want to believe him. I reached over and locked my passenger car door.

The confession from Marie that she was struck across the face and slammed into a wall shocked me, but the one in which she said, "I was made to feel worthless and consequently deserving of the punishment," I could identify with. "Worthless" was a word Ronnie used on me and our children when I was married to him; thus, I kept trying to please him. Physical abuse was never part of my life, but I now realized it could happen.

I knocked on Gary's office door. "What is on your mind, Sherrie?" he asked.

"Gary, I've talked to Angie and Marie as their lawyer," I said. "You are the shelter therapist. What would you say is the difference in their cases, and how are you helping them? I'm floored by their stories." I leaned against his door as I didn't want to come in, because it was after five already.

"Sherrie, you've opened up hours of conversation. The main difference is Angie is not ashamed to tell her story because it is a common one in her world, but it is harder for her to get away. She has no money and nowhere to hide. Marie had extreme abuse for someone in her position, but she had money and people around she could get help from. Affluent people that are abused fear the loss of esteem, and try to justify and hide the abuse."

"Thanks, Gary, It's late, but I would like to discuss this further on another day. Shirley put me into a job I'm not familiar with."

I left his office thinking about how I never admitted to anyone but Lizzie that I was emotionally abused, and my mother never told me anything about her own abuse. I gathered my coat and briefcase from my office and headed to my car, still shook up over my interview with Marie.

The sense of fear and anxiety I lived with Ronnie was gone now; actually, *almost* gone. I was busier but calmer; even my breathing was better. I was now becoming afraid that work at the shelter may re-open things in my mind.

Chapter Twenty-Nine

Gary left an electric typewriter in my office with a note that said, "No need to schlep your typewriter up and back." It was nice of him, but I had never used an electric typewriter, and I was lost. I worked right through lunch, trying to figure it out. I was a fast, accurate typist on my old manual. On this one, I made mistakes.

"Mrs. Paul, you've missed lunch," said Jean, a short, plump, gray-haired woman probably in her sixties—the shelter's house mother. "The cafeteria is closed already. Here, I've brought you some soup."

I stopped to sip the hot chicken noodle soup and took some bites from the Italian bread. "Jean, you are a godsend," I said. "This typewriter has been driving me crazy, and I've lost sense of time."

"Mrs. Paul, just ask Dr. Bernstein for help," Jean said. "He is the sweetest, most patient man I've ever known. All the women love him." Her face lit up while talking about him.

When she left, I went back to trying to type on the electric typewriter. I wasn't going to look like an idiot in front of Dr. Bernstein. If worse came to worse, I would take it home and ask Lizzie or my kids for help. So far, my take on Dr. Bernstein was still in the voting booth. One day he was friendly and helpful, and the next, all business. Oh, well. No matter how hard we women tried, it was still a man's world. I needed Ronnie's help in getting my own credit, for a lower-priced mortgage, and to get a bank credit card. Even though the Equal Credit Opportunity Act was signed in 1974, women still had a hard time getting credit in their names, especially credit at a low rate. I was paying twelve percent on my mortgage.

I put everything away, including my two typewriters, gathered my files, and closed my office. On my way home, I stopped at Kentucky

Fried Chicken. I needed to start cooking again. This wasn't fair to my kids. That night Jim asked, "Why don't you go on any of the field trips with my class or do any baking for the carnivals?"

Yes, Shirley and I, and the other women we worked with, had been telling women they could have it all—a career *and* motherhood. Could we, without killing ourselves?

On a cold and snowy Sunday morning in February, Lizzie came to pick up Babs and Jim for the Temple's Purim party.

While my kids were pulling on their boots and heavy winter coats, Lizzie stood, feet apart, mouth pouted.

I knew what was wrong without her saying a word. We grew up together and could read each other.

"OK, Lizzie, I'll meet you Friday morning," She had been bugging me for weeks to join the temple, and I kept putting it off.

The temple was a massive, gray stone building located barely a mile away from our home. The interior decor was modern, even though the temple was conservative. Every wall had bright, shiny chrome to match the stainless steel kitchens now in vogue—that is, until we entered the main prayer room. Biblical scenes on the stunning floor-to-ceiling stained glass windows in the main sanctuary glowed as the sunlight struck them. The wood-paneled walls gave the room warmth. The bi-mah was traditional, with four very decorative Torahs, which meant it was a wealthy congregation. Torahs were not cheap.

Lizzie's opinion on the children was right: Babs at thirteen and Jim at eleven were almost too old to start Hebrew school at a conservative temple, so it was time to approach the temple personnel. They both had a year of school at the Reform temple in Glencoe. Though the goal was to learn about their heritage, Aunt Tillie had already bribed them with the promise of fancy bar and bat mitzvah parties. Still, Babs decided to go for confirmation instead of a bat mitzvah. It only required Sunday

School. Jim, as a Jewish boy from our family, didn't have a choice. He would go to Hebrew School and be bar mitzvahed at thirteen.

Lizzie, who just about ran the temple, walked into the office with me.

"Sherrie, you will be so happy that you joined," she said. "The women are so nice and friendly, and the rabbi is wonderful."

"Lizzie, I'm working now and cannot become involved in sisterhoods and mah jongg games," I asserted.

She gave me one of Aunt Tillie's head shakes, and I shivered knowing that busy or not, I would be passing through these doors with Lizzie often. I agreed to join their book club because I would be reading books no matter how busy I was. My thoughts went to my so/so friends among Chicago's wealthy and prominent group; not a one had called me since the divorce. I was never comfortable with them, anyway. *They must be too busy going for facials, massages, or under the knife for more facelifts.*

Right after signing the kids up for religious school, Ronnie and I had our first conflict over religion.

His phone call came while the kids were in school and I had a morning off of work. It interrupted my re-reading of my transcript on the Wilson case, which was probably why I answered so defensively.

"Sherrie, my mother is having a big Easter party with many prominent people," Ronnie explained. "I want my children to be there."

I slammed down my coffee cup, spilling some on the Formica table. "Ronnie, this year Easter and Passover are on the same day, and it is my weekend," I replied. "I want them to be at Aunt Tillie's seder."

"They are with your aunt constantly," he replied coolly.

"Not my fault," I countered. "Your mother never asks for her grandchildren." I could swear I heard his eyes narrowing.

"I never before asked for extra time to see them," he argued. "Be reasonable."

Frustrated, I stood up and yelled into the phone, "Extra time!" I explained. "You cancel half the time. I'll think about it and get back to you." I hung up, furious.

Having no mother, I called Aunt Tillie.

"Sherrie, you complain that he cancels a lot," she said. "Let the children go with him early and have them home after sundown for the end of the seder, or for the second seder on Monday." She threw in the second seder to make me feel guilty.

The Passover table was set with Grandma's—"Ma's"—gold Austrian china, and the old worn *Haggadahs*, the books that tell the story of the Exodus, were next to each setting. The matzah plate covered by the embroidered scarf from Poland brought back memories of the family building where we were all together; all conversation quieted as Aunt Tillie struck a match, covered her eyes, and chanted the blessing over the candles.

Afterwards, Yale broke the silence by asking, "Where is everyone?"

"Yale, you never listen to me," Aunt Tillie said. "I told you, Izzy broke his wrist, so he and Dora are staying in Florida, and their kids are going down there, and Sherrie's kids are with their father."

Lizzie, said, "Your sister's family and your cousins Sherrie, Rachel, and Gail are here. Don't we count? Where is your girlfriend?"

Nobody mentioned my dad, who was in a nursing home due to his dementia. He had stayed with Aunt Tillie until things deteriorated. Twice he disappeared, causing a village alert and frantic searches. Poor Dad kept trying to go to his store in South Shore. I went to visit him the day before, hoping he would respond to me, and then I could bring him here for the Seder. He didn't even recognize me, however. "Bess?" he

231

uttered with a quizzical look. So heart-wrenching was this disease. Except for Pa, the men in our family didn't live long. Lizzie and I had been helping our aunts, who were in their late sixties, with finances. The men of their generation took full responsibility of paying bills and investing, leaving their partners clueless.

Chaim, Lizzie's husband, picked up a Haggadah, broke the matzah, and performed the honor of conducting the seder, which we mechanically followed. For years in the spring, Jews celebrated the holiday of Passover, where we remembered being slaves in Egypt, and how Moses liberated us. We ate the matzah to remember when the Jewish people had to bake no-yeast flatbread to leave Egypt in a rush, the horseradish to remember the hardships we endured as slaves, dipping wine into a dish to remember the ten plagues, and praying, singing, drinking wine, and, finally, eating. Jim, who was with his dad, missed doing the four questions—an honor for the youngest in the family.

David was on everyone's mind. No one had heard from him in well over two months. Aunt Sarah was beside herself. Aunt Tillie had exhausted the Jewish pipeline in California and Chicago. Lizzie had probed the Chicago gay community.

There was a rapid-fire conversation.

"Lizzie, have you contacted Barry and Gino?"

"Yes, they haven't heard from him, either."

"What about Jeffery?"

"No, they broke up at least ten years ago."

I said, "Yes, but they stayed friends. Jeffery knows everyone in the gay community. I'll try to find him."

Back home, searching through an old address book, I found the number of David's ex-boyfriend friend Jeffery. Luckily, he answered the phone when I called.

"Jeffery, this is Sherrie Paul, David's cousin," I said. "We haven't heard from him in over a month, which isn't like him. Do you have any idea where he is?"

Jeffery hesitated before saying, "He's at a hospital in Los Angeles."

"What did you say?" I shouted. "He wouldn't be in a hospital without notifying his mother and the family. Was he in an accident, or is he unconscious?"

"I'm sure he didn't want anyone to know that he has AIDS," Jeffery replied.

"What is AIDS?" I asked.

I wasn't happy with his answers. I hung up the phone in disbelief. I didn't want to believe. David had a homosexual disease that could kill him. I never heard of it before. I sat still for a few minutes while I tried to process this information. I would have to contact David, and his doctors, plus all resources and health officials who knew anything about this disease before talking to the family.

Chapter Thirty

I met Shirley for lunch at the Vernon Park Tap, an iconic, family-run, Italian restaurant in business since 1930. It was located on the Near West Side. Most of the customers were lawyers or young medical or dental students, or city politicians. The place was always packed to the point that the smells of perfume and after shave lotion hung in the air. I scanned the menu for something besides a salad and settled on an Italian beef sandwich. Shirley was late. Fidgeting with my files instead of a cigarette didn't help me pass the time. My kids were on my case to stop smoking. Damn those ads about the dangers of smoking!

Twenty-minutes later, Shirley made it to our table after stopping to say hello to half the patrons. I realized she had made quite a name for herself while I was home raising kids. She was single, with out-of-the-house grown children, so her tireless, demanding personality helped her achieve success. Once Shirley took on a project, there was no stopping her. Several years ago, Paula had fully retired to spend time with her family.

Shirley took the files. "Thanks for getting them done so quickly," she told me. "You do understand what is going to happen with Angie. If Angie testifies, Tyrone may get a few months in jail, after which she will go back to him. The courts do nothing for cases from the ghetto community. We are trying to expose the judges who shrug off these cases, but it isn't easy. Maybe we can make some headway."

"It is hard to believe women are still disregarded so in court."

"Sherrie, we weren't granted the right to vote until 1920. Think about how men thought about our intelligence."

"Maybe they are afraid of us taking over," I said while grabbing another garlic roll.

Shirley smirked as she lit another cigarette. "Good thought,"

"Back to Angie. Do you really think Angie will go back to Tyrone?"

"She has no money, no job, and that is the only life she knows," Shirley explained. "We volunteered to relocate her in Michigan, but she won't do it. Now, the Wilson case could be our chance to make the world aware that abuse of women isn't just something done to the poor and uneducated. We have a team on this case. I'll need you to join us. It will require some evening hours and extra time on research."

The waiter came with our food. "So, what do you think of Gary?" she asked in between bites. "He's single."

I squirmed in my seat. "Shirley, I'm only divorced eight months, and at this point, I think I hate all men. I believe Gary isn't sure what to do with me."

"He'll figure it out," she said slyly as she reached for the check.

"What do I owe?"

Shirley shook her head as she took a credit card out of her purse. "Business lunch," she said, matter-of-factly. "By the way, you need to get a credit card in your name. Ruth Ginsburg has paved the way with her win on the Reed v. Reed Supreme Court case, so you should have no trouble getting your own credit card. If you need my help, let me know."

On the way out, I grabbed a handful of mints to satisfy my sweet tooth, because I was aggravated. The Supreme Court case win was making it easier, but I would still have to deal with Ronnie for help to get things into my name. I had no credit on my own. He was avoiding it. What a dumb lawyer I had been during our marriage and divorce. So many things I missed or was just afraid to bring up.

* * *

I went home early, stopping by Sunset Foods to load up on special groceries. For dinner, I made Jim's favorite—chicken parmesan with garlic bread. Today, June 8, was his twelfth birthday. It being a Saturday, he was able to spend the morning with his dad and the evening with Babs and me.

As he swung through the garage door carrying gifts from his dad, he asked "Mom, can I invite one more kid to my party at the batting cages tomorrow?" Jim asked.

"Who is it?"

"Terri's son,"

I saw Babs sink into herself as she followed her brother into the house.

I asked, "Who is Terri?"

"Dad's girlfriend," Jim said.

"I don't think that is a very good idea," I responded. "His girlfriends helped break up our marriage."

"Not what Dad says," Jim argued. "He said it's your fault we are not a family."

My blood boiled. Babs, who glared at Jim, quickly joined the conversation before I exploded. "Mom, why don't you talk to Dad about it? Terri's son probably can't come anyway."

I tried to keep calm. "For sure, I will talk to Dad,"

Early the next morning, after a sleepless night, I called Ronnie. "How could you suggest that your girlfriend's son come near me? And you told . . ."

"Sherrie, calm down," Ronnie-interrupted, "I'm sorry about that. There is something more important we have to talk about. Babs told me that your cousin David is sick from a rare disease that starts with an A, and he is going to stay at your house. I am guessing he has AIDS. I want you to know that if that degenerate homosexual gets near my children, I'll sue you for child custody!"

I slammed down the phone, turned off the lights in my bedroom, and stubbed my toe on the bed frame. I rubbed my toe while I counted to ten before going downstairs to make breakfast for my children. On the way down, I heard both phones ringing. I refused to answer them.

In 1985, very little was known about AIDS (Acquired Immune Deficiency Syndrome) or HIV, as it also was called. It was like something out of the movie *The Andromeda Strain*. We knew it was contagious and it attacked mainly homosexuals and drug addicts. Most patients lived in California and New York. It was met with suspicion, concern, and prejudice by everyone. The virus destroyed the immune system and over eighty percent of the patients died of an infection. No medicine or treatment tried so far made a difference.

After Passover, Lizzie and I made arrangements to fly out to California to see David and find out what was going on with his disease. The news we received there was not good. The doctor told us that David, against all odds, had come through his first infection, but he most likely wouldn't be able to ward off the next one, and at this time there was no cure and little treatment.

Dr. Brenner suggested we take him home to be with family.

"Is it contagious?" we asked. We both had kids.

"As far as we know, only through sex with gay partners or through drug needles, but we still know so little about it," the doctor answered.

Visiting David was an eye opener. His tremendous loss of weight gave him a skeletal look. The red and blue bruises due to his weakened immune system were downright alarming to behold. The only positive thing about his condition was that he had just made it through pneumonia. He couldn't even talk to us. His breathing was still shallow. All we got was a smile across his hollow face, and a weak handhold. In fact, he had only been off the ventilator five days. It would be a little while before he could travel, I believed. Dr. Brenner suggested we transfer him to the Sable/Sheerer AIDS Clinic in Chicago, which was near Cook County Hospital and near the shelter where I worked. I wondered if he could make the trip. I was afraid the good doctor just didn't want another death in his hospital.

Lizzie and I returned home. We had spent the whole plane ride back, crying, reminiscing, and planning what to do. This was a family problem. Yale, who didn't have a family yet, came out to be with David when we left.

I was furious with Ronnie because he was partially right. We weren't sure if it could be transmitted in ways beyond sex and needle use, and I was devastated over the diagnosis. I loved David so. He was my idol, and so young, just two years older than I was. I dreaded telling the family.

I chose a Friday night Shabbat dinner to talk to the family. I waited until the teacups and the strudel were on the table, and everyone was done serving and seated. I received some help from an odd place.

"Everyone here knows that Lizzie and I have been going back and forth to California to visit David while he is recuperating from pneumonia," I began.

Aunt Sarah sat on the end of her chair, bouncing up and back. "When can he come home?" she asked. "I can't even talk to him on the phone."

"*Sha*, let her talk," Aunt Tillie said.

I started my talk with, "Did you hear about Rock Hudson? He just revealed a secret he has hidden for years. That gorgeous movie heart throb is a homosexual, and he has a new fatal disease called AIDS."

Everyone started to murmur about the shock of it.

238

Lizzie said, "Beautiful, sexy Elizabeth Taylor stood by him, with several other actors and actresses when he made this announcement. I don't know much about this AIDS business, but it sounds like he is very sick and could even die."

Aunt Sarah waved her hands in the air, stood up, and said, "Enough with Rock Hudson. Tell me about David. When can he come home?"

All eyes turned towards me. I took a deep breath. My insides churned. This was going to be hard. I remembered when my mother helped David tell the family that he was a homosexual.

"We brought up Rock Hudson because David is gay and also has AIDS," I said.

"What is this AIDS business?" my family asked.

I tried to explain it.

For a short time, no one said a word. Then the crying, praying, and questions came. Unfortunately, I really couldn't answer them positively.

"I don't know if David will make it," I said. "Right now, there is no cure for the disease. He has recovered from pneumonia and is getting better. When he is more robust, we will bring him home. Yale is in California with him now."

"I'm going to my son," Aunt Sarah asserted. "What is this AIDS business? Where did he get it?"

Tillie laid her hand on her sister's shoulder and said, "You aren't well. Lizzie will go back and help Yale bring him home. David is young and healthy. He will be fine."

"From your lips to God's ears," Sarah said in Yiddish.

Lizzie's husband, Chaim, brought her a cup of tea, which she sipped slowly. Nobody wanted Sarah to see David until he gained some weight and looked more like the David we knew and loved.

That night, I conferred with Lizzie, Chaim, and Yale. We formed a plan to get David home. It would require an ambulance plane, and it would not be cheap, but I had some funds that I had hidden for a rainy day, and this was one.

I had taken a week off for David and needed to go back to work. It wasn't comfortable, with David on my mind. The weather was warm and humid, so I made sure the air conditioning was on in the office. Today I needed to talk to a new occupant of the shelter, and I couldn't concentrate enough to do my job.

Up and back, I paced. When I bent down to search through my purse for some aspirin, I became aware that Gary was standing in the doorway, watching me.

I swung around and demanded, "Why are you spying on me?"

"I guess your vacation wasn't that great," he offered.

"My week off was not a vacation," I said. "It is too painful and too private to discuss with you, so leave me alone." I grabbed the file and walked down the hall to my interview.

To make matters worse, my next interview was with a sixteen-year-old girl who had run away from her pimp. Her tight jeans and short top exposing her belly button went with her defiant attitude. A large black-and-blue mark encircled her eye and cheek. Her swollen, bruised lower lip made it difficult for her to talk. After fifteen minutes in which she revealed very little, I realized she was just using us to heal and rest before going back, especially since she defended her pimp and wouldn't tell us his name. Plus, the information she offered about family didn't check out. I couldn't do my job, so I left her room.

I had lunch on one of the wooden benches outside of the cafeteria in the enclosed park. Not in the mood to talk to anyone, I stared out at the sun shining through the full leafed trees. New buds on the spring greenery meant life everywhere but in our family.

Gary sat down next to me. I glared at him.

He put his hand up as to ward off an attack. "Don't get angry," he said. "I know you have a problem today, and I think you should go home. Now, if you want to talk, I am a psychologist."

I burst into tears and said, "My cousin David, my best friend and soul mate, has AIDS and will probably die. I was not on vacation. I was in California with him."

"Wow," he said. He put his arm around me. I rested my head against his shoulder and closed my eyes. It was a comfortable place.

Gary encouraged me to talk, and I did for the next forty minutes. "We grew up together in the family building," I explained. "When we were young, David and I pricked our fingers to make a blood pledge to not tell on each other. Now, he looks like a skeleton with gray skin and cold bony fingers. He used to be gorgeous, tall, and muscular. I accepted him as gay when no one else would. Where did this AIDS come from? A death sentence out of nowhere. He is going to die. It will kill his mother; we've lost so many. Lizzie's husband and my ex don't want David near their kids. What do I tell my children about AIDS and homosexuality? They don't know anything about sex. They loved David."

Gary listened patiently, saying very little: "I'm sorry, Sherrie. Since they know so little about AIDS, anything can happen with your cousin. Sounds like he made it through his first trial." He walked me back to the office. "You didn't touch your lunch," Gary observed. "Let's call it a day and go out and get something decent to eat."

I let him help me gather my things, and I followed him out of the office. I suddenly felt comfortable and protected, and a tingling in my body that I hadn't felt in months. I looked at Gary differently, and he gazed at me with emotional eyes.

We took a cab to Tuscany, an Italian restaurant on Taylor Street. He helped me remove my sweater and get seated. He asked what wine

I wanted, and if I would like an appetizer. He suggested the chicken parmesan but didn't push it. In my world, men ordered for me instead of allowing me to make so many choices. After crying about David some more, our conversation centered on learning about each other instead of about our work.

"Did you really grow up in South Shore?" I asked.

He answered, "I graduated from South Shore High School in 1965."

I touched my chin and thought about his age. "You are a baby," I said. "I graduated Hyde Park in 1961. I'm sure we could spend a day playing Jewish geography. Gary, why did you specialize with abused women?"

He took a bite of the garlic bread while I sipped my white wine.

"Actually, I was working for Cook County Hospital, and I met Shirley," Gary explained. "She convinced me that I wanted to work at her shelter."

Still holding my fork in the air, I burst out laughing and said, "When Shirley wants you, you are hooked."

"What about you? How did you end up working for Shirley?"

I replied flippantly, "Oh, hell, I worked with her and another lawyer who was her first partner back when I graduated from law school. We worked on Roe vs. Wade. She was tough back then, but now she is unreal. Shirley is smart, a maneuverer, and always one step ahead of everyone else. She has a goal to help women by getting new laws passed, not by rallies."

"Wow, you have her figured out," Gary said. "Do you have the same passions and goals as she does?"

"The same goals, but not the passion and time."

"You seem to be someone who is very passionate,"

Our eyes locked. I quickly looked away, and Gary changed the subject.

"Where have you been working recently?" he asked.

I stiffened. "I was married for twelve years, and am divorced ten months, and I think I better finish eating and head home to my kids."

I just wasn't ready to start answering questions about my divorce, especially in an Italian restaurant where Ronnie and I had dined frequently. I was still a mess over David.

Silently, we finished our meal.

The waiter, all smiles, approached our table, and said, "We have some special desserts today. They go great . . ."

I cut him off and said, "The check, please."

Gary reached for the check, but I insisted that we split it.

We hardly talked in the cab. He walked me to my car. As I opened the door, he stopped me.

"Sherrie, I enjoyed getting to know you," he said. "I understand that you are hurting, I'm here if you need someone to talk to."

I shook his hand and thanked him. On the way home, I had mixed emotions. I clearly felt that he was something more than a friend, and I think he did too, but too much was happening now between David, my kids, and I was not over Ronnie yet. Gary tried hard to be witty and comforting, and I blew it with my behavior in the restaurant and then, a handshake?

In front of my house was a furniture delivery truck. Two young men were carrying a huge box to my front door. I pulled my car behind them and exited in a fury.

"What are you doing?" I shouted. "I didn't order anything. Put it back in the truck."

"Is this the Green/Paul Residence?" one of the men asked.

"Yes, but I didn't order anything. What is it, anyway?"

"A waterbed," the man said.

"A waterbed?" I asked incredulously. "Are you crazy? Take it back! You have the wrong place. I'm a lawyer and I will sue you for trespassing."

Feeling a little tipsy from the wine, I stationed myself in front of the package moving up and back so they couldn't get around me.

Jim came running out of the house yelling, "It's mine. A present from Dad."

Then he turned to the delivery men and said, "I'll show you where it goes."

I stood there in shock as Jim led the delivery guys into my house and up the stairs to his bedroom.

Ronnie was buying this kid everything he asked for. We needed to talk. A waterbed!

Enough was enough. Last visit, Jim came home with a portable tape player called a Walkman. My kid ran around with his ears plugged and loud music coming out of a box. It put him in his own world, and he couldn't hear anything anyone said to him.

One of the young delivery kids gave me a sarcastic grin as we passed each other in my hallway. I felt like giving him the finger as he left, but my kids were there. I ran straight to the phone in the kitchen. As I dialed Ronnie's number, the last conversation entered my mind. I hung up. Every conversation with him recently ended with David and our children. There was so much discrimination against AIDS patients now. I didn't know what to do. Jim still hadn't adjusted to Northbrook and the divorce. Possibly the waterbed would help. Babs wanted a puppy. Why not make her happy too? She never asks for anything.

I had never had a dog of my own. The building had Uncle Hymie's dog, Prince, who was always in trouble with Aunt Tillie for accidents in the house, fearless barking at every noise, and most of all, stealing food off the table. I had a grudging empathy for the poor dog. Waterbed for a twelve-year-old? Is Ronnie crazy? *I better get flood insurance,* I thought miserably.

I sat down in my dad's old brown leather lounge chair, leaned back, closed my eyes, and quit thinking about anything.

Chapter Thirty-One

I was busy unloading my box of files when Gary entered my office. "Good morning."

I murmured back, "Good morning."

He paused at my desk and asked, "How is your cousin?"

"Better. In fact, we are thinking of bringing him home."

"If you do, you will need a doctor that specializes in HIV," Gary explained. "Not all doctors will treat AIDS patients. Don't go near County Hospital. I know a homosexual doctor at St. Joseph Hospital in Lincoln Park who specializes in AIDS and really cares about his patients. If you are free tomorrow, maybe we could discuss the best way to help your cousin."

I felt a twinge of excitement, like a high school teenager. Before saying yes, I remembered something.

"Gary, we will have to pick another day," I explained. "Tomorrow is Saturday, and I promised my daughter Babs that we would go looking for a puppy."

"Where are you going?"

"I'm not sure," I replied. "She has her heart set on a collie puppy. Once she saw Elizabeth Taylor in the movie *Lassie Come Home,* and since then she has wanted a collie."

"Oh, Sherrie, I have the perfect place to take you. My friend in South Holland runs a collie rescue."

I shook my head and started to laugh. "My God, you are a walking Yellow Pages with a solution for all my needs."

He chuckled, "Tell me what other needs you have, and I'll see what I can do."

"Let me check with my kids . . ." I started to reply when Jean came into the office, looking concerned, "One of you better do something. Angie is packing up and leaving."

We both flew down the hall, just in time to catch her.

"You two leave me alone," Angie said. "I ain't going to no court."

She pointed to the newspaper she was holding and said, "This kid that got himself shot in Englewood—I know him, and the ones who shot him." Her face was drawn and set, and her breathing was heavy.

I called Shirley while Gary tried to talk to Angie. We had to let her go, even though we were afraid for her life. Englewood, where I went to high school, was now a gang haven with constant shootings.

On my way home, I weighed how things were evolving between Gary and me. After all, Ronnie wasn't sitting home alone. I, too, possessed emotional and physical needs that didn't end with the divorce.

During a dinner of Chinese take-out, I told Jim and Babs that tomorrow we would be going with Gary to look for a collie puppy. I didn't expect the response I received.

Jim stood up and, in an angry voice, said, "Who is this Gary? Do you have a boyfriend?"

In shock, I answered, "No way! He is my boss and my friend, and he knows someone who raises and rescues collies."

"Why a collie?" Jim asked. "Instead, let's get a German shepherd."

Babs turned towards him and said, "You got a waterbed. It's my turn!"

Feeling guilty and confused, I started to clean up. Jim went to play on his Atari, and Babs joined me in the kitchen, saying, "Mom, I'm all excited about the puppy, and if you like your boss, so will I."

My stomach churned. She tried so hard to please, and Jim was more and more acting like his dad. I was all for women's lib until I faced a strong man, or boy.

* * *

Late spring was my favorite time of the year. The rains were slowing down, and everywhere there was color - green, white, yellow, pink. The trees, the plants, and the animals all were coming back to life. I opened the window to hear the blue jays, cardinals, and sparrows chirping while I finished my morning preparations.

I dressed carefully to match the warm weather and the casual day's activities: blue jeans, patterned blouse, and sneakers. I caught my reflection in the mirror and was pleased for a change. I added the pair of long beaded earrings I had purchased in California to be with the new fashions. I realized that I had better enjoy this weekend. Yale was bringing David home next week.

On the way down to the kitchen, I decided to make chocolate chip pancakes. The kids loved them, and Gary may want to join us for breakfast, I thought smiling.

Gary, in blue jeans and a t-shirt from a lung cancer run, came in through the garage door, carrying a dog crate full of puppy food, squeeze toys, and leashes.

"Why did you bring all that stuff? We don't even have a dog yet," Jim said as he descended the stairs.

Gary smiled, put the things down, and offered his hand to Jim, saying, "You must be Jim. I'm Gary."

Jim gave him the Ronnie stare that said, "Are you nuts? Who else would I be?" It took everything to keep me from laughing.

Babs, who walked in front of her brother, saved the day by saying, "Gary, this is wonderful. Now we are prepared for the dog." She shook Gary's hand.

All I could do was smile while thinking *my little girl is growing up.*

"What if we don't get a dog?" Jim's icy voice chimed in. When he narrowed his eyes and pouted his lips, I saw Ronnie, especially now that Jim had sprouted into a slim, five-foot-eight twelve-year-old.

"I'm sure you will fall in love with the collie puppies, but if not, I can use everything I brought with my dog, Barney," Gary replied.

"Please, everyone, sit down and eat," I said as I put the chocolate chip pancakes and the pitcher of orange juice on the table.

Gary asked, "Does everyone have a special seat?"

"Sit anywhere," I answered. "Coffee?"

Gary sat down next to Babs on one of our blue padded swirling chairs. "Yes," he replied, "coffee with cream, please."

Babs turned towards Gary. "What kind of dog is Barney?"

In between bites, Gary answered, "He is a border collie, not as big as a real Lassie, but he does an excellent job of keeping my cat, Tyrone, in line."

"I would rather have a cat," Jim said flatly.

"You have a waterbed," said Babs, just as evenly.

Wow, I thought. *She needs to speak up like that more often.*

Gary looked like he was in thought, and said, "Jim, a cat could puncture a waterbed. I always wanted to try a waterbed. How do you like it?"

Jim didn't answer.

"More coffee or pancakes? Finish up so we can get going. It's a long ride to the farm."

On the way, Gary tried hard to engage my children in conversation. Babs responded. Jim didn't. They both came alive at the collie rescue. Never had we seen so many collies as there were on the farm. The new ones were in cages, the older ones in fenced in yards. Black fur, tri-colored fur, dark brown fur, caramel light fur, and all types of mixed fur and sizes, something we didn't know before coming out.

Gary and I, with Lily, the owner, leisurely strolled among the dogs while Jim and Babs ran back and forth from one to another. I was impressed by the gentle, friendly, manner these beautiful animals displayed. No dog jumped on us, but many spent time wagging their tails and sniffing us. Babs was set on a Lassie look-alike, so Lily brought us into her home where two Lassie's look-alike had six puppies. We went home with a fluffy, thick-coated sable-and-white, ten-week-old collie puppy whom Babs named Lassie.

Gary's gold Honda van, with the large open spaces, allowed kids and puppy to stay in the back and get to know each other. Because we were afraid to let Lassie stay by herself, we missed going to Gary's favorite restaurant, so I decided we would have dinner at home.

Babs and Jim were busy making Lassie explore her new home while Gary and I made dinner. While I boiled spaghetti and found a jar of Prego tomato sauce, he chopped tomatoes, onions, garlic, and basil for a bruschetta. We talked freely.

"Gary, why haven't you ever married?"

"I did when I was young and foolish back in the sixties," he explained. "We divorced because I gave up drugs and went back to school, and she didn't. I've dated, but until now, I've never found someone I thought I could care about." He put his hand on mine and smiled at me.

I released his hand, pointed towards Jim, and said, "He is still having a hard time with the divorce. It may be too early for me to bring another relationship into our family, even though I would like to."

"I can wait," Gary said. "It seems to me though, Jim is still in an angry state and needs to talk to someone outside of the family, and you shouldn't let Babs just disappear because she hides things."

I pressed my lips together, "I'll consider your advice." Realizing that I was acting negative, I added, "I really appreciate your help with the puppy. It was a nice day, thank you."

Gary left after dinner, saying goodbye to Jim, Babs, and Lassie. I thought about his acute observations, realizing that was his job. I would pay more attention to Babs, my quiet one.

The poor puppy was wiped out and slept ten hours, even when Jim and Babs tried to play with her. I felt envious as I cleaned the morning breakfast dishes, and swept the floor. Gary was on my mind when the phone rang.

"Oh, Yale, that is wonderful," I said. "When will you and David be home?" I was so happy that David had improved enough to bring him home—for his sake, and for Aunt Sarah.

Chapter Thirty-Two

David and Gary had to be put on the back burner for a couple of weeks. I thanked God David was doing better, and the family was working with his doctors while I took a back seat because I found myself part of one of the Chicagoland area's most sensational divorce trials. Besides a divorce between two wealthy society members, there was the accusation of extreme mental and physical abuse.

Shirley was busy working towards new laws to protect abused women, and she understood that abuse between poor people received no interest, but she also knew that a case between the likes of Marie and Daniel Wilson would put the topic right on everyone's mind.

Our team consisted of three women, while Daniel Wilson's four-member team had one high-class female Harvard Law School graduate named Ellen Wosak, whom Shirley knew and wasn't fond of.

Our staff meeting at Shirley's office brought up many problems.

"Shirley, does Marie realize that, if she doesn't settle for a plea bargain and go quietly, they will fight back by exposing her background?"

Shirley, in her professional black knit suit and high heel pumps, was chain smoking and pacing back and forth. "I talked to Marie about that," Shirley said. "She was a showgirl in Vegas and doesn't care if it becomes known. In fact, she believes it will embarrass Daniel more than her, and it's been years since she has had contact with her own family.

Lunch was brought in so we could work all day. A major decision had to be made.

"I have years' worth of abuse testimony taken by Sherrie and me," said Denise, a recent law school graduate who joined our crew. She reminded me of myself. She was very conscientious, but she frowned when she talked, which made it look like she was questioning every-thing.

Shirley picked up the documents and asked, "Do you have any wit-nesses to confirm the testimonies by Marie?"

Denise became upset. "Not really. I've tried to talk to some of the servants Marie talked about. They are not around or won't speak to me."

Shirley turned towards me. I had just taken a bite out of my sand-wich. "Sherrie, the burden of proof is on us," she said. "Do you believe Marie?"

I put down my Italian beef sandwich, wiping the juice off my hands, and asked, "Aren't we ethically responsible to defend our client no mat-ter what we think? I do believe most of it. I understand that she is furi-ous and wants to get back at him."

Shirley shook her head and mused, "It would help if we could find someone who could corroborate at least one of her physical or emo-tional abuse stories, or it becomes her say against his, and the man is still the one believed, especially one from money and breeding!"

"Marie does have pictures of her bruises, scars on her arm from one of them," Denise said. "But I'm having a hard time believing that a man like Daniel Wilson could physically hurt anyone. Why, he is so refined, rich, and important."

I answered, "Denise, his status helps protect him. Our problem is she took the pictures, so they don't prove the bruises were from him."

"Have either one of you found servants or some friends she has talked to that we can subpoena?," Shirley asked.

"Well, I did talk to a sister of a maid who once worked for the Wil-sons," Denise said. "She confirmed that her sister said Mrs. Wilson was afraid of her very demanding husband, and hardly left the house with-out him."

"Where is the sister?" I asked Denise.

"She died," Denise replied.

Both Shirley and I said, "Hearsay!"

"We don't have a lot of time," I added. "Daniel offered a very generous financial settlement if she forgets the abuse case."

Shirley finished her coffee and walked over to the window, standing silently before she turned around and spoke. "This would be a great case to make people aware of the abuse some women must put up with, and a perfect time to influence the legislature, but we can't sacrifice Marie," Shirley said.

"What does she want to do?" Denise asked while she nibbled on French fries.

"Marie wants to expose her husband as a physical and emotional abuser," Shirley replied. "That is why she chose our law firm. There is a hearing with Judge Albert Collins next week."

"Shirley, you are frightening me," I said. "You are usually so confident and full of enthusiasm for whatever project you are working on. Remember I was with you on Roe v. Wade."

Enviously, I watched Shirley take out another cigarette. My kids were making me quit, and I missed those puffs. I walked over to the lunch table and grabbed a leftover cookie.

"Of course I want to win for my client, but I need to be fair in letting her know how good our chances are," Shirley said. Then, looking at Denise, she added, "Wife assault cases without enough proof are still looked upon as private matters between husband and wife and not open to legal responses."

Shirley's narrowed eyes, pinched lips, and the glance she sent my way said, "You and I know how the game is played, Denise is new!"

My colleague, like me, had learned that change did not come easily, and right and wrong were not always defined as they ought to be.

We continued to toss through books and discuss ways to work the case while we drank endless cups of coffee.

Shirley glanced at the clock, "It's past six, we've been here all day. Let's get going." She gathered her documents and walked towards the door.

I emptied the overflowing garbage cans, boxed the sweets, straightened the chairs, picked up my papers from the table, and put on my light, spring cloth jacket before exiting.

"Have a good weekend. See you Monday, and remember, not a word to the press," Shirley said as she turned off the lights and locked up the office.

The press! "Shit," I said aloud. *Ronnie will be upset. His firm does work for Wilson's company.*

* * *

Babs at fourteen and Jim at twelve were old enough to leave alone for a few hours every night, but I refused to give Ronnie any ammunition for a custody battle, so I had hired sixteen-year-old Joy to help out.

I walked into the house tired and hungry. Lassie greeted me with barks and jumps. I really loved her. She was my therapist.

"Hi, girl, where is everyone?" I said to the dog, as I petted her. Then I remembered Babs had a Girl Scouts meeting to which Joy was taking her.

"Jim," I called. No answer. I ran around the inside and outside of the house calling his name. He wouldn't be caught dead at a Girl Scouts' meeting. I picked up the phone and made some calls. Neither the two friends he had nor Lizzie had heard from him. I panicked. Keys in hand, I was about to go searching the neighborhood when he walked in through the garage with, of all people, Gary.

Seething, I shouted, "Where were you? I've been worried to death!"

Gary answered, "Sorry Sherrie. I dropped by to see how Lassie was doing, and Jim was home alone. We talked and then decided to try out my new bike. We should have left you a note."

I looked at how happy Jim was and calmed myself down. "Jim knows to leave a note," I said sternly.

"We were about to go to Barnaby's for a hamburger, will you join us?" Gary asked.

I guessed that Jim would like me to stay home, so I said, "Thank you, but I am beat. Next time."

They left, engaged in conversation about a banana-seat bike. Gary did say he was willing to talk to Jim. He should have warned me, however. I wanted to kill them both for worrying me! Then again, Jim seemed so happy, I had better calm down and let their friendship develop on its own. Gary was a respected psychologist, and a good person.

In my hour-and-a-half of quiet, I took a hot bubble bath and consumed a tall glass of white wine. I reasoned that I deserved it after working so hard and too many hours on Marie's case.

Jim came running into the house with Gary following.

"Mom, you know that yellow banana bike you want me to get rid of because Dad bought me a new Schwinn racing bike? Well, Gary said it will be a collector bike, so I'm keeping it," Jim said breathlessly. "Can I go to Gary's house Saturday to see his antique bikes?"

"Of course," I said while thinking that Jim had just blurted out more words than he'd said to me since we moved here.

Gary smiled and asked, "How is the case going?"

"Not good," I answered.

He picked up his jacket off the sofa and said, "Good luck. I have faith in you and Shirley. See you Saturday, Jim."

Gary was halfway out the door when Babs came in, loaded down with boxes of cookies.

Gary helped her with the boxes and asked, "Can I buy some?"

"These have been ordered, but you can have one of mine. I hope you like peanut butter," she said as she handed him a box of cookies.

"Thanks," Gary said as he took the box. Then, Lassie either wanted his attention or his box of cookies. She jumped him and he fell down. Jim ran over and helped Gary up. I stood there, arms folded, laughing. He turned towards me, shrugged his shoulders, and said, "I'm really leaving this time."

He walked out, put on something like a football helmet, got on his bike, and disappeared.

"Where is his car, and what does he have on his head," I asked.

Jim answered, "Mom, Gary, bikes everywhere. He wears a bike helmet to be safe, and he is bringing me one next time. Gary left his car at the Botanical Gardens. You really don't know anything about your boss, do you?"

Jim was right. One important thing I knew about Gary, however, was that he made me smile, and another was that my son liked him.

Babs went to her room, Jim to his, and Lassie, who was becoming my dog, slept by my feet on the sofa while I went over the Wilson case.

One quote from Marie struck me like an arrow into my soul. She said, "I'm so happy to be done with Daniel's commands that started with, *You will* . . . When I heard that phrase, I would drop everything and obey the command even though I knew there was no way that I could do anything right for him, and I consequently I would be punished."

I re-read those words knowing that I, too, lived with them for twelve years. Just last weekend, Ronnie told me, "*You will* dress the children appropriately."

Yes, I lived under emotional abuse. When I heard those words, I jumped back, and I do so even now that I am supposedly free of him.

I put the Wilson file down. *Enough for tonight.* I let my mind shift to thoughts of David. He came home to his mother that morning, so Sabbath dinner at Aunt Tillie's was delayed. He sounded so exhausted on the phone. I hoped Lizzie and I would be able to see him tomorrow as planned. Lizzie's husband was taking the girls to sell Girl Scout cookies. A reluctant Jim was scheduled to go along with them, and, luckily, Gary had solved that problem.

After waking up, I turned over and blinked twice to make sure I was reading the clock correctly. It said 8 a.m. I had slept through the alarm with so much to do that morning. It was the open window. I had smoked a cigarette I found in an old purse, and I didn't want the kids to smell it. This quitting smoking was hard to do, especially with the pressures from the case and David's illness.

The doorbell rang. I was in my PJs, moving the laundry from the washer to the dryer. As I thought about opening the door not dressed, I heard Jim bouncing down the stairs.

"Mom, it's Gary," Jim shouted. "I'm leaving."

"You haven't had any breakfast yet,"

Gary's mellow voice answered, "We'll stop for something to eat on the way."

Babs yelled out, "I'll have breakfast. What are you making?"

I put another load of laundry in the washer, thinking about how it wasn't easy being a working mother, but that it was exciting to be part of both worlds.

* * *

I made pancakes, and Babs helped me with the laundry and dishes. She was growing up so fast. Already she was two inches taller than I, with dark, curly hair and a pretty, narrow face. Lizzie's husband, Chaim, knocked on the door. I told Babs, "Go, honey. I will finish the dishes."

With Babs away with Lizzie's husband and daughter, and Lassie fed and walked, I was ready to pick up Lizzie before heading to Aunt Sarah's. I honked and Lizzie joined me in the car. She was very quiet, contrary to her normal self. I drove slowly and concentrated on the traffic on the expressway. Finally, I asked, "Besides David's AIDS, what's the problem?"

"Oh, I've been fighting with Chaim all morning," Lizzie said, sighing. "He doesn't want me near David in case it's contagious, and the idea of how David got the disease disgusts him."

"Ronnie feels the same," I said.

"You're not married to Ronnie anymore," Lizzie said. "Also, some kid named Ryan got AIDS from a blood transfusion. So Chaim feels they really don't know enough about it."

"Lizzie, I wouldn't judge you, if you want me to take you back home," I said. "For me, David has always been like a brother, and I will do anything I can to help him. I've never judged him, just accepted."

"No, keep going. David is family," she answered as she turned away from me.

I decided to change the subject and said, "It is so nice of Chaim to take Babs with, today."

"Babs is never any trouble," Lizzie said. "She is so good, and she takes care of everyone."

At Aunt Sarah's apartment building, I reached in the back seat of the car for a package, "Polo shirt for David in a smaller size. He complained that nothing fits him anymore." I added sadly.

Instead of using the elevator, we walked up the stairs to the second floor and knocked on Aunt Sarah's door. She looked like hell—messed hair, no lipstick, wrinkled house dress, but David looked much better than he did in California. There was color in his cheeks, a little meat on his bones, and he was sitting up by the kitchen table eating a piece of challah. We expected him to be in bed.

I hugged David and handed him my gift.

He shook the box and said, "Sherrie, I hope it's not an umbrella, because I won't need it. I'm going to be fine."

We laughed and cried together while David took out the Polo shirt and everyone else looked at us for an explanation. Aunt Sarah asked, "Is it raining?"

"Private joke between Sherrie and me," David said.

When David retired to his bedroom, Aunt Sarah shook her head, put her wrinkled hands together in prayer fashion, and said, "He can't drive, he sleeps so much and hardly eats. What can I do?" Lizzie and I assured Aunt Sarah that we would help get David to his doctors, and wherever he needed to go, and that it would take time before he felt better. I felt bad for David and Aunt Sarah. Since David's diagnosis, she aged tremendously. Her gray hair from constant worry, her double chin, and her limp from her bad knees didn't help. I couldn't even imagine what it would be like to lose a child.

On the way home, the thought occurred to me that I hadn't been a good mother lately. Lizzie and Gary were taking care of my kids. Between David and the Wilson case, I haven't had time to do anything else, and I had been losing sleep too.

Chapter Thirty-Three

I sat in Shirley's office waiting for her and Denise to show up. I checked my watch again; 9:15 a.m. She did say 9:00. They were late, and I was early, as usual. I re-read the last interview I had with Marie when she described one of her abusive situations:

"I had been making dinner when I heard his call," Marie had said in the interview. *"Normally, I would drop everything and run into his study. That day, I didn't come right away. When I entered his study, his cold blue eyes stared at me. 'When I call you, you come. Do you understand that you are nothing but a whore without me?' Then he grabbed me by the hair and slammed me against the wall. As Daniel walked out of the room, he nonchalantly said, 'Clean up the blood before the housekeeper comes in.' "*

I looked away from the document and pressed my lips together to avoid the tears. I took off my new cheaters glasses and rubbed the bridge of my nose. How many times did I hear similar words come out of Ronnie's mouth? The difference was the punishment. Never had he physically abused me—just made me feel like shit. On occasion, he broke antiques that were mine from Aunt Tillie. He, like Daniel, was a highly respected member of the community who would never be suspected of any kind of abuse. People have many sides.

Shirley swept into the room, dropped her purse and piles of documents on the table, filled her coffee cup with black coffee, took out a cigarette, and announced, "We're up shit's creek. Interviewed a dozen witnesses and none of them will say a word against him or substantiate her claims. We can't go to court with the word of an ex-Las Vegas showgirl against the Almighty Daniel Wilson III. The pictures of her bruises were taken by her, so they are no good. Any ideas?"

Denise asked, "Could we get his financial records to see if he paid the witnesses off?"

I smiled while Shirley gave her a stern look, eyebrows knit, lips pursed, shoulders raised.

"Honey, he's no dummy," Shirley said. "They will have been paid off with cash. Do some research on similar cases, and, next time, make the coffee stronger and make sure I have a new pack of cigarettes."

I watched Denise sink into her chair.

Shirley turned to me. "I'm thinking we should check how he acted while out of town on business," I suggested. "Call girls, a mistress. The type of abuse Marie talks about doesn't stop with one person."

"Good thought," Shirley said. "Sorry, but I have to go. I actually have another case, a small one, but it needs me now. I'm counting on you to find the missing witness. Dismissed, go home. Sherrie, if you get a chance this week, go by the shelter. Nice young mother with a nine-year-old and a six-year-old could use some comfort. Thanks. Denise, close up and let's move."

On my way home, I felt slightly annoyed with the way Shirley treated Denise. Shirley, a powerful advocate for women, sometimes acted like a tough male boss. Denise was a lawyer, not a secretary. Also, Shirley dragged me out for about an hour-long meeting where she threw the major job of finding a miracle witness at me.

* * *

David did get stronger, and for a while, it looked like he might beat the odds of over fifty percent deaths from the virus. Gary's friend, Dr. Fine, an immunologist at St. Joseph Hospital, became David's savior. Dr. Fine, gay himself, dedicated his practice to working with AIDS patients. His tall, muscular build didn't match his quiet, competent nature.

He made me think of Rock Hudson, who was diagnosed with HIV in 1984 and had announced it to the public just a few months ago.

While David was getting blood tests, I walked into Dr. Fine's office. He was sitting at his small oak desk, staring straight ahead. The black headpiece of his phone was laying on the desk next to his hand. There was no sound coming from it. The setting sun passing through the window was focusing on his gold watch, causing it to sparkle.

I started to back out when he looked up and said, "The hospital called. We lost another patient to AIDS. There is no cure. Over fifty percent die within fifteen months."

"David?" I asked after taking a deep breath.

He gave me a half-smile and said, "For now, David is doing great. He is infection-free, and so very determined. There is a new drug, AZT, that may prolong life. When it is available, we will get it for him." Dr. Fine walked over to me and put a consoling hand on my shoulder, saying, "He is a special young man."

* * *

Four weeks after David came home to Chicago, I took him to the shelter for a professional decorating job. Ironically, when I was married to Ronnie I donated to the shelter, so it had some money to spend.

We walked into Gary's office. David looked around, and said, "This place is terrible, depressing. It needs some light, some color."

Gary went over to him and shook his hand, saying, "Glad to meet you, David."

I shook my head, and said, "Don't spend all our money in Gary's office. We want to cheer up the abused women." I left for my meeting with Shirley and Denise concerning the Wilson case, and said, "He's yours, Gary."

I reported on my progress, saying, "I interviewed the chief of police in Marie's town because Marie told me that she had called the chief of police when she was alone after Daniel attacked her. But he was of no help. He listened to her, then hung up and called Daniel when Daniel arrived home. When Daniel got off the phone with the chief, he slapped Marie and locked her in the guest room for two days with no food or drink."

I paused before continuing.

"The chief told me he called Daniel because 'Danny' was so admired and considered so important in the community," I said. "Plus, he knew if he hadn't called him, Daniel would get the chief fired. Daniel's excuse to the chief was that sometimes Marie drank too much. Over a drink of Jack Daniel's, he asked the policeman to keep it quiet. Chief Whitehall couldn't possibly believe that Daniel would beat anyone."

Shirley paced as usual, as she reported to us, "I met with Daniel's lawyer, Miss Fancy Pants in her red wool Chanel suit. This is what she told me: *'It's obvious Marie is suffering from a mental breakdown. Several of the help will testify to her drinking and her strange behavior. Nobody will believe your client. My client denies all allegations. We are willing to give Marie a generous settlement just to keep these fake accusations out of the paper.'*"

Shirley sat down and took a short drag on her cigarette and a gulp of coffee before talking. "I may have to tell Marie to go along with it," she said.

I took a bathroom break. When I came back, it occurred to me that Daniel's secretary had mentioned that he went to Los Angeles to see a friend who was severely injured in a fight. "What if it was a mistress he beat up?" I asked. "Let me explore this."

"Anything we can find to substantiate her claims would be significant," Shirley noted. "We need a decision in the next two weeks."

I picked David up from Gary's office. The two of them were like long-lost buddies. They already had plans for the shelter and a date to go to the Merchandise Mart. On the way to Aunt Tillie's, David couldn't stop talking about Gary.

Friday saw me at Shabbat dinner at Aunt Tillie's, even though I just wanted to go home, take a warm bath, and go to sleep. But my children were already there with Lizzie's family, so I knew I had to be there. Hugs and kisses, traditional food, and love coming from every corner brightened my day.

David grabbed me and said, "Sherrie, I have some great ideas to brighten up the shelter. Can you go with Gary and me to the Mart this week?"

"David, I would love to, but I'm working on this case that is in a dead-end place, and we have to get something on the guy in the next two weeks, or we lose it," I explained. "In fact, maybe you could help me with the hospitals in LA. I need to find out if there is a hospital in L.A. that someone could maneuver." I then told David about the Wilson case.

"The hospital I was in is a small, privately owned clinic that caters to AIDS patients," David explained. "They are very secret."

"I'm looking for something like that place that may have treated one of Wilson's mistresses or a call girl he picked up," I said. "An abuser doesn't just abuse one person." I thought about how Ronnie talked to his father and to the help in our house.

David answered, "Why does it have to be a woman mistress? It could be a gay lover, especially since you believe it was from someone out of town. In fact, one guy at the hospital I was at was close to death from a lover's beating."

"I never thought of that," I said. "Of course, a mistress would be accepted in Chicago, but a gay lover wouldn't. Is there a way you can check out that guy for me?"

"I still have contact with him. I will give him a call, but I think that would be too much of a coincidence," David mused.

"Thanks for the thought," I said, and then went into the bedroom and used the phone to call Marie.

She answered, "Daniel had real estate in California and was always flying to L.A. without me. I thought he had a mistress there, which was fine, because it gave me a break. He could be a closet gay. He hated women, and we never had normal sex. It was usually akin to a rape scene."

I went home all fired up with a new angle to check.

* * *

My life over those past few days had consisted of washing, ironing, shopping, and packing. After canceling out of most of his weekends, Ronnie was suddenly Super Dad, taking his kids on a week-long trip to London. I'm sure it would be a combination of business and pleasure like he did on our honeymoon. They were excited, so I tried to be, too. Babs told me his girlfriend Jill was no longer around so we would have to see who Ronnie's new girlfriend was. I'm sure there would be one with him.

After Jim and Babs were picked up by their dad's driver, I went up the wide carpeted stairs to check on their rooms, and to collect laundry. Babs' room was neat and orderly. Only a few stuffed animals were on the bed, the rest were away in her closet. You could tell she was approaching her teen years by the pictures on the wall of different rock stars, such as Bruce Springsteen. I then went into Jim's room to grab his laundry. He was the collector who had too many things and knew where everything was among what looked to me like chaos. I just shut the door and sighed.

I then settled into the rocker on our pine patio with a large coffee, a donut, a book, and a collie puppy who was now around fifty pounds. I vowed to take some time off while my kids were gone. I slowly inhaled the scents of late summer, the freshly cut grass, and the variety of blooming flowers. My favorite fall backyard foliage was the strong, large sunflowers. The variety of sunflower and fruit seeds Gary brought to our bird feeders were a favorite of birds such as chickadees, cardinals, and blue jays who brought sweet melodies and sharp calls to the yard. We added the chain-link fence to make life easier with Lassie, though she still loved to go on walks, especially when we stopped at 31 Flavors to get her a vanilla ice-cream cone.

I still missed living on Lake Michigan, but I did not miss the house. Probably the thing I missed the most about my house with Ronnie was the underground irrigation system that watered the lawn and flowers. There had been no rain for almost ten days, and I was just too lazy to get up and hand water.

I re-filled my coffee cup and Lassie's water dish. I petted Lassie, and said, "Hey, girl, we get a week's rest." She looked up at me like she understood. She was such a good gentle dog, nothing like the dog I grew up with within our family building, the one who stole food off the table and chewed Uncle Izzy's socks.

The light wind shook the trees and moved the fallen leaves about, reminding me that Fall was not far away.

I thought about Gary, and that maybe I should call him and see what he was doing. It had been almost two years since my divorce. I wasn't even forty yet, too young to be celibate, while Ronnie went through girlfriends regularly. I had refused to be fixed up by friends, mainly because of Babs and Jim. My figure was still decent; maybe it would be better with fewer pounds, my hair was turning salt and pepper, but I declined to color it; I was hoping to end up with a beautiful head of silver hair, like Aunt Tillie's.

I jolted upright at the sound of the phone. Back in the kitchen, I caught it right before it stopped ringing.

Gary's mellow voice asked, "Did Babs and Jim get off okay?"

"Yes," I responded. "I will miss them, but I need a week on the case and to rest."

"How about I help you with the rest part starting with dinner tonight," Gary asked. "What if I pick you up at seven?

"Sounds good."

"What do you have a taste for? How about Italian?" He always asked, which was so nice.

Lately, I was branching farther and farther away from kosher, though I still wouldn't eat pig or shellfish, or mix meat and milk products, and I had separate dishes and silverware for *milchet* and *fleishig*.

I glanced at my chipped nails and humidity damaged hair, and picked up the phone. Chuck fit me in for an appointment in the next hour, so I needed to hustle. So much for my rest, but possibly an answer to my thoughts. It will be nice to go out without worrying about getting home to my kids.

I barely had time to apply fresh makeup and change from jeans to a new pair of brown slacks and a tan and green silk blouse after coming home from the beauty shop. Lassie must have sensed that I was going out because she barked until I filled her food and water dishes. I had taken over Babs's job, and Lassie was smart enough to not trust me.

Gary picked me up promptly at seven. He was dressed in a brown patterned suit, instead of his normal blue jean outfits. He handed me a beautiful bouquet of red roses.

"They are gorgeous," I said as I went to put them in my crystal water vase.

"You are beautiful too, especially in that pretty outfit," he said.

Gary had been in my house a dozen times before, but this time was different. He was more reserved, even to the way he treated Lassie. It felt like I was on a first date with a new boyfriend.

We decided to go to one of my favorite restaurants in Lincolnshire called Phil's. He helped me into his van. "Babs and Jim in London, wow," Gary said. "I never got out of Illinois until I was in my late twenties."

"Their departure was hectic, but all went well," I said. "Their father travels a lot for business. I'm guessing he is combining both for a nice write-off." I refrained from mentioning that he combined our honeymoon with business in London.

I knew Gary would like the restaurant because it was located in an old, converted painted lady mansion. The wooden porch surrounded most of the building and featured an enormous old swing. Gary sat down on the swing, and I sat next to him.

"Sherrie, this place is heavenly," Gary said. "Breathe in the aroma of the flowers around the porch. Check out the stained glass windows. How did you find it?"

"Lizzie found it. I knew you would like it," I said as a plump blonde hostess directed us into a room decorated with blue-flowered wallpaper and old converted gas lights. We sat down on wooden captain chairs and checked out the menu, especially the many fish items. I ordered salmon; Gary, wine and a shrimp entree.

Gary raised his glass of wine and said, "Red wine, the nightingale cries to the rose."

I raised my glass and, clinking it on his, I answered, "To Omar Khayyam." I would have liked to have finished his quote, but I couldn't remember it. Anyway, Gary was delighted that I knew where it had come from. He reached across the table and squeezed my hand.

"It is hard to find one who knows Omar Khayyam," he said.

"What other poets do you like?" I asked.

"There are so many I love from the past and present," he answered. "I was an English major in my undergrad days."

"There is a new up and coming poet doing excellent work," I informed him. "I can't remember her full name. The first name is Bella."

"Yes, there are many, but Khayyam's quatrains tell you to live for today, and I am in favor of that," Gary said.

"I thought psychologists help you deal with your past," I responded.

"Only when it helps you deal with today," Gary said.

"Interesting," I said, thinking about letting go of my mother and Ronnie so I could deal with today.

The conversation slowed down when our meals arrived.

I started it up again by saying, "You know and have met most of my family. Tell me about yours."

He put his hand on his chin, thought a moment, and answered, "Had you and Shirley been around championing for women's rights, I might have been aborted! My mother had me at age forty-four. She was a very practical person. I can just hear her telling the doctor that he was crazy when he told her that she was pregnant. My sister, Sage, was married at twenty to a dentist and living in Arizona. My dad was fifty and sick with heart disease. He died when I was eight, so I lived a geriatric's youth."

"No wonder you like thousand-year-old poets," I said with a smile.

Gary laughed, while I tilted my head back, and used my hand to brush away hair from my forehead.

He grabbed my hand. "Stop, I love the way your hair rests on your forehead."

We stared into each other's eyes, and something clicked between us.

We took a pass on dessert and talked little on the way home. Without speaking, Gary followed me into my house and up to the master bedroom. I was excited and nervous.

Gary pulled me towards him, passionately kissed me on the lips, and held me close until I eased away. With his cute devilish smile, he said, "From the moment you walked into my office, I've wanted to do that."

"I hope you want to do more now," I answered.

With a chuckle, he picked me up and put me on the bed where he gently removed my clothes and hurriedly dropped his on the floor, as the heat between us grew. Soon, we were moving in perfect rhythm, his lips against mine, our breath mingling, and our orgasms together. Afterward, we lay in each other's arms, smiling.

"Gary, do you need to go home to your pets?" I asked, playfully.

"I already asked my neighbor Jill to look in on Barney and Tyrone," he said, smiling.

I raised up on my arms, turned towards him, and said, "A-HA! So this *was* pre-meditated!"

He pushed me back down among the covers, kissed me gently, and said, "*Mmm,* you smell like a rose."

I laughed. "It's rose-scented soap. You too can get the same wonderful scent if you will join me in the shower."

He did.

Chapter Thirty-Four

Gary and I didn't get much work done the week my kids were gone. We just went to work for necessary appointments and spent the rest of the time getting to know each other. Shirley wasn't happy with me.

He was a much different lover than Ronnie had been - romantic, compassionate, and always trying to please. He was a talker, and funny too.

During sex he whispered, "How would you like to be tickled all over by my new mustache?" I burst out laughing. With Ronnie, we never said a word.

There was an ease and comfort with Gary vs. a type of fear and excitement with Ronnie. I had hidden parts of myself from Ronnie, but not from Gary. I was free with Gary.

He took hold of my hands and, while looking into my eyes, said, "I love you, Sherrie."

I gave him a tender kiss and wrapped my arms around him, but I wasn't ready to say I love you.

His interests were definitely different too. Gary introduced me to the Botanical Gardens in Glencoe, where we took a long walk through the magnificent grounds. Most of us are content to look and not see. Not Gary. On our walk, besides the vegetation, he pointed out the different patterned butterflies, the robins digging for worms, the bikers without helmets, the happy-faced walkers, the annoyed walkers, lost toys, lost hats, ignored pennies, etc. He made me aware of my surroundings.

"This place is so beautiful. The flowers, the bushes, the varieties of trees, and the ponds filled with goldfish. It is hard to believe that I've never been here." I stopped a minute to inhale the scent of lilacs and to take in the fluttering of butterfly wings.

"Jim and I biked through here. Wait until I get you on a bike. A whole new world will open up."

"No way, I haven't been on a bike in twenty-five years," I said. Gary just smiled.

We found a romantic outdoor cafe in Evanston, where we sipped white wine and shared a salad and a quiche, while that big orange ball of sunlight retreated into the West, and he analyzed the latest book I had read, making me realize I held too much to facts and missed so much of nature, and the emotional side of things.

Another day, Gary found a farmer's market. We came home with three flower boxes filled with clusters of petunias and geraniums. My deck was starting to look like the Botanical Gardens, and my kitchen, like a vegetable garden. I watched him chop vegetables together and add them to the already cooking spaghetti sauce, like he was creating a precious new formula.

"You really enjoy cooking," I observed. "I love a good meal, but I'm always in a hurry, substituting things." I glanced out the window at the cardinal perched on the feeder Gary had installed, thinking, *Gary is really more domestic than I am.*

He turned to me in fake horror, and said, "You substitute! You are right, I do love cooking. As soon as the right ingredients are united, something magical happens. While cooking, you need to engage all your senses. It is an experience, a job that needs to be done perfectly."

"Cooking and serving her food is like that to my Aunt Tillie," I said. "I guess my *freyd* is getting someone to understand my theories, or seeing a woman surprised that she won a case against a man." I stopped talking to inhale the delicious aroma of the bubbling sauce. "*Mmm . . .* whatever you are making smells *wonderful,*" I exclaimed, sighing.

"This sauce needs to simmer for an hour, and you look delicious. Any idea of what we can do while waiting to eat?"

* * *

On one of the days we ditched going into the shelter, Jean, who was covering the clinic for us, called, sounding frantic.

"A truck is unloading furniture and boxes!" Jean yelled. "What should I do?"

I called David, who said, "I'm on my way there. Doesn't she know we are fixing up the shelter?"

"How are you getting there?" I asked. "I could pick you up."

"No, you enjoy Gary," David replied. "He is a great guy. I'll take Uncle Izzy's Cadillac."

"Stay in budget," I warned as he hung up on me.

I turned to Gary and relayed the conversation. Then I said, "I guess Lizzie can't keep a secret, even when I asked her to. Family never could. Everything was worked out and talked about. What do we do when my kids come home?" Maybe he had an answer worked out, I thought.

"You worry about everything," Gary said as he moved around the kitchen, flipping homemade pancakes and pouring fresh squeezed orange juice. "Your kids will be okay with us being a couple. They know and like me."

"Babs will be, but Jim will feel betrayed," I reasoned. "He thinks you are his playmate. We better take it slow, with a lot of family time."

"So, now that I finally got you in bed, we have to stop sleeping around," he said as he gave me a screwed up funny face and dropped two more pancakes on my plate.

"I don't know," I answered, then switched topics.

"On another subject. I'm so happy that David is improving so much," I said. "He loves that doctor you recommended. Though Uncle Izzy's car is about twenty years old, and he shouldn't be driving it. That can kill him faster than AIDS."

Gary sat down near me, reached across the table for my hand, and said, "Don't get your hopes up. There is no cure for AIDS. Only twenty percent of patients survive over five years. He has done a remarkable recovery, but he still has that telltale look and the black and blue marks."

"And you told me I worry too much. You are totally pessimistic about David."

"No, I'm just stating facts. Believe me, I wish it were different. David is a great guy, and not the first one I know with AIDS."

I pushed my plate away, pursing my lips together. Grief welled up in me. I didn't want to face the fact that there was no cure for AIDS, and David was on borrowed time.

"Let's pick up David and go to the shelter," I suggested.

Gary turned to Lassie who was hanging around the table for leftovers, and said, "Our first disagreement in six days, not bad. What do you think, girl?" With that, I laughed, and Lassie devoured the pancake he put in her dish.

I was still in my robe, and Gary was unshaven in his t-shirt and shorts. I was ruining the leisurely last day we had planned, but Gary was a good person who would understand, and David still needed help. I glanced at the clock over the sink before calling David to tell him we would pick him up. He sounded relieved.

"Gary, can you be ready in a half-hour?"

"I'll try, Speedy," he answered with the new name he gave me. I was always early, while Gary was usually late. I watched him continue to stack the dishes in the dishwasher. His bare muscular arms were covered with thin light brown fuzzy hairs. *That's it*, I thought. *If he continues to call me Speedy, I can call him Fuzzy.*

In the week Gary and I were playing, David, with the help of his old partner, Jeffery, had started to transform the shelter. Rooms were glowing with color from new paint and wallpaper. When David started to direct the movers on where to put the furniture, he received a standing ovation from the seven occupants of the shelter.

Emily cried when her two boys, six and eight, ran to the toy room. They stopped and looked at David. "Can we play with the toys?" they asked. When David said yes, they carefully took down a few toys from the many red, yellow, and blue painted shelves of toys and games. Though they settled at one of the low light wooden children's tables and started to play, they kept a cautious eye on David.

Emily grabbed David and said, "Thank you! My husband wouldn't allow them to have toys. If anyone gave them anything, he threw it away. If he caught any one of them with toys, all three of us would be beaten."

The other occupants of the shelter and the help stood up and clapped. They thanked David for brightening up the place, and David assured them this was only the beginning. I slid down in my seat thinking about where I would get the money, as our budget from Shirley had already been spent.

David was so happy to be back in design and appreciated, and the shelter occupants were so thrilled, that I knew I would find a way to finance it.

By the time we traveled home, Gary and I were tired, and David was beat. He slept in the back of Gary's van. I worried about him, as he was suffering behind his act of everything being great.

It was hard for Gary and me to part, but it was time. The next day my kids came home all excited from their week's trip in London. There was a very nice English girlfriend who entertained them while Ronnie was working. They were loaded with gifts from their rich father. Babs' room, always neat and clean, was now cluttered with stuffed animals, clothes, and records, while Jim had more Atari games, Matchbox cars, music videos, and video games.

Truthfully, I was glad they had a good time, but also, I was jealous, as I remembered our honeymoon in London. I picked up one of Jim's Matchbox cars. "Honey, did you ride on one of the double decker buses?" I asked. "I was fascinated by them when your dad and I were in London."

He looked up. "You were in London with Dad? When?"

I felt like my children believed there were no days with Ronnie and me before they were born. I mumbled, "Our honeymoon," as I handed the bus back to him.

Death is horrible, but final. Divorce with kids is never final, and it is hard to let go of the hurt and anger when your ex is still in your life.

I then sat back down on our couch, kept my mouth shut, and listened to my kids' stories of their trip with their dad. I thanked them for the miniature English tea kettle and put it in my china cabinet. Tomorrow they would be mine again. Summer would end, school would start, and our family routines would be back.

* * *

The trees rustled in the wind, dropping their leaves all over. A cloudy day in late summer that felt like fall. Luckily, I left a sweater in my car. I breezed into Shirley's office, where I received an unexpected hug from her.

"You are brilliant!" she said. "We've been looking for a mistress, while it is a gay lover. We found him through the house telephone records. Daniel made several calls to him. He is an interior decorator named Jordon and he lives in L.A. They've been lovers for two years."

I smiled, thinking of David, and asked, "Was the lover abused by Daniel?"

"Yes, but right now, he is reluctant to come here and testify," Shirley replied. "I have someone going out there to at least get something on paper."

"Shirley," I offered, "let me contact my cousin. He is a gay interior decorator too, and he just came back from LA. I hate to say this, but we may want Marie and Daniel tested for AIDS."

"Shit, I never thought of that," Shirley said as she lit another cigarette, and Denise, asked, "What's AIDS?"

"What about Marie?"

"She was shocked," Shirley said. "Never thought his lovers could be men. How did it come to you?"

I went for the donuts before answering. Quitting cigarettes was resulting in adding on pounds, as sweets had become my cigarettes substitute. "My cousin David," I answered as I dripped chocolate on my nice new top.

Meanwhile, Denise sat there with this dazed expression, which made me think back to when I first moved out of the family building to face the real world. I pushed the hair off my face as I tried to give Denise a short explanation of AIDS.

After leaving Shirley's office, I stopped at the shelter to get David. I told him about Shirley's discovery. David asked, "Do you have pictures of Daniel and his lover? The gay decorator community sticks together. I may know them or someone I know in L.A. does. They may go under different names if they haven't come out to the world yet."

"I'll get pictures," I said. "You have been such a great help, both with the shelter and my work." I gave David a hug before dropping him off at Aunt Sarah's. As I watched David maneuver up the stairs, I cringed at how thin and slow he had become. The small Polo shirt I bought for him was hanging loosely. At least he was alive and improving every day.

The next day at work, Gary pulled me into his office, shut the door, and hugged and kissed me. "Please don't," I said, as I pulled away. While straightening my blouse, he stared at me, "I haven't seen you in over a week. Is something wrong? Did I assume too much?"

"Gary, first of all, we are at work, and second, I'm confused," I replied. "We had a great week, but now my kids are home, and I don't know what to do."

"Jim called and asked me to come to his baseball game Saturday," Gary said. "We could tell them then."

"Tell them what, that we are dating?" I replied. "The problem is, Jim thinks you are his best friend."

He chuckled, "Dating. I feel like a teen again. I'm in love with you, and I've been there since you first walked into my office. I love the way your hair falls across your eye, the way you care for others, your silly grin and your . . ."

Just then, Jean, our helper, knocked on the door. We stopped talking and let her in.

"You won't believe this one," Jean began, "we have a forty-year-old man here with a black eye and a bruised lip. His mother has been abusing him for years. Do we take men?"

"I'll take care of him," Gary said as he rushed out of the room.

"Jean, domestic violence isn't isolated to one race, one socioeconomic group, or one gender," I told her, trying to be professional.

"I guess you are right," she said as she sat down by my desk, huffing and puffing from her brisk walk down the hall.

I didn't see Gary again until he showed up at Jim's game on Saturday. I did care for Gary, but I worried about the kids, especially Jim. I wished he could relax more, laugh more, not have his father's view of life that winning was all that counted. Once Babs got away from her fear of her own father, she had really blossomed. She was small, pretty, and popular with a large group of friends. Everyone liked her. She was more of a pleaser than I was.

I decided to go to the game. Because of work, I had missed most, and Ronnie never came. The game was a third over by the time I got there. So I slid onto a backbench which was shaded by an old oak tree. Even though it was a hot humid day, the baseball field was thick with parents, siblings, dogs, bicycles, and baby carriages.

The small, white-and-red painted wooden snack stand that sold colas, chips, candy, hot dogs, and ice cream bars was the gathering place for family and friends. I rested my gaze on my daughter. Dressed in formfitting blue jeans, a skimpy top, and makeup, it suddenly dawned on me why my fourteen-year-old Babs always went to the games. Tall, muscular, attractive Brian, a friend's son who was in a class ahead of Babs, handed her an ice cream bar while she coyly leaned against the big old oak tree. In her soft, steady voice, she said something to him before she took a small bite of the ice cream. My daughter was flirting. I had wondered why she had not written any poems or wanted to review any books with me. I missed our private time together on those projects. Now that I thought about it, the dolls and stuffed animals had disappeared from her bed, and now pictures of Madonna and Bruce Springsteen were taped to her walls. Maybe it was time for me to talk to her about the facts of life. *God, I hope I'm not too late . . .*

I watched Gary, too. His shaggy, curly brown hair made him look boyish, except for his brown mustache. He enjoyed interacting with the children and their parents. With his playful grin, he focused on each one individually, like he was genuinely interested in what they said. At the moment he was quietly asking a child about her stuffed bunny. He was talking to her like she mattered, with words such as, "Tell me about your bunny. Is it a boy or girl? Do you think she is too warm with a sweater on, should we take it off and make her more comfortable? Susie is a pretty name." He helped her take the sweater off the bunny and off herself. I knew he wasn't acting; that that was his personality, and one of the reasons I cared about him. He had this ability to put people at ease.

I took my heavy, blue fleece sweater off too as I directed my attention to the game. I grew up believing sports belonged to the males in the family. We did cheer for the White Sox in 1959 when they won the pennant and the air-raid sirens went off, but truthfully, I couldn't tell you the rules of the game. I knew winning the game was very important to my twelve-year-old. Already, Jim towered over everyone on his team, reminding me of Ronnie's six-foot frame. I turned towards him; he was up to bat and he took his stance, clutched the bat, and moved his arms into position to connect with the ball.

People in the stands stood up and cheered when he not only connected with the ball, but hit a home run, sending the ball past the outfield, and bringing two other players besides himself in. In that instant, I realized he was a good player, appreciated by his team members. That home run helped his team gain a victory. I stood up and joined the clapping crowd.

"Mom, what are you doing here?" Jim later asked as he and Gary walked over to me. Jewish guilt set in! Embarrassed, I answered, "I wanted to see you play a game!"

"Well, you picked a good one. Join us at Barnaby's for pizza. Gary, can you take care of Mom?" he asked, then ran back to join his teammates. I looked for Babs, but she most likely left with her friends.

Gary gazed at me, and with his cute grin, he said, "Nice that you made it to today's game."

I shook my head and grinned back. "I'm sorry I haven't made time to come to more of them."

"Your children have learned how to survive with a working mother," he said as he backed up to the bleachers and picked up my sweater.

"Thanks," I said, grabbing the forgotten sweater. "Good to have you around."

In the middle eighties, working mothers were still an unusual group for the affluent suburbs. He was right. My children had become more independent in the last few months. Jim quit slamming doors in anger, and Babs spent less time seeking my approval. Both seemed to find the dinners I left in the fridge and join carpools for their activities when I was working late.

Gary looped his arm into mine, leaned over, and whispered into my ear, "I would love to take care of Mom, but we better join the team for pizza first."

I laughed as we walked along the gravel path to our cars. Before getting into my car, I pulled Gary towards me and whispered back, "Ronnie has Babs and Jim next weekend."

We spent a fun weekend together, that is, after a command Sabbath dinner at Aunt Tillie's. This time we took Lassie to Gary's house, where she met Barney. They hit it off right away. Lassie had been spayed, while Barney had not yet been fixed, so we were safe leaving them alone, though Barney kept trying.

To my delight Mitchell's Ice Cream, a South Shore favorite, had opened in Homewood, so I enjoyed a memorable hot fudge sundae and purchased some sauce to take home. Those cute, little white round tables with the small, black wrought iron chairs were still in use.

I had to admit, the South suburbs felt more like South Shore than my home in Northbrook. Maybe it was the apartment buildings with friendly neighbors or my more relaxed feeling. Gary had a two-bedroom apartment on the third floor of a twenty-unit building near the Homewood train station. I wouldn't say he was a hoarder, but more of a major collector of books, gadgets, toys, Jewish items, etc. Very organized, even though there were more things than a two-bedroom could hold.

The best room was the kitchen, which Gary had totally remodeled. I knew he loved to cook, and the aroma of fresh herbs such as thyme, basil, and garlic, plus the copper pots, extra-large Kitchen Aid, and the kitchen block of Cutco knives really confirmed it. I sat down on a patterned stool near the high counter, shook my head, and said, "This kitchen is awesome."

"Next time, I will cook," Gary said. "This time, I want to take you to my favorite South Suburban restaurant." With that said, Gary handed me wine in a crystal glass and leaned towards me to click glasses. I moved towards him, missed his glass, and soon wine and glass spilled and shattered all over the quartz counter.

I jumped back, "Oh no!" I called out. Gary was suddenly on top of me. "Are you Ok? Did you get cut?"

"I'm fine," I replied. "What about your mother's crystal?"

Gary laughed and said, "Material things can be replaced, never *you*. Sit over here. I'll clean it."

A collection of old Schwinn bicycles occupied his second bedroom. This was what Jim was bragging about.

Aunt Tillie already liked Gary. Once she heard about his apartment, she would love him. It had a much warmer feel than Ronnie's sleek, modern apartment on the drive.

"Gary, what is this?" I asked. "It looks like a miniature old-fashioned circus."

With a flip of a nearby switch, the music started while the merry-go-round, the rollercoaster, and another miniature ride moved for the small figures seated on them.

"When I had a children's practice, they loved this," Gary said.

"I bet they did," I mused. "You should have children. You are so good with them."

He avoided the subject.

"Dress casual," Gary said. "I'm treating you to the best pizza restaurant anywhere. It's called Aurelio's."

Gary entered the bathroom while I was trying to put on makeup without my magnifying mirror. He turned me around and said, "Stop, you don't need makeup. You are a natural beauty, and I love you just the way you are, raw and tender."

How could I not love him?

Aurelio's was a multi-floored restaurant with rafters and hidden booths everywhere. Upon arrival, we were greeted with delicious smells of garlic mingled with laughter and lively conversation. The owners and several of the customers familiar with Gary greeted him warmly, and we were shown to a wooden table with cozy, red leather booths.

"Heh, Gary, good to see you! The usual?" the young waiter asked.

"Garlic rolls, sangria, and a menu. It is Sherrie's first time here," Gary answered, smiling at me.

The wine and rolls came. I savored the garlic and olive oil yeast rolls. "Gary, you order," I said. "Remember, I only do cheese pizza."

Conversation flowed between us, covering all topics from Reagan and Gorbachev to Coca-Cola changing its recipe. Back at Gary's place, we watched television, made love, and fell asleep early.

The next morning, I woke up, lazily stretching across the whole bed hearing pots and pans banging in the kitchen. The sun peeked through the opened shutters, and I inhaled the sweet scent of lilacs and pungent coffee. I threw on my blue silk robe and entered the kitchen to see Gary chopping onions and tomatoes. Soon he was beating eggs and cheese.

"I hope you like omelets," he said as he poured the eggs into the pan and added the other ingredients.

"Delicious," I said as I sat and savored the taste of his omelet. Gary smiled at me from across the table. "I love you and want to be with you always. I'm terrible at hiding my emotions, and worse at keeping secrets. Babs and Jim are fourteen and twelve. They can handle the fact that we love each other. Look at their dad and all *his* girlfriends."

I wanted to say, "Maybe we are going too fast. Love takes time. We are on our best behavior now. Until you live together you never really know each other," but I was afraid of hurting our relationship.

On the whole ride home, my head hurt and my stomach churned at the thought of telling Babs and Jim. I had to sort out my feelings toward Gary. So far, there hadn't been another man in my life. It did feel good to be wanted and loved again. The sex was nice, but the cuddling and touching were what I had really missed. I turned the radio on to avoid conversation.

When we arrived home, I went straight upstairs to find some Advil. I was no good at helping Gary make dinner either, and he was a master at chopping away at vegetables and making special dinners from whatever he found in the kitchen. Tonight would be shish kabob on the new grill he bought me.

We sipped some white wine before Jim and Babs came swinging through the garage door, dropping their backpacks on the sofa and petting Lassie, who was jumping all over them.

Jim sat down at the dining table while Babs headed for the bathroom. "Something smells delicious. I'm starving," Jim said as he grabbed for a hot, homemade garlic roll.

When Babs came out of the bathroom, she asked, "Did Jim tell you about Dad's new girlfriend? She is a vegan, which means we had the worst food ever—no meat, no fish, no dairy, no sweets, and she spent the weekend trying to convert us. This food is great. I hope you also have a decadent fattening dessert!"

We were passing the food back and forth, all seated around the dining room table, when Gary took the conversation about Ronnie's new girlfriend as an opportunity to say, "Guess who *my* girlfriend is?"

I choked on my wine. "No," I tried to say.

Without looking up from their plates of food, both kids said, "Mom."

Gary grinned at me, and his hand covered mine with a light squeeze.

Looking up, I asked, "How did you know?"

Jim said, "Gary is always talking about you when I am with him."

"You look at Mom the way Brian looks at me," Babs offered, smiling at Gary, then at me. "At least you don't have your hands all over Mom the way Trish is with Dad."

Gary turned to me, and I just started to laugh.

Both kids stared at me. "Are you okay, Mom?" Babs asked.

Gary got up to go to the kitchen.

"*Now* I am," I answered, as Gary returned to the dining room with a homemade chocolate cake.

That night, Gary took the kids to the movie theater to see *Risky Business,* while I worked on the Wilson case with Lassie curled up on the sofa next to me and my nearby pot of coffee. Gary had lit the fireplace—something I never did. The crackle of the fire and the sweet smell of burning wood helped to keep me calm and focused.

Chapter Thirty-Five

When Shirley summoned, I came. Shirley had become a strong domineering boss who was respected and feared in the legal community. Her small eyes, set into a round face, seemed to pierce into one's soul. At her request, I brought David with me to Shirley's conference room. Besides Denise, there was a very thin, dark-haired man around thirty with several bruises on his face and arms, sitting by the long wooden table. Before Shirley introduced him, he and David acknowledged each other and hugged.

"John, what are you doing here? I thought you were a goner," David said as a greeting.

John smiled at David and said, "They lured me here with you as bait. How did you recover from AIDS? Three of my buddies from Grant Hospital are dead."

I turned to Shirley and said, "You just told me to bring David, not that they knew each other."

She gulped down her coffee, and sat at the head of the table, not answering me. "Let's get started," she ordered.

As we all took our seats, Shirley tossed a picture at David and asked, "Do you know this man?"

To me, it was a blond-haired Daniel Wilson in blue jeans and gold jewelry, instead of the bald, conservative-suited Daniel Wilson I knew from the museum, but the facial expression was the same.

To David, it was Daniel Warburg, lover and partner to John. As he handed the picture back, David said, "I will always remember his small, cold, narrow eyes, and his indifference to the nurses and doctors."

Shirley asked, "David, when did you meet Daniel Warburg?"

"Only at the hospital when he brought John wine and an envelope of cash," David replied. "John and I met each other at the hospital. I was there because it was one of the few hospitals that took AIDS patients, and John was there because Daniel was hiding him."

The leather on the chair made a screeching sound as John had squirmed in his seat at the mention of cash.

Shirley grinned and said to John, "I guess he tried to pay you off. I want you to think carefully when I ask the next question. Will you both be willing to testify at a trial? Daniel Wilson is a ruthless and a powerful man, as you probably already know."

David and John looked at each other before clasping hands.

Then John announced, "We both have AIDS, what else can he do to us?"

Shirley stood up and clapped. "We are going to put this bastard behind bars," she asserted. "Denise, bring in the champagne! Sherrie, go get Marie. She is in the main office. With John and David's assistance, we put Daniel Wilson in jail for domestic abuse—not as long as we wished, but long enough to ruin his life."

Unfortunately, the press spent more time on the gay connection than on the domestic abuse. Homosexuals, with the current AIDS epidemic and the Harvey Milk case a few years ago, made good headlines. The press loved catching Wilson.

For me, the highlight of the case was when Ronnie congratulated me. It felt good that he acknowledged I had succeeded as a lawyer, and that he also acknowledged women can accomplish things. I couldn't deny that I still had feelings for him, but the flow of girls through his life and the authoritative way he still spoke to me assured me that he hadn't changed.

Marie told me the highlight of the trial for her was the look on Wilson's face when John entered the courtroom. She could see drips of perspiration sliding down Daniel's white face as he tried to disguise his shock. She had the satisfied smile of the Cheshire Cat on her face when she told me this.

Laughing, chatting, eating, and drinking in a private room at Don Roth's Blackhawk restaurant to celebrate winning the case went on until well into the night. Ties came off the guys and heels off the women. The wine flowed loosely, and I actually became drunk, something I hadn't done since one, maybe two times in college. Instead of driving home, I stayed over at Shirley's downtown condo while Lizzie watched my kids. I slept like a baby despite the wailing sirens, and it took me a few hours in the morning to get going, and my new, blue St. John tweed suit looked like it had been in a war. Shirley loved it. I was sure she would tease me about it for years to come.

John and David went on to work for organizations that were raising money for AIDS research. Their determination kept them going, even though both had been compromised by the disease. AZT, the new drug, kept them going for longer than anyone could have imagined. They spoke in front of Congress, they marched on Washington for gay and lesbian rights, and even met with President Reagan. I found myself watching the news for word about new AIDS medicine or a clip of David from one of the ads he was in.

On a trip home from his traveling for AIDS research, Lizzie and I met David for lunch at The Claim Company on Clark Street. His enthusiasm for the mission was overwhelming, but his appearance was alarming. My head pounded with fear as David walked into the restaurant. Lizzie and I exchanged looks. My lips tightened. Again he was emaciated, and his breathing was labored. He wore a herringbone jacket over too large jeans. My enthusiasm for his successful mission was tempered by reality and real fear for his life. There were better treatments to prolong life, but no cures yet. I wondered how he could be so enthusiastic for a cause that was killing him. Again, I went back to my role playing with David. I became the google-eyed cousin who admired everything he said and did.

Both google-eyed Lizzie and I asked him to tell us about his meeting with Elizabeth Taylor!

"We met with her and probably twenty-five other people," David said. "She told us about how she and a group of physicians formed the American Foundation for AIDS Research. She is the spokesperson for the organization, bringing an awareness of the disease to the public. We were asked to give our stories on film to be used at one of her promotions."

Lizzie and I looked at each other, and I said, "David, we want to know what she wore, and what was she like in person."

David chuckled and said, "I don't remember. She was beautiful and charming, of course. Her eyes were violet because they reflected the color off her purple necklace. I was more impressed with Reagan."

Lizzie looked at us with a puzzled expression as if a question just popped into her head. "I just don't understand you two," Lizzie said. "We came from the same family building. You should be happy sticking together with us at family gatherings and other clan activities. Instead, you are always running after these impossible causes."

"Lizzie, Lizzie, part of the Jewish tradition is to make the world a better place - *Tikkun Alum*," David said.

Lizzie put her sandwich down and ate a few of the sweet potato fries. "Sherrie, I really wish you would take some time off from your women's crusade to learn how to play mah jongg and bake challah." She turned to David. "And, David, you look like hell, so *skinny*! And is that some kind of rash on your arm? I am worried about you. Stay home for a while!"

David took a small bite of his hamburger and a gulp of his Pepsi as he moved his chair forward and said, "Lizzie, I always wanted the part of you that made the family happy. You fulfilled their expectations, and you are the one the rest of us count on to keep the family members and our history together. I couldn't because I was born different. I know the consequences of what I am doing, but I am finally at peace."

I went to the salad bar to refill my plate with some tuna salad and pasta while I thought about our conversation. I loved that Lizzie was following in Aunt Tillie's footsteps and keeping the family together, something I wanted—so long as I wasn't the one to do it. Maybe we love people who fulfill a part we are missing. Ronnie and Shirley had the self-confidence I often wished for, and Gary had a loving child-like openness.

I picked up the tab, gave David a kiss goodbye, visited the ladies room, and left Lizzie to take David home while I went back to the shelter to catch up on a new occupant. As I drove down the street, tears streamed down my face. I wondered if I would ever see my cousin again.

I thought about what Lizzie said and decided my kids did need a domestic mother around sometime, especially now that the trial was over, so I invited all to our house for the Passover Seder. Two days Babs and I worked. We took out the good English china, linen table-cloths, sterling silver, and Passover *Haggadah,* the central Jewish text of Passover. We ironed and polished silver. I found myself on the phone to Aunt Tillie often to check recipes, especially the Passover plate which held the paschal lamb bone, *maror* (bitter herbs), the *charoset,* (consisting of wine, apples, and nuts), salt water, the *beitzah* (a hard-boiled egg), and parsley, used to dip into the salt water.

The best of the preparations was the fun we had working together. "Mom, are you sure Aunt Tillie told you to put that greasy stuff in to the liver?" Babs asked as I added schmaltz to the chopped liver while she rolled the meatball appetizers.

"Yes, schmaltz is a Jewish staple, kind of a butter substitute for meat dishes," I replied.

"Did you and the family really use different dishes for Passover and clear the house of all bread products?" Babs asked. "Wasn't that difficult and costly to do?"

"Yes, it was a cleaning ceremony for the whole family," I explained. "We gave all bread products to the cleaning lady. I don't remember food pantries then."

"Did my non-Jewish grandmother participate?" Babs asked as she finished loading the dishwasher with the pots.

"It was a different time," I explained. "Remember, my mother pretended to be Jewish, otherwise, Pa wouldn't have allowed her and my dad to be part of the family. Hasidic and Orthodox Jews still practice that religious rule. During the years I was growing up, most Catholics and other religious groups expected their children to marry within the group."

"You're kidding," Babs said. "If I marry Brian, who isn't Jewish, would you kick me out?"

I dried my hands on the dish towel, turned the dishwasher on, and thought about how Reformed Jewish I had become. I answered her, "Honey, whoever you love, I will love and welcome into my home. I would prefer he be Jewish, but it's your life. Anyway, you are only fourteen. Let me worry about all that in a few years, okay?"

I smiled and said, "Let's go to bed, it's late. Thanks for your help."

We embraced, turned off the lights, and went upstairs together. Jim, after bringing up the extra chairs from the basement, had been in bed for at least two hours.

Chapter Thirty-Six

"Mom! Flowers!" Babs yelled from the open front door. "What do I do with them?"

Just out of the shower, I quickly threw on my bath robe and ran down the stairs to help her find a vase. In a hurry, I stood on a chair to open the top kitchen cabinet where I reached in to grab my cut glass vase. Not secure enough, the chair rocked, and I dropped the vase. Babs tried to save it. I screamed as I watched the vase hit the counter and shatter across her arm.

"Oh, no!" I screamed louder as bright red blood ran down her hand onto the blue tile floor.

Babs stood very still in a type of shock as I grabbed a dish towel and applied pressure to stop the bleeding. It made me think of Judy, my old roommate, and I panicked when it wouldn't stop bleeding, I called for the paramedics.

Sitting in an emergency room, watching my white-faced, scared, fourteen-year-old daughter get eight stitches in her arm made me aware of what was important in life. My head pounded and my heart beat overtime from fear and guilt. It was my careless fault; I should have been the one to get hurt. A thought occurred to me—because of the scar, my daughter would be wearing long sleeves from now on, no matter what I said to her. Thank God no artery was involved.

Babs was so good about it, consoling me with, "Mom, it was an accident, calm down." Lizzie, who met us at the hospital, apologized for suggesting I become domestic. She then reminded me of the Jewish saying, "Man plans and God laughs."

Passover is a two-day Seder holiday, so with Aunt Tillie's help, we celebrated at our house for the second Seder where Babs was the star of the evening, and Gary apologized for sending us flowers. I sat back and watched Babs, who could accept things and just move forward, while it horrified me that my haste caused disfigurement and pain to my daughter.

Eighteen months after the Wilson trial, I received the phone call I had been dreading. When the doctor identified himself from a hospital in San Francisco, I swallowed hard to keep back my tears. Again, Lizzie, Yale, and I brought David back to a hospital in Chicago. We tried so hard to be positive, but every test proved otherwise. His blood counts showed how anemic he was, while his white tongue exhibited the telltale thrush fungus, and his chest x-ray showed the pneumonia associated with the disease.

I spent every day that week in the hospital watching David go further downhill. The cold cement walls, the sterile metal furniture, the closed window shade, and the uncomfortable chairs added to my grief. At least we were in a private room at the end of the hall—the room they gave to dying AIDS patients, the room where many visitors could come at the same time to say good-bye. The unconscious man in the bed with yellow skin had no resemblance to our David. If not for the breathing machine, I wouldn't know he was still alive. The room was so silent. When my mother died, I was too young and naive to really understand what was happening.

Yale entered the hospital room and moved towards the bed. He turned towards me, "Hell, what happened to him? Last week he was sitting up and talking to me. Okay, he was as skinny as a Holocaust victim, and he was coughing constantly, but he was *alive.*

"The antibiotics for the pneumonia aren't working any more, and the pills for the fungus have quit too," I said, swallowing.

"Sherrie, we better call the family to the hospital."

I knew this for the last two days, but I couldn't admit it until Yale showed up. David was the brother I never had. I left Yale in the room and took a break. Hurrying down the steps, I pushed open the door to the outside. I remembered the day David told me he was a homosexual. We sat on the concrete rocks watching the blue Lake Michigan water splashing against the shore. This spot, two blocks from our family building, was our favorite place to exchange secrets. He was nineteen and I was seventeen. It was 1962 and I had no clue what he was talking about, and I don't think he knew what sacrifices he would make with that commitment. I told him I would love him no matter what, and I still do.

The street in front of the hospital was busy with cars moving fast in both directions. The burst of leaves on the trees, and the sprouts of red, pink, white flowers spoke of life, but not for our family. I stood half in and half out of the door until someone tried to enter. Reluctantly, I went back into the hospital and called family.

David died surrounded by close friends and family. I held his hand and told him how proud we were of him. Aunt Tillie held her crying sister, who kept calling, *min kin, min* kin (my child). Aunt Sarah had buried a twenty-six-year-old husband and now her forty-two-year-old son. The first thing we did was to convince our Reform Rabbi to perform the service for David, and the second was to put on his headstone, *Son of Irving and Sarah Paul* in English under the traditional Hebrew. We almost took the cemetery to court. We paid extra for a burial team that wasn't afraid of the disease.

He was buried on a beautiful, sunny spring day. Weinstein's Funeral Home in Skokie had to set out additional chairs to accommodate the large crowd, and more tables to accommodate all the flowers. Jeffery, David's long-time friend, asked to speak at the funeral. He spoke with such intense emotion concerning their first attraction, and the pain he and David endured coming out in the early sixties. The young and gay crowd couldn't stop the tears from flowing, while some of the older crowd actually left the funeral parlor. Even though homosexuals and AIDS were all over the news in the eighties, it still wasn't accepted by all as a way of life.

Sarah asked, "How did my son get to know so many people?" as several celebrities spoke about David's relentless dedication to AIDS research. We were hoping Elizabeth Taylor would show up as David had worked with her, but it didn't happen. She and the late Rock Hudson set up the American Fund For AIDS Research. David worked with the fund, traveling all over the country to make people aware, and to collect donations.

Most of the people who came to Aunt Tillie's house were strangers who brought candy, cakes, and casseroles. I know they also enjoyed the deli trays from Max and Benny's and, of course, Aunt Tillie's strudel, kugels, and challah. Aunt Sarah insisted we sit the traditional shiva—seven days—but we refused to cover mirrors and keep the crowd quiet, though I knew the bursts of laughter irritated my aunt. Only for the Kaddish did we quiet everyone down. David loved parties and would have been awed to see so many colleagues there. Pa would have probably been sitting shiva long before David died, but times were changing.

"Aunt Sarah is lucky to have my mother," Lizzie said. I hugged her and whispered in her ear, "I'm lucky to have you."

On the way home, I could hardly concentrate on the road. Cars honked at me when the stoplight changed to green. I hadn't realized until today that my aunt hadn't accepted her son as a gay decorator. Maybe that is why he traveled so much. I walked into my house, carrying an award President Reagan had given David for his work on the President's Commission on the HIV Epidemic. Aunt Sarah gave it to me because she wanted no part of what it represented, not because she thought I would like to have it. I went to bed with a terrible headache.

Jim and Babs came to the funeral and to two days of shiva. They, like everyone else, had to go back to living. Gary stayed with them at our house while I went daily to Aunt Tillie's house, where we sat shiva. Cars flew by, shoppers shopped, children went to school, bicycle riders went about their business, and life went on, even though for me and my immediate family life stood still. I had lost my cousin who was my best friend. So few of the family building members were still around. They, like the South Shore we once knew, were disappearing from my life.

In one of our last conversations, David said, "Sherrie, I know you were always angry with me for abandoning decorating, but I found my real calling this last year. I believe my work for AIDS research will save so many lives in the next few years, and your work for equality for women, gays, white, or black—will make the world a better place to live."

By the nineties, AIDS awareness spread as more and more prominent actors and athletes such as Arthur Ashe and Magic Johnson admitted to having AIDS and pledged money to research. Finally, a treatment was found to contain and maintain the disease, but not cure it. I thought about continuing David's campaign for AIDS, but I couldn't do it. The best I could do was to continue donating in his name and to take care of his mother.

Chapter Thirty-Seven

Marie Wilson took her large divorce settlement and left town. The last we heard from her, she was in Las Vegas. Shirley used her popularity to develop more shelters and domestic abuse programs throughout the United States. We were successful in getting the Violence Against Women Act passed in 1994. The Federal bill provided close to $1 billion to fight domestic violence through shelters and the training of judges, police officers, social workers, etc. Shirley never gave up. Right before she left for Washington to put in her opinion on the Violence Against Women Act, she gave her team, which now included a young man named Henry, a new job. I was ready for a rest and time with my kids after fourteen-hour days, but Shirley had other ideas.

During a downpour, I scrambled from my car with a newspaper over my head, saying, *David, can you believe I don't have an umbrella in this pouring rain?* I arrived in the conference room and, like Lassie, I shook myself off

Shirley gave me her impatient look, lips pursed tight, eyebrows knit. "We are ready to start, Sherrie," she said tersely. "I have a plane to catch.

I slipped into my seat, and Shirley started to talk.

"This law firm has worked mainly with women, divorced women, widows, abused women, underpaid women, sexually harassed women. There is one thing I found in common for almost all. Even though it's the nineties, most of these women had no knowledge of how to invest their finances.

We will meet again in two weeks. I would like us to put together some seminars on Finances for Women. I need to take off, but you are welcome to stay and throw this around among you. Henry, I believe finance was your major. Remember, this will be a beginner's course for women who had allowed their spouses to handle everything.

Shirley gathered her things. On the way to the door, she turned around and said, "We are in the process of installing an IBM computer. Denise and Sherrie will need to take lessons. I related to the group, "A few days earlier I had taken my Aunt Tillie to the bank because her CD was up for renewal. She was upset because in a year the rate had dropped down to ten percent, but the bank gave her a toaster as a gift for renewing. When her husband died, she knew nothing about investing, or where or how much money they had. Because of me she now checks the paper for the best CD rate. Unfortunately, she never learned to drive."

Denise smiled sheepishly and said, "I'm a lawyer, and I allow my husband to take care of everything, using time as an excuse." Henry admitted he never thought of this subject, though he wasn't married. I was surprised this tall, broad-shouldered man with a full head of auburn hair, thirty to forty-years-old, was single. He agreed to explore the mechanics of putting together public seminars, and Denise and I decided to explore topics and ways to present them. When Shirley left Henry asked, "Do you ever deal with racial injustice?

I replied, "We are a firm that deals with injustice towards all women no matter what color or religion. We have at times even taken cases of male abuse.

Denise and I took bathroom breaks before leaving. "Do you know anything about computers? They scare me," she said as she applied fresh makeup.

"My ex gave my son an Apple computer," I replied. "He has spent hours playing games. They aren't cheap. I'll call you with some ideas before we meet with Shirley."

"I never heard of Apple computers," Denise said. "I thought they were only IBM or Radio Shack. Thank you for all your help. I know you realize Shirley scares me." She gave me a quick hug. I grinned, thinking only the tough women can make it in this man's world, and Shirley has become one. We needed to change things, to make the world a place where all women had a chance.

True to Chicago's weather, the rain had disappeared, and the sun was pouring red, blue, green, yellow, and purple rainbow rays across the sky. It was now a balmy fall afternoon. I took the long way home, enjoying Lake Shore Drive for a change. Chicago had a fantastic sky-line, with all the new glass high-rises sticking out against the azure blue sky and the wavy icy blue waters of Lake Michigan, now mainly empty of her summer boats and yachts, and many fishermen. Coming from South Shore had always been the prettiest route. On the drive, my mind was exploding with memories of days gone by, pleasurable memories of life in our family building, instead of worrying about working on the new-fangled computers. Communication in the South Shore days was by talking or writing to each other.

Saturday afternoon, while driving with my son Jim to Radio Shack for our first computer lesson, I heard a loud ringing. I slammed on the brakes. Of course the guy behind me hit me. Jim, who didn't have his seat belt on, slammed into the dashboard.

With his hand over a bleeding chin, my son said, "Mom, you are an idiot. The car phone rang!" I stared at the new-fangled wonder gadget that cost a fortune and took up my whole car trunk. Jim talked me into it.

He loved any new technical gadget.

The knock on my car window brought me back to the present. I exchanged insurance information with the guy behind me, but didn't call the police like I should have, because I needed to get Jim to emergency where he received three stitches on his chin. I never did find out who called, nor did I reprimand Jim for speaking to me in such a derogatory way. I know he was hurting, but he was always quick to point out my mistakes. A week later, when the stitches were taken out, I watched Jim frowning and checking his chin in the mirror.

"Now you have that sexy look, like Kirk Douglas," I said, trying to console him.

He turned and looked at me, his eyes wide open and mouth closed in a pinch. "Mom, I have no idea what you are talking about," he said.

When we finally made it to a computer class, I realized this was going to be more challenging than college, but I needed it if I wanted to do the lecture series. I was destined to be called an idiot many more times by my son while we studied computers together. He understood what they were talking about immediately, while I was lost. I realized today's and future children would not take ballet and piano lessons as we had, It was a new era—one belonging to computers. The one in the law firm's office took up a whole wall. Shirley hired someone to create programs for the series. The Apple Jim had was smaller, but still a considerable size with its screen, keyboard, and large separate disc case. It took up his whole desk. He did his homework on the kitchen table.

On the coffee break at the Temple Book Club meeting, I asked, the twelve participants, "If I was to do a seminar on finances for women, what questions would they have?"

It took me a while to open my fellow women to talk about the subject. Most just hemmed and hawed. I had brought along some wine and cookies to loosen the group up. Lynn admitted to knowing nothing about the stock market. Karen, a recent widow, couldn't even balance a checkbook. Sandra, a divorcée, wanted to know about investing and insurance. De, another book club member, complained that we were there to critique books, and Susan said, "I take care of the kids and household, and Phil takes care of the finances."

I started to ask this question wherever I went. The more women I talked to, the more I realized even though women were college graduates, they were still stuck in the fifties where the men took care of the finances and the women took care of the kids and the household.

I called Denise, "Meet me at the law school library. Shirley has a great idea. Women need our help."

I really got into this project. It became something I believed in. It also was a way to stop thinking about David. I still couldn't believe he was gone. I thought about working for AIDS research, but I was too angry about what this disease was doing to young people. I was a lawyer, not in the medical field.

Denise and I spent the next month researching finance, meeting with financial planners, and interviewing women. I found out there was a lot I needed to do to get my own finances, wills, and trusts into order. One of the better things I did while preparing for the seminars was to open a stock account and buy some Apple stock. I wanted to have some experience trading stock, and Jim loved his Apple computer. Most people owned IBM or Radio Shack when they thought about computers. We were ready for Shirley.

"So, what do you think of my idea?" Shirley asked as we once again sat at the gigantic wooden conference table in her new, bigger office. Smiling, Denise and I, in unison, said, "We love it. There is a definite need." Henry replied after putting up a large screen, "We can start with videotapes and slides until I finish my computer course on something new by Microsoft called PowerPoint."

We started a series of seminars at schools throughout Chicago and suburbs. Videotapes, slides, written material, and discussion were used until Henry figured out PowerPoint. It took us months to put it together, as we needed to go from law jargon to laypersons' language. It took many trials to get there. We called the series, "What Women Should Know About Family Finance," and our charge was minimal at the beginning. Attendance was small until we realized husbands weren't happy paying for this topic. Attendance doubled when we moved to restaurants and called the series "Luncheon Seminars on Family Finances." Food always brought people in. In fact, we had several retired men join us too.

Speaking in front of an audience usually scared the hell out of me, and I normally wrote the script for someone else. But I found that I enjoyed doing these seminars, more so than the court cases, so Shirley turned the seminars over to me.

Before the first one, Gary coached me. I stood up in front of a makeshift podium he put together from a footstool. I stood with my speech on the stool facing Gary who was sitting on a chair with his stopwatch in order to time me.

"Sherrie, you need to relax," he said. "Remember everyone out there is the same as you. Take a deep breath. If you believe in what you are saying, they will believe you."

I stood before him and started to speak. He stopped me and said, "Honey, you are using hand gestures too much, and talking too loud."

"I'm Jewish from a big family."

Gary smiled. "Try it again. Remember, the audience is on your side. Make eye contact." He brought me a glass of water.

I started again. Gary asked me a question, "Why do you think women need this? We take care of the house and the men the finances."

"What are you doing?" I asked as I stopped talking.

"I want you to answer a question like this without antagonizing the person asking," Gary explained. "No Shirley band-wagoning."

I sat down on the sofa with watery eyes. "I can't *do* public speaking. I always wrote the programs and let someone *else* do them."

Jim entered the room with a Dove ice cream bar. "You do suck at it," he said, honestly. "Pretend that you are convincing me what I need to accomplish for my own good."

As always, he irritated me, but he also helped me. The next presentation I practiced was done with conviction.

Gary sat in the front with encouragement for the first two seminars. I was determined to do them instead of turning them over to someone else.

My first seminar was in the side room of Max and Benny's Deli in Northbrook. There was a podium, but no stage. Metal chairs with red vinyl seats next to metal tables filled the room. We brought our own screen and slide projector. Most of the women were retired Jewish women who came for the corned beef sandwiches. One whiff of garlic upon entering let us know where we were. Before I went home, I had spent most of the profits on bagels, cream cheese, and lox.

My hair was cut in a stylish Rachel from *Friends* cut, plus pink polished nails went with my gray and pink St. John knit from Neiman Marcus for the occasion. The suit was identified by one of the women in the audience, so I guess it was a good choice.

Since so many of the audience members were older, I started out with, "The purpose of this seminar is to make you aware of your finances in case you become a widow, divorcee, or your spouse becomes sick."

I did the *ptew, ptew, ptew* to ward of the evil spirit. This brought a laugh.

"So many times, we women leave all the business decisions to our husbands, while we take care of the household," I said.

I went to my slides, leaving off the charts for this audience, going to a list plus an explanation of things every woman and man should know about their finances.

"Decision making should be made together," I explained. "Starting with simple things like, Where do you bank? Whose name is on the accounts? Do you have both checking and savings accounts? How do you write checks, read a statement?

"Do you have a lawyer? Where can you reach him or her? Do you have wills, trusts, insurance?

"Who is your accountant? Could you do your taxes at the end of the year? Can you read your tax return?

"What do you owe? Rent, a mortgage, business loans, utilities, car payments?

"Where can you get money when you need it to pay bills?

"Where is everything kept?

"What are your investments—stocks, CDs, bonds, real estate, jewelry, gold?

"Do you have access to your credit cards and credit reports?"

We sent everyone home with handmade pamphlets outlining what we talked about, and bags of cookies.

This was the simple beginning seminar. We offered the first for free. The next six came with lunch and a more complex agenda. We moved downtown, first at the Hilton, then farther north at the Marriott. The most amazing aspect I found was when I asked the question, "Why did you hesitate to find out and take part in your family finances?" most answered, "To avoid disagreements with my spouse," and not that they weren't interested. This came from working women too. A few older women felt like my aunts, stating, "It's the man's job."

When those first twenty-six people left with their black and white cookies I wondered if they would recommend the seminar for the content or the food. We grew into two different types of seminars, beginners and advanced. I spent many days dozing on airplane seats, and existing on pasta and junk food as we expanded our seminars across the country.

Soon we had to hire lawyers and financial planners in several major cities to conduct the seminars, which were now attended by women and men of all ages. Slides were replaced by computers and PowerPoint programs. To get the content together was easy. Constantly learning new computer skills was the hard part. Jim, who majored in computers, became my technical advisor.

Settling back in the limo that was now picking me up at the airports I visited I thought about where my life was heading. Surprisingly, this program to alert women to their need for financial awareness was a success for me both monetarily and personally.

On a clear sunny day, beautiful snow-capped mountains came into full view. I was in Aspen, the place I once hated, the place where my ex-husband, Ronnie, took his girlfriends during our marriage. Now I was here to do a seminar. By divorcing him, I found my calling.

* * *

By the nineties, Gary and I were living together. He had retired from the shelter and practiced psychology three days a week in a shared office with a friend in Highland Park. Without Gary, I would have had a hard time being a single working mom. Gary took care of the home front, surprising us with home improvements like ponds, newly wall papered rooms, expanded patios, or new delicious recipes. *Tonight we will have apple pie,* I said to myself as I watched him climb the ladder, wicker basket in hand while he reached up to find the ripest apples from the trees he planted. His constant companions were Lassie and Barney's puppies. Yes, the vet forgot to spay Lassie.

I realized Gary and I were better suited than Ronnie and I had ever been. Gary was reliable, a stay at home guy, always there to comfort me, and, most important of all, we were friends beside being lovers. Through Gary, my in-house psychologist, I realized that I, too, was like my Aunt Tillie and Lizzie, and that I, in my quiet manner, enjoyed being in charge and creating something that benefits others. Always in the back of my mind was the abuse my mother suffered from her alcoholic father, and the abortion Judy received from a back-alley butcher. Most of all the love and guidance I received growing up in my family building, where the woman actually had more control than was apparent, became the major influences in the way I've lived my life.

* * *

It was the year 2000, and Shirley, along with over one hundred other women, was raising her glass to me in a toast, saying, "To Sherrie's successful Women In Finance Series!"

I looked around the beautifully designed Conrad Hilton Hotel banquet room with the traditional large, heavy-draped windows, the chandeliers, and fresco painted ceiling. Groups of tables covered by white linen tablecloths adorned with bone china plates, crystal glasses, and white lily bouquets were arranged throughout the room. Smartly dressed working and stay-at-home women sat on the silk-covered chairs, conversing with one another.

Among these women was a very special guest, my eighty-year-old Aunt Tillie, the last of the family-building matriarchs. Her daughter Lizzie made sure her gray hair was styled, and that she was out of her house dress. The black silk dress with a gold *chai* was perfect. I almost didn't recognize her. It was then I realized that soon, the family mantle would be passed down to me, Lizzie, and the other cousins. Our job would be harder as family members were no longer in one spot like they were in the three-flat building in the South Shore. They were scattered across the world, but family is still important.

Shirley tapped her glass to get the crowd to quiet down. After giving me a glowing introduction, I rose with wine glass in hand and tears in my eyes. "First of all," I began, addressing the room, "I need to thank everyone for your help in making our seminar series successful. It was Shirley who realized all women needed to be aware of how to take care of their personal finances. She handed me the ball and I ran with it. Over the last fourteen years, we've developed Women In Finance Seminars across the country and on a weekly TV show. We are getting so many men joining us; we may have to change the name."

There came a pleasing laughter from the audience.

"When I was one of the two women in my law school, a male fellow student said to me, 'You are taking up space for a man who will practice a lifetime, while you will get married, have babies, and stay home.' He was only partially right. Men still haven't realized that women need to use their intelligence to better the world and keep their sanity. They need to be involved in business and industry, as well as raising a family. We have been working diligently to not take jobs away from men, but to get them to be equal partners at home and in the workplace. Men need to help take care of their children and the house while women also bring home their share of the income. Financial ignorance for any adult, rich or poor, alone, married, or in a relationship can be catastrophic.

"Besides the seminars, I am so proud of the advances we have made in equality rights for all, but our fight isn't over," I continued. "For example, the Equal Rights Amendment is still out there. Women are now in important places such as the heads of major corporations, and even the Supreme Court, but their achievements are still not admired the same as men's. Our ultimate goal should be a woman in the White House!"

I turned to my right where my daughter Babs was sitting. She looked so grown up in her red wool suit and matching black and red, thigh high suede boots. I loudly asked her, "Tell the audience, how many students in your law school class are women?"

"Almost half, Mom," Babs replied. "I would like to see a male student today try to tell them they are taking up space for a man who would practice a lifetime, while they would stay home with babies!"

All two hundred women stood and clapped for a viewpoint that would have been inconceivable to the women of the family building.

Today was a different and better time for women, though. Farewell to South Shore!

About the Author

Native Chicagoan Charlene Wexler is a graduate of the University of Illinois. She has worked as a teacher and dental office manager and as a wife, mom, and grandmother.

In retirement, her lifelong passion for writing has led to her creation of several essays, short stories, and novels. Among her books are: *Lori, Murder on Skid Row, Elephants in the Room, Murder Across The Ocean,* and *Milk and Oranges*.

Coming Soon!

CHARLENE WEXLER'S

MURDER ON SKID ROW

"Spare any change?" and "I don't know nothing" were the watchwords on Chicago's Skid Row in the 1960s. Located on Madison Street, a little west of the city's bustling and prosperous downtown, Skid Row was home to hustlers, winos, addicts, bums, lost souls, ripoffs, and kickbacks. Everyone, it seemed, had a secret.

Into this shady society steps Dr. Mel Greenberg, who opens his new dental office "to help the downtrodden," he says. Instead, he finds himself in a world for which his working-class upbringing never prepared him, where a day might bring anything from a philosophy-quoting patient to a knife held at his neck. Eventually, he finds himself a suspect in murder.

Based on a true story, Charlene Wexler's *Murder on Skid Row* takes the reader back to a place that was an integral part of Chicago for decades—but one today's public officials and city-beautiful boosters would rather have us believe never existed.

**For more information
visit:** www.SpeakingVolumes.us

Upcoming New Release!

MURDER IN GEORGETOWN
BY
JACQUE ROSMAN

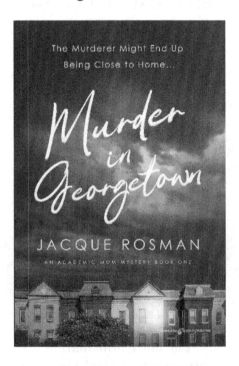

Murder in Georgetown is the thrilling book one in the Academic Mom Mysteries. If you like amateur female sleuths in academia, moms struggling with work-life balance, and the backdrop of the nation's Capital, then you will love Jacque Rosman's cleverly constructed new mystery.

For more information
visit: www.SpeakingVolumes.us

Made in the USA
Monee, IL
15 February 2024

53505873R00187